Praise for *Blown Red*

"If you like Rick Mofina's novels, you'll love *Blown Red* . . . a pacy action-packed thriller that will leave you gasping. Finally! A kickass female protagonist in a thriller who rings true."

—Peggy Blair, best-selling author of *Hungry Ghosts*

"Plucky heroine Signy Shepherd never backs down from a fight and has all the odds stacked against her. You'll cheer her on as you blow through the pages of *Blown Red*."

—Deryn Collier, author of *Open Secret*

"Gripping from the very beginning! Philpott's suspenseful storytelling and unique characters will pull you in."

—*New York Times* bestselling author Laura Griffin

"Philpott's guiding hand is sure, and the tension radiates throughout the cross-country trip. . . . Philpott has a knack for creating compelling relationships."

—*Quill & Quire*

Also by Susan Philpott

Blown Red

Dark Territory

Susan Philpott

Published by Simon & Schuster
New York London Toronto Sydney New Delhi

SIMON &
SCHUSTER
CANADA

Simon & Schuster Canada
A Division of Simon & Schuster, Inc.
166 King Street East, Suite 300
Toronto, Ontario M5A 1J3

This book is a work of fiction. Any references to historical events, real people, or real places are used fictitiously. Other names, characters, places, and events are products of the author's imagination, and any resemblance to actual events or places or persons, living or dead, is entirely coincidental.

This Simon & Schuster Canada edition January 2016

For information about special discounts for bulk purchases, please contact Simon & Schuster Special Sales at 1-800-268-3216 or CustomerService@simonandschuster.ca.

Manufactured in the United States of America

10 9 8 7 6 5 4 3

ISBN 978-1-4767-6531-0
ISBN 978-1-4767-6532-7 (ebook)

For Andrew, Sarah, and Abby

dark territory: a section of railroad tracks without functioning signal lights

Chapter 1

Lizzy Stone hurried down the deserted corridor, its concrete walls plastered with fluorescent biohazard warnings. Clutched under one arm like an overinflated football, Justin screamed bloody murder, his furious cries echoing through the underground maze. Clamping a hand over the baby's mouth, Lizzy darted a quick look over her shoulder.

She skittered to a halt in front of a heavy steel door. Ignoring the Do Not Enter sign, she swiped the access card she'd stolen and shouldered the door open. Flipping on the lights, she whirled round, slammed the door shut, and then clicked home the dead-bolt. Only then did she lean against the wall and close her eyes.

She breathed in the familiar mix of pine disinfectant and chlorine bleach, and it was a minute or two before she noticed the baby's squirms grow weaker. She glanced down. His nose clogged, he was struggling to breathe. She whipped her hand away from his mouth, and after a couple of sputtered cries, he let loose again, every muscle in his body quivering with rage.

Swinging him up onto her hip, she patted his back while completing a quick survey of the room. She was surprised to see that nothing much had changed in the laboratory since she'd last been allowed down here. On one wall, a gleaming stainless steel lab bench held an array of scientific equipment, autoclaves, a centrifuge, flasks, and test tubes.

Tears pricked behind her eyes when she saw that the caricature she'd had made for Solomon at the New York State Fair still occupied its place of honour on the centre of the bench. The artist had drawn him hunched over a microscope, a white lab coat hanging around his knees, his hair wild, à la Einstein. Surrounding him, a ring of smiling children held up Thank You signs in a variety of languages.

Turning her back on the drawing, she examined the class II safety cabinet that dominated the opposite wall. With its separate environmental controls it served to keep the operator safe from both biological and chemical agents.

"No," she cried, prying the baby's grasping fingers from her long brown hair. She held his writhing, sweat-slick body out in front of her, his tiny feet windmilling. She grimaced as his screams rose in an almost unbearable crescendo.

Striding over to the safety cabinet, she bent forward and peered inside. The empty interior was sparkling clean. Using her hip, she opened the glass shield and set the baby inside.

His shrieks abruptly halted as he stared open-mouthed at this novel environment.

Her shoulders relaxed a fraction of an inch. She'd suspected a stint in Daddy's sanctum sanctorum might do the trick. As if he were reading her mind, the baby burst out into a babble of infant chatter.

Lizzy slid the door shut, then glanced at the temperature gauge. If she cranked the dial even a little, the temperature inside the cabinet would climb to unbearable levels. Like a dog left in a car on a sweltering summer day, he'd be cooked within minutes.

Shaking her head, she stepped over to a refrigerator-sized incubator. A quick check of the gauges showed that the temperature, humidity, oxygen, and carbon dioxide were ticking along at optimum levels. Peeking through a small window on the door, she could see tightly packed culture dishes. Each dish had a white screw top at one end and a thin layer of pink nutrient medium lining the bottom. Not bothering to don a mask, she reached in and extracted one of the plastic containers.

She peered closely at the contents, noting with satisfaction the fuzzy dark spots that marred the clean surface of the medium. Carrying the culture dish over to a deep metal sink, she twisted off the white cap. Bringing the mouth of the dish under the tap, she turned on the hot water. The little container filled almost immediately, and she watched as grainy splotches of cell tissue broke free of their life-giving moorings, floated to the surface, and rode a torrent of water out into the sink.

She repeated the process until every scrap of her husband's work met an unceremonious end in the sewer tank deep underground.

Tossing the last culture dish into the garbage, she stepped over to a large metal desk that held the computer in which Solomon recorded his data. She turned it on, and scrolled through the contents. She dragged the cursor past scores of files containing years of raw data and statistical analyzes, as well as a series of scientific articles Solomon was poised to send to peer-reviewed journals.

She paid no attention to the research files. She wanted the videos, and there they were. Hundreds of them. She chose one at random, her lips twisting with disgust as the familiar images flickered to life.

Shuddering, Lizzy grabbed a USB key from the desk drawer and copied the file onto the key, slipping it in her pocket as soon as the transfer was complete. Then she spun the computer tower, opened the back, and slid out the hard drive. Glancing around the lab, she found what she was looking for over by the door. Dropping the hard drive onto the concrete floor, she picked up a heavy metal doorstop and used it to crack open the drive.

Tossing the battered casing in the sink, she found a flask of hydrochloric acid in a glass-fronted cupboard. She poured the entire bottle over the hard drive, watching as the delicate inner workings dissolved into a smoking lump of twisted metal.

Certain that Solomon's work had been obliterated, she returned her focus to the baby's miniature prison. He'd managed to roll over onto his side, his fuzz of blond hair dark with sweat. Her hand hovered over the temperature dial. With what his father had planned for him, the poor little thing would be better off if she simply cranked the knob.

The baby stared back at her with his sparkling blue eyes.

"Just like going to sleep," she whispered through the glass.

Justin grinned, then plugged a thumb into his mouth.

Lizzy shook her head. "Come here, little monkey," she said, sliding open the door and lifting him free of the stuffy cabinet. The baby wrapped his arms around her neck and she pressed his impossibly soft cheek to hers.

She was turning to leave when she caught sight of a black marker. Ripping the cap off with her teeth, she walked over to the wall and scrawled the word *Murderer* in ten-inch-high letters.

Back in the hallway, she spotted a trail of evenly spaced marks marring the concrete floor. Inspecting the bottom of her feet, she found the offending stain on the sole of her right foot. She discounted the idea of returning with a bucket and mop. She'd be long gone by the time he discovered the bloody footprints.

Wiping away an errant tear, she choked back a hysterical giggle. By then, a little extra cleanup would be the least of his problems.

Chapter

2

Bursting into the kitchen, Signy Shepherd slid across the polished concrete floor, barely hanging on to a silver tray laden with champagne glasses. Behind her, the swinging door boomed against the wall, while overhead, rows of copper pots shivered on their hooks.

"Good Lord!" Grace Holder cried, flinging her tea towel into the air. "Are you trying to scare me to death?"

Squaring her shoulders, Signy tottered across the slippery floor with as much dignity as she could muster. Setting the tray on the counter, she flipped up one foot, pointing a dagger-like stiletto at Grace. "I'd like to see you wear these. I should be getting danger pay."

Grace hummed an apology.

Flashing a smile, Signy threw back her head and inhaled. "God, that smells good." The kitchen was redolent with the glorious odour of roasted chicken and groundnut stew, plantains in coconut milk, spicy okra and sweet mango banana pie.

"Any sign of our passenger?" Grace asked, removing dirty glasses from the tray and placing them into an industrial-sized dishwasher.

Shaking her head, Signy retrieved the tea towel from the floor. "Are you sure you want to go through with this?"

"I doubt you could have missed her. Maitland says she's a real showstopper," Grace said.

Signy eyed her mentor, taking in the sheen of sweat on her forehead and the hot blush creeping up her plump cheeks. "If you're not feeling up to it, we could try another way."

"Drop it, Signy," Grace warned. "I'm fine."

Signy held up her hands, and then wobbled across the slippery floor and pulled open the door to the walk-in fridge. "Should I open more champagne?"

Grace nodded. "If she's going to be late, we need to draw this out as long as possible."

Signy shivered as she walked inside the fridge, her skimpy serving uniform no protection against the chilly interior. Spying the last few bottles, she clutched them to her chest, then teetered back into the kitchen, shutting the heavy door with a jerk of her shoulder.

"She'll be wearing purple," Grace said.

Setting all but one of the bottles down on the counter, Signy clamped the remaining bottle between her thighs, wincing as the icy glass pressed against her warm flesh. She twisted a dishcloth around the cork. "Definitely haven't seen anyone like that, just a bunch of stuffy government types sucking back free booze." Squeezing the bottle with her knees, she gripped the cork and heaved. She sniffed with disgust when the cork refused to budge.

Snatching the bottle out of Signy's hand, Grace gave the cork an expert twist, a muffled pop heralding her success. "When we get home,

I'm having you over for dinner. You may be an excellent conductor but you have a thing or two to learn about elegant wine service."

Signy sighed but watched carefully as Grace filled each flute without spilling a drop.

When the tray was laden with glasses, Grace handed it to Signy. "See if you can find out what's happened to the target. We don't have a plan B if she doesn't show tonight."

Tucking the tray into her waist, Signy turned to go.

"It's a conspiracy, you know," Grace said.

"What is?"

Grace ran her eyes over Signy's outfit, the tight white blouse, the black pencil skirt that barely covered her bum, the ridiculous high heels. "The sexy server costume." Grace grinned. "Clearly a manifestation of the subjugation of women."

Signy laughed and felt the worm of anxiety that had taken up residence inside her stomach uncoil. That Grace was back on the job only four months after her near death was nothing short of a miracle. She undid one more button on her blouse. "Conspiracy or not, next time *you* get to be the bait."

Grace laughed aloud, her wild Marge Simpson hair jitterbugging on top of her head. "Flattery will get you everywhere." She flicked her fingers. "Now go do your gorgeous thing."

With an exaggerated wiggle of her hips, Signy sashayed out of the kitchen.

The tinkling champagne glasses rang like tiny alarm bells as Signy made her way to the grand ballroom. Rescuing a diplomat's wife from inside a foreign embassy was her toughest assignment to date in her role as a conductor on the modern Underground Railroad known as the Line. Although the dedicated volunteers that made up the Line tried to plan for complications, Signy had learned the hard way that even the simplest job could fall apart in the blink of an eye.

She shouldered her way through the door and back into the dreary reception hall. She'd expected opulence, but the folding wooden tables and dust-coloured walls reminded her more of the endless strawberry socials and ham dinners she'd been forced to attend at the local Legion hall when she was a kid.

As did the smell. Embedded in the aging green carpet, the familiar odour of ancient beer and musty tobacco smoke wafted into the air with every scrape of a shoe. Overhead, banks of fluorescent fixtures cast a stark light over the cavernous space.

The guests, on the other hand, did not disappoint. Gliding around the room in colourful robes and exotic gowns, the distinctive men and women of the host country put to shame the ubiquitous Ottawa blue suits. Threading her way through the crowd, Signy despaired that she'd ever spot the young woman in the purple dress amid so much exotic beauty.

Across the room, she heard the hearty cries of the ambassador proclaiming the arrival of more guests. Peering through the throngs of people, she caught a glimpse of the newcomers. She immediately recognized the press secretary from the photo she'd been shown. A thickset man with a neck as broad as his shoulders and a face like a pit bull, he had a balding head that shone as though he had polished it with wax.

He shrugged his overcoat into the waiting arms of a liveried footman. Underneath, he wore a snowy white jacket cut military style, adorned with official-looking baubles and braids. A pair of knife-edge black trousers and a black bow tie completed the look. A phalanx of black-clad security guards piled into the foyer behind him, their eyes roving ceaselessly around the room.

It was the woman in purple standing demurely by his side that caused Signy to let out her breath with an inaudible whistle. The young woman was stunning. She wore a flowing linen caftan the rich purple of African violets. A tribal pattern was woven into it with fine gold threads, the dress shimmering as though lit by an internal fire. Dangling gold earrings and a chunky necklace complemented the matching headdress.

Signy had no doubt that this was her new passenger. Binah Jakende's story was a tragic one. She'd been only fourteen years old when the press secretary to the ambassador of a small West African country had spotted her working the fields in her home village. He'd offered twenty cattle and a shiny zircon for her hand in marriage, a proposal her widowed mother had been eager to accept.

Life with her new husband at his home in the capital city had been brutal. In addition to almost daily beatings, Jakende had infected his young wife with some of the nastier STDs he'd picked up from his frequent visits to a local brothel. Left untreated, Binah suffered through painful bouts of pelvic inflammatory disease, which had left her unable to conceive.

Binah made no complaints, but Amara Ngozi, the wife of the ambassador, well acquainted with the press secretary's vile proclivities, was outraged. Jakende's three previous wives had suffered in the same way, each one eventually falling victim to a fatal "accident" after proving unable to present him with an heir.

Amara was determined to rescue this poor child. There was nothing to do at home—Jakende's influence was far too powerful throughout the country—but with her husband's posting to Canada, Amara knew she finally had the opportunity she'd been seeking.

From the moment Binah touched down on Canadian soil, Amara Ngozi worked doggedly to find a way to help Binah escape the clutches of the ruthless press secretary. It had been the friend of a friend who'd put her in touch with Maitland McGuinness, the storied engineer of the Line.

Just as the Underground Railroad had helped American slaves escape their barbarous masters, the Line shuttled women away from all sorts of dangerous situations. Maitland had founded the Line as a way to bring some meaning to the senseless murder of her own daughter, gunned down by a barbarous husband only weeks away from giving birth to their first child.

Appalled by Binah Jakende's sad story, Maitland swept into action. Learning from Mrs. Ngozi that Binah would be attending an embassy function later in the week, Maitland arranged for a local catering firm to provide the food and a van while she provided two of her favourite conductors, Signy Shepherd and Grace Holder, to attempt the tricky extraction.

Wielding her tray like a machete, Signy sliced through the crowd until she was standing in front of the new arrivals. Offering the tray of champagne to the man Mrs. Ngozi had described as the cruelest man she had ever met, Signy had to fight to keep a smile on her face. He exuded a sense of raw power that caused the tiny hairs on her arms to stand to attention.

He picked up a flute glass, downed the contents in one gulp, then set it back on her tray. His eyes darted to her shining high heels, then travelled slowly up the length of her long thighs before lingering on her cleavage. "I haven't seen you before," he said.

His breath burned like sulphur in the back of her throat, but she managed an inane titter before turning and offering the tray to Binah.

"Not for her," the big man snapped.

Binah peeped at Signy from under thick lashes.

"Of course," Signy said, "I'm sure I can find something more refreshing in the kitchen. Would you care for a diet soda or sparkling water perhaps?" She held the young woman's eyes and was rewarded with a spark of comprehension. Mrs. Ngozi had done her part. The girl understood that she was to proceed to the kitchen to meet up with Grace.

"Just some water, please," replied Binah, in a singsong lilt, "but first, may I ask the location of the ladies room?"

Signy bobbed as though in the presence of royalty, a pretty little gesture that diverted the press secretary's attention away from his wife. "Down that hallway and through the double doors at the back." She indicated the direction of the kitchen with a nod of her head.

"Thank you, miss," Binah said, holding Signy's eyes for a moment longer than necessary. She slipped away.

Returning her attention to the press secretary, Signy leaned in and spent several long moments examining his gaudy medals. "Wow," she said, finally, "very impressive."

The press secretary puffed out his chest. "There is much about my country that you would find remarkable. Have you seen our collection of ancient bronze statues? They are on display upstairs." He winked. "I'd love to show them to you."

She felt a spray of spittle on her cheek and for an instant was almost overwhelmed by the urge to smash her elbow into his filthy mouth. Instead, she forced herself to giggle.

He was leaning in for another pass when a loud crash brought him to an abrupt halt.

All eyes turned toward the kitchen.

"Oh my goodness," Signy murmured, "I should see about that." She whirled away.

As she made her way back through the crowd, she heard the press secretary bark out an order. Hazarding a quick glance over her shoulder, she saw the medals on his chest sparkle in the bright fluorescent lights as he waved over one of his security detail.

She doubled her pace, weaving through the crowd as quickly as she could without breaking into a run. As she approached the metal door that led to the back hallway, she could see, reflected in its shiny surface, a uniformed guard shoving his way through the crowd not far behind her.

She straight-armed her way through the heavy door. Ahead, the long hallway was deserted.

She ran.

Chapter

3

Lizzy Stone stared at the ATM, unwilling to believe what she was reading on the small screen. *Funds Unavailable—Please see your branch.*

"No, no, no," she said, removing her bank card from the machine and then pulling her American Express from her wallet with numb fingers. She was standing on the sidewalk in front of a poorly lit machine, near the outskirts of Rochester. The cold was frightening. She didn't think she'd ever felt anything like it. Her shearling coat was gorgeous—Solomon had bought it for her as a birthday gift—but it was useless against the bitter wind. She inserted her American Express card into the machine.

Please, please, please, she chanted internally, hoping to manifest the power of positive thinking as the machine took her through its automated instructions. She punched in her four-digit PIN and waited, hardly daring to breathe. Once again, the dreaded message scrolled across the screen: *Funds unavailable . . .*

Her wallet slipped from her numb fingers, its contents spilling out onto the frozen pavement. She was tempted to leave it all there, just hop back in the car and drive west until she ran out of gas. Instead, framed in the headlights of her idling car, she bent down and retrieved the scattered coins, paper bills, gift cards, and the other remnants of her old life.

Clutching everything that she could find, she stumbled back inside the car. Strapped into his car seat in the back, the baby slept. She tossed the detritus onto the seat beside her, then warmed her hands in front of the blaring heater.

Solomon must have cut off her access to their joint bank account, to her credit cards, everything. Pawing through her cash, she almost cried when she realized that she had a grand total of sixty-one dollars and thirty-seven cents. Enough for one fill-up, but what about hotel rooms? Food? Not to mention formula and diapers for the baby.

She stifled a cry of panic. If she couldn't get out of town, and in a hurry, she had no doubt what would happen when Solomon found her, and he'd track her to the ends of the earth if he had to. Glancing over her shoulder, she checked on the baby. He was awake. He stared back at her with wide eyes, then jiggled the set of brightly coloured plastic car keys clutched in his fist.

"Right," she said, "I'd get moving if I could. But where?"

The baby smacked the keys up and down.

"If you have any ideas, I'd be happy to listen."

He dropped the keys on the floor.

"Nothing, huh?" Sighing, Lizzy rested her forehead on the steering wheel and forced herself to think. She needed to go home to California, and yesterday wasn't soon enough. To get there she needed cash, and sixty-one dollars and thirty-seven cents wasn't nearly enough. The power of positive thinking provided its usual result, a big fat zilch. Nor did she have anyone in her life she knew well enough to ask for help. Not that it mattered. Who would ever take her word over that of the sainted Dr. Solomon Stone?

The baby squawked.

Lizzy crawled over the seat and retrieved the plastic keys from the floor, then handed them back to the baby. "Last chance, big boy. Any suggestions?" she asked.

He answered by blowing a huge spit bubble, his eyes crossing as he examined his creation.

That made her laugh, and she tried again, flipping through the pile of detritus from her wallet. She found a business card. Priya Subramanian, the executive director of the local women's shelter, had handed her the card after they'd had lunch together at a conference a couple of years ago. She held it up to the weak overhead light, wondering if Priya was still working at the shelter. Not that it mattered. All she had to do was call and they'd have to help her.

A frisson of hope zipped up her spine, and she picked up her cellphone, then realizing that Solomon would be able to access her phone records, tossed the phone back into her purse. Her frosty breath had steamed up the driver's window. She cleared a peephole with her fingers, then scanned the strip mall looking for a pay phone. She could see nothing but an empty sidewalk and the dark windows of closed shops.

Twisting round, she looked over her shoulder, trying to get her bearings. She thought she remembered passing a public pay phone a few blocks up the road. She'd make the call to the women's shelter from there.

She put the car in gear. Under her breath she hummed an old railroad song she'd learned as a child, and in the back seat, the baby settled down again and slept.

Chapter 4

Signy rushed into the kitchen, her mouth dropping open as she took in the dreadful tableau. A security guard, barely old enough to have hair on his chin, lay crumpled on the floor amid morsels of chicken, carrots, and squash spilling from an overturned tureen. Blood dripped freely from a nasty gash above one of his eyes, staining the front of his white shirt a vivid scarlet.

Binah Jakende stared at the guard, her eyes wide, the hem of her lovely dress soaked with fragrant peanut sauce. Grace Holder, her lips peeled back in a rictus of terror, clutched a butcher knife in her hands. The insistent ping of a timer alarm lent a macabre soundtrack to the scene.

"Grace," Signy said, taking a step forward.

Grace raised the knife over her head. "The Nembutal didn't work," she said, her eyes glittering like black diamonds.

Signy looked over her shoulder, the sound of heavy footsteps coming closer. "We have to go."

Grace peeled her fingers from the knife, one by one, until it slipped from her hand.

"Now," Signy said.

Nodding, Grace stepped over the body and, grabbing hold of Binah's arm, hustled the girl across the room.

Hoping to create a momentary diversion, Signy whipped her serving tray Frisbee-style through the open door of the walk-in cooler, where it smashed into a tower of sparkling water bottles. With the sound of shattering glass ringing in her ears, she followed Grace down a back corridor.

At the end of the hallway, the trio pushed through a heavy door and into the freezing garage. Signy flipped on the lights. She was relieved to see the broad side of the white catering van, its side doors open, nose facing the street, just as they'd left it. She'd been afraid that the young guard might have disabled their getaway vehicle. The only other car in the garage was a black Mercedes Benz sedan parked on the far side of the van.

Struggling to keep up with Grace's longer strides, Binah tripped, landing heavily on one knee. She stifled a cry of pain.

"I'm sorry," Grace said, stopping to help the girl back onto her feet.

The exterior garage door was open, and through the clouds of frozen breath, Signy could see the flash of headlights as cars whizzed by out on Range Road. She hoped the traffic was light.

Binah had just made it to her feet when the guard who had followed Signy from the banquet hall barrelled through the door behind them.

Stepping in front of Binah, Signy watched the guard approach. Built like a front-end loader, he had a head like a shovel and fists made for crushing rocks. If she let him get any closer, she wouldn't stand a chance.

She took a step back, pretending to stumble.

The man sneered.

"Please don't hurt me," she said, letting a squeal of terror ring through her words.

He ran his eyes over her, taking in the black miniskirt and high heels. With a dismissive snort, he dropped his fists.

"I was only trying to help," she said. "That man over there tried to kidnap Mrs. Jakende." Signy pointed to a spot behind the big thug. As she waited for his eyes to follow her finger, she calculated the exact length and number of strides she would need to ensure that she had her weight planted firmly on her left foot when she reached him.

In the instant he looked away she exploded forward, managing to land a devastating kick on the inner aspect of his right knee before he saw her coming. She felt a sick satisfaction as the knee gave way with a horrible crack, and he crashed to the floor.

"Go," she shouted, turning back toward the van. She could see Binah Jakende, her purple skirt hiked up around her knees, crawling in through the side doors, but slumped against the side of the van, Grace wasn't moving.

Signy raced to her mentor's side. Falling to her knees, she conducted a quick visual assessment but could find no sign of injury. "Grace? What is it? What's wrong?"

Arms limp by her side, Grace stared straight ahead, her eyes blank. Her skin was grey, and beads of sweat the size of pearls stood out on her forehead. Globules of groundnut stew clung to her frizzy hair.

"Get up," Signy yelled, grabbing the front of Grace's blouse, prepared to haul her up by force if necessary, when Grace suddenly began to gasp for air, her breath steaming between them like white thunderclouds.

"Ethan," Grace said, her hands clawing at her face.

"Can you help?" Signy called to Binah.

They almost had her on her feet when Signy felt a massive hand clamp her around her waist. Shrieking with surprise, she dug her fingernails into the leathery skin—to no avail—and then a powerful arm swung her up off her feet and sent her flying through the air. She collapsed in a heap on the cold concrete.

Binah screamed.

Ignoring the sudden flare of pain in her hip, Signy flipped to her feet, horrified to see the injured guard limping toward her. "Grace!" Signy shouted, glancing over her shoulder. "I don't know what you're trying to pull, but I could use some help here."

There was no response.

The thug launched himself at her.

Signy got in two quick blows to his face, but she might as well have been slamming her fist into solid rock. She tried again, driving her knee into his injured leg. The move had the desired effect; the big man fell heavily back down to the ground. Unfortunately, he dragged her with him.

Half pinned under his body, Signy looked wildly around the cavernous space, searching for anything she might use as a weapon. If she let him get the rest of his huge body on top of her, she'd be doomed. She could see an assortment of steel gardening tools hanging from hooks on the wall, but they might as well have been on the moon. "Grace!" she shouted.

Growling, the man tried to heave the rest of his body over hers. He pawed at her flesh, and she knew what a rabbit must feel like inside the jaws of a python. When he swung his good leg up over her, exposing his injured knee, she saw her chance.

Gritting her teeth, she drove the heel of her shoe deep into the flesh between his shattered patella and dislocated knee joint. For one horrifying moment, she thought her effort had been in vain. The giant uttered an agonized grunt but refused to roll over. She jammed the heel in deeper, twisting her foot back and forth, feeling the strain as tendons and ligaments resisted the pressure before tearing apart with a staccato *pop*, *pop*, *pop*.

His mouth opened wide, and a river of hot saliva poured from his trembling lips onto her cheeks. He stared down at her, uncomprehending. Then his eyes rolled back, and he was out.

Crawling out from under his inert body, Signy raised her head, thankful to see Grace finally hauling herself to her feet.

"You okay?" she asked.

Grace wiped sweat from her eyes.

"Time to go," Signy said, before slamming the side doors and running around to the driver's side.

Grace climbed slowly into the passenger seat.

Just as Signy cranked the engine, two more guards rushed into the garage. Outside, a third guard was hoofing through the deep snow, trying to close the wrought iron gate out by the road. She had only a few seconds if she hoped to beat him.

She put the pedal to the metal, the back wheels squealing as they failed to catch on the smooth concrete floor. With her brain screaming in protest, she released the pressure on the gas. She heard hands pawing at the back door handle just as she applied a gentle pressure to the gas pedal and the tires caught. The van leapt forward.

Fishtailing down the icy driveway, Signy fought with the wheel, the back threatening to slip sideways and shoot the awkward vehicle broadside into the perimeter fence. The outside security man heaved his shoulder against the frozen gate. Her heart sank when she saw him finally manage to get it moving.

In the rear-view mirror, she could see the two inside men pile into the black Mercedes. "Hang on!" she shouted, feeling the rear tires come back under her control. She shot forward, her lips curling into a triumphant grin as she watched the guard at the gate leap to one side as the heavy catering van barrelled past him.

Bumping the van out onto Range Road, she wrenched the wheel to the left and once again slammed her foot on the gas.

Behind her, the big Mercedes shot through the gate and made the same sliding turn.

Signy cursed when the clumsy van refused to give her more speed. Ahead, a green signal turned amber. She flew toward the intersection, the van exploding over the icy ruts in the road. Crumpled in a heap in the back of the van, Binah Jakende shrieked.

As Signy whizzed through the intersection, she saw a red Ford pickup truck about a block in front of her lose control of its back end as it slid over a patch of black ice. "Bloody hell," she shouted, steering the van directly toward the hazardous section of road. Behind her, the huge German car was so close she could no longer see its front grille in the mirror.

Signy waited until they were almost upon the shimmering patch of black ice before yanking the wheel to the left. The van responded, sliding sideways for several long moments before roaring down a side street.

The Mercedes was not so lucky. Signy touched the brakes, watching the black sedan spiral out of control on the black ice before climbing up and over the curb and onto the snow-covered park area that separated Range Road from the frozen Rideau Canal.

With screeching metal and flashing sparks, the Mercedes rocked up on two wheels, slid on its side for one precarious moment, then rolled over onto its roof, spinning toward the ice-covered canal like a badly thrown curling stone.

With a grim smile, Signy hit the gas and shot off into the night.

The driver of a silver SUV pulled to the curb on Range Road. He peered down the side street and watched the red brake lights on the catering van wink on briefly before it shot forward, only to disappear over a small rise in the road. Grinning, he glanced over his shoulder at the Mercedes, watching it spin in lazy circles toward the Rideau Canal.

Snaking through the city of Ottawa for almost eight kilometres, the Rideau boasted the world's longest skating rink. Whenever he travelled he enjoyed exploring the world's biggest this and the city's longest that, and he'd checked the canal out earlier while waiting for Signy and her partner to arrive at the embassy. He'd enjoyed watching the crazy Canadians gliding and twirling and swinging hockey sticks, their brightly coloured toques like winter blossoms in the snow.

He watched the Mercedes, hoping it would slide into the canal, break through the ice, and sink to the bottom. No luck. The heavy car came to rest on its roof, just shy of the icy waterway. Shouted imprecations erupted from inside the vehicle, and he watched a booted foot emerge from one of the side windows. Excited skaters approached the scene from both directions.

Relaxing in his seat, he smiled. She could drive; he had to give her that. Despite the insane risk she'd taken, it had been a pleasure to watch her in action. Still, he'd been hanging around this frozen city a tad longer than he found prudent. It was time to return to his home in the desert.

He heard the strained squawk of his cellphone.

Frowning, he clicked on the phone. "What is it?"

"Hello to you too, Alex."

"Helen, you are a ray of sunshine." Hired as his administrative fixer, Helen had become much more than that, and although he was loath to admit it, he enjoyed talking to her.

"I'm glad you finally noticed," she replied. "Listen, you asked me to let you know if there was any action on those fishing lines you set."

Alex felt his heart thump inside his chest. "And?"

"You had a nibble. Tiny, but it was there."

"You're sure?" said Alex, his mouth dry.

"No doubt about it. Someone has definitely been poking around."

"Excellent. Can you get me on an earlier flight home?"

"Already done."

"Helen?"

"Yes, Alex?"

"You're too good to me."

"I know that. Oh, and Alex?"

"Hmm?"

"I'd love to put a face to your beautiful voice. There is a fabulous new steak in town. What do you say? Tomorrow night, eight o'clock? I assume you know where I live?"

"Can't. I'm a vegetarian."

"Yippee. I love tofu."

"Helen?" he said, chuckling.

"Yes, Alex?"

"Soon." He hung up the phone before she had a chance to say anything more.

Chapter 5

Dr. Solomon Stone gazed out over the audience, soaking in the admiration. The who's who of New York City had gathered in this luxurious ballroom just to see him. Loosening his tie, he ran his fingers through his hair, giving it the tousled look he'd practiced repeatedly in front of a mirror at home.

"In conclusion," he said, flashing his most charming smile, "I would like to thank all of you. Due to your generous support, thousands more of the world's most vulnerable people have access to timely and effective trauma care."

The crowd rose in a spontaneous ovation.

In the front row, a pretty little redhead caught his eye and he stepped behind the podium lest his excitement show. Behind him, the final slide of his PowerPoint presentation shone on a large screen. It was a picture of him, dressed in green medical scrubs. He was standing in front of a medical tent, surrounded by a crowd of smiling African faces. Keeping his eyes off the sexy little thing in the front row, Stone beamed as the walls shook with the rolling thunder of mutual appreciation.

Eventually, Stone invited the crowd to resume their seats with a wave of his hand. In the shuffle of chairs and murmuring of voices, he tapped a few keys on his laptop. "If you will allow me, I would like to take a moment or two more of your time."

On the screen, Stone's face was replaced by the image of a gaunt young man with no legs. Hunkered down on a makeshift scooter that was no more than a sheet of plywood fitted out with caster wheels, the man was holding out a tin cup on a crowded street corner.

"As you're aware, I've been taking this little canned presentation around the country for too many years now. The faces change from year to year, of course, as do the hot spots. Lebanon, Sudan, Darfur, Syria." He gripped the sides of the podium with both hands and leaned forward. "What doesn't change, year after year after bloody year, is how relatively little we've been able to help."

A murmur of compassionate dissent filled the room.

Stone hung his head, and then waited until he could hear a pin drop before pacing across the small stage, his fingers tented in front of his chest. "For too long now," he said softly, forcing the audience to lean forward in their chairs, "my team and I have tried our best to patch the wounds, to heal the burns, to save lives." He spread his arms wide, palms up. "But at what cost?"

He looked out over the sea of puzzled faces, his heart pounding in his chest. He'd imagined this moment his entire life, and now that it had finally arrived, he wanted to savour every second.

"Despite our best efforts, the level of tissue repair we can manage in the field is woefully inadequate. We don't have access to sophisticated technology, nor do we have the time or resources to manage the weeks, months, or even years of treatment that many of our patients require to return to a functioning life. Instead we patch them up as best we can, pump them full of antibiotics, and then send them home to towns and villages where there is no medical follow up."

A flurry of appalled head shaking broke out in the crowd.

"And don't think that we in the developed world are immune." He pointed to one of the grand windows overlooking the New York skyline. "Out there, some of the finest hospitals in the world are doing cutting-edge research for wound and burn repair. Yet even in the most technologically advanced city in the world, people are burdened with horrific scars, open sores that refuse to heal, or wounds that are simply too extensive to repair with the skin graft technology that currently exists."

Stone paused for several long moments until he was sure that every face had turned toward him. "As the people who have supported my independent research, I wanted you to be the first to know that I am on the cusp of introducing a new technology that will put an end to the expensive, painful, and barbaric methods the medical community currently employs to treat catastrophic wounds."

Listening to the buzzing crowd, Stone had to struggle to maintain a professional demeanour. He walked over to the podium, wiped the perspiration from his hands with a handkerchief, and then pressed a key. The image of a plastic petri dish dotted with a living culture coalesced onto the screen behind him.

"As you know," he continued, "many breakthroughs in science

have come about by lucky chance. Penicillin, for example, was discovered because Alexander Fleming forgot to clean up his lab before going away on holiday." He chuckled. "Lucky Dr. Fleming. I can't remember the last time I took a vacation." He paused to allow a wave of laughter to peter out, then pointed at the screen. "The amazing discovery I am about to share with you was also discovered by accident, deep inside the skin cells of one very special donor."

He heard a shuffling of chairs as members of the audience leaned in closer. "As many of you know, I have been working for many years now trying to improve skin-grafting techniques." He refastened the buttons on his suit jacket. "Let me provide some context for those of you who are new to the field. Currently, our best option for graft success is to harvest the patient's own skin cells and then grow those cells on a biological latticework in order to create enough skin to cover the superficial top layer of the wound. The process takes weeks, and the resultant tissue is fragile and subject to a high rate of graft failure."

"There are other methods, of course. Xenografts, where skin from another species such as a pig is utilized on a temporary basis, is sometimes helpful. Artificial skin also shows promise. Full-thickness grafts, where an entire section of cadaver skin is grafted onto the recipient, results in minimal scarring but is subject to high rates of donor rejection."

He shrugged. "These methods are adequate to some degree, but as you can imagine, they are not terribly practical in the harried and poorly funded medical theatres common to conflict zones. What we need in a field hospital is the technology to quickly grow a full-thickness skin graft that the patient's body will not reject." He paused and looked out over the crowd, revelling in the moment.

He took a deep breath. "I am thrilled to announce that I have developed that technology."

He waited for the excited murmurs to die down before continuing. "I have been experimenting with various types of human skin cells, trying to find a way to enhance their growth rates. I was working with one particular specimen when I noticed something very unusual.

"These particular cells," he said, turning to the screen and running his laser pointer over a dark smudge in a petri dish, "did not die out, as most cells do over several days or weeks, but continued to grow at an unprecedented rate. In fact, when kept under controlled conditions, these cells never died. They are, for all intents and purposes, immortal."

There was a scrape of chairs as members of the audience sought to get a better look at the image on the screen. The redhead in the front row was leaning forward and he could see down the front of her blouse. A spray of freckles dotted her alabaster skin and she had the creamiest breasts he'd seen in some time. He forced himself to look away.

"To put this into perspective, to date, the only truly reliable immortal cell line originated from cancerous cervical cells removed from a dying patient in the nineteen fifties. Known as HeLa cells, they are still alive over sixty years later and continue to be useful in a multitude of experimental studies all over the world. The skin cell line I have discovered shows similar properties."

He leaned over and tapped a key on the computer. A new image popped up on the screen, a section of thick tissue about five inches square lying in a medical tray. "When I observed the extraordinary characteristics of this new cell line, I attempted to grow them on a biological lattice. In just days, those few skin cells differentiated into all the layers that make up human skin and spread throughout the lattice to create a perfectly formed, full-thickness graft."

A hum ran through the crowd as those with even a rudimentary scientific knowledge took in the implications.

"A thrilling development indeed," Stone said, with a pleased smile, "but before I got too excited, I needed to explore the issue of compatibility. The skin is an organ, just like the heart or lungs or corneas. And because the body is geared to reject all foreign matter, antirejection medications are key after organ transplant." He shook his head. "Unfortunately, developing nations have limited access to antimalarial drugs, let alone antirejection medications."

He gave up trying to mask the joy he was feeling. "I discovered that not only is this very special skin cell line immortal, it is also supercompatible, meaning that it is not recognized as foreign by the human body's immune system. The body does not attempt to reject this new skin. Instead, it is accepted and integrated into the host, as though it were just another part of the host's own body."

The crowd roared its approval.

Stone beamed. "Imagine," he continued, his voice growing thick with emotion, "that instead of condemning a man to a life of chronic pain and poverty, we send him home a fully functioning husband and father. Instead of amputating the leg of a ten-year-old girl, we have the ability to repair the catastrophic damage so that once again she might run and play.

"Imagine," Stone shouted over the crowd, "skin cells that grow at an incredible rate, and will not be rejected by the host. Immortal skin cells that can be transported anywhere in the world and grown wherever needed. If my initial results prove as successful in clinical trials, and I am certain they will, then with your help, we will have revolutionized the treatment of wound repair, not only in the world's hot spots, but also right here at home."

The crowd jumped to its feet, the applause deafening. In the front row, the gorgeous redhead laughed and clapped, her emerald eyes sparkling.

Solomon Stone drank in the adoration, higher than he'd ever been in his life.

Chapter 6

Slicing through the volcanic bedrock that makes up the southern edge of the Canadian Shield, the highway between Linden Valley and Ottawa seemed almost deserted. Signy steered around a jutting rock face, the road lit only by the weak light of a quarter moon. In the passenger seat Grace sat quietly, while Binah dozed in the back.

They'd left the catering van in a long-term parking space at the Ottawa Airport and transferred into Grace's Prius. If the van was discovered by embassy security, they would waste time poring over flight manifests searching for Binah Jakende.

Signy had tried to start a conversation once they'd cleared the outskirts of Ottawa, but Grace had shut her down with a muttered "Later." The steady roar of the heater, set to high against night air that had plunged far down into subzero territory, acted as a further buffer. Sick at the thought that she'd ruined everything, Signy silently replayed the events in the embassy.

The press secretary's sulphurous breath, groundnut stew splattered on the floor, blood spraying from the young guard's forehead. Grace leaning against the van, her eyes blank, overwhelmed by the mind-robbing, gut-wrenching dread that gets people killed. Mostly, she remembered her angry shouts, demanding that Grace snap out of it.

The car jolted over a deep pothole in the frost-torn tarmac and Binah mumbled something unintelligible. Signy flicked her eyes to the rear-view mirror but the girl did not wake. In the passenger's seat, Grace reached out and clutched the door handle.

"Terrible road," Signy said, just loud enough to be heard over the heater.

Grace's only response was a grumbling noise in the back of her throat before she leaned her head against the cold window and closed her eyes.

Sighing, Signy tried to concentrate on the road, but in her heart, she could see nothing but darkness ahead.

Signy was listening to late-night talk radio on the CBC as she drove into the outskirts of Linden Valley. In a charming story plucked from the archives, an elderly man from Wales was waxing poetic on a colony of ring-necked parakeets that had taken up residence in his back garden. She felt her stomach relax. She couldn't remember the last time she'd been quite so relieved to be home.

Situated in the Lake District north of Toronto, Linden Valley is a mid-sized Ontario city with a population of ten thousand. Those ranks swell in the summer when local cottagers pour into town, but close to midnight in the dead of winter, the town seemed devoid of life.

Signy buzzed down the main drag, sailing through one green light after another. She flew past the mall, the vast parking lot empty except for the ever-growing mountain of plowed snow. Only the twenty-four-hour McDonald's, with its bright golden arches lighting the dark sky, showed any activity. A few cars idled in the parking area while their owners ran in to stock up on late-night grease.

Grace shifted in her seat. "Home?" she said, without looking at Signy.

"Almost," Signy said. "Grace? Can I ask you—"

"I can't tell you how much I'm looking forward to a hot bath," Grace interrupted, "right after we get this poor thing settled." She leaned over into the back seat and touched Binah lightly on her knee.

Binah Jakende's eyes flew open, and she scrambled upright.

"It's okay. We're here," said Grace, as Signy made the turn onto the quiet side street that housed the women's shelter.

"Here?" Binah whispered.

"Safe and sound," Grace said, pointing out the shelter to Binah. Vicky's Place sat just off the main drag, far enough from the busy downtown to provide a semblance of normality for the residents, but close enough that needed services were within walking distance. Constructed in the classic Ontario style, the building was a red brick box with a peaked roofline, trimmed in whimsical, Victorian white millwork. Over the years, the need for more beds had necessitated an addition that took up much of the backyard. At peak capacity, Vicky's Place could house as many as twenty women and children.

Signy flicked on the turn signal, then bumped the Prius up and over the compacted ridge of icy slush blocking the driveway.

"What happens now?" Binah asked.

"A conductor named Thelma is flying in from Calgary tomorrow morning," Grace said, "She'll take you the rest of the way."

"I'm not staying with you?" Binah said, her voice squeaking with alarm.

"Thelma's great," Signy said. "I worked with her last year, although you might want to bring some earplugs."

Grace fired an exasperated look at Signy, who responded with a contrite shrug. "Please, try not to worry," Grace continued. "Thelma is wonderful."

"Never mind me," Signy said. "You'll like Thelma, I promise."

Binah tried to smile.

The car rocked over a snowbank as Signy squeezed it into the one remaining parking spot. A motion-sensitive security lamp flickered to life, and within seconds, the cluttered backyard blazed with light. Twisting in her seat, she looked over her shoulder at Binah. "We'd better get you bundled up. You'll freeze to death in that dress."

Binah plucked at her beautiful but useless gown. "My mother would have loved this dress. When he was alive, my father used to call her his little magpie. She couldn't resist pretty things." Binah's bottom lip quivered.

Signy and Grace exchanged a dismayed glance.

"She sold me to that terrible man for the price of a few cows and a shiny stone. Why?"

"I'm sorry, honey," Grace said.

Binah's teeth began to chatter.

Leaning into the back seat, Grace shook out the brown parka that Binah had been using as a pillow and pressed it into the girl's hands. "Let's get you inside. What you need now is a warm bath and some sleep."

Clutching the jacket to her chest, Binah offered a wan smile.

"I can't even imagine what you've gone through," Grace continued. "It's going to take time to process, but I promise, as soon as you're settled, we'll make sure you have someone to talk to. You won't have to do it alone."

Binah's eyes welled with tears. "No. I don't want to talk about . . ."

"You certainly don't have to, but I hope you change your mind," Grace said, kindly. "Talking can help."

"I couldn't agree more." Signy held Grace's eyes with her own.

Grace opened her mouth to speak, then shut it again, the whites of her eyes glittering in the dark car.

"I understand that," Binah said. "It's just that—" She cleared her throat.

Grace closed her eyes, and Signy felt a sudden drop of pressure inside the car, as though a bad storm were rolling in.

A crease formed between Binah's brow and she glanced at Signy.

"Just what, Binah?" Signy said, jumping in to fill the sudden silence. "What are you afraid of?"

Binah brought a hand to her throat and shook her head.

Signy waited, the silence crackling between them like lightning.

It was Grace who broke the impasse. Opening her eyes, she said, "I know what she means. Binah is afraid that if she opens her mouth to speak, she might start screaming and never stop."

Her dark eyes fixed on Grace, the girl nodded.

Grace inclined her own head in response.

"That won't happen," Signy said. "The fact that you made it this far speaks volumes. You have people who are willing to stand by you, no matter what. You will come through this an even stronger person. I promise. Now let's get inside Vicky's, where it's warm."

Tumbling out into the frigid night air, the trio skated across the frozen lot, Binah held securely under each arm by Grace on one side, Signy on the other. Safely inside the alcove, they stomped snow from their boots while staff examined them by remote camera. After a few seconds, the inner door clicked open, and they piled inside.

Martha, who had worked the overnight shift for longer than Grace could remember, bustled down the hallway to greet them. She wore a pair of loose sweats and a bulky sweater. Faded skin hung like a loose curtain on her rod-like cheekbones, bony protuberances jutted from her wrists, and her head was bald save for fine brown fuzz, but her blue eyes sparkled. "You made it," she exclaimed, a relieved smile on her face.

"Martha," Grace said, "I'm so glad to see you back."

"Not as glad as I am to be here," Martha replied. The two women shared a brief hug and an even shorter back and forth about Martha's improving health status.

Breaking free, Martha turned to Binah. "Welcome," she said, warmly.

Binah stared at her, dark circles like bruises under her eyes.

"My goodness, you poor thing. To bed with you," Martha said. She began to lead the young girl down the hall toward the stairs that led up to the bedrooms. "We have a lovely room made up."

Binah whispered something in Martha's ear.

"Of course, dear," Martha replied.

Binah turned back to Signy and Grace. "I want to thank you, ladies. So much. I don't know what would have happened if you hadn't come for me." Tears sprang to her eyes, and her voice trailed off.

Grace stepped forward and gave the girl a warm hug.

Signy hung back, grinning stupidly.

"What you need is a good sleep and a hot bath," said Martha, touching Binah's arm.

Grace smiled. "Yes, indeed. A hot bath cures all ills."

Binah nodded, and then followed Martha upstairs.

After the two women had disappeared, Signy turned to Grace. "What about you?"

"What about me?" Grace said.

Catching the warning look in Grace's eye, Signy swallowed hard, the questions she was dying to ask sticking in her throat like a bitter pill.

Grace attempted a smile. "How about you? Will you be able to sleep?"

"Like a log," Signy said, and meant it.

"Because if you need to debrief . . ."

"I'm fine," Signy said. Taking a deep breath, she plowed ahead. "What about you? I mean, shouldn't we talk about what happened back there?"

"The only thing I'm going to do is have a long soak, then fall into bed and die." Grace shooed Signy toward the door. "I suggest you do the same."

"Are you sure?"

Grace tugged Signy's hood tight around her cheeks. "Go home."

Signy felt suddenly very young.

"Good," Grace said. "We meet with Maitland at one-thirty, so I won't expect you in the office until noon. Sleep well."

Signy nodded and turned away.

"Oh, Signy, by the way?"

She turned back.

"I'd appreciate it if you didn't mention my little bout of opening night jitters to Maitland. It would only worry her, and I'm fine now. Really."

Working hard to keep her expression neutral, Signy felt an uncomfortable warmth rise in her cheeks. She dropped her eyes to the floor. Feeling suddenly adrift, she clung to the thought that it was Grace Holder who had given her a second chance when no one else would, and Grace Holder who had offered friendship when everyone else turned away. Hell, this crazy woman with her Marge Simpson hair had even taken a bullet for her. If she let Grace down in any way, she would never forgive herself. Signy felt her toes brush solid ground.

"Are we good?" Grace asked.

Signy held Grace's eyes. "I won't say a thing. You have my word."

Pulling open the door, Signy hurried outside before Grace could read the doubt in her eyes. She coughed reflexively as a wave of icy air bit the back of her throat. Head down against a bitter wind, she picked her way across the slippery parking lot. She hated leaving the cozy warmth of a toasty building to face subzero temperatures and hazardous footing. The only thing she loathed more was trying to start her frozen car.

It took several tries before her ancient Saturn finally chugged over with a long, low groan. It was a few minutes more before the car warmed up enough to shift into drive. Shivering uncontrollably, Signy decided to set aside her concerns about Grace's frightening behaviour, the potential fallout from their botched extraction, and her scheduled debriefing with the Engineer.

She had other things to think about, like the brunch in the morning she'd been anticipating with a mix of excitement and dread since the unexpected invitation had arrived in her inbox a few days go. Right now, however, all she wanted was to get home, crawl under the covers, and crash for twelve straight hours. The light turned green. Sighing, she pressed down gently on the gas pedal and steered the car north toward home.

As she pulled into her own driveway, the image of Grace's odd behaviour at the embassy was still with her. Who was Ethan, and why had Grace called his name?

Chapter 7

Burying her head in her pillow, Signy sighed. As if the incessant *plink-plink-plink* of the bathtub faucet wasn't bad enough, she was sure she'd heard furtive scratching coming from under her bed. A mouse must have decided that braving the gauntlet of traps she'd set around her small apartment was preferable to freezing to death outside.

Her nose felt like an ice cube. The baseboard heater had been fighting a losing battle all night with the frigid winter chill. Even so, under the heavy duvet, her skin was clammy with sweat. She'd had a restless night, her sleep fractured by the spectre of last night's debacle at the embassy. She rubbed her hip. It was still sore where the big goon had tossed her onto the hard concrete. She wouldn't be surprised if she had a huge bruise.

She gave up any hope of catching a few extra winks when the guy next door fired up his truck, revving the diesel engine until her windows rattled. When he finally took off in a howl of grinding gears, she relaxed, telling herself that at least she didn't have to put up with that barrage every morning. She usually left for work long before he did.

Her eyes flew open. Fingers scrabbling across the surface of her nightstand, she grabbed for her cellphone but only managed to sweep it onto the floor. She had to reach down and claw under the bed to retrieve it.

Checking the time, she threw off the bedclothes and leapt to her feet. The anemic winter light filtering through the blinds on the window had tricked her. It was a quarter to ten in the morning. She was due to meet Ben Tran for brunch in fifteen minutes.

She flew into the bathroom. A quick glance in the mirror confirmed her worst suspicions. There was not a chance in hell she was leaving the house without a shower. She looked like death, dark circles under eyes, face blotchy, her hair tangled into a squirrel's nest.

She thought about sending Ben a quick text to let him know she'd be late but didn't know his number. When he'd disappeared last fall, he'd left no forwarding information. For the millionth time, she wondered why he'd left Linden Valley so quickly, and without a word to anyone.

Without a word to me, she amended as she stepped into the shower. God knew she had pathetic taste in men. Certainly, her on-again, off-again flings with Zef couldn't be more wrong for her. Still, she'd given him his marching papers right after she'd arranged for his release from jail a few months earlier, and so far, and she'd managed to stick to her guns.

Ben was different. She appreciated his sweet smile and shy phone calls. They'd had a couple of memorable dinner dates last fall. He had a goofy way about him that put her at ease. Even though it was against policy, she'd opened up about her work as a conductor on the Line. It had been a relief to be honest with someone about her moonlighting gig. Better still, he'd made her laugh. A lot. Which was why his sudden disappearance had been so strange.

Stranger still was the voice mail he'd left yesterday on her work phone letting her know that he was in town for a couple of days and asking her to meet him at the diner this morning. From the businesslike tone of his voice, she could tell he'd made the call from the precinct, and all the hours of tossing and turning had left her no closer to solving the mystery of why he wanted to meet.

Out of the shower, she twisted her wet hair into a neat braid and then, on the off chance that this might be some sort of a date, she applied a dash of makeup. Dropping her towel on the bedroom floor, she slipped into a pair of black jeans and a white sweater, then wound a blue scarf around her neck, hoping that it brought out her eyes. At the door, she pulled on a navy pea coat instead of her bulky parka and a pair of equally impractical knee-high leather boots.

Before slipping her cellphone into the pocket, she checked her email. There was always the chance he'd cancelled on her. She didn't want to show up looking like an idiot if he wasn't even going to be there.

She found nothing from Ben, but the presence of a message in her inbox from Grace gave her pause. She opened it, not sure what she was expecting to find, and was relieved to see that it was just a group email reminding all staff of a new safety policy that took effect that day. She tucked her phone away, determined not to think about Grace, Maitland, or the Line, until she absolutely had to.

At ten minutes past ten, she was behind the wheel, struggling to get her car started. Every time she turned the key, the groans of protest from the car's aging engine grew more plaintive. Finally, the useless hunk of crap couldn't even muster a sigh of protest. If the engine still had any life left in it at all, she'd probably just drowned it.

Signy slammed her palms against the steering wheel. "Get ready for the scrapyard, you lousy shit box." As she lurched out of the car, she forgot she had chosen form over function with her cute leather boots, slipped on a patch of ice, and almost fell flat on her face.

After a graceless recovery, she glanced up the road. Plowed and sanded, the sidewalk seemed safe. If she really hoofed it, she might still be able to make her breakfast (date?) with Ben Tran. Picking her way down the treacherous driveway, she made it safely to the sidewalk, then started to jog.

She could do the route with her eyes closed. She ran this circuit toward downtown almost every day during good weather. Most of the time she enjoyed watching the scenery go by, the rows of red brick houses, the imposing new library building, the charming tourist shops. At this time of year, however, she kept her eyes prudently on the sidewalk, taking care to sidestep patches of black ice.

She held a glove to her nose and mouth in a losing battle to filter the toxic clouds of vehicle exhaust unable to escape into the atmosphere due to a massive low-pressure weather system. A leaden stratus cloud deck had settled over the city, and Signy thought she could reach up and touch it.

Only February, and she was already sick to death of winter. Worse, she'd heard on the news that the damned groundhog had seen his stupid shadow, which meant at least six more weeks of icy weather.

Rounding the corner onto the main downtown circle, she slowed to a walk. She wasn't about to let Ben Tran see her running. She checked the time on the tower clock that crowned the town hall, cheered to see that she was only fifteen minutes late.

When she finally stepped into the delicious warmth of the diner, however, she was irked to find no sign of Ben Tran. Spotting the lone server, a wiry woman sporting hair the colour of Kraft Dinner, Signy asked if an Asian guy, about yay high (she held her hand just inches above her own head), had been in.

"Sorry, honey," the server said, with a gruff, smoker's voice, "you're out of luck."

Signy shrugged. "Story of my life. If I didn't have bad luck, I'd have no luck at all."

The server, who had the name *Wanda* embroidered onto the left breast pocket of her green cotton blouse, let loose a barking guffaw. "Take a seat. I'll fix you something warm and we'll compare notes."

With a chuckle that was half amused and half despairing, Signy rolled her eyes. "We'd be here all day." She was turning to leave when the door opened and a gust of icy wind sliced through the cozy room. A table of gossiping retirees joined Signy in gawking at the good-looking newcomer, who was shrugging his apologies to the room for letting in the cold air. Dressed in full dress blues, right down to the gold braid and spit-and-polish shoes, he cut quite a stunning figure.

Catching sight of Signy, he flashed a delighted grin.

Her knees took on a distinct wobble that had nothing to do with her recent spill.

"I'm so sorry I'm late," he said, removing his stiff blue hat, revealing neatly trimmed dark hair.

“I wouldn’t make a habit of being tardy, young man,” Wanda said, standing in front of him with her fists jammed into her bony hips. “There are plenty of other fish in the sea, especially for a girl this pretty.”

Signy shot a horrified glance at the server, who smiled sweetly in return.

“Never again, ma’am,” Ben said, solemnly, “I promise.”

“Kill me now,” Signy muttered.

“Shall we?” Ben said, pressing his fingertips to the small of her back and guiding her over to a booth in the corner.

As she put one foot in front of the other, her brain struggled to come up with a plausible excuse should her body suddenly collapse in a twitching heap of sexual tension right there on the floor of the diner. The thought made her giggle, and she had relaxed somewhat before they finally sat down.

He leaned forward and, after swearing her to secrecy, began to tell her what he’d been up to over the past several months. Caught up in his fascinating tale, she forgot all about her nerves.

Chapter 8

The Tracker pulled his ball cap down low over his eyes as he pushed through the exit doors of the Albuquerque International Sunport. Low in the sky, the winter sun fought a losing battle with the morning chill. He rolled his head, trying to work the kinks out of his neck. The best flight Helen had been able to arrange was a seven-hour overnight marathon with two plane changes. Still, it was good to be home and he was eager to find out who, or what, had nibbled at his fishing lines.

Bypassing a line of idling taxis, he wheeled his carry-on bag behind him, threading his way through rows of vehicles in the cavernous parking garage. Behind his sunglasses, his eyes worked a grid pattern, searching for anything out of the ordinary. A hint of movement, a shadow, the squeal of a tire. His internal alarm system remained silent. Not even a faint ping.

He'd expected as much. He went to great lengths to fly under the radar. In his line of business there was always some malcontent itching to take him down. Angry relatives, disappointed clients, former runners seeking revenge. The list was endless, really. Not to mention that somewhere out there, he had poked something with a stick. He would be wise to take even more precautions than usual until he determined exactly who, or what, that something might be.

His footsteps echoed in the hollow parking garage, dim amber lights casting a sickly glow. He spotted his Ford F-150 in a back corner but, instead of heading toward it, made a ninety-degree turn and strode toward the elevator. Enclosed in a concrete structure with windows on the north side, both the elevator and adjacent stairway appeared deserted. A quick glance inside confirmed that no one was lurking in the small lobby. He moved around the back of the structure and waited.

Tuning in to his nerve endings, he listened for a cautionary ping. Nothing. Of course, inside the parking structure it was possible that a hitter could be hunkered down with a rifle, but he doubted it. It was too enclosed, and the angles were all wrong. A few more minutes of patient observation confirmed his hypothesis. He was alone.

Two and a half hours later, he pulled up to the front of his double-wide trailer deep in Navajo country. Exiting the truck, he stepped down onto the clean sand.

February was typically the driest month of the year in New Mexico, and yet a hint of creosote on the wind suggested it had rained while he was away. Shading his eyes with his hand, he peered out over the vast expanse of desert and felt a shiver run down his spine when he saw the sun flash scarlet off the monolithic peak of Shiprock in the north.

Rain in February? Blood on the Shiprock? Two bad omens in one day. A superstitious man would consult with the local medicine man, but he was a modern man. He did not believe in the Witchery Way.

With a shake of his head, he pulled open the door and stepped inside. "I'm home," he called, and was rewarded with the house springing to life. Recessed incandescent lights powered up, the coffee maker ground the dark-roast beans he'd preloaded, and a series of clicks and buzzes indicated other essentials had whirred to life.

He felt his shoulders relax, happy to have returned to the only place he felt truly comfortable. "Report?"

"All systems within normal limits, zero probability of incursion." A mechanical voice issued from speakers located at strategic points throughout the trailer. He'd installed the voice recognition technology as a means of efficient communication with the computer mainframe that controlled many of the functions of his home. With simple commands, the system monitored power, water, and ambient light levels, regulated all appliance usage, monitored internal and exterior security, and even watered his plants.

"How was your trip, sir?"

"A bit of a hoot, actually." He scrubbed at the stubble on his jaw, then decanted a cup of dark roast from the coffee maker.

Striding over to the bank of computers sitting atop a steel and glass table, he examined the indicators that scrolled continuously across the twenty-seven-inch Apple monitor, and he confirmed the computer's assessment that his home remained a safe haven.

He strolled into the living area, his feet gliding over the honey blond hardwood, waxed and shining. Arranged in front of a picture window, a matching couch and love seat of crisp white leather formed a perfect L shape. Sleek black end tables completed the arrangement in dramatic fashion.

After hours of sitting cramped in airplanes and his truck, he ignored the couch, preferring to stretch his back in front of the window. Gazing out over miles of wilderness, he was thrilled when, not twenty feet away, a lone coyote loped across the open ground at a steady pace, his tail ramrod straight behind him.

As if sensing the intrusion, the coyote swivelled his head, glaring at the Tracker with golden eyes.

Alex raised his cup in salute.

With a swish of its tail, the animal picked up his pace and disappeared behind a grove of mesquite trees.

Alex turned away from the window. It was time to ramp up his efforts. He needed to find out who had tugged on his fishing line.

Outside, the coyote howled.

Chapter 9

"That food is not going to eat itself." Coffee pot in hand, Wanda glared in mock disapproval at Signy and Ben's untouched plates.

Signy offered a conciliatory smile, then dug her fork into a mound of cold scrambled eggs.

"It's my fault," Ben said, picking up a slice of dried bacon. "I seem to be a bit of a motormouth this morning."

Wanda grinned down at him. "Whatever you're doing, keep it up. The young lady seems enthralled."

Signy almost choked on her eggs. "Hey," she said, holding up her coffee cup, "I can manage on my own, thanks."

Wanda topped up their coffee, then winked at Signy before heading back to the kitchen.

"Manage what?" Ben asked, dipping into an egg yolk with a wedge of toast.

Waving the question away, Signy leaned across the table and whispered, "So, basically, you're like a real-life Jason Bourne?"

He laughed. "It wasn't quite that dramatic, but I have to admit it was a nice break from working the streets."

"Seconded to the Canadian Intelligence Service? I'd say that's a bit of a big deal. And it sounds like you played a key role in bringing down a terrorist cell. How cool is that?"

Ben's cheeks coloured.

"So, what's up with the fancy dress?" said Signy, taking pity on him. "If you were trying to impress me, it's working." She coughed reflexively when she realized she'd said that last bit aloud.

"Impressing you is my number one priority, of course, but I'm also in town to testify at the Asian fisherman case."

She recalled the crime spree that had first brought Ben to Linden Valley. Local thugs had been assaulting anglers of Asian heritage coming up from the city to fish at a local lake. Vietnamese on his mother's side, Ben had worked undercover, eventually flushing out the posse of ignorant, young perpetrators. The trial for the ringleader started this week. "Too bad the Crown couldn't lay hate crime charges," she said.

Ben shrugged. "We nailed them on aggravated assault."

"Will you be coming back after the trial is over?"

"To police work?" He smiled sideways at her. "Or to Linden Valley?"

She felt a butterfly take wing inside her stomach. "Oh, I don't know," she said, laughing in an effort to disguise the sudden, intense longing that washed over her. "Both, I guess."

"Unfortunately, my days as an international man of mystery are over for now." He chuckled. "I've been assigned to forty-two division in Toronto. Gang unit."

Signy couldn't hide the look of disappointment on her face.

"I take it this means I'm forgiven?"

"For what?" she asked.

"For skipping out on you last fall."

"Skipping out?" she said, with a casual shrug, "We only had a couple of dates."

Ben leaned forward over the table. "I hated that they wouldn't allow me to tell anyone where I was going, not even you."

A flock of delicate wings fluttered madly inside her chest. She liked the sound of that "not even you." It made her feel special to him, even if it wasn't true. She brought the napkin to her cheeks, afraid that she might spontaneously combust at any moment. "They wouldn't let you tell your family?" she said, in a desperate attempt to change the subject.

He shook his head. "My mother was furious. Still hasn't forgiven me."

Signy smiled. "Mothers can be like that."

He flicked his eyes to the ceiling. "You don't know the half of it. I was born in 1979 in a refugee camp in Thailand. We spent three years there before she was able to emigrate to Canada. Three years alone in a refugee camp, with an infant to care for."

"She sounds like a strong woman."

"You could say that," Ben said. "Once here, she left me with a neighbour and worked three jobs. It took her only two years before she was able to buy a decent-sized house in Toronto. She set it up as a boarding home. A few years later, she'd bought her own hotel."

"And your dad?"

"An American soldier. He probably never knew I existed. Still, she married a great guy when I was ten." He threw his head back and laughed.

Signy felt a shiver run through her body at the sight of his soft, black hair settling over his warm eyes.

"Talk about yin and yang. Angus MacDonald is a great big, red-headed Scot who looks like he could take down an ox with his bare hands. In reality, he's about as sweet a man as you'd ever meet. He was a great father."

"Lucky," Signy said.

Ben nodded. "My mother, on the other hand? Let's just say she didn't appreciate my sudden disappearance."

"I can imagine. What about the whole cop thing? Did she approve?"

"She didn't talk to me for months." Ben grimaced. "But enough about the indomitable Kim-Ly. How about you? What was your family like?"

Signy popped the last bite of toast into her mouth. Ben obviously didn't know about the Dumpster Baby saga. She hadn't felt like enlightening him last fall, and she still didn't. Instead, she leaned forward and said, "If I were to tell you something, could you keep it under your hat?"

He touched the side of his nose with a forefinger. "If you can't trust Jason Bourne, who can you trust?"

Signy eyed him speculatively. He had an air of solidity about him she did find trustworthy. As far as she knew, he hadn't spilled the beans about her work on the Line. She supposed that was why the Canadian Security and Intelligence Service had requested him, while someone like her would never make it past their front door.

She leaned forward. "We had a real screw-up yesterday on the Line."

He peered at her over the edge of his coffee cup.

She liked the way he waited for her to speak without jumping in with a bunch of questions. "Grace Holder and I were working a job in Ottawa. You remember Grace?"

"The legendary Ms. Holder?" He smiled. "She'd be a hard one to forget. How's she doing?"

Signy frowned. "She's recovered physically from the shooting, but I'm not so sure about her mental state." As soon as the words left her lips, Signy felt a thousand pounds lift from her shoulders. It was as though by putting her fears into words she had magically stripped them of their power. "I mean, think about it. That psycho Volkov invaded her home, tied her up, and shot her."

"Not to mention almost choking you to death."

Signy shrugged. "It was different for Grace. This wasn't the first time she's been hurt, and her partner couldn't take it anymore. Kim walked away from the relationship. I don't think she even visited Grace in the hospital."

"Harsh," Ben said.

"It took her months to fully recover. She only just came back to work at the Women's Centre a few weeks ago. I don't think she should have jumped back into her work on the Line quite so quickly." She lowered her voice even further, forcing Ben to lean forward to hear her. "We were doing an extraction at an embassy in Ottawa. The plan was to spirit the wife of the press secretary out of the compound in the back of a catering van."

Ben whistled under his breath.

"Everything was going well until one of the guards caught wind of what we were up to. Normally, Grace would have taken care of it. Nothing violent, mind you, she just has this uncanny knack of talking her way out of anything. But not this time." She shook her head to clear the sight of Grace leaning against the van, eyes blank as she mumbled the name. *Ethan.*

Ben reached over and squeezed her hand.

"I'm okay," she said, enjoying the warmth of his hand on hers. She paused to clear her throat. "I don't know if it was PTSD or what, but she really freaked out. We ended up having to fight our way out of there."

"Fight?"

Signy cleared her throat. "There may have been a few injuries."

Ben frowned. "Let me get this straight. You engaged in hand-to-hand combat inside an embassy in Ottawa?" He pinched the bridge of his nose with his thumb and forefinger. "Please tell me it wasn't with the ambassador himself?"

Signy sniffed. "Don't be ridiculous. It was just a couple of the security detail."

"More than one?" His eyes widened.

"One, two?" She shrugged. "Does it really matter at this point?"

Ben sighed. "You understand that embassy personnel enjoy diplomatic immunity?" He paused for effect. "You, on the other hand, are subject to the full extent of the law. Pardon me for saying this, but it doesn't seem very professional to me."

"Professional?" Signy frowned.

He held up a hand. "I'm just saying."

"You don't get it, do you? With the exception of a few support staff in Toronto, the Line is run by volunteers."

Ben cocked a brow.

"That's right, and believe me, I'm no Jason Bourne. Most of us are social workers, for God's sake."

Ben sat back. "So why do you do it?"

Signy shrugged. "We're talking about women who can't find help anywhere else. Take the girl at the embassy, for example. Do you really think the RCMP is going to march into a foreign embassy to rescue her?"

Ben shook his head.

"No kidding. Besides, even if they did, their solution would be to stick her in a local shelter somewhere. Before you know it, her husband gets her back. What do you think happens to a young woman who has the gall to defy a man like that?" Signy sat back and crossed her arms over her chest. "We may not be professional, but we do the best we can with the resources we have."

"Point taken." Ben sipped at his coffee. "You're full of surprises; I'll say that for you. I heard how you took care of that asshole Dick Dalton."

Signy shuddered. "Talk about psychopaths. There's a man who shouldn't see the light of day for a long time."

Ben raised his coffee cup in a congratulatory salute. "Anyway, I assume by the fact that you're not cooling your heels in a jail cell in Ottawa that you rescued the woman?"

Signy nodded.

"And you're okay?" he asked, in a more serious tone. "You weren't hurt?"

"Nothing I couldn't handle. Easy as mango banana pie."

He raised a brow.

"Never mind. Left over adrenaline, I guess." She cleared her throat. "Can I tell you the worst part?" In for a penny, in for a pound, as her foster father had been fond of saying.

He gave her fingers an affirmative squeeze, then leaned forward.

Gazing into his soft brown eyes, she almost forgot what she was going to say. It took a few seconds before she was able to blurt out, "Grace made me promise not to tell Maitland about what happened."

Frowning, Ben brushed a stray crumb from the front of his jacket. "That's a tough one."

"I know," Signy agreed.

"An unfair request, if you ask me."

Signy fiddled with her napkin. "That's not all. While she was out of it, I yelled at her. She hardly spoke to me on the way home. I'm afraid I really screwed things up."

"Listen," he said, searching her eyes, "I'm free tomorrow night. How about we get together for dinner?"

"Can I bring you two anything else?" Wanda loomed at the side of the booth.

Signy dropped her napkin, then shook her head.

"You sure?" the woman asked. "I just brewed a fresh pot."

"No, thanks," said Signy, gathering her coat and purse, "I should have been at work ages ago."

Ben glanced at his watch, "And I'm due in court."

"Was everything okay?" asked the woman, slipping the bill from her apron pocket, then setting it down in front of Ben.

Signy struggled into her coat. "Everything was great. Fantastic."

"Hope to see you both in here again real soon," said the woman, winking at Signy as soon as Ben turned away to pick up his hat.

Ben handed Wanda two twenty-dollar bills, waving away her offer of change, and she hustled away, a pleased smile on her face.

"You okay?" Ben asked, as they got to their feet.

"Look, forget I said anything. I really shouldn't be talking about any of this."

He tapped his hat onto his head, then tucked his arm through hers and steered her slowly between the tables toward the door. "Consider it forgotten. The only thing I do know is that keeping secrets often makes things worse."

Signy hunkered down inside her thin coat.

Ben pulled open the door. "God, it's freezing out here," he said, dancing from foot to foot. "Can I drop you somewhere?"

Signy thought about the geriatric heap in her driveway. "No, thanks, I'm okay. I could use the walk."

He glanced at his watch. "Damn. I should have been in court fifteen minutes ago."

"Go," she said, giving him a little shove. She smiled as she watched him stride away, his long blue coat flapping around his knees, his hat square on his head. He looked so together, so professional, so damn sexy. It was only then that she realized she hadn't answered his question. *I'm free tomorrow night. How about we get together for dinner?*

Damn, she thought, remembering her flippant statement to Wanda: *If I didn't have bad luck, I'd have no luck at all.* She turned and began the long walk home.

Chapter

10

After leaving Ben, Signy stopped in at her local garage. After a little sweet-talking, the mechanic agreed to come over to the house and jolt the Saturn back to life with a set of jumper cables. Still, it was almost twelve-thirty before the old car wheezed into the parking lot of the Women's Centre.

Located in a nondescript office complex on the other side of town, the Women's Centre provided administrative support to Vicky's Place as well as supplying community outreach to Linden Valley and surrounding areas. As the executive director of the entire agency, Grace Holder oversaw the daily functioning of both locations.

Knowing that staff at the shelter had to deal with a grinding 24-7 schedule, Signy was grateful for the steady nine-to-five routine at the Women's Centre. She thrived on the endless variety. On any given day, she might show a battered woman how to navigate the complex legal system, arrange a new school for a displaced child, or help a homeless family to find permanent housing.

Pulling open the door, she tiptoed around the minefield of toy cars, Lego blocks, and picture books scattered across the floor of the deserted client waiting area. A motherly type named Audra, headset on, conversed with a client on the phone. From the serious look on Audra's face, the call seemed to be a heavy one.

Signy slid by and a few seconds later squeezed into her cramped cubicle. Unlike the older staff, who longed for the good old days of private offices, Signy didn't care where she sat. She only ever used her small space as a convenient spot to keep her office supplies and to plug in her laptop. Although other staff enjoyed the social aspect of being in the office, Signy preferred meeting her clients at their homes or in a local coffee shop. She learned far more about how well a woman was coping when she met her in the client's own environment.

After firing up her computer, she checked her schedule, then spent the next half-hour making some follow-up phone calls. She was trying to arrange a presentation to the local high school for the following week but had been playing telephone tag with the guidance department. Unlike most of her colleagues, she actually enjoyed visiting the local schools and talking about violence in the home. When she stood in front of a classroom full of rowdy teens, she felt like she became a different person.

She had a few canned presentations on PowerPoint but she preferred winging it, assessing the mood of the room and adapting accordingly. Sometimes she stuck to the script, but more often she veered wildly off topic, following the lead of the kids. She felt confident and funny and in control. The kids liked her too. After some initial catcalls and disparaging hoots, the boys usually settled down.

The girls, on the other hand, usually proved to be an attentive audience, and by the end of the talk, one or two girls were likely to request a private meeting. She always booked a room in the guidance office for just such an event. She was gratified that her intervention might save a young girl from further abuse, or that she might be instrumental in opening the minds of the boys.

After a quick visit to the loo, she saw that she had a new voice mail on her personal phone. Her heart flipped over when she heard Ben Tran's voice. *Hi, Signy, we didn't get a chance to talk about dinner. I have a thing for work tomorrow night, but how about Winston's on Saturday. I'll pick you up at eight. Let me know if that sounds good to you.* There was a long pause and then, *This is Ben, by the way, Ben Tran.*

She thought she heard him swear softly to himself as he hung up. Trying not to laugh, she sent him a text. *Winston's is perfect. See you on Saturday.* Winston's was an English-style pub in town that served excellent steaks in addition to the usual pub fare. Best of all, they had a dartboard and a pool table if the conversation dragged.

She wasted a few minutes thinking about what she might wear and then remembered she was way behind in her case notes. Because the agency was government-funded, workers were required to document every client visit in a common database within two business days of the appointment. Signy didn't know how she'd let herself get so behind. She put her head down and got to work.

Lunch was over and the office was alive with activity when she finally came up for air. Feeling a sense of accomplishment, she pushed her chair back, then made her way to the tiny staff kitchen. Painted hospital green, the square, windowless room consisted of a table with four chairs, a coffee maker, and a kettle.

Signy opened the cupboard and, eschewing the dull white cups provided by the agency, removed a bright yellow mug belonging to one of the trauma therapists. She grabbed an Earl Grey tea bag from a glass jar, then plugged in the kettle. While she waited for the water to boil, she picked up a *Toronto Star* newspaper lying unopened on the lunch table.

She flipped through the paper looking for anything about events at the embassy the night before. She found a brief article about the Mercedes spinning out by the canal but nothing to indicate it was anything more than a typical car accident. The longer the incident stayed under the radar, the more likely that embassy staff had deliberately chosen to keep a lid on it. She wondered briefly about the condition of the two men who'd attacked her but put them out of her mind. They deserved what they got.

A merry bubbling sound from across the room announced the water had boiled. She filled her mug, mashing the tea bag around with a spoon, when she felt a presence behind her.

"Hey, Signy."

"Hey," Signy said, her heart sinking. She turned around to find Suzette Wells blocking the doorway. A petite brunette, Suzette was pushing fifty but dressed and talked in the style of an urban teenager. She was wearing a white Oxford shirt over a pair of shiny black leggings. A red belt and matching spike boots completed the ensemble.

"Where did you get those awesome boots?" Suzette asked.

Signy shrugged. "Just that discount place in the mall."

Suzette sighed. "I wish I had your height. Tall people can pull off anything."

"Right. Well," Signy said, trying to squeeze by Suzette, "places to go, people to see, you know the drill."

"Have you heard the latest?" Suzette continued, stepping into Signy's path.

Signy felt her shoulders rise up around her ears. She shook her head.

"Word on the street is that something is going down with Grace." Suzette leaned in, her bright eyes avid, her nose twitching.

Signy had a sudden image of a jubilant rat, nose deep in a stash of fragrant garbage.

"You know me, I *never* gossip, but the fact is we're all worried."

Suzette stood aside as three more women shuffled into the kitchen and mumbled their hellos. Signy gathered their sudden appearance was anything but accidental.

"Have you noticed anything?" Suzette asked.

"Nope," Signy said. She turned and casually set the yellow mug into the sink after noticing that its rightful owner was among the group of newcomers. "By the way," she said, over her shoulder, "did you guys get the email about that policy change today? I'm not sure I understand the second paragraph."

"Did you know she's been sleeping in her office over at the shelter?" Suzette said. "She's been skipping meetings too. You know Grace. She'd rather die than keep someone waiting, especially ministry reps."

Signy kept her expression neutral but knew Suzette was right. Grace would never inconvenience anyone if she could help it.

"And the week before that she tore a strip off Angela in the finance department. Grace accused her of deliberately screwing up the budget." Suzette glanced over her shoulder before continuing. "Angela told us later that it was Grace that had messed up and I believe her. The poor woman was almost in tears. Everybody's talking about it."

Signy felt her stomach lurch. As usual, she was the last to know.

"We thought maybe you could talk to her."

"Me?" Signy stared at the woman as though she'd just grown a second head.

Suzette pointed her sharp little chin. "Well, sure. You're Grace's flavour of the month."

The other women bobbed their heads in agreement.

Signy scowled. "What the hell are you talking about?"

Suzette slapped Signy playfully on the arm. "Don't freak out. *Everyone* knows it."

There was that *everyone* again. Signy felt her jaw tighten.

"Good afternoon, ladies." Grace Holder appeared in the doorway. "Is that coffee fresh?"

Signy took a cold pleasure in the sudden scrape of chairs and the mass exodus as the rats abandoned the kitchen.

Grace waited until the room cleared before pouring herself a cup of coffee. As she stirred in a dollop of cream, she cupped a hand in front of her mouth and blew into it. Sniffing the contents, she shook her head. "Can't be my breath."

Signy mumbled something about everyone being behind in case notes.

"Don't worry about me," Grace said. "A thick skin comes with the job. That's something you'd be wise to learn. Ready to roll?"

"I have a client appointment at four. Will we be back by then?"

Grace checked her watch. “It’ll be tight, but if the traffic holds, we should be okay.” She turned and led the way out to the parking lot.

As she and Grace passed by Suzette’s desk, Signy caught a loaded glance pass between Suzette and another of her gossiping cabal.

For an agency that was all about fighting oppression, Signy thought, these women sure could dish dirt. She sighed. She wasn’t going to change human nature. She’d just have to find a way to live with it without resorting to the pepper spray she kept handy in her purse.

As much as she was tempted.

Chapter

11

The Tracker spent the morning catching up on his own business. He'd been working on a relatively simple skip trace when he'd discovered Signy's daring plan for the embassy extraction. She'd freak out if she ever found out he was monitoring her activities, but the stakes had been too high for his comfort level. He'd contacted his client, explained that he needed to postpone the job a few days, and flown to Ottawa.

Still, the woman he'd been hired to locate wasn't going to find herself, so he got to work. Evelyn Walker, age fifty-two, had been working for Howard Klemper Construction for over half her life.

A creature of habit before the incident that had changed her life forever, Evelyn arrived at the offices of Klemper Construction every day at eight a.m., sharp. She ate lunch every day (Cobb salad with a diet Coke) at the same café with her dear friend, Periwinkle Swanson. Evelyn was the only person who had permission to address Ms. Swanson by her full name. Everyone else called her Peri.

Every evening, Evelyn Walker left the office at five o'clock, on the dot. Unfortunately, on Halloween night of the previous year, she'd left the office as usual but had made it only half way home before realizing that she'd forgotten the two-pound bag of bite-sized Smarties she'd purchased during her lunch hour. Unwilling to disappoint the trick-or-treaters, she'd made a quick U-turn and returned to the office.

When she opened the door to the reception area, she could hear Mr. Klemper, whom she still called Mr. Klemper, despite the fact that, when the fancy struck her, she provided an occasional Monica Lewinsky–style extra to his daily routine, arguing with someone in his office. She tiptoed over to her desk so as not to disturb the two men.

She had just pulled open the drawer when she heard the sound of a struggle, a strangled shout, and then the loud report of a handgun. She'd dropped to the floor, trying to make herself as small as possible, and thank God and Moses, as she'd proclaimed later, the killer hadn't noticed her as he'd rushed from the office.

Conversely, she'd certainly seen the murdering swine, and over the course of the next few months, she proved to be a big help to the police, the FBI, and the subsequent grand jury investigation.

Unfortunately for poor Evelyn, the man who'd hired the killer didn't take kindly to witnesses of any kind, let alone the chatty type. The police had tried their best, of course, bundling Evelyn off into the Witness Protection Program. They'd explained the rules and warned her, and Evelyn had been conscientious.

She didn't try to phone her aging mother: truth be told, she was relieved to have an excuse not to call the miserable old biddy. She always remembered to use her new name when talking to bank managers, doctors, and the like, and she never, ever struck up a conversation with a stranger.

What the Witness Protection officers hadn't counted on, however, was Evelyn's need to stay in touch with the Pomeranian Rescue Society, of which she'd been a huge supporter over the years. She knew her own two Poms, Chip and Dale, would never forgive her if she let her responsibilities slide. She checked in now and then, sending generous cheques—under her new name of course.

Sadly, Evelyn just couldn't stand that Periwinkle Swanson, the founder of the PRS, would not know that it was she, Evelyn Walker, making the hefty donations. So she'd let Peri in on her secret and the two agreed to stay in touch. Surreptitiously, of course.

That was how the Tracker found her. It had been pathetically easy. Evelyn had taken to having long chats with Periwinkle every Friday evening, five p.m. on the dot, from a local pay phone that she assumed must be safe. It was a pay phone after all, and Evelyn believed that one couldn't trace the identity of a person using a pay phone.

She was mistaken. It had taken him less than an hour to access Periwinkle Swanson's phone records and determine that she was receiving weekly calls, all of them originating from the same phone booth. It took another hour to confirm that it was, indeed, Evelyn Walker making the calls.

He tapped into a local traffic camera, and there she was. Every Friday at five, one fluffy mutt under each arm, the receiver tucked under her chin, her dark sunglasses doing nothing to disguise her distinctive horse face.

The Tracker contacted the client and gave him the news. If he wanted to pick up Evelyn Walker, he'd be wise to be at the phone booth on the corner of Main and Sixteenth on Friday afternoon at five o'clock. He hadn't hung up until he'd watched his payment roll into his offshore bank account, pleased that so little effort had netted him such a hefty payday.

Suddenly starved, he stood up, stretched his arms over his head. He whipped up a spinach salad topped with onions and peppers, mandarin oranges, goat cheese, and a handful of pine nuts. He splashed some homemade citrus vinaigrette on top and ate the entire thing standing by the window. The coyote did not reappear.

After lunch, he strolled into his bedroom. The room was almost obsessively neat, the white walls a match for the decor in the living room. He found the monochromatic design relaxing. The only splash of colour glowed from a turquoise and gold Navajo wall hanging. He wasn't sure why, but the intricate thread work and colourful design helped to create a fertile landscape space for his imagination. As he lay on the edge of sleep, he'd gaze at the shimmering messages hidden in the design, transported to a land of dreams where anything was possible.

He picked up the cellphone he'd left on his bedside table and checked the blank screen. He wondered how long she was going to make him wait, then shrugged off the useless question, turning his attention to more immediate worries.

With a little pressure from his knee, the king-sized bed slid on hidden tracks, revealing the outline of a door in the floor beneath. The Tracker padded into the bathroom, opened the medicine chest, and moving a tin of talcum powder out of the way, arranged his eye in front of a retinal scanner secured to the back wall of the chest. He stood, unblinking, as the scan passed across his eye, and was rewarded when he heard the distinctive thunk of the hidden door under his bed as it popped open.

He'd created this underground chamber himself, shoring up an old mining test-hole with concrete and elbow grease. Hidden under his mobile home, it provided him with a safe space in which to conduct the work that had become his all-abiding passion.

Climbing down into the hidden room, he touched a button and the bed slid back into place. It would be virtually impossible for an intruder to breach these walls, so the space served a dual purpose as both a private workspace and panic room. Not that it was likely he would ever require such a contingency, but in his line of work, it was wise to be prepared.

He looked around. Four months ago, the walls had been plastered with photographs of women. Women who, by virtue of the blue-grey colour of their eyes and forceful personalities, joined his short list of candidates matching his memories of the sister he'd been separated from so many years before.

His search had come to a dramatic end during his hunt for the long-lost granddaughter of an elderly Russian assassin. Strange, the way the universe unravels, he thought. Two lost girls, Signy Shepherd and Elena Morozov, set on converging paths pointed straight at him.

Since finding Signy, his focus had changed. Now, instead of photos, paper-thin LCD screens covered the walls. Fishing in his pocket, he removed a USB key and slid it into the port of a computer sitting on a metal desk. He fired up the computer and tapped in a series of commands. The lights in the underground bunker dimmed slightly and the LCD screens glowed to life. He took a seat in a well-worn chair situated dead centre in the room.

The screen directly in front of him began to play a silent video. He watched, mesmerized. Signy Shepherd sat in a Toronto restaurant, sipping a mocha latte, chatting with one of the more formidable members of the Line.

He'd researched Grace Holder extensively over the past four months, the results confirming the old adage, that one should never judge a book by its cover. Despite her dumpy appearance, Ms. Holder was no mere steam locomotive. Over the years, she had become the high-speed bullet train of the Line.

He paid particular attention to Signy, from the thick blond braid that ran down her back to the flashing blue eyes so like his own. He chuckled when he saw her expertly sidestep Ms. Holder's proffered hug as the two women rose to leave the restaurant. He wondered if she would ever come to know how very alike they were.

Contrary to his disdain for whiny mea culpas, he indulged himself in a few moments of mental self-flagellation. He had found her only to lose her in a series of disasters for which he had no one to blame but himself. He felt a familiar tightness in his chest. Was he destined to let down every woman that he cared for?

For an instant, he was back in her apartment that terrible night, sitting at her kitchen table, watching her blue eyes grow stormy as he confessed his multiple betrayals. The shock and hurt he had seen in her eyes continued to eat away at him. Haunted by the wreckage he had left behind, the Tracker could only hope that if she ever gave him another chance, he would not fail her again.

Chapter

12

Fighting to keep the wheels inside a narrow set of frozen ruts, Signy steered Grace Holder's Prius down a boulevard in North Toronto. City employees had been working for days trying to clear away the third massive snowfall of the season. Highways and major arteries took priority, leaving homeowners to fend for themselves.

Signy wondered why the residents of this particular neighbourhood hadn't hired a private company to keep their roads cleared. They could certainly afford it, judging by the gracious estates that lined both sides of the boulevard.

As she picked her way along the road, she couldn't help but stare. Each one of the exquisite estate homes, with its sweeping front lawn and towering windows, seemed more opulent than the next. It wasn't until she caught sight of the last house on the dead-end street that she uttered a soft "*Wow*."

"What did I tell you," said Grace, who'd been snoozing in the passenger seat for most of the drive down from Linden Valley.

"Welcome back," Signy said.

Grace rubbed her eyes. "Ugh, I shouldn't have done that."

"You probably needed it." Signy shot a quick glance at her passenger.

Grace pointed at the house Signy had been admiring. "Amazing, isn't it?"

"Incredible," Signy said. "It looks like someone dropped a castle in the middle of the city."

"Welcome to Grand Central Station."

Situated well back from the road, on a spectacular property overlooking a wild ravine, the dramatic manor home had a magical feel. Leaded windows set deep into the limestone block exterior ran in precise rows across the two lower storeys, while four copper-topped dormers accented the third floor. Craning her neck, Signy counted three massive chimneys.

A single-lane drive led up to a gatehouse that was larger than the sprawling farm home she'd shared with her foster brothers and sisters. Bypassing the side entrance, Signy turned left up the main entranceway, negotiating her way through stately wrought iron gates, along a cobblestone drive cleared of ice. A hint of afternoon sun threw long shadows on the thick blanket of white powder shrouding the front lawn. A manicured twelve-foot cedar hedge tipped with snow ringed the property, while two ancient blue spruce trees soared high above the green copper roof.

Pulling to a stop, Signy turned off the ignition. She sat still for a moment, listening to the tick of the engine as it cooled in the frigid air.

"You okay?" Grace asked.

Signy twisted in her seat. "Are you sure about this?"

"What do you mean?"

Signy stared out the window.

"Look," Grace said, "if you're worried about yesterday, don't be. I was out of practice, that's all. It won't happen again."

"It was awful to see you like that." Signy scrubbed her face with her hands. "I didn't know what to do."

"Oh, honey," Grace said, clutching one of Signy's hands in her own, "I'm so sorry. I should have realized."

"Don't worry about me. It's just—I mean, are you sure you don't want to tell Maitland?"

Grace smiled. "You know what? I haven't told you yet how amazing you were. You got us all out of there, safe and sound, against incredible odds."

"Are you trying to butter me up?" Signy said with a lame chuckle. She could feel the worm of anxiety squeezing its coils around her heart.

"Don't be silly. You showed incredible grace under pressure. That's what I want to tell Maitland."

"But—"

"But nothing. I'm fine. I promise it won't happen again."

"Can I ask you something?" Signy asked.

"That depends," Grace responded in a lighthearted tone, although her eyes were sharp.

"Who's Ethan?"

Grace slipped her hand away. "What?"

"Ethan. You called that name while you were . . ."

"Having my opening night jitters?" Grace finished the sentence for her.

Signy frowned. "Who is he?"

"Ethan?" Grace said, casually. "I can't imagine why I would have said that. I'm sure it's nothing important. Now, can we go inside, please? I don't know about you, but I'm freezing to death."

Signy squeezed into her coat and jammed her hat down around her ears. She kept her mouth firmly closed as she trailed Grace over frozen cobblestones sprinkled with rock salt toward the imposing entrance.

Standing in front of the gleaming door, Signy examined the brass knocker. Its intricately carved mane and gaping jaws reminded her of Leonid Volkov, a.k.a. Leo the Lion, and she shivered at the memory of his powerful hands around her neck. Squaring her shoulders, she reached up to grab the knocker but stopped when Grace placed a restraining hand on hers.

"Grand Central Station is always open," Grace said.

Signy glanced at her in surprise. "What about security?"

"It's everywhere," Grace said. "You just can't see it. Maitland wants people to feel welcome, not like they've entered a police state." Grace pushed open the door, then ushered Signy inside.

In the grand foyer, hit by a blast of heat emanating from a vent hidden somewhere overhead, Signy felt her muscles relax. On the floor, a round art deco carpet with a dazzling black and white geometric pattern covered the marble tile floor. Grace slid open a closet door, cleverly disguised behind smoked glass. After hanging her coat, Signy followed Grace into the main reception area.

Just like its New York City namesake, Grand Central Station was alive with activity. Signy tried not to stare. A dignified-looking woman, her black hair streaked with grey and tied in a tight bun, swayed gracefully over the white marble, murmuring softly in

Hindi. Beside her, a younger woman, exotic in a scarlet sari, her hands painted with an intricate henna design, kept her kohl-lined eyes on the floor.

Racing down the grand staircase, two boys no older than ten shrieked at each other. As they launched themselves off the final step and slid across the floor, arms flapping, Signy thought of Canada geese attempting a slippery landing on a frozen pond.

Seated behind an ornate desk in the centre of the foyer, a plump woman wearing a royal blue pantsuit leaped from her chair and whirled on the youngsters, chasing them away with good-natured threats. She waited until they were gone before smoothing her jacket and turning back to the new arrivals.

"Grace, dear, how are you?" the woman said, in a rich Jamaican accent. She shuffled forward, enveloping Grace in a pillowy hug. "I am so happy to see you back on your feet, honey. We were all so worried."

Grace returned the hug, and then the two women turned to face Signy.

"Signy Shepherd?" the woman asked.

Her attention caught by the ornate dragonfly brooch the woman sported on the lapel of her jacket, Signy sputtered a quick affirmative.

"I'm Henrietta," said the woman, holding out her hand. "So wonderful to finally meet you, honey. We've all heard so much about you." Shaking Signy's hand, Henrietta exclaimed, "Look at you, such a skinny little thing. From what Maitland said, I expected a giant killer, fourteen feet tall and swinging a mighty sword."

Hearing Grace's amused chuckle, Signy felt a blush rise to her cheeks.

The woman clapped her hands. "I mustn't keep you. Maitland is waiting." She turned and swept her hand toward the grand staircase. "It's a bit of a maze but Grace knows the way."

Trailing Grace up to the second floor, Signy decided the magnificent staircase was wide enough to drive a Volkswagen up if one were so inclined. The gold runner, edged with black, showed signs of heavy wear. Sliding her hand up the ebony banister, she admired a series of exquisite paintings hanging on the wall. She paused in front of an Alex Colville, depicting two young girls laughing by the seaside. "Wow," she said.

"You think that's neat? You ain't seen nothin' yet," Grace said.

At the top of the stairs, Signy's breath caught in her throat. A massive painting by Emily Carr dominated the space. Expertly lit, it portrayed an empty beach at sunrise, the vast sky glowing pink and purple.

"Every time I see it, I feel hopeful," Grace said.

"Not me." Signy shoved her hands in her pocket. "I feel nervous. It's like the National Gallery around here. What if I break something?"

They stood aside for a woman dressed in a tailored business suit clutching a stuffed leather briefcase under her arm. The woman nodded pleasantly before expertly clicking down the stairs in a pair of heels even higher than the ones Signy had worn at the embassy. Signy shook her head. "Now I'm really intimidated."

Grace laughed, then set off down the hall.

Signy hustled to catch up, and it wasn't long before she lost all sense of direction. She stopped counting rooms after passing the tenth doorway, and she felt a moment of relief when Grace finally lumbered to a halt in front of a rather imposing set of double doors.

"All aboard," said Grace, with a grin. She swept open the door with a flourish and stood back to allow Signy an unobstructed view.

Signy's eyes widened. The space that had once been a dazzling ballroom now resembled a NASA command centre. If she'd thought the main house was abuzz with activity, this room was crackling. Everywhere she looked, she saw women and men chatting in small groups, hunched over computers, or sitting in front of humming machinery.

"Pam?" Grace called in a cheery tone, then stepped inside.

A wide-hipped technician tending a towering bank of hard drives whirled at the sound of her name. She broke into a gap-toothed grin when she saw Grace. "Grace, baby! How's it hanging?"

The two women exchanged a fist bump before Grace asked, "Is she here?"

Pam nodded, then jerked her chin down a long row of cubicles. "Over in documents."

Grace smiled. "Where have you been? It seems like ages."

The tech nodded. "Setting up the new Atlanta office. Great town but it's good to be home. I missed having a real winter."

"Ha. I'll bet you'll be singing a different tune in a few months. Winter seems to last forever these days. Damned polar vortex."

Pam laughed. "Hey, do you want to get together?"

"Sure," replied Grace. "Maybe catch a Leafs game?"

"Awesome," said the tech. "Can't wait to see Kim. Remember last time?" She threw back her head and laughed. "Sandy and I had to spend two days in bed just to recover."

Grace's smile froze.

Signy felt her stomach sink. Grace's friend obviously hadn't heard the news. She stepped forward, waving her hand at the rows of incomprehensible computer hardware. "Is this the central server?"

Pam turned to her with a bright grin. "Oh ya, baby. This is where the real action goes down. Let me show you."

After an interminable few minutes, during which Pam explained everything Signy had never wanted to know about the benefits of heat-assisted magnetic recording over the old low-density parity check codes, Grace came to her rescue.

"Damn," said Pam, smiling at Signy. "I wanted to show you the multiple backup systems. I always get carried away when I meet a fellow tech geek. Next time, eh, babe?"

Signy smiled weakly.

Pam turned back to Grace. "I'll call you."

Grace planted a quick kiss on Pam's cheek, then turned to Signy. "Thanks," she mouthed. She indicated a set of doors leading off the north end of the room. "Ready to see where the magic happens?"

"There's more? I had no idea there was this level of support behind the scenes."

"At any given time we usually have close to a hundred passengers on the move."

Signy's jaw dropped.

Grace nodded. "And every one of them has complex needs. Money, new identity, housing, employment, schools for the kids, you name it. Not to mention the support and coordination required by the conductors."

"A hundred," Signy said, shaking her head. "Maitland must be a magician to keep everything operating smoothly."

Grace chuckled. "It is a bit like Alice in Wonderland around here."

When they pushed through a set of double doors at the end of another long corridor, Signy saw that Grace was right. Maitland McGuinness, the storied Engineer of the Line, elegantly dressed in a wool skirt and silk blouse, nibbled on a pair of gold pince-nez glasses. Her white hair, gathered into a formal bun, was pinned with a diamond-encrusted comb. She stood beside a tall window, the soft light lending a warm glow to her paper-fine skin.

Maitland was peeping over the shoulder of a skeletal man, his long white hair swept into a ponytail, a snowy beard flowing down over his chest. He was wearing a purple lab coat and peering through a magnifying glass.

"That man," Signy whispered. "Is it just me, or does he look like—?"

"Dumbledore?" Grace sniffed. "Harry Potter's a party magician compared to this guy. Come on," she said, grabbing Signy's arm and pulling her into the room, "let's go say hello. His name is Percy, and I'm ninety-nine percent sure he won't bite."

Chapter 13

Solomon Stone scrutinized the woman heading his way with a mix of anticipation and revulsion. The pink tweed suit was Coco Chanel, and the artful palette of blond masking the grey in her thinning hair must have required hours in the chair of a master. Unfortunately, whoever had done the work on her face was a hack. She'd had an old-school skin pull leaving her with a distinctive windswept look.

"I was most impressed by your talk yesterday, Dr. Stone, most impressed," said the woman in a warm New England drawl that spoke of summers on Nantucket.

Stone shook her proffered hand with a gentle touch, the fragile phalanges evident through the paper-fine barrier of mottled skin.

"So much suffering," she continued, gazing up at him through rheumy eyes.

Stone inclined his head in a courtly fashion. "I don't believe I've had the pleasure, madam."

"Madam?" She swatted playfully at his arm. "My chequebook will remain firmly closed if you persist in using that vile form of address. My name is Honoria, Honoria Cabot."

She leaned in and Stone could feel a thin rope of breast tissue press against his chest. He took a deep breath. "My apologies, Mrs. Cabot." He smiled warmly. "In answer to your question, it is difficult work but it is also intensely rewarding."

She sidled in even closer, raking scarlet claws across the front of his Armani suit. "And dangerous, I would imagine. Quite, quite dangerous?"

"Oh, yes," he breathed into her ear, falling easily into the familiar game.

She grimaced, the resultant rictus of her mouth and eyes turning his stomach. He glanced away. He really ought to get the name of her surgeon. The man was a butcher. He should have his medical licence stripped.

"Those pictures you showed. Those ghastly wounds . . ." Her voice trailed off.

He gazed down at her, his voice solemn. "The day that I become immune to the suffering endured by my patients will be the day I throw in the towel. Until then, my colleagues and I are grateful for the support of caring people like you, Honoria." He allowed the syllables of her name to spill from his lips with the grace of a lover.

The aging benefactor tittered although paralyzed by Botox injections; her face offered no emotional giveaways. She might have been clearing phlegm from her throat. Stone considered the wisdom of asking the name of her surgeon, then thought better of it. He didn't want to risk what might prove to be a considerable donation.

"Honoria!" A great bear of a man sporting waves of shining white hair and a well-aged Florida tan came up behind Stone. On his arm, the lovely redhead from the front row who had caught Stone's eye the evening before. "May I present my daughter, Krystal."

Honoria glared at the man but was gracious enough to exclaim over the young woman.

The man turned to Stone. "Krystal is only in grade nine, but she already knows what she wants to be."

"And what would that be?" Stone asked.

"I'm going to be a doctor—like you," the girl said.

"How wonderful," he said, offering her a dazzling smile.

"I loved your speech, Dr. Stone. Your work is amazing."

"Forgive me for the interruption, but might I have a word with Dr. Stone?" Wilkington smiled apologetically at Honoria Cabot.

The old lady glared up at the intruder. "Must it be this instant, Wilky? I was hoping to have the good doctor escort me to the luncheon."

The newcomer grasped her wizened hands in his. "You don't mind do you, darling? I'll give him back shortly, I promise." He pushed his daughter forward. "Meanwhile, Krystal would love to take you into lunch."

Honoria narrowed her eyes, then, gathering her dignity around her like the tattered remains of a matador's cape, swept back into the crowded reception, the gorgeous redhead bobbing along beside her.

"If that was meant to be a lifeline," said Stone, waiting until the mismatched pair was out of earshot before clasping the older man's outstretched hand, "I was holding my own."

"Honoria Cabot would have consumed you, bones and all."

George Wilkington threw a big arm around Stone's shoulder, then added in a conspiratorial whisper, "I've heard she can do things in the sack that would curl your toes."

Stone sneaked a glance over his shoulder at the retreating dowager and shuddered.

"Trust me," said Wilkington, moving Stone toward a side room where they could talk in private, "you don't want to go there. The woman is like a zebra mussel; she gets into everything and is almost impossible to scrape off." He gave Stone a reassuring squeeze on the arm. "Don't worry, though. She'll still write you a fat cheque. She has more money than she knows what to do with."

"I'll find some way to restrain myself."

Laughing, Wilkington held up a bottle of Scotch he'd snagged from behind an unmanned but well-stocked bar. When Stone nodded, Wilkington sloshed the amber liquid into two highball glasses. "How's the haul so far?"

"Good, excellent, as a matter of fact. For another year, at least. I can't thank you enough, George. It would have taken me months to raise this kind of cash."

"If you were smart, you'd get yourself and that young family of yours out of that ridiculous backwater. This is where the real power lies." Wilkington handed Stone a glass, then swept his arm toward the window, where the lights of Manhattan glittered against the jagged skyline. "And from the sounds of your announcement this evening, you're going to want to be in the thick of things." He slammed a thick paw on Stone's shoulder. "I wouldn't be surprised if there's a Nobel Prize in your future."

Stone scoffed but inside he felt his heart soar. He had little doubt that the precious tissue samples growing in his lab were going to earn him the highest of honours. His days of begging for scraps from the tables of the wealthy were almost over, and he felt himself flush with pride.

"Congratulations, Solomon," Wilkington roared. "I couldn't be more pleased for you."

"I couldn't have done it without you, George. Your support has been invaluable."

Wilkington looked at Stone, a wily glint in his eye. "That's why I called you in here. I'd like to have first crack at the investment as soon as you're ready to launch. Once this thing takes off, we're talking billions, man."

Stone held his breath and allowed his smile to die. He turned and gazed out over the city.

Wilkington clamped a gentle hand on Stone's shoulder. "What is it?"

"I can see why you are so popular with your patients, George." Stone sipped at his drink and swallowed hard. He opened his mouth, tried to speak, then looked down at the floor and shook his head.

"Is it Lizzy?"

Stone allowed the barest hint of grief to cross his face. "Am I that easy to read?"

Wilkington shrugged. "Patty mentioned just the other day that none of the girls have seen her in months. Not since the baby was born at least."

Solomon shook his head. "Lizzy would kill me if she knew I was talking to you about her."

Wilkington nodded. "If it makes you feel better, I'm donning my psychiatrist's cap. This conversation is privileged. So, tell me. What's happening?"

Stone let out a deep sigh and paused as if he couldn't find the words, then let the story explode from his mouth in a desperate rush. "Something is terribly wrong. It started right after the baby was born. I thought it was a typical case of baby blues. I'd been ready for it, just between you and me." He leaned in. "Lizzy has never been what you might describe as emotionally stable. She's always had her ups and downs."

Wilkington nodded. "Patty has mentioned Lizzy can be moody now and then."

"I wasn't sure anyone else had noticed." Stone grimaced. "After Justin arrived, things just got worse. At first, she cried constantly, retreated to her room, wouldn't eat. I chalked it up to feeling tired and overwhelmed. Justin is a wonderful kid, don't get me wrong, but he has a set of lungs on him that could bring down the walls of Jericho."

Wilkington winced. "Our number one daughter was like that. I thought I'd go mad."

"Right," said Stone, "but you cope, right? I mean, he's only a baby, and it's not as if we don't have help. There's more," he continued, his voice ragged. "It's hard to put a finger on, but there's something about the way she looks at Justin that bothers me."

Wilkington raised a brow.

Stone shrugged. "I'm probably being overreactive."

"Have you taken steps to protect the child, just in case?"

"Of course," Stone confirmed. "The nanny has mental health experience. She's worked with mothers who struggled with postpartum depression." Stone shot a look at the older man. "That's what this is, right? In your professional opinion?"

Wilkington nodded. "I'd have to evaluate her more formally,

of course, but it certainly seems to be leaning that way. I'm sorry, Solomon."

Stone looked down at the floor. "I've never told this to anyone, but Lizzy has attempted suicide before."

Wilkington nodded, calmly. "Was it a serious attempt?"

"She was in a coma for two weeks, does that count as serious?"

Wilkington poured another drink for each of them. "Look, in most cases postpartum depression is highly treatable. Rest, medication, perhaps even a brief inpatient stay and she'll be as right as rain. Still, we have to act fast. When do you get home?"

"Home?" said Stone, checking the date on his watch. He smiled weakly. "I can't even remember what day it is. Maybe she has a point. Maybe I do spend too much time away. I should be focusing more of my energy on her and the baby."

"Could be," said Wilkington, "but your presence, or lack thereof, isn't causing this level of illness."

Stone let out his breath in a long stream. "So, she really is sick? It's not just me?"

Wilkington shook his head. "Tell you what. How about you clear the decks and get home ASAP. I can be in Rochester by the end of the week. I'll do a thorough assessment and we'll go from there."

Stone shook his head. "There is no way she'll agree to see you."

"Let me worry about that." He smiled. "I have my ways."

Stone held the older man's eyes for several seconds before sighing heavily. "Thanks, George. Thank you so much. At the very least, I'm relieved to have finally told someone." Stone held out his hand.

"Come on," said Wilkington, "there's a rubber chicken with my name on it out there, and big fat chequebooks just waiting to be laid bare before the young Turk. Are you ready?"

Stone swiped at his eyes.

"Just remember," said Wilkington, pointing at his own chest, "you're looking at your number one investor."

"If you can help Lizzy, I'll give you forty-nine percent of the company," said Stone, forcing a grin. "I love her, you know?" Solomon followed George Wilkington back into the grand ballroom, his head bowed.

Chapter 14

The white-haired man in the purple lab coat shoved his beard to one side as he squinted through a monocle. He appeared to be fixing a wax seal to some sort of legal paper.

"Make sure it's centered properly," Maitland murmured. "It won't pass muster otherwise."

The man glared up at her, then swept a liver-spotted hand over the document. "I bow to your superior skill level, madam. Would you care to take over?"

"Excuse me," Grace interrupted, pushing Signy in front of her, "I come bearing gifts."

Maitland straightened her back in a fluid motion that belied her eighty-plus years. She whirled round. "Grace Holder, how many times have I told you not to sneak up like that on an old woman?"

The wizard snorted, mumbling something to the effect of "Old woman, my ass."

Signy thought she must have misheard until Maitland rapped him smartly on the top of his snowy pate with her pince-nez reading glasses.

He chuckled but did not raise his head.

"My conquering heroes return," Maitland said in her distinctive Lauren Bacall drawl. She walked over and took each of them by the hand. "I presume all went well?"

"A hiccup or two, but it could have been worse," Grace said, not glancing at Signy.

Maitland tucked in between the two women. "Sounds like a story that should be told over drinks. Shall we retire to my suite?"

"Fun fact," said the Dumbledore look-alike. "Excessive alcohol intake has been linked to diminished mental acuity in women of a certain age."

"Indeed? Here's another." Maitland tossed her head. "It seems that excessive irritability has been correlated with the onset of stodginess in fussy old fossils."

"I try my best, madam," he said, his bushy beard shaking with laughter.

Chuckling under her breath, Maitland swept out of the room. In the hallway, she tucked an arm through Signy's and leaned in. "I have been terribly remiss in not touching base earlier. Grace has kept me abreast of your adventures. Flown solo more than once, I hear?" The question must have been rhetorical because Maitland chattered on without waiting for an answer.

As they strolled through a maze of quiet oak-lined hallways, Maitland paused now and then to elucidate on some particularly interesting object. She spent quite a bit of time on the medieval origins of the stained glass that graced an oval window at the top of the third-floor stairs. After that there was an Inuit soapstone carving of a polar bear, an original Robert Bateman wolf painting, and a haunting yet vibrant portrait of a tribal elder by Norval Morrisseau.

Grace interjected with a knowledgeable question now and then, but Signy kept her mouth firmly closed. She knew nothing about medieval stained glass or Henry Moore sculptures or the Group of Seven for that matter. She was almost certain that neither Grace nor Maitland would care to hear her expound on the finer points of mucking out horse stalls.

Signy was relieved when Maitland ushered the two women through a heavy oak door. The decor in Maitland's living quarters was muted in comparison to the museum quality of the rest of the house. Signy felt immediately at ease surrounded by pale yellow walls and the natural light pouring in through expansive windows that overlooked the ravine.

Seated on pale blue, silk-covered chairs, she and Grace watched Maitland pour Dubonnet into three old fashioned glasses, then add a dollop of bitter lemon. Using a pair of ice tongs from a silver service laid out on a fine mahogany coffee table, she dropped one cube of ice into each glass. With the drinks handed round, Maitland took a seat opposite, smoothing her grey wool skirt over surprisingly shapely knees. "Why don't you tell me about those hiccups, Grace?"

Over the next several minutes, Grace gave a sanitized version of the events at the embassy in Ottawa, leaving out the part where she left Signy to do battle on her own. Occasionally, Maitland glanced at Signy, who nodded enthusiastically to everything Grace said.

To her credit, Grace was clear that the operation had not ended well. She was open about the fact that they had been chased from the embassy by a car full of security men, and that the only thing that had prevented them from being caught was a patch of black ice.

"My word," Maitland exclaimed, fiddling with the gold chain holding her pince-nez. "Do we know the condition of all concerned?"

Signy shook her head. "There was mention of a car spinning out along the canal but nothing else."

"No news is good news, I imagine." Maitland peered into space for a few moments, then smiled brightly. She set her glass down on a crystal coaster and then walked over to a large mahogany desk situated under a west-facing window.

Grace shifted uncomfortably in her seat. "I wouldn't want to sugar-coat the situation. I'm afraid we can expect potentially significant fallout."

Removing a key from her skirt pocket, Maitland opened the bottom drawer of the desk and removed a red file folder.

Glancing at Grace, Signy saw her own dismay mirrored in Grace's eyes. A red file could mean only one thing. There was another passenger in urgent need of transport on the Line.

Tucking the file under her arm, Maitland resumed her seat. She picked up her glass of Dubonnet and peered up at Grace. "I imagine your actions in the embassy garage were caught on camera?"

Grace shrugged. "I think we have to assume so."

"Not to mention that embassy personnel are aware that it was the catering staff who helped Mrs. Jakende escape and that it was the ambassador's wife who hired said staff." Maitland grimaced. "I imagine things are not too pleasant for the poor woman right about now."

"No," Grace agreed.

"Not your fault, my dears," Maitland said, tossing the red file onto the coffee table. "It was a very difficult extraction. I'll take over from here."

Grace sat back in her chair.

Maitland glanced at the red file. "I'm sorry to spring a new case on you quite so soon, but unfortunately, the circumstances require a speedy response. I have another asset driving up from Chicago to help, but she can't start for a couple of days."

Signy leaned forward, taking a polite sip of the vile Dubonnet before setting her glass down on the table.

"Grace, have you met Priya Subramanian?" Maitland asked.

Grace frowned, her eyes scanning the ceiling. "She's the executive director at the shelter in Rochester, New York, I believe? I met her at a conference about a year and a half ago." She turned to Signy. "You hadn't joined the Women's Centre then, but there'd been quite a spate of missing street youth around that time and not just in Toronto but also Rochester, Syracuse, Buffalo, and even as far west as Detroit. The police set up a fact-sharing conference for law enforcement and community agencies on both sides of the border. There was a suggestion at the time that missing kids might be getting caught up in a cross-border sex trade."

"What was your impression of Ms. Subramanian, Grace?"

"I liked her. She has a good head on her shoulders."

Maitland nodded. "I've worked with her once before and she struck me as quite capable. What we know so far is that a young woman arrived at the shelter last night along with her seven-month-old son. She's not saying much, except to insist that Priya not contact the police."

"Why?" Signy asked.

"An excellent question. Priya knows the woman. Her name is Lizzy Stone and she's the wife of a prominent plastic surgeon. I've done a very preliminary background check on the man. In addition to his private practice, Dr. Solomon Stone is quite the humanitarian. He spends a lot of his free time in various war zones offering his services free of charge."

She leaned over and brought up the home page of the *Rochester Democrat and Chronicle* on an iPad sitting on the coffee table. She held it up, showing them the front page. "There's a story this morning about their hometown hero. They picked it up from the *New York Times*. It seems Dr. Stone has developed a revolutionary new form of skin replacement for the treatment of burns." Maitland handed the device to Grace.

"How does Priya know Mrs. Stone?" asked Grace, as she scanned the story featuring Dr. Stone.

Reading over Grace's shoulder, Signy found the article on Dr. Stone tucked among stories lamenting the closing of a local tire factory, reminding the public about the anniversary of the case of a missing street kid known only as Kit Kat, and warning of an approaching nor'easter predicted to dump significant snow over the next several days.

"Lizzy Stone used to volunteer at a local youth shelter," Maitland said. "They've met professionally on occasion. Priya tells me that Lizzy is claiming that her husband is telling anyone who'll listen that she is suffering from postpartum depression and is on the verge of suicide. Priya also says that Lizzy vehemently denies the claim. In fact, she insists that it all comes down to Dr. Stone's wanting her out of his life—permanently."

Grace peered at Maitland. "You don't seem entirely convinced."

Maitland gave an almost-imperceptible shrug. "Unfortunately, I've been unable to find a shred of hard evidence supporting Mrs. Stone's claims."

She picked up her drink, swirling the blood red Dubonnet around the glass. "In the unlikely scenario that Mrs. Stone is trying to circumvent a legal custody determination, I'd like to be certain. Unfortunately, it's happened before."

Grace nodded. She turned to Signy and filled her in on the case of a woman in the United States who'd accessed the Line, claiming her husband was sexually abusing their young daughter. Before verifying the story, a conductor down in Boston had jumped the gun and sent the woman and her child into hiding.

It wasn't until the young child began turning up in the emergency room with bumps and bruises indicative of physical abuse that Maitland became aware of the mistake. The story had gone public and the very existence of the Line had been touch and go for several months.

Since that case, every volunteer on the Line forwarded all cases involving children directly to Grand Central Station for consideration. Grace knew, however, that if the case had made it this far, then Maitland must be generally satisfied with Lizzy Stone's story.

"Priya suggested that we take the woman and her child underground until the investigation is complete," Maitland continued. "Given the seriousness of Mrs. Stone's claims, and the fact that Priya knows her personally, I'm wont to agree. What do you think, Grace?"

Grace handed the iPad back to Maitland. "I trust Priya Subramanian's judgment."

Maitland set the glass down on the table beside her with a definitive *whump*. "That's settled then."

"What happens next?" Signy asked.

"Should we bring her into Canada?" Grace asked. "There would be little chance of her husband finding her and it's just across the border if you determine she needs to go back."

Maitland shook her head. "Canada might be safer, but despite his many talents, even Percy can't have an adequate passport ready in time."

"Which would mean a record of her crossing the border under her own name would be readily available for anyone who came looking," Grace added.

Maitland nodded.

"Why don't we put her in a car and just start driving? We could meet up with the woman coming from Chicago," Signy said.

"I'd rather she not stray too far from home until we are sure what we are dealing with," Maitland said. She turned to Grace. "If I recall, you have a ski chalet near Lake Placid?"

Grace nodded. "I haven't skied in years but I have a man down there who can get the place ready for visitors."

"Excellent." Maitland asked, "I imagine it will only be for a few days. Could you leave tomorrow?"

Signy turned to Grace. "Why don't I go?"

"Really?" Maitland asked.

"Sure. I don't mind. I'm feeling up for a challenge."

"Are you sure, dear?" Maitland asked. "No one would fault you if you wanted to sit this one out. It sounds like you went above and beyond in Ottawa."

Signy held Grace's eyes for a long moment.

Grace said, finally, "I'm all right with that, and Signy doesn't have to stay. John can protect Mrs. Stone until the other conductor arrives. I'd trust him with my life." Grace smiled. "I have on one or two occasions, if memory serves."

Maitland glanced at Signy, one eyebrow raised.

Shoving away thoughts of her date on Saturday night with Ben Tran, Signy nodded her agreement. With luck, she could make the drive to Lake Placid and back in time to make it.

Maitland nodded. "Excellent. Thank you, dear."

Grace set her glass on the table and made to rise.

"If you're up for it, Grace, there is one other thing."

Grace plastered an expectant smile on her face and settled back into her chair.

"I'd like an experienced person to get a feel for Dr. Stone. I'll do the hard research of course, but I would like your general impression of the man. Just a quick in and out. Use the Abigail Lieberman alias. I've spoken with Rachel at *Sift* magazine. She'll back you up if Dr. Stone checks your credentials."

Grace glanced over at Signy, then back at Maitland.

Maitland peered closely at Grace. "Certainly, if you'd prefer, I can find someone else."

Grace waved a hand. "Not at all. I'm happy to go."

Maitland turned to Signy. "You still have the Carole White identity?"

Signy nodded.

"I believe we set up Carole White as a reporter, as well?" Maitland asked.

Signy nodded again. "Same magazine. *Sift*. I've used the alias a couple of times. Rachel knows me."

"Excellent. Check in with Percy on your way out. He'll have some new identity documents ready for Mrs. Stone. Oh, and give me a call tomorrow around noon. I hope that I'll have some further information on our new passenger by then. One way or the other."

Grace rose to her feet. "I believe Signy has a client appointment later this afternoon. We should be on our way."

"Of course," Maitland said. Getting to her feet, she reached out and took one of Grace's hands in hers, looking hard into the taller woman's eyes. "Is there anything else I should know?"

Grace shook her head.

Maitland turned her attention to Signy. "How about you, dear? Anything further you'd like to share?"

Signy forced a smile. "I'm good."

"It sounds like a fairly straightforward operation," Grace said, slipping her hand out of Maitland's, "like you said, a quick in and out."

Hearing Grace's confident pronouncement, Signy felt a strange foreboding settle in the pit of her stomach. Sure, she thought, a quick in and out.

Easy as mango banana pie.

Chapter 15

The Tracker pinched the bridge of his nose with his fingers. Pinned to the north wall of his underground lair was a record of everything he'd been able to glean about the events that had led to his mother's murder. The whitewashed surface was almost empty.

He moved closer, peering at the map of Ontario and Quebec that he had fixed to the centre of the wall. At the very least, he now had a location and a date, somewhere concrete to begin. He'd marked the street location in Toronto, where he'd abandoned Signy inside the Dumpster when she'd been just a toddler and he'd been not much older.

The horrifying little scene flickered to life inside his head. The two of them, bound together by a red ribbon, cowering in the back seat of a car, a car driven by the monster who had just murdered their mother.

The vehicle jerking to a halt in a sea of traffic, and Alex seizing the opportunity to grab his sister, open the door, and flee. Sometimes, when he lay on the verge of sleep, he could still feel the shock of icy cold against his bare skin and hear the slap of his shoes as he raced down the street. He could feel the terror as he skittered sideways on the ice and careened into the alley.

The alley. That dark and horrible place where, with a strength born of terror, he'd lifted his baby sister high in his arms and tossed her into a filthy Dumpster like garbage. And pleading with her to stay quiet, he'd turned back the way he'd come, willing to sacrifice himself to the monster if there was even the slightest chance that doing so could save his sister.

Moreover, to discover all these years later that he had prevailed. His joy knew no bounds. He could only hope that his true mother was finally at peace. He shook the memory away.

Getting to his feet, he paced the small room. If he wanted to solve the puzzle, he had to focus on the present. He walked over and stood in front of the area where he'd posted every newspaper article written in the Toronto newspapers about the angelic "Dumpster Baby" discovered in a back alley by a student on her way to work. December 19, 1986—sky overcast with snow predicted for later in the evening, temperature a chilly minus five degrees Celsius.

Running his finger over the picture they'd taken of Signy just after her rescue, he speculated for the hundredth time how long they'd been held captive in the monster's car. In the photograph, Signy was wearing a T-shirt with a yellow smiley face on the front, indicating the monster had not had the time to find them proper clothing.

Turning away from the newspaper accounts, he examined the big map of Ontario and Quebec. On it, he had drawn a series of concentric circles. The first circle encompassed the city itself. The next took in the greater Toronto area. From any point on the circumference of that circle it would take a car no more than two hours to reach the inner core of the city where Signy had been found.

After that, a series of circles fanned out like the rings on a pond, the final circle reaching out to a distance of twenty-four hours by car from the city. He had not included the United States, even though there were several border crossings that were only a few hours away from Toronto. He was almost certain that a lone man transporting two scantily clad, traumatized youngsters, neither of whom had a passport or any other ID, would not have made it across the border.

In fact, he doubted that he and Signy had been in the back of that car as long as twenty-four hours, perhaps not even eight. When he'd escaped the car with Signy in tow, he'd felt strong and alert, not exhausted and numb, as one might expect had he been in the car with the monster for many hours.

Nor had he been hungry. He remembered the monster passing him a box of fries, telling him to eat. When he and Signy had refused, the monster had shouted at them. He remembered a taste like acidic sawdust as he'd forced the soggy fries into his mouth. They had to have travelled far enough that the monster had decided they should be hungry, but not far enough that they had built up an appetite. Three hours? Four? Maybe even as many as six or seven?

As he examined the circles he'd traced on the map, he knew from bitter experience that there were hundreds of small towns, mid-sized cities, and even larger urban centres from which to choose. Raking his fingers through his hair, he swore under his breath. Half the population of Canada seemed to live in the area in question.

The few memories of his home life before his abduction were of no help. He thought he remembered playing with Signy in a sandbox inside a yard surrounded by a high wooden fence. There might have been a swing set and a blue plastic wading pool in the summers. He did not recall ever attending school or having any friends other than his baby sister.

He'd done some research on childhood memory formations and learned that for most children, events before the age of four or five are ephemeral, eventually eclipsed by newer memories. It is not until about the age of ten that the memories begin to crystallize and can be accessed as the person moves forward into adulthood.

The fact that he could not remember much more than a lush backyard didn't mean he had never attended school or had friends. On the other hand, perhaps his family had been hiding from the outside world long before disaster struck.

Clasping his hands behind his back, he stared at the map. He could speculate until the cows came home, but until he had some concrete evidence one way or the other, it was nothing more than guesswork. To that end, he'd done a data search. For the week leading up to December 19, 1986, he'd looked into every murder investigation in Ontario and Quebec.

He'd learned that at a rate of 1.8 homicides per 100,000 people, the murder rate in Canada paled in comparison to some American cities where the rate soared as high as 64 deaths per 100,000 citizens. In fact, in 1986 there had only been 761 homicides in the entire country.

If he went with the assumption that his mother's body had been discovered, then somewhere a murder investigation had been initiated. In the course of their probe, police would have learned that the dead woman had left behind two young children and launched a frantic search into their whereabouts.

In the past four months he had checked out every case of a murdered woman as well as every report on missing children. The only thing he'd found was what he already knew—that a female toddler had been found in a Dumpster in downtown Toronto. There'd been no report of a missing boy, or girl, anywhere in Ontario or Quebec. He'd even widened his search to include the states that bordered Ontario and Quebec and come up empty.

Similarly, he'd been through every pertinent murder file with a fine-tooth comb, but not one of them seemed to fit the facts as he remembered them. He recalled his mother's death well enough. He'd sat in her blood, holding her hand as she wheezed out her last few breaths.

In the days leading up to December 19, 1986, he'd found records for three women murdered, none of whom could have been his mother. Two of them had been too old. The third had been strangled by her husband, who had then killed himself.

It seemed that whoever had taken away his family had gone to great pains to ensure that they were erased from the face of the earth. Not even their dead bodies had been allowed to remain as witness to their passing. Why he and Signy had survived remained an even greater mystery.

He could feel his stomach rumble. He checked his watch, surprised to see that he'd been in his bunker for almost an hour already. He turned away from the screens and maps hanging on the wall. He needed a diversion.

When he'd done his Canadian data mining, he'd set up a trolling line, a clever cybertrap that would alert him should anyone, or anything, show any interest in his online footsteps.

According to Helen, he'd gotten a bite. He felt his blood burn inside his veins. Why, after all these years, would his investigation into an ancient murder trigger a response? Who was out there watching him, and why?

Chapter 16

Signy idled outside Linden Valley's only high-rise building waiting for her chronically late client, the crotchety Mrs. Nagy. For once, she didn't mind cooling her heels. She couldn't shake the unsettling feeling that something was seriously wrong with Grace.

As soon as they left Grand Central, Signy had tried one last time to get through to her mentor. She'd asked if it might not be prudent to have someone else go down to Rochester to interview Dr. Stone.

"I've been dealing with men like him for over twenty years," Grace said. "I can spot a liar a mile away. One hair on the back of my neck stands to attention, and I'm out of there. I'll fly back and be in Linden Valley by the time you make it to Lake Placid with his wife. Satisfied?"

"All right," Signy said, out of options.

Fishing in her purse, Grace had extracted a single house key attached to a key fob shaped like a pair of crossed skis. "The chalet is near Whiteface Mountain in the Adirondacks. It's remote, with no neighbours. It's set up as a safe house. It'll have everything you need. Food, money, and clean cellphones. I'll email you the directions. John will be waiting for you."

Glancing through the frosty windshield, Signy could see Mrs. Nagy in the lobby of her apartment building, doing up the buttons on her coat. She tried to relax. Grace's lapse at the embassy was a blip. She was worrying about nothing. She settled back in her seat and hiked up the heat.

As she watched her dour client pick her way down the sidewalk in her practical galoshes, she heard her cellphone chirrup with an incoming text message. She picked it up, grateful for the distraction. *Could this trial get any more boring? Can't wait to see you!!!*

She smiled. Three exclamation points had to mean something. She thought about warning Ben that she might not be able to make their date on Saturday but decided against it. She'd give him a call tomorrow if the situation changed.

Signy said hello as Mrs. Nagy pulled open the passenger door and climbed inside. Mrs. Nagy didn't reciprocate and, before she'd even done up her seat belt, started in on a litany of complaints. The weather was too cold, her condominium too warm, her doctors too unfeeling.

Sighing, Signy pulled out into traffic. There was a good reason she was a support worker and not a therapist. She was self-aware enough to realize that some days she just didn't have the necessary patience or skill to help others achieve new insights. Hell, half the time she wouldn't know a decent insight if it hit her on the head, she thought, with a rueful smile.

Letting her left brain take over the conversation with Mrs. Nagy as they drove across town, she listened to the older woman list a variety of reasons why her therapist was an ineffective boob. After validating her concerns, Signy tried to suggest that a broader perspective might be helpful. That went nowhere, so after a while she stuck to listening only.

With her right brain, she thought about Ben Tran, allowing herself a moment of hope that their dinner tomorrow might be the beginning of something she'd never had before. A real relationship. Flowers, chocolates, long walks on the beach, the whole nine yards. She rolled her eyes. Not bloody likely.

She dropped Mrs. Nagy at the front entrance of the hospital with the promise she'd be waiting in an hour, and then thought about going to the coffee shop across the road for something to eat. Grace had had no goodies in her car, and the disgusting Dubonnet that Maitland had served was percolating in her stomach.

She put the car in gear and rolled away from the curb but instead of heading over to the coffee shop, the damn car turned left into the hospital's short-term parking lot. What did Zef call her Saturn? A shit box with a mind of its own? If not the car, it certainly looked like someone had other plans for her this afternoon.

Parking the car, she turned off the engine and sat for a moment debating with herself. Grace had asked her not to tell Maitland about what had happened at the embassy and she'd honoured that promise. On the other hand, Grace hadn't said anything about telling anyone else.

She grabbed her purse, then hustled across the frozen parking lot, barely feeling the cold. There was only one person who would have the cojones to ask Grace not to go down to Rochester, only one person who might convince Grace to take the time she needed to get her feet back underneath her.

Signy pulled open the door to the emergency department. For the first time since the shooting, she was going to confront Grace's ex-lover, the intimidating Dr. Kim Blackwater.

After polishing off a late lunch of refried beans and rice with a fresh tomato and mozzarella salad, the Tracker sat down at his computer, determined to find some clue as to who had been nibbling at his fishing lines. At first, he thought the process would be easy: follow a few IP addresses back to their source and voila, he'd have the identity of his cyberstalker.

A half-hour later, he quashed that foolish hope. He'd followed the trail down one dead end after another and was beginning to think that the stalker had deliberately sent him on a wild goose chase, when his search came to an abrupt halt.

He slid his chair in closer and frowned at the screen. It took several minutes before he was sure what he was looking at. It took several more before he could believe it.

He'd run up against an impenetrable wall of encryption code written with a level of sophistication he'd never seen before. What the hell was going on? His fingers flew over the keys as he attempted to back out, but no matter where he turned, he hit one blind alley after another. It was as though someone or something was deliberately toying with him.

The screen went blank.

Leaning back in his chair, he was about to check the power connection when a line of text began to scroll across the screen. He squinted at the message. "What the fuck?"

Alex . . . You must suffer me to go my own dark way.

The cryptic message repeated five times before his computer abruptly powered down, then began to reboot. He sat in shocked disbelief for almost a minute before exploding from his chair. "Report!"

"All systems within normal limits, zero probability of incursion," answered the mechanical British voice.

"Time of last scan?" he called, rushing over to the picture window. He could see nothing outside but a rogue tumbleweed speeding across his driveway, heading north toward Shiprock.

"Last scan performed at one five zero five point seven seven seconds."

The Tracker raced back across the room and hunched over the computer screen. The most recent scan had occurred less than one minute ago.

He placed a hand on his heart, feeling the heavy beating through his chest wall. He could smell a sour tinge of sweat and noticed with disgust the damp crescents under his arms. "Unacceptable," he shouted at the white walls.

"Please rephrase the question," said the mechanical voice.

Gritting his teeth, he said, "No question."

"Very good, sir."

He dug his fingers into his blond hair and tried to think. He'd done nothing more than attempt to discover the circumstances behind a twenty-five-year-old murder-kidnap and seemed to have unleashed a massive shitstorm.

Whoever was watching him was good. Very good. The stalker had breached his firewalls with alarming ease. He thought about the words on the screen. *You must suffer me to go my own dark way.* What did that mean?

He dragged his chair back in front of the desk and performed a quick Google search. Almost immediately, the exact quotation popped up.

You must suffer me to go my own dark way. Written by Robert Louis Stevenson in 1886, in *The Strange Case of Dr. Jekyll and Mr. Hyde.*

"You must suffer me to go my own dark way?" he whispered, as he stared at the screen. "Dr. Jekyll and Mr. Hyde?" He raked his fingers through his hair. What the hell did it mean?

Chapter 17

Signy's first stop was the hospital cafeteria. She paid for a large take-out coffee but held off on the doughnut. Her stomach was doing flip-flops at the thought of facing Grace's ex. The last time she'd seen Dr. Blackwater, the ER team was prepping Grace for an air ambulance trip to a trauma center in Toronto.

Maintaining that Signy's reckless negligence had exposed Grace to the murderous intent of a violent assassin, Kim had stalked from the treatment area spewing fire and brimstone. At the time, Signy meekly accepted Kim's vitriolic accusations. She'd felt she deserved it all and more. She tapped a couple of packets of sweetener into her cup, then added a dollop of cream.

Things were different now. Grace had helped her to realize that although she might have made some better choices during her first solo job with the Line—chief among them learning to ask for help when needed—she was not responsible for Grace's injuries. Leonid

Volkov was a psychopath who enjoyed hurting people. It was as simple as that.

As she pushed through swinging double doors that led to the ER waiting room, Signy doubted she'd be able to convince Kim of that. Feeling her pulse flutter at her neck, she called up a gem of wisdom she often shared with clients. *You can't control what others think or do. The only thing you can control is how you choose to respond.* Talking the talk is easy, she thought.

Walking the walk was a different thing altogether. Take Mrs. Nagy for example. The old bat rarely treated her with the respect she deserved as a social worker. In fact, Mrs. Nagy had made it patently obvious that she viewed Signy as nothing more than a rather annoying taxi driver. Still, Signy vowed to be a bit more pleasant with her recalcitrant client on the drive home.

She scanned the board that indicated which physicians were on duty. Spotting the green flag beside Kim's name, she squared her shoulders and approached the triage nurse. "Hi, I'm Signy Shepherd from the Women's Centre?"

"Sure," said the nurse, offering a weary smile. "You bringing someone in?" She glanced over Signy's shoulder.

Signy shook her head. "I see that Dr. Blackwater is on today, and I really need to speak to her. Any chance I could go back and try to catch her for a second?"

"I don't see why not," said the nurse, glancing at the half-empty chairs in the waiting room. "Now is as good a time as any."

The Linden Valley ER was not much more than six or seven curtained beds crammed into a wide hallway. In the center, a glass-enclosed trauma room housed an array of basic life-saving equipment. Signy hustled past the trauma bay without looking, the citric odour of industrial cleanser not quite masking the reek of human suffering.

She squeezed by an ancient man, his sagging bottom only partially covered by a blue paper gown. Clinging to the arm of a young nurse, the old farmer seemed on the verge of tears, insisting that he needed to go home and milk the cows. Beyond them, a child shrieked in pain.

Signy felt her stomach lurch.

At the nurses' station, a diminutive man in a white coat sat at a computer console. Signy saw him grin at the hapless nurse, then turn his face toward her. His eyes flew open, and Signy thought he couldn't have appeared more surprised if Elvis had just popped his head out from one of the curtained beds and called for a fried peanut butter and banana sandwich. Did she know him?

A bone-rattling cough from behind one of the green curtains caused her to reach for an antibacterial dispenser that hung on the wall. Just as she finished dousing her hands with far too much gel and wiping them dry, the pint-sized physician was up and hustling away. He glanced over his shoulder at her before disappearing into the doctors' lounge. She could have sworn he had an avid little grin on his face.

She edged down the hall after him, her heart beating a little faster with each step. As she approached the open door of the lounge, she heard two people talking in low tones.

"Quit yanking my chain," whispered a female voice.

"I kid you not. It's the girl. Plain as the nose on your face, which in your case is—"

"You're hilarious, Paul."

Signy stopped dead in her tracks. For one crazy moment,

she contemplated pulling a George Bush, as Zef called it. A good old-fashioned cut-and-run. In any case, the decision was taken from her. Without warning, a figure loomed in the doorway, and she found herself face to face with Grace Holder's former lover.

Taking in Kim's dishevelled appearance, Signy tried to keep a neutral expression on her face. Kim's spiky black hair had grown out and now hung in greasy strands below her chin, the fuchsia stripes faded to a sickly salmon hue. Unlike Grace, Kim had lost weight since the breakup, her newly carved cheekbones emphasizing the fierceness in her dark eyes.

"Signy?" Kim asked, a hint of breathlessness in her voice. "What's wrong? Is Grace okay?"

"Kim, I'm sorry. I didn't mean to scare you. Grace is okay." Signy frowned. "Sort of, anyway. I think."

"You think?" said Kim, taking a step forward.

"Could we talk somewhere private?" Signy flicked her eyebrows at the tiny doctor, who was watching the encounter with great interest.

"Paul?" barked Kim, over her shoulder. "Can you give us a minute?"

The doctor yanked both ends of the stethoscope tight around his neck, then squeezed his way between the two women and out the door. Signy watched him flash Kim a look loaded with anticipatory delight. She had no doubt he'd be waiting for the scoop with bated breath.

Kim waited until he was gone and then turned back to Signy. Her face had drained of colour. "What are you trying to say?"

"I don't know," Signy said.

Kim reached out blindly behind her and grabbed the back of a chair.

"She's okay, physically," Signy added quickly.

Kim stared at Signy for several moments, then clearing her throat, moved over to a small kitchenette in the back corner of the room. She turned on the kettle, reached into a cupboard, and took down a mug. By the time she'd prepared a mug of steaming orange pekoe a few minutes later, her eyes were dry. "Are you still working for Maitland?" she asked, breaking the tense silence.

Signy nodded.

"Grace too?"

"She is."

"I should have known that nothing would stop the mighty Signy Shepherd," said Kim, her tone slipping into belligerent territory, "but I'd hoped Grace would have more sense."

Signy examined the floor tiles and noticed a pattern of indistinct brown stains. It looked as though a careless physician had tracked blood into the room on the bottom of his surgical booties. She held the warm paper of her takeout coffee cup to her cheek.

"Does she know you're talking to me?"

Signy shook her head.

Kim barked out a laugh that was devoid of humour. "She'll kill you if she finds out."

"I know that."

Kim held Signy's eye. "So talk."

For the next minute Signy told Kim everything. The whispers at the office, the debacle at the embassy, the unreasonable promise Grace had exacted from her. When she finally sputtered to a halt, she searched Kim's face.

Swearing under her breath, Kim looked away.

"This isn't the first time, is it?"

Kim stared into space for almost a minute before seeming to notice that Signy was still in the room. She shook her head. "Any more good news?"

Signy cleared her throat. In for a penny, in for a pound, as her foster father used to say. "She's going on a job for the Line tomorrow. It should be a quick in and out, nothing dangerous, but I think she should send someone else."

"Did you talk to her?"

"I tried."

A ghost of a smile flashed across Kim's face. "And you think she'll listen to me?"

"She misses you terribly, if that counts for anything."

Kim gave an almost-imperceptible shrug of her shoulders.

Getting the message that the interview was over, Signy walked to the door. She paused for a moment, then turned back. "Do you know who Ethan is? Or, why Grace called out his name?"

"I do," Kim said.

Signy waited, but Kim did not elaborate. "Okay. None of my business, I get it."

Kim snorted, and began to turn away.

"Um, Dr. Blackwater? Could I ask you one more thing?"

"What?" Kim asked coldly.

Signy swallowed hard, feeling as if she should have a yellow stripe painted on her back. "Can you please not tell Grace that I talked to you?"

Kim shrugged again, her dark eyes impenetrable.

Signy backed out of the room and closed the door behind her with a quiet click.

Chapter 18

It was dark by the time Signy pulled her Saturn into the driveway of the old Victorian house where she rented the third floor. Her headlights cut across the red brick siding and lit up the narrow alleyway that led round to the back parking lot. She snugged the Saturn in beside a row of grey garbage bins, then, head down against a wicked wind slicing between the houses, inched her way over black ice to the front entrance.

She climbed the two flights of stairs to her apartment and shut the door tight behind her, making sure the deadbolt she'd had installed a few months ago was firmly engaged. Before joining the Line, she'd played it loose and easy, confident in her "it could never happen to me" attitude. She'd learned the hard way the folly of hubris.

She used her toes to kick off her boots, shrugged her coat onto the floor, and then walked into her bedroom. She'd purchased a pretty duvet cover in an effort to abolish the memory of Big Dick Dalton attacking her in her own bed. It worked. Most of the time.

Squeezing past the end of the bed, she opened the pine wardrobe in the corner of the room. She changed into a pair of loose sweats and a T-shirt and strode back into the living room, casting a regretful glance at the kitchen. She hadn't eaten since breakfast and she was dying to whip up an omelette with cheese.

Instead, she spent the next half-hour performing the fifty-four ritualized thrusts and parries associated with the kata she practiced as often as she could. She enjoyed performing the familiar routine. It was a relief to focus only on her body for a few minutes a day, allowing her mind to take a break from its constant chatter.

By the time she wrapped up the final move, she thought about rounding out her workout with a run, but she could hear the block of old cheddar she'd picked up at the market last week calling from the fridge.

Twenty minutes later, having scarfed down a gooey omelette, two pieces of rye toast, and a huge glass of freshly squeezed orange juice, she pushed back her chair. She had a few things left to do to get ready for her trip tomorrow, but after that, she was going to sleep like the dead.

Grabbing her keys, she walked back into the bedroom and opened the door to the wardrobe. Things hadn't gotten any better inside her closet, she noted with disapproval. Doing laundry was her least-favourite thing, especially when it meant a two-hour trip to the Laundromat downtown.

Grumbling, she stuffed the mound of dirty clothes into a laundry bag and tossed it aside. She'd deal with that when she got back. Once the wardrobe floor was clear, she spied what she was looking for, a locked metal container about the size and shape of a safety deposit box. She popped the lock and opened the lid.

Inside, a passport, driver's licence, and three credit cards all in the name of Carole White were fastened together with an elastic band. She extracted the bundle and removed the band, then shoved the passport into the front pocket of her backpack. She tucked her legitimate passport into the false bottom of the bag. It was a risk to carry two passports, but she liked to have a backup in case her alias was blown. The driver's licence and credit cards went into a pink wallet she found near the bottom of the box.

Stuffed with typical detritus—library card, movie ticket stubs, doctor and dental appointment cards, and a pocket full of jingling coins—the wallet was well-worn. Also included was a press card from *Sift* magazine, identifying her as an investigative reporter for the webzine. All in the name of Carole White and all of it apparently utilized on a regular basis should anyone go so far as to check her recent library checkouts or Aeroplan points.

Reaching back into the metal box, she lifted out a two-inch-thick brick of cash provided by the Line, to use when needed. In denominations of tens and twenties, it added up to about seven thousand dollars. She picked out five hundred in twenties and stuffed them into the pink wallet.

She closed the lid and clicked home the lock, then slid the metal box back into the back corner of her wardrobe. She was about to get to her feet when she caught sight of the little cherrywood box her foster father had carved for her when she'd been just a girl.

She lifted it gingerly from its hiding spot, then set it down on the bed. She hadn't opened it in months. She didn't need to. She knew the location and significance of every object inside: the crumbling roach wrapped in a twist of plastic, a reminder of her first night with Zef; a couple of her favourite childhood photographs; a score card of one of the few times she'd beaten her childhood friend Jilly at cards.

It was the legal-sized envelope tucked on the bottom that took her breath away. It contained the DNA report that had unlocked the mystery of her identity, a white business card, blank except for a ten-digit phone number she'd long since memorized, and two lengths of scarlet ribbon, braided together to form a perfect whole.

She held the box in her hands, her fingers flicking open the tiny latch and then closing it again. Open, closed. Open, closed. She could hardly believe she'd actually contemplated driving down to New Mexico to visit the lying bastard. After what he'd done, he'd be lucky if she ever saw him again.

After what felt like an hour, she tucked the box back into the corner of the closet. Enough time wasted on memory lane. Tonight, she had other things to do.

She stuffed the pink wallet into the backpack, then hefting it to her shoulder, walked back into her small living room. She couldn't risk bringing her Taser or a canister of pepper spray across the border. In the unlikely event that push should come to shove, she'd just have to make do with whatever was at hand.

Satisfied that she had everything she needed, she took a shower, then flopped into bed. She was nodding off when she heard a scratching sound coming from inside the bedroom wall. The mouse was back. She smiled and rolled over. The little creature was a survivor; she had to give him that. A few minutes later, she fell asleep and didn't dream once that she could remember.

Chapter 19

Grace tried not to watch the door. Chilled to the bone when she first arrived, she'd chosen the booth next to the potbelly stove, but now she was too warm. She inched further into the booth and picked up the menu for the third time.

Opening the cracked plastic cover, she scanned the words without reading. The selections at the Manor House hadn't changed in the ten years she'd been living in Linden Valley. Thick cream soups, house and garden salads with heavy dressings, and the usual burgers and fries, western sandwiches, and spaghetti and meat sauce.

Thank God, the house white was passable. She was well into a carafe and thinking she should have ordered a bottle when she felt a whoosh of cold air on her feet. Her eyes darted to the door. A group of young people tumbled inside, chattering happily. Co-workers looking to unwind at the end of a long day. Not the party she was waiting for.

Her heart thudded painfully in her chest, and for a moment she wondered if she might be having a heart attack. At the very least, a quick cardiac arrest would make the nightmares stop, she thought wryly. The months of recovery had given her a desperate fear of hospitals and doctors and pain. She couldn't do that again.

She picked at a greasy spot on the tablecloth and thought about her conversation with Signy on the way home from Grand Central. She'd laid on the BS thicker than peanut butter on her morning toast, but Signy wasn't stupid. She knew something was wrong. She was just still too intimidated to do anything about it.

"God," Grace whispered, sending out another silent prayer of thanks. When Signy had asked about Ethan, she'd almost stopped breathing. She really must be losing it if she was talking to her dead brother in the middle of a crisis. Ethan Holder had thrown himself off the Don Valley Bridge years ago. Why was she thinking about him at all? Grace caught sight of her face reflected in the glass window, her eyes fixed and staring.

Looking away, she wondered if perhaps Signy was right. Perhaps she should send someone else down to interview Dr. Stone tomorrow. Melissa Chang was the executive director of the shelter down in Niagara Falls. She occasionally did some work for the Line. Maybe she'd be willing to hop across the border to check out Lizzy Stone's husband.

Grace pulled out her cellphone and punched in Melissa's home number. The line rang once, then clicked over to voice mail. Grace left a brief message explaining the urgency of the situation and asking if Melissa had a couple of hours the next day to conduct the interview.

She was tucking the phone back in her purse when the tiny

hairs on her arms shot to attention. She felt a chill on her ankles as the outer door whooshed open. Grabbing the menu with numb fingers, she stared unseeing at its sticky pages, seized by a strange paralysis as though the world around her had slowed. She could hear Nick behind the counter calling out to the cook for two halibut specials, his words a garbled drawl like a record playing at half speed.

"Hi," said a female voice.

With Herculean effort, Grace shifted in her seat and turned to face her dinner companion.

Kim Blackwater removed her coat, hung it on a hook by the booth, and then slid into the vinyl bench seat across from Grace. She unwrapped a scarf the colour of cranberries that was gathered at her neck.

Grace watched, her eyes glittering.

Kim glanced at the empty carafe. "Am I late?"

Grace gave Kim an appraising once-over. "You've lost weight."

Kim fumbled a menu out of the metal stand.

Grace felt a blush rise to her cheeks and was glad when Irene arrived with the fresh carafe of wine and a glass for Kim.

"I haven't seen you two in here for ages," said Irene. "I'm glad you're back."

"Me too," said Kim, then buried her nose in the menu.

Grace's heart skipped a beat.

"You need a minute?" asked Irene, pen poised over the pad. "Or will it be the usual?"

"You know what?" said Kim, with a smile. "I'll have the fish and chips for a change. Take a walk on the wild side."

"I wish someone would tell Hank that," said Irene. "I've wanted to go on a cruise for years but that man thinks a trip over to Stanton is adventure enough." She turned to Grace. "What about you? Are you going to take a chance?"

"I'm with Hank," said Grace, forcing a smile. "I like things the way they are. Fish and chips for me too, Irene."

Smiling, Irene tucked the pad back into her pocket and turned away.

"I thought the road to hell was paved with trans fats," Grace said.

"Oh, it still is," said Kim, with a small laugh, "but if I've learned anything in these past few months, it's not to take things quite so seriously."

Digging her fingers into her bushy mass of curls, Grace piled her hair high over her head.

"So," said Kim.

"So," echoed Grace.

The two women examined each other.

"How's Chivas?" asked Kim, finally.

"He's good," said Grace. "He misses you." She felt her cheeks flame hotter and rushed on. "He dug up all the tulip bulbs you planted last year."

"Sneaky little shit."

They both grinned.

"Work?" asked Grace.

Kim shrugged. "Same old, same old. Did you hear Paul is separated?"

Grace snorted. "Another one bites the dust?"

Kim flicked her eyes heavenward. "He has a replacement already, a young nurse from the obstetrics department. She's about five foot nothing and cute as a button."

"At least they'll be a matching pair," said Grace.

Kim smiled, then took a long sip of wine, "What about you?"

"What about me?"

"Any replacements on the horizon?"

Grace cocked on eyebrow.

"Sorry. Stupid question." Kim scrubbed a hand through her choppy hair.

"You've let the colour grow out," said Grace.

"Not feeling very wild and crazy these days, I guess."

Irene appeared with two plates heaping with fried fish and home-cut fries. A small dish of creamy coleslaw with wedges of fresh lemon perched on top. After setting the plates down, she stepped back and asked, "So far, so good, ladies?"

Grace held up the empty carafe. "Might as well bring a bottle."

They passed the rest of the meal in semi-awkward conversation, both of them steering well clear of perilous waters. When dessert arrived, chocolate cake and an Irish coffee for Grace and a bowl of fresh fruit for Kim, Grace could feel the alcohol coursing through her body. She felt relaxed for the first time in months, and suddenly bold. "All right, let's hear it. Why now? Why the sudden interest?"

Kim speared a raspberry with her fork.

"Four months without a word from you," Grace said. "No card, no call, nothing."

Kim pushed the berry around the bowl.

"I'm fine, by the way," said Grace, crossing her arms over her stomach.

"Any complications?" Kim asked.

Grace shrugged. "Who needs a spleen?"

Kim inserted a fork full of fruit into her mouth and chewed slowly. "I guess it was all worth it, then?"

"Their lives for ours, you mean?"

"Seriously, Grace. Do you think any of it makes a difference in the long run?"

"Why don't you tell me," Grace retorted. "You patch them up night after night, then watch them come back for more, over and over. Is that any different?"

Kim stared off into space for a few moments. Finally, she said, "Do you remember Nikki?"

Grace closed one eye and made a show of concentrating.

"Gorgeous Nikki, the triage nurse?" Kim lifted one corner of her mouth.

"Oh, *that* Nikki," said Grace.

"She's pregnant," Kim said. "She and Jean are going to have a baby. A daughter."

Grace looked down and fiddled with the napkin in her lap. "That's wonderful," she mumbled.

"It is, isn't it? They are over the moon. The thing is, Grace, Nikki works in the ER, just like me. But what you do, sweetie?" said Kim, sliding a hand across the table. "We can't bring a child into that life, can we?"

Ignoring Kim's hand, Grace wrapped her napkin around her knuckles.

"What if I'd been home that day? What if I'd been upstairs with our baby?"

Grace twisted the napkin tighter.

"You see, don't you? It is different. What you do is noble and brave and amazing." Kim covered Grace's hand with her own. "And I love you for it."

"But?"

Kim pulled her hand away. "I have to move forward. That's what I wanted to tell you. I've accepted a position at Vancouver General."

Grace stared at her for several long moments, then drained the remainder of her Irish coffee.

"I leave at the end of the month."

Grace slowly set her glass back on the table. Lifting her napkin from her lap, she folded it repeatedly until it was the size of a deck of playing cards.

"Will you please say something?"

"I never took you for a coward, Kim." Grace slid to the edge of the booth. Swinging her legs into the aisle, she had to take a moment to get her equilibrium. The room was spinning.

"Grace, don't."

Grace tried to get up but couldn't get her feet under her.

"Grace, wait," said Kim, opening her wallet and tossing several bills onto the table. "At least let me drive you home."

"I don't think so." Grace struggled to her feet. Taking a moment to steady herself, she plucked her coat from the hook and threw it over her shoulders.

Kim stood up. "It's happening again, isn't it?"

Grace froze.

"At least tell me you're talking to someone." Kim reached out and touched Grace on the arm.

Grace stared into Kim's eyes, then her mouth twisted downward. "I should have known. That's what this is about, isn't it?" She shook Kim's hand off her arm. "Signy Shepherd strikes again. All for one and one for all, my ass."

"Don't blame the brat, she's worried about you." Kim bit her bottom lip. "She told me you're planning on doing a job for the Line down in the States. She doesn't think you're ready."

"She doesn't think—? Are you serious?"

"Please don't go. Get someone else."

Grace glared at Kim, a cold rage extinguishing her last ember of hope. "Go to hell." She gathered her coat around her, barely able to do up the buttons.

Kim stepped into her path. "Grace, please, will you just listen to me for a minute?"

Grace's cellphone rang. Holding up a hand to still Kim's pleadings, she fished her phone from her pocket and brought it to her ear. She listened for several seconds, her eyes not leaving Kim. Finally, she flashed a tight smile and said, "Thanks so much for getting back to me, Melissa, but I've had a cancellation in my day tomorrow, so I'll be able to go down to Rochester after all." She listened to the other woman's answer, then said, "Yes, I'm sure, but thanks anyway." Grace hung up.

Kim held her hands in front of her in an attitude of prayer. "Grace, please. Don't go."

Smiling thinly, Grace stepped around Kim, taking care not to let even the hem of her coat touch her former lover. She yanked open the door and stalked into the cold night without a backward glance.

Chapter 20

Signy stomped snow off her boots in the chilly alcove of the Rochester women's shelter. She'd set off from Linden Valley before dawn. With a silver Chevy Tahoe rented at the Toronto International Airport, the drive to Rochester had been a breeze, the big SUV handling the winter conditions with ease. Crossing into the United States had gone smoothly too, the US Customs officer accepting her bogus passport without incident.

Signy checked her watch. Grace would be flying into Rochester soon. Shivering, she crossed her arms over her chest, uncertain whether her sudden case of the shakes was a result of the glacial temperature inside the alcove or of the idea of Grace meeting alone with Solomon Stone.

The door to the shelter swung open and a heavy-set woman, clad in a green sari, stood in the entranceway. "Ms. Shepherd?"

Signy cracked a smile, her cheeks stiff with cold.

The woman tucked an errant strand of black hair back into

her tight bun. "Thank you for coming," she said, ushering Signy through the door. "I'm Priya Subramanian."

While Priya took Signy's coat and boots and placed them in a front hall closet, the two women exchanged the standard weather talk common to people who spend half the year battling snow and ice. Both women downplayed the dire predictions that the approaching winter storm was going to be one for the record books, agreeing instead that it would probably follow the usual pattern and peter out over the Atlantic.

A few minutes later, Signy trailed Priya through the shelter's communal living space: a homey circle of comfortable, plush chairs that actually matched the couch, and a freshly washed, scratch-free pine floor. Modern prints brightened the walls. Signy thought it very different from the hand-me-down look of Vicky's Place in Linden Valley.

She tiptoed through the room trying not to interrupt a group of residents learning how to conduct an employment search after having put their careers on hold. A grey-haired woman with washed-out blue eyes and deep lines on her face smiled at Signy, who wiggled her fingers in return.

Leaving the group behind, Signy followed Priya into her office, immediately struck by how different it was from Grace's workspace. No stacks of files teetering on the edge of the desk, no half-empty coffee mugs scattered about like land mines, no crumbling remains of homemade cupcakes. Though the orderliness was refreshing, Signy found she missed the bright model train that chugged along a set of tracks suspended from the ceiling in Grace's office.

Priya's office was bare except for a sleek desk and chair, a round meeting table surrounded by four smaller chairs, and a shelving unit, neatly stacked with books and journals. The only hints of disarray were a jumble of policy notices and posters pinned on a corkboard. Grace had one just like it in her office.

While Priya took a seat behind her desk, Signy walked over and examined one of the posters. It was a missing persons notice, decrying the disappearance of more than a dozen young women and girls. She peered at the faces, discerning no obvious pattern. Eye colour ranged from black to brown to blue, face shapes varied widely, and hairstyles were all over the map.

She read a few of the names: Janelle, Akilah, Bridie, Muhubo, Sandra, and Kit Kat, the girl featured in the newspaper story she'd read at Maitland's place. A diverse bunch. She sighed. Things might be bad in the States for women, but they were no better in Canada. Indigenous women, in particular, went missing or worse in alarming numbers, with a rate of victimization almost three and a half times that of nonindigenous women.

She recalled a recent news item detailing the tragic outcome of a yearlong investigation into a brutal cross-border sex-trafficking ring. Young indigenous woman from both sides of the border were lured aboard Great Lake freighters with offers of drugs and money, kidnapped, and used as sex slaves.

"Coffee, tea?" asked Priya, her hand hovering over the phone.

"Just some water, please," said Signy. She wondered how many of the heartbreaking young faces peering out from the missing poster had met a similar fate. She couldn't imagine a more poignant reminder of why she was risking her own freedom to spirit Lizzy Stone and her baby to safety.

Priya poured a glass of water from a pitcher on her desk and handed it to Signy. "Lizzy will be down shortly. Tell me. What do you know of postpartum depression?"

Signy swallowed hard. Priya's question felt like a test, or perhaps the woman just had an unfortunate way of speaking. Either way, Signy took a moment to pull out a chair and sit down. "I know it's a serious psychiatric condition," she answered, after collecting her thoughts.

"Indeed," Priya replied, "very different from the 'baby blues,' which, as you probably know, is characterized by a couple of weeks of irritability, tears, moodiness, and insomnia."

Signy nodded.

"True postpartum depression is a different kettle of fish altogether. A major depression that builds slowly, peaking at around three to four months after the birth of the baby. Some mothers even have thoughts of harming their babies, although that is usually more of a fear than an urge."

"Do you think Lizzy Stone has it?"

"Not at all," Priya said, "but it certainly looks like her husband is on a campaign to have it appear that way. I had a call this morning from the wife of one of Dr. Stone's business associates. I know her slightly. She occasionally brings in donations. She asked if I had heard from Lizzy lately."

Signy raised a brow.

"Of course, I said nothing one way or the other. She went on to say that Dr. Stone had confided his worries to her husband, and she felt compelled to spread the news in order to prevent a possible tragedy, as she put it." Priya shook her head.

"And you don't agree."

"Absolutely not." Priya shoved the errant strand of hair away from her eyes. "I've known Lizzy for several years. She used to volunteer over at the youth shelter. The young people there adored her."

"Really?" Having worked as a counsellor at a youth shelter, Signy knew how difficult it could be to forge a connection with street-hardened kids.

Priya nodded. "And I see nothing about her current demeanour to indicate anything has changed. Despite the fact her baby can be quite the handful, she seems to be holding up very well."

A terrible caterwauling exploded outside in the hall.

Priya winced. "Ah, it seems young Justin Stone has arrived. There was very little sleep in this house last night, I must say."

Signy grimaced. The kid had to be registering in the 120-decibel range. Somewhere between jackhammer and jet engine.

Priya strode over to the door and pulled it open.

Framed in the doorway was a young woman, no bigger than a minute, as Signy's foster father used to say, her straight brown hair caught back in a rough ponytail. Wearing black yoga pants and a matching top, she looked over at Signy with chocolate brown eyes that seemed far too large for her face.

Could this really be her new passenger? The girl looked no older than fifteen or sixteen, and it was only a pair of obviously fake double Cs and the squalling baby clinging to her hip that hinted at her real age, which, Signy knew, was closer to thirty.

"Please," said Priya, holding out her arms, "let me take him."

Lizzy Stone placed the baby into Priya's arms with a relieved smile.

Bouncing the squirming infant on her hip, Priya ushered the woman inside the office. She waited for the baby's cries to hiccup to a halt, and then said, "Lizzy? I'd like you to meet Signy Shepherd. She's the one I told you about."

Peeping up at Signy through impossibly long eyelashes, Lizzy said, "Hi, nice to meet you."

Signy echoed the greeting, then performed the obligatory inspection of the baby. "He's adorable," she exclaimed, after what she hoped was an appropriate number of oohs and aahs.

"You really think so?" Lizzy looked unconvinced.

"For sure," Signy lied, glancing at the sweaty, red-faced creature who appeared to have a misshapen pumpkin growing out of his shoulders instead of a baby's head. "He's as cute as a bug in a rug."

"I don't know. I've always thought his head was too big for his body."

Pretending to cough, Signy covered her smile.

"He's beautiful, absolutely gorgeous," said Priya, making a tut-tutting noise with her tongue.

Lizzy glanced at Signy, her brown eyes sparkling.

"Don't ask me," Signy said. "I know nothing about babies."

"Neither did I," Lizzy said. "Having Justin has been an eye-opener."

"Not to mention an ear-opener," Priya added, chucking the baby under his fat little chin.

"Yes." Lizzy raised her eyes heavenward. "That too."

Rising to her feet, Signy asked, "You ready to go? I'd like to get you to the safe house as soon as possible. Your husband returns today?"

"Unfortunately."

"When do you expect him?"

"He flew in this morning, but he should be spending the day at the office. With luck, he won't be home until after six at the earliest."

"Plenty of time," Signy said, thinking about Grace.

Priya was standing in front of the window, showing the baby a pair of blue jays flitting about a bird feeder hanging outside. "The sky is getting darker," she said.

"Time to go," Signy agreed.

Lizzy nodded but gave no indication that she was ready to move.

Signy noticed that the young woman's hands were shaking. "Is there something else?"

"When Solomon finds out that Justin is missing, he'll go ballistic." Lizzy added, "I mean really nuts."

"We'll be expecting a visit from the police, of course," Priya said. "Don't worry, we'll tell them nothing."

"The cops will be the least of it. Solomon is a very dangerous man."

Signy and Priya exchanged a troubled glance.

"I know what you're thinking," Lizzy said, "but I'm not crazy."

"I don't think that at all," Priya said.

"Nor do I," said Signy, surprised that she truly meant what she said. Even in this brief interaction with Lizzy, she saw no signs of mental illness. On the contrary, she thought Lizzy came across as a competent, caring mother, genuinely terrified of her husband.

"I'd be in California by now if he hadn't blocked my access to our bank accounts. He's been planning this for some time." Lizzy flicked her eyes at the baby. "I don't want to think what might happen to Justin if Solomon finds him."

"What do you mean?" Priya asked.

Lizzy looked at the baby and frowned. "Solomon has a different plan for our son."

"What are you saying?" Priya said. "Is the child in danger?"

Lizzy nodded. "Very much so."

"If there is anything you're not saying," Signy added, "now would be a good time."

"I'm sorry," Lizzy said, holding Signy's eyes with her own, "I know it sounds nuts, but I can't tell you anything until we're safely away. It would be too dangerous for all of us."

Signy shot a questioning look at Priya, but the older woman had her eyes fixed on Lizzy.

"All right, Lizzy," Priya said, "you know best. Just remember, the more information Signy has, the easier it will be to help you."

Lizzy walked over to Priya. As she held out her arms for the baby, her sleeves slipped up her wrists, exposing a criss-cross of fine white scars on the inside of both arms.

Signy filed that complicating information away for future discussion.

Priya handed the baby back.

Lizzy turned to Signy. "All I know is that Solomon will do everything in his power to get this baby back. You and me? We're nothing to him. He'd slit our throats as easy as look at us."

Signy stared back at her, sending up a prayer of thanks that Grace was meeting with Stone in his public office.

"I just want you to know what you're up against before you go any further." Lizzy bit her lip.

"Nothing is going to happen to you or the baby, I promise," Signy said, drowning out the internal voice that was admonishing her for making promises she might not be able to keep.

Lizzy let out her breath with a loud whoosh.

Signy smiled. "If we're going to outrun the storm, we'd better get a move on."

Clutching the baby close to her chest, Lizzy followed the two women out of the room, a sad smile playing around her lips.

Chapter

21

Solomon Stone rolled the Cadillac to a stop in front of the sleek wrought iron gate. Sliding down the window, he winced at the sudden blast of frigid air. The heater had been working overtime in the hour it had taken him to make the drive home from the office, and he was sweating under his suit jacket. Swiping his access card through the security box, he opened the gate. He shivered as the moisture cooled on his skin.

Once the gate creaked open, he pulled the Caddy ahead, the tires crunching on the frozen gravel drive. He'd deliberately chosen to leave the driveway unpaved, not because at almost a mile in length the cost would have been exorbitant, but because he preferred the rustic nature of the small roadway as it wound its way through the impenetrable woods that surrounded the house.

He felt his usual thrill of pleasure upon seeing his home come into view. Faced with limestone and towering three storeys into the sky, the place had a fortress-like air. Surrounded by a blanket of pristine white snow, the main building sat high on a cliff, standing sentry over the vast expanse of Lake Ontario.

More snow on the way, he thought. Craning his neck, he peered up at heavy clouds, so laden with unshed snow that they brushed the peak of the slate-tile roof. Punching the garage door opener, he took a moment to stretch his neck from side to side as the door rumbled slowly open.

He felt sluggish. He'd tossed and turned for hours, his sleep fractured by disturbing dreams, despite his overwhelming success at the conference. The East Coast investors had come through in a big way, and he'd even managed a pleasant chat with George Wilkington's gorgeous redheaded daughter.

He was not fazed to see that Lizzy's car was not in its spot. Lizzy and Katy sometimes did the grocery shopping together. He'd check the chalkboard in the kitchen. The girls knew to leave a detailed note anytime they went out. He hung up his coat, then walked quickly into the kitchen to check the board.

He was pleased to see a scrawled note from Lizzy saying that she and Katy had taken the baby into Rochester to do some shopping and would be home later that afternoon. Trudging wearily out of the kitchen, he started down the long hallway that led to the grand foyer, where a stunning Scarlett O'Hara staircase wound up to the second floor. With luck, he could catch forty winks before meeting with the Canadian journalist, Abigail Lieberman.

He'd been ready for more media attention since the article on his discovery ran in the *Times*, although the Canadian webzine article was not exactly the international attention he'd been expecting. The editor who'd contacted him had said they were interested in a human-interest piece about his work in war zones. No matter, it wouldn't be long before real reporters were knocking down his door, which is exactly the way he'd orchestrated it. He wanted the buzz to be huge by the time he announced the results of his work in Atlanta next month.

He smiled. He could hardly call what he did work. He was one of those lucky few for whom work was a passion, a true joy. To think that all those long years of trial and error were finally paying off was almost too good to be true.

A puff of warm air brushed across his nostrils as he passed over a brass heat register, and he thought something smelled a little off. The feed line from the propane tanks outside had been giving him trouble of late, but the furnace seemed to be getting enough fuel now. The house felt toasty.

Scuffing at a small smudge marring the hardwood floor, he thought about going down to the lab and checking on his tissue cultures but decided to wait until he felt more rested. Katy would have made sure all was well before going out.

He allowed himself to dream about the luxuries of a publicly funded research lab, with skilled staff on call 24-7. Operating a private laboratory had never been his preference, but it was the only way to avoid the scrutiny of the animal welfare nuts.

What did the PETA crazies want? He erased another little smudge on the floor. Flesh torn by bombs, faces marred by acid, limbs blown off by land mines. How did they expect scientists to find affordable and effective means to repair such catastrophic damage without utilizing live animal testing? He'd like to see what one of those misguided fools would say if they found themselves with third-degree burns. He doubted they'd be complaining then.

Catching sight of yet another blot on the floor, he stopped abruptly, a crease forming between his brows. Bending down, he drew a moist fingertip through the stain. His frown deepened when he saw the brown stain resolve into a deep red smear on his skin. He looked up the hall and picked out two more spots although they were so faint as to be almost invisible.

Jumping back up, he looked behind him. He could see them clearly now, a series of evenly spaced spots. He felt a white-hot dread explode in his gut. Racing back down the hallway, he followed the row of bloody dots to where they disappeared behind the basement door.

His heart hammered painfully, and he couldn't catch his breath. His vision blurred and sweat poured down his forehead and into his eyes. When he pulled open the door and saw the bloody footprints on the stairs leading down to his lab, he flew down the steps, already knowing in his heart what he was going to find.

Chapter 22

"I am so dead," Lizzy Stone said.

Signy gripped the wheel, the dull strip of Interstate 90 stretching out in front of her as far as she could see. Which, as luck would have it, was less than a few hundred feet. Fat snowflakes had started to fall, making the tarmac feel greasy under her tires. Easing back on the gas, she glanced over at Lizzy. "Why do you say that?"

Lizzy chewed on a fingernail. "When Solomon finds out—" Her voice trailed off.

"Finds out what?" Signy asked.

"Justin and me. Missing. When he finds out we're gone, he'll freak."

Signy glanced over her shoulder. The motion of the car had done that magical thing that cars do to babies. Justin was fast asleep in the car seat the shelter had provided. The air smelled of baby powder and warm milk.

Twisting in her seat, Lizzy peered out the rear window for the hundredth time. "He's coming. I know it. And when he finds me—"

"There's no one following us, I promise," Signy said. Which was true, as far as she could tell. She'd been varying her speed now and then, watching for any vehicles that were keeping pace with her. So far, she'd seen nothing suspicious. Still, she felt a shiver of unease lift the hair on the back of her neck and, despite her assurances, found herself checking the mirror again. Lizzy Stone's fear was starting to infect her. "But I have to say, it would help if I knew exactly what we're dealing with. Just how bad is this guy?"

Lizzy bit her lip. "It's complicated," she said, finally.

"We have time."

Lizzy peered out the front window. "How long until we make Lake Placid?"

"A few hours."

Lizzy shook her head. "I'd need ten times that to tell you the full story, and even then, I doubt you'd really understand."

Recognizing the futility of a head-on approach, Signy tried another tack. "What's in California? Family?"

"Not really, but I did grow up in Los Angeles."

"Cool. Did you ever meet any movie stars?"

Lizzy chuckled without humour. "I didn't really run in those kind of circles. I ran away from home just after my thirteenth birthday."

Signy made a sympathetic noise in the back of her throat.

"My new stepdad had a thing for young girls." She stared out the window. "My mom refused to believe me, so I had no choice but to get the hell out of there."

"I'm sorry."

Lizzy shrugged. "The good thing about L.A. is that it's warm most of the time, so living on the streets is doable. Besides, I got hooked up pretty quickly with some awesome youth workers in the local shelters."

"Priya told me you have a fabulous rapport with the kids at the Rochester youth shelter."

Lizzy smiled. "The kids open up a lot faster when they know you've been there, done that."

Signy silently agreed. Having grown up in foster care, she had a better understanding than most about how tough it was on kids to live in a constant state of chaos, never knowing what would happen next. It had made her a better worker with young people, but she certainly had no idea what it was like to survive on the streets.

"That's how I met Solomon, you know."

"What? Volunteering at the shelter?"

Lizzy shook her head. "When I was *living* in a shelter. In L.A."

"That must have been years ago." Signy flicked her eyes in the rear-view mirror.

"Did you see something?" Lizzy asked, craning her neck to stare over her shoulder.

Signy shook her head. "All clear. When did you meet him?"

"Almost fourteen years ago."

Signy did the math. "That would have made you, what, fifteen?"

"Fourteen and a half."

Signy hung on tight to the wheel as a pickup truck passed her on the left side, dousing the SUV with wet snow. She flipped on the windshield wipers.

"He was a plastic surgery resident at one of the big hospitals but spent time doing pro bono work at the street clinic where us kids got free medical care."

Darting her eyes at Lizzy, Signy asked, "He was your *doctor*?"

"The girls adored him." Lizzy stared straight ahead, a faraway look in her eyes. "But he chose me."

Signy digested that for a moment, then cleared her throat. "When you say chose, do you mean . . ."

"Was I sleeping with him?"

Signy nodded.

"Sure."

Signy drew in a deep breath, trying to maintain a professional demeanour.

Lizzy waved a hand. "I know what you're thinking. I was only a kid. He was in a position of power, blah, blah, blah. But he was the best thing that ever happened to me and it wasn't like I hadn't slept with a ton of older guys by then."

"I get that, but still—"

"I don't think you do get it. When you live on the street, you do what you have to. That's why the kids at the shelter like me. I don't judge them."

"I'm not judging you," Signy said, although inside her head she was picturing various ways to cause pain to the detestable Dr. Stone.

"Sure you are," Lizzy said, her voice tight. "I don't blame you. It's hard for someone who's never been there to know just how easy it is to cross over to the dark side when you don't have enough to eat."

Signy felt the back tires slip sideways on a patch of black ice. She steered into the skid until the car came back under her control.

"Besides, until the baby came, we had a great life. Nice houses, great clothes, trips south in the winter, and gifts. He used to love to give me pretty things." Lizzy cupped her hands under her large breasts. "He gave me these for my sixteenth birthday."

Hammered by a powerful gust of wind whipping through a break in the trees, the SUV rocked to one side. Signy gripped the wheel tighter.

Lizzy shrugged. "The problem is I'm almost thirty now, and apparently, no amount of Botox or plastic surgery can turn me back into a child. Not that he hasn't tried." Lizzy hunkered down inside her seat belt and chewed on a thumbnail. "Anyway, do you mind if we don't talk about it anymore?"

"Sure," Signy said, glad of the reprieve. The thought of a physician using his position of privilege and power to abuse young girls was monstrous. That he used surgery to mould Lizzy into his ideal child-woman was turning her stomach.

After a while, Lizzy began to babble away on a variety of inconsequential subjects. Signy understood the woman's need to fill the dead air. She'd learned that her passengers often used mindless chatter to stave off the dreadful void they knew was coming. She didn't interrupt and the miles passed quickly.

After exiting Interstate 90 near Syracuse, Signy headed north toward Watertown on Interstate 81, using the change of direction to bring the subject back around to Lizzy's current dilemma. "If you're going to disappear," Signy said, "you'll have to go off the grid. No more Lizzy Stone." She rummaged in her bag, slipping out a manila envelope, which she handed to Lizzy. "Here's your new ID. From now on, you are Marianne Bridges." Signy pointed at the baby. "His name is Dylan. You live in Watertown."

Reading her new driver's licence, Lizzy mouthed the address.

"My name is Carole White and I'm an old college buddy of yours. I live in Toronto. I came down a few days ago to do some shopping at the outlet mall in Rochester. There's a bag of clothes from the mall, along with the appropriate receipts. I stopped there on my drive in from Ontario."

Lizzy raised her brows. "You really are prepared."

"Always," Signy said. "And from now on, you have to be the same. Being ready for anything needs to become your full-time job."

In the back seat, the baby stretched and yawned, squawked and fussed, until finally, having built up a full head of steam, he opened his mouth and screamed.

"He's hungry again," Lizzy said.

"Hold on," Signy said, "there's a turnoff just ahead."

Lizzy stiffened in her seat. "We should keep moving."

The snow had let up and the driving was easier. Even the cloud cover appeared to be lifting. It appeared as though the so-called storm of the century had petered out over the Atlantic. Signy breathed a sigh of relief. The sooner Lizzy Stone was safe at the chalet, the better. She steered into the well-plowed turnoff and pulled to a stop. "We'll be okay here for a few minutes."

Signy watched with approval as Lizzy made note of each vehicle in the lot before popping open the buckle that held the baby inside the car seat.

Freeing him from the restraining straps, Lizzy lifted the child up and over the seat, snuggling his plump body into her lap. The baby clawed at her blouse. "The shelter prepared a couple of bottles for me. Do you mind grabbing one? They're in my bag."

Signy leaned over into the back seat and rummaged through the girl's bag. Pushing aside a small bundle of clothes and what appeared to be a mini laptop computer, she snagged one of the bottles. "It's not warm."

"That's okay. This guy will eat anything." Proving her right, the baby latched on to the bottle and attacked the nipple as though he hadn't eaten in days.

Trying to tune out the moist gulping sounds, Signy asked, "That thing in your bag, is it a laptop?"

"What?" Lizzy said, mopping at the overflow trickling from the corner of the baby's mouth.

Signy extracted the item from the bag and held it up for Lizzy to see.

Lizzy flicked her eyes in Signy's direction. "It's a DVD player."

"Does it have Wi-Fi or any smart functions?"

"It only plays movies. I brought some cartoons for Justin."

"Okay, but be careful. No Internet, no smart phones, nothing."

"I know. Priya gave me the lowdown."

Remembering that Maitland had asked her to call in for updates, Signy dug the burner phone from her purse and punched in the number for Grand Central Station. The line rang several times before she heard a click and a whispered hello.

"This is Signy Shepherd; I'd like to speak with Maitland, please."

"Good Lord, Signy. It's Henrietta speaking."

"Hi, Henrietta. Maitland asked me to call in. Is she there?"

"Listen, honey, I'm afraid she can't come to the phone right now."

Signy glanced over at Lizzy. "Why? What's wrong?"

Lizzy stared back at her, her own eyes dark with concern.

"I can't talk long; we have government men crawling all over the place," Henrietta continued.

"What?" Signy drew in a sharp breath.

"Seems there's been a bit of a brouhaha regarding the embassy assignment. A wall of black suits showed up a couple of hours ago with warrants. All hell is breaking loose here. Pardon my French."

"Shit. I should be there."

"Please, don't worry. We can handle things on this end. Nevertheless, I'm glad you called. We just heard from the Chicago connection. She can't make it. Family emergency. Maitland wants you to hang out with your friend at the ski slopes for a while. She'll call when she can."

"Sure, I can do that," Signy said.

"Oh, and you'd best get rid of that phone. We're not sure about the lines here. Find a way to get in touch as soon as you're safe."

"What about Grace? She should be back by now. Is she there?"

"Honey, now is not the best time for a chat."

"Sure, sorry." Signy broke the connection. Glancing over, she saw that Lizzy's cheeks had drained of colour.

"Solomon knows, doesn't he? I told you he'd find out. He's coming for me."

"Can you get him back in his car seat?" Signy said, in as calm a tone as she could muster.

To her credit, Lizzy didn't argue, merely got the boy buckled back into his seat, a turn of events he was finding less than ideal, judging by the volume of his shrieking complaints.

Signy removed the SIM card and battery from her cellphone, then slid down the window and tossed the tiny square card out into the snow. Putting the SUV in gear, she eased the car forward. Before exiting the turnoff, she tossed the cellphone battery under the massive tires of a tractor-trailer idling on the shoulder of the road.

Lizzy stared at Signy.

"Don't worry. It's nothing to do with you." Signy rejoined the traffic on Interstate 81. "Just a small problem back at HQ. We'll be in Lake Placid in no time, and everything will be fine," she said, with more confidence than she felt.

Feeling Lizzy's terrified eyes boring into her, Signy flashed a bright smile, then rolled down the window and whipped the phone out into the snow.

Chapter

23

Stone flew down the basement stairs, his feet hardly touching the steps. With one eye, he followed the trail of bloody footprints down the dim hallway, the neurons in his brain sparking randomly as he raced through the underground maze. The sound of his desperate breathing was eclipsed only by the roar of blood as it pulsed through his veins.

Hurtling toward the door to his lab, he slid the last few feet, the scrape of his leather shoes on the concrete floor like the hiss of a lit fuse. He slipped a key card from his pocket. He had no doubt that his world was about to explode as surely as if Lizzy had cut the propane line and lit a match. He stood frozen before the door, the card jittering between his trembling fingers.

How could she have done this to him? When he'd first laid eyes on her, she was a foul-mouthed street punk. He'd devoted himself to transforming her into the dazzling butterfly she'd become. He'd given her everything she'd ever wanted, and more. For what?

Gritting his teeth, he swiped the card and shoved the door open. His breath caught in his throat as he took in the horrible scene. The jumble of empty culture dishes scattered across the floor like murdered children. Globs of pink medium clinging to the drain in the sink, a bitter reminder of the tenacious life he had so lovingly nurtured. The shattered and chemically burned computer hard drive.

Stone sank to his knees, his legs no longer able to hold his weight. A sudden gush of acid scorched his throat. His mouth hung open, drool dangling from the corner of his mouth like spider silk. He felt as if he'd been punched in the gut. Blinking away furious tears, he fought for breath.

It was several minutes before he was able to sit back on his heels and survey the carnage. Lizzy knew that he hadn't yet shared his findings, hadn't yet sent samples of the precious tissue to other labs to have his results duplicated. She was well aware that this small incubator contained the only samples of the immortal cell line that he had so carefully tended.

Struggling to his feet, he felt his brain begin to fire on all cylinders again. Lizzy had a decent head start, but he'd taken the precaution of freezing her bank accounts. She had no friends or family, nowhere to run. Most importantly, he was certain she'd keep the child safe. She knew a bargaining chip when she saw one.

He walked over to the sink and splashed cold water on his face, then plucked a paper towel from a dispenser. Lizzy was a clever girl, but if she thought that by destroying the computer she had saved herself, she'd made a serious miscalculation.

Backing up data was an almost religious obsession for him. Multiple times per day, he saved his findings on a secondary hard drive. Every scrap of raw data, every note, and every scientific paper he'd ever written. Every single video.

Mind racing, he contemplated and discarded potential options before finally settling on the most viable solution. He stepped over to the wall phone and tapped in the three numbers.

"Nine-one-one, what is the nature of your emergency?" a female voice asked.

"My name is Dr. Solomon Stone," he said, allowing his voice to crack just a little. "My wife and son are missing."

The operator took the required information, then asked, "How long have they been gone?"

"I'm not sure, several hours?"

"Have you checked with friends? Family? Is it possible your wife simply—"

"I'm a doctor," he interrupted. "My wife recently had a baby and is suffering from postpartum depression."

"Are you concerned about her safety?" the 911 operative asked.

"Yes, and not just hers. I'm very worried about my son."

"I'll send an officer over immediately."

After hanging up the phone, Stone remembered the bloody smudges. His eyes swept the floor, and he could easily read the story in the pattern of rusty spots. He could see how she had walked over to the fume hood after entering the room and then crossed to the incubator. He noted the cluster of spots in front of the sink where she'd shifted from foot to foot.

The delicate pattern was puzzling. He'd expected to find the great splotches of blood she enjoyed leaving for him when she was cutting herself. He'd come to understand this bizarre form of communication. The blood loss was never life-threatening but was dramatic enough to get her point across.

He frowned. These marks were less histrionic. She obviously hadn't used a scalpel, as was her typical style. The size and shape of the drops were all wrong. He glanced at the orientation of the stains near the door and saw his mistake. She'd had blood on the bottom of her feet *before* she'd entered the lab.

His eyes flew open, his brain reaching its unthinkable conclusion at the same instant as his feet began to run. He dashed out of the lab and up the stairs, then back through the kitchen. As he raced down the long hallway that led to the foyer, he realized that the odour he smelled earlier had grown stronger.

He took the stairs to the second floor two at a time. The police would be arriving at any minute. If they found anything untoward, they would swarm his home like a pack of locusts. If that happened, he had no doubt that his life would be over.

Holding his hand over his nose against the foul smell, he raced toward the bedrooms.

Grace steered her rented Nissan Sentra into the Rochester University Medical Center parking garage, then used a skyway to cross into the office complex where Dr. Solomon Stone maintained an office.

Her head was still pounding from the copious amounts of wine she'd swilled the night before, not only during her ill-fated dinner with Kim but also from the additional half bottle she'd downed after stumbling home. She stopped at a small cafe in the lobby and bought a bottle of pomegranate juice, then popped two Advil.

She walked through a hollow atrium on her way to the banks of elevators, the chatter of patients and medical personnel almost too much to bear.

The ride up in the elevator wasn't much better. An elderly woman with a face as dried out as a wizened apple sat in a wheelchair, her bony legs draped in a blanket. Standing behind the chair, a younger replica of the chair-bound patient stared into space, her head bowed as the old woman assaulted her with a litany of complaints.

Grace stared at the floor, trying not to listen as the old woman tore a strip off her daughter on an astounding variety of subjects.

"And that breakfast, Maria? I wouldn't be surprised to discover you're trying to poison me."

"All I did was open a carton of yogurt, Mother."

"Yes, and it had strawberry on the bottom. You know I like vanilla," the woman countered.

"I know, Mother. I just thought you might like a change."

"Change can be deadly at my age, Maria."

"I just thought—"

"Well, don't."

When the bell finally rang for the twelfth floor, Grace couldn't wait to make her escape. As she hurried out into the hall, she made brief eye contact with the beleaguered daughter, sending her a compassionate look of understanding. She was heartened to see the daughter flick her eyes heavenward in response, then muster the ghost of a smile.

As she thudded down the corridor, looking for suite 1224,

Grace ran through her agenda for the meeting with Dr. Stone. After a brief introduction, followed by a few questions having to do with his recent discovery, she would steer the conversation toward his charitable work and the impact his long periods away have had on his own family. She wanted to study his behaviour when he talked about his wife.

Finding Dr. Stone's office, Grace stood in front of the door and checked her watch. Eleven a.m. Right on time. She pressed her fingers over her right eye, trying to ease the spike of pain, and then pushed open the door.

She was surprised. She'd expected chrome furniture, smoked glass, and walls covered with glamour photos of gorgeous women showing off their enhanced breasts and faces. Instead, the outer waiting area was modest: six chairs arranged around a central coffee table strewn with a variety of magazines along the lines of *Cosmo* and *Vogue*. The air had a flowery scent, and Grace wondered if the doctor preferred to evoke a calming walk-in-the-park mood for his clients as he discussed the merits of peeling the skin off their bones.

She walked over to the reception area, where a slim woman with doe eyes and a blond pixie cut walked on a miniature treadmill attached to one of the ergonomic stand-up desks Grace had read about. People were starting to use them as a way of combating the plague of sitting that had gripped the plugged-in world.

Seeing Grace, the woman looked up from her computer screen and offered a dazzling smile. "Good morning."

Grace smiled, tipping her head at the treadmill desk. "I haven't seen one of those before."

"Isn't it awesome?" the pixie exclaimed. "No way am I dying of heart disease by the time I'm forty."

Grace sucked in her gut. "Dr. Stone must be a good employer."

"The best," the pixie gushed.

"Good to know. My name is Abigail Lieberman. I have an appointment."

"Oh, right. The reporter." The pixie tilted her head and her smile slipped sideways. "I'm so sorry, Ms. Lieberman. Dr. Stone apologizes but he needed to head home earlier than expected."

Grace felt a stab of anxiety in her stomach. "I hope nothing is wrong?"

"Not at all. In fact, he felt bad that you've come all the way down from Toronto and was wondering if you'd mind meeting at his home. He often has reporters out to the estate. The place is a showcase. You can get some amazing pictures there."

"Oh," Grace said, her mind whirling. "Is it far?"

The pixie dipped her chin in apology. "Not too far. Dr. Stone said that he could meet you at one o'clock."

Lots of time to put something in her stomach. Grace smiled. "That will be fine."

Flashing impossibly white teeth, the pixie slid over a sheet of paper on which she'd printed directions to the Stone estate. "He'll be pleased."

Grace smiled. "One last thing: is the food in that café downstairs any good?"

The pixie gave her an appraising look. "Lots of grease, if that's what you're looking for."

"Just what the doctor ordered."

The pixie chuckled, her laughter like tinkling glass. "Oh, by the way," she said, when Grace turned to go, "drive safe. They say there's a big storm on the way."

Grace glanced back. "Not to worry. I plan on being long gone by then."

"I hope so. Dr. Stone's estate is in the middle of nowhere. You wouldn't want to slide into a ditch out there. It could be spring before they found you."

A few minutes later, as she made her way along the buffet-style line in the café, loading up on eggs, bacon, soggy pancakes, and fries, Grace thought about the pixie's warning and hoped Signy was well on her way to Lake Placid by now. As for herself, she'd be in and out and on a plane for home well before the snow started to cause problems at the airport.

Grace groaned as she tucked into the fat-saturated fry-up, her head already beginning to feel better as the grease hit her system. If the storm arrived earlier than expected, then she'd just have to deal with it. She shovelled a forkful of gooey egg into her mouth. There was nothing like driving through a blizzard to hone the senses.

Her thoughts drifted to the dinner the night before. Kim had made it perfectly clear she intended to fly off to a new life in Vancouver. With that melancholy prospect heavy on her heart, sliding off the road seemed the least of her worries.

Chapter 24

"Excuse me, sir?"

The Tracker opened his eyes. A pretty flight attendant hovered in the aisle next to him.

"Sorry to wake you, sir, but we're on our final approach into West Palm Beach. Would you mind popping your seat back up?" She waited for him to comply before moving on to the next passenger.

Covering a yawn with his fist, the Tracker glanced out the window. Far below he could see fishing vessels bobbing on the dazzling blue ocean and the white flash of rolling breakers as they crashed against the creamy sands of the South Florida shoreline. The inland waterway stretched on forever in a ribbon of blue-grey. The same distinctive blue-grey as Signy Shepherd's eyes.

Shaking her image from his mind, he stretched his legs, wincing as the blood flowed back into his limbs in a fizzy burst of pins and needles. He checked the display on his personal cellphone and, finding nothing, folded his lean frame back into his seat.

Squinting into the mid-afternoon sun as the plane prepared to land, he admired the checkerboard of shimmering swimming pools and the majestic rows of royal palm trees lining the clean, white streets. It felt good to be back in the balmy South.

By the time the aircraft docked at the terminal, however, the blazing Florida sun had turned the aluminum fuselage into an oven. Loosening his tie, he thought about the last twenty-four hours.

The job had been straightforward enough. The meeting with the client had taken place the night before in the Tracker's hotel room. He'd chosen a chain hotel in a suburb outside Boston at the client's request. The client was the mayor of a mid-sized Massachusetts city, and with scandal swirling around him, he had the press dogging his every move.

"We alone?" said the client, shoving his way into the room. "I just spent the last hour touring all around this fucking place. Last thing I need is the press to find out I'm meeting with someone like you. No offense."

"None taken," said the Tracker, trying not to show his surprise. The pictures he'd seen of the man were misleading—deliberately so, he surmised. He'd read the mayor was a health nut, but the man had obviously taken the wellness craze a shade too far.

His collar was loose around a sinewy neck; the bony wrists that poked from beneath his sleeves, as fragile as a young girl's. Without an ounce of extra padding, his angular cheekbones and hooked nose suggested a bird of prey. As did the bright blue eyes that burned with a wily intelligence.

He paced the room, energy sparking from his small frame. "Slimy fuck always had it in for me."

"Why don't you start at the beginning," said the Tracker, tossing over a bottle of water from the mini-fridge, "and don't hold back. Every detail helps." Leaning against a desk, he crossed his arms and listened as the mayor outlined the entire sordid story.

A reporter at a local TV station claimed to have viewed a cellphone video in which the obviously inebriated mayor is cavorting in hotel room with two scantily clad and underage girls. The reporter went on to say that an anonymous source, claiming to be a long-time friend of the mayor, had shot the video. The source insisted that his motivation was noble, that he was an honest whistleblower, only seeking to expose the mayor's predilection toward pedophilia.

As a show of good faith, the seller had provided a screen shot showing the mayor, obviously intoxicated, his tongue shoved down the throat of one young thing and his hand dabbling inside the halter top of another.

The mayor extracted a copy of the photo in question and slid it across the desk. "Fucking bullshit."

The Tracker gave the picture a cursory glance. He'd already examined the evidence and, in his opinion, the picture was authentic. Altering a cellphone video was almost impossible without access to the type of sophisticated equipment reserved for agencies like the NSA or the CIA. Nonetheless, he kept his expression neutral. The guilt or innocence of his clients was of no interest to him.

"This friend," continued the mayor, drawing air quotes around the word, "then offers to sell the video for a hundred grand. A real public servant." He shook his head. "You got anything harder in there?" he asked, waving a hand at the mini-bar.

The Tracker slid a bottle of Dewar's from the fridge and held it up. When the mayor nodded, he poured it into a plastic cup and handed it over. So much for the health-nut myth. The way he was sucking back the booze, the Tracker figured he was jonesing for something harder.

"Anyway," the mayor continued, after coming up for air, "the local bloodsuckers decide to run with the story, despite the lack of any concrete evidence. As we speak they're scrambling to raise the cash."

The rest of the tale, the Tracker already knew. The picture would go viral. Worldwide, the press would have a field day. Late-night comedians would think they'd died and gone to heaven. Schoolgirl Sexcapades, they'd dub it.

"Bunch of liberal worms," said the mayor, finally winding down.

The Tracker shrugged. "What aren't you telling me?"

"Whaddya mean?" the mayor asked.

"The way I figure, your boy had a surefire payday coming his way. If he's in the wind, then something must have spooked him."

The mayor turned a hard blue stare on the Tracker. "A friend of mine did attempt to pay him a visit, but the shit managed to high-tail it down the fire escape."

The Tracker nodded. "Anyone else know he's on the run?"

The mayor shook his head.

"Good," said the Tracker. "The fewer people on his tail, the easier my job. Tell me about him."

"His name is Lenny Screed," the mayor began, tossing back a huge gulp of Dewar's. "I knew him in high school. A total loser. Didn't make it past grade ten. Spent his time smoking pot and watching TV."

The mayor paced the small room. "Anyway, he comes to me a couple months ago—I have an open door policy, you know?" He bared his teeth in a politician's grin that spread nowhere near his eyes. "I make it a point to be available to my constituents. Jesus, I hardly recognized him. He looked like a bum. Still, I let him in, we shot the shit for a bit, and then he asks me if I could maybe do him a favour."

"What kind of favour?"

"The green kind," the mayor snorted. "He was overly fond of the slots. Wanted a loan."

The Tracker raised his brows in question.

"Of course, I didn't give him anything." The mayor drew himself up to his full five foot five inches. "Welfare rolls are down thirty-five percent since I took office. No work, no pay. Sometimes a kick in the butt is all it takes, know what I mean?"

The Tracker understood perfectly. Nothing spoke louder to an unschooled and complacent public than the demonization of one minority group or another. A surefire election ploy. "So, you kicked his butt?"

"What? No. I passed him off to one of my assistants, asked her to get him in touch with gambling treatment, bankruptcy services, that kind of crap." The mayor shrugged. "I knew he wasn't happy, but what was I supposed to do, bankroll his addiction? Jesus Christ."

The small man slammed a fist into his palm. "Before long, I start seeing him everywhere, heckling me from the crowd at community functions, blitzing the office with fake complaints, following me after hours, shit like that. So when this so-called video turns up, I know exactly who's behind it."

"What about the two girls? Has anyone tried asking them about it? Maybe they could discount the whole thing?" the Tracker said, in a neutral tone. He already knew the answer but wanted to hear the mayor's take.

"Incognito, said the mayor, "both of them. Probably gone underground, waiting for the whole thing to blow over. Can't say I blame them."

The Tracker doubted that explanation. Madeline Raines, age fifteen, and fourteen-year-old Jasmine Parker had disappeared around the time the photo surfaced. He was under no illusions. The person most likely to benefit from their disappearance was standing two feet away from him.

"All right," said the Tracker, ushering the man toward the door. "I should have something for you by tomorrow afternoon at the latest."

Stopping in his tracks, the mayor looked at the Tracker and cleared his throat. "When you do find him, then what?"

Staring hard at the smaller man, the Tracker thought about the unacceptable invasion into his life by the mysterious Dr. Jekyll. Tracking the bastard was going to cost money. Lots of money. "That depends on how much you're willing to spend," he said, finally.

"Whatever it takes to make the problem go away—all the way, if you know what I mean," the mayor said.

Tight-lipped, the Tracker scrawled a figure on a slip of hotel stationery and handed it over.

After glancing at the number for less than a millisecond, the mayor nodded. "Fair enough. Do it."

The Tracker ushered the mayor to the door and watched until the man was out of sight. Then he walked into the bathroom and scrubbed his hands clean.

Chapter 25

Justin Stone screamed.

Gritting her teeth, Signy glanced over her shoulder. The baby's face was the colour of raw beef and his downy hair lay plastered to his skull in sweaty strings. His legs pumped furiously inside his puffy snowsuit.

"Maybe he's too hot?" Signy asked, trying not to let her growing desperation show in her voice. The baby had been screaming nonstop for what seemed like hours, and no amount of fussing by his mother seemed to have any effect. Fed, changed, a soother popped in and out of his mouth about a hundred times—nothing had worked.

Jamming her fingers into her ears, Lizzy let her head drop onto her chest.

The nurse at the shelter had tucked a tincture called gripe water into Lizzy's bag, but several generous doses had failed to quell the incessant crying. Signy winced as the baby redoubled his efforts. The kid didn't need gripe water, she thought, he needed a slug of demon water, preferably eighty proof.

"We're turning east at Watertown," Signy shouted. "There's a Superstore there. Let's stop. Maybe get him something lighter to wear."

Fingers plugged firmly in her ears, Lizzy didn't reply.

Taking that as a yes, Signy took the off ramp on the fly. A few minutes later, she pulled into the parking lot of the Superstore, relieved to find a spot available near the front entrance.

Lizzy unhooked the shrieking baby from the car seat while Signy wrestled with the cumbersome stroller that Priya Subramanian had squeezed into the back of the SUV. As soon as Lizzy secured the kid in the stroller, he quieted. Signy and Lizzy had both begun to shiver but the arctic chill seemed to invigorate the baby. He looked around wide-eyed, his tears freezing on his swollen cheeks.

It took a few minutes of heavy slogging before they rolled through the sliding doors and into the warm store. Stomping snow off her boots, Lizzy walked over to the rack and grabbed a cart. It wouldn't budge. "Ah, come on, you stupid piece of crap."

"Forget it," Signy said.

Ignoring Signy, Lizzy gave the cart a couple of rough jerks. "Get out of there, for Christ's sake."

"Language!"

Wheeling around, Signy glared at the strident critic, a cadaverous man with a face so pitted with pockmarks, he appeared to have been burned in a fire. He was wearing a black suit that had gone shiny with age, a white shirt frayed at the collar, and a bolo tie secured with an iron cross slide. He had a ruler-straight part carved into his oil-soaked hair, and he reeked of faux piety.

Alarmed, Signy jerked her eyes toward Lizzy. "Do you know him?" she asked, relieved when Lizzy shook her head.

The man pointed an accusatory finger at Lizzy, and Signy saw that he had sharpened his nails into points.

"*Do not be deceived*," he said. "*God is not mocked, for whatever one sows, that will he also reap*."

Signy watched the dull red colour that had been creeping up her passenger's face during the struggle with the cart bloom into a fiery scarlet.

"Galatians six seven," the man concluded, pulling his lips into a thin line.

"Why don't you take that holier-than-thou bullshit and shove it up your tight ass," Lizzy hissed.

"Walter!" A round-faced man wearing a blue Superstore vest barrelled onto the scene. He glared at the odd man. "Do you really want to get banned from the store again?"

Scuffing a pointed toe across the grimy floor, Walter glared at the staffer.

"You let him talk to people like that?" Lizzy asked, outraged.

"Don't mind him. He's harmless—for the most part."

"For the most part?" Lizzy asked.

"He can get a bit testy when he's hungry. How about you leave these ladies alone and head over to Mickey D's for some lunch, Walter."

"*Life is more than meat, the body more than raiment*."

The blue-vested employee crossed his arms over his chest. "Perhaps you'd rather I give Officer Bromwell a call? They'll be serving lunch down at the lockup just about now."

Grumbling under his breath, the odd man shook his head.

The Superstore employee turned toward Signy. "My apologies. Walter is a bit of a fixture around here. He's usually pretty quiet, but every once in a while he gets a bee in his bonnet."

"No harm done," Signy said, and then turned to Lizzy. "Let's go."

As if suddenly remembering her presence, the man swivelled his scrawny neck up, fixing a pair of oddly reptilian eyes on Signy. "*Make no friendship with a person given to anger, nor go with a wrathful woman, lest you learn her ways and entangle yourself in a snare.*"

"Walter!" the other man warned. "Enough."

"Colourful advice," she replied, smiling politely. "I'll take that under advisement."

"You've got to be kidding," Lizzy said.

"Keep moving." Signy turned and pushed Lizzy further into the store. As soon as she felt they were far enough away, she turned to check over her shoulder.

The strange man hadn't moved but he was following their progress with his eyes. Signy could see his lips moving slowly, as though he were praying—or casting a curse. She felt an involuntary shiver run down her spine.

As they headed toward the baby section, Signy noticed the glowering expression on Lizzy's face.

"Remember what I said about being prepared for anything? Sometimes shit happens. The important thing is to not draw attention to yourself."

"But that guy. . ." Lizzy's voice trailed off.

"There was obviously something wrong with him," Signy said.

"No," Lizzy said, "no way. He knew what he was saying." She glared at Signy for several seconds before her shoulders relaxed.

"You're right," she said, tossing a lightweight snowsuit and several pairs of sleepers into the cart. "I'm overreacting. It's just that I've been putting up with crap like that from Solomon ever since Justin was born."

Picking up one of Lizzy's hands, Signy held it tight. "You're doing great. Don't let anyone tell you otherwise."

Lizzy offered a tentative smile. "You really think so?"

"Hey," said Signy, glancing at the baby, "he's a cute kid, but he's high maintenance. I'm amazed you're hanging in so well."

Signy was relieved that her words had the required effect, and the storm seemed to pass. After Lizzy turned to examine a stack of diaper boxes, Signy exclaimed over a tiny pair of leather boots. They were an exact replica of the hiking boots she wore at home, right down to the orange and black laces.

Gnawing on his thumb, the baby grinned up at her.

Signy couldn't help but smile back. Despite his incessant crying, his weird pumpkin head, and the spittle pooling between his double chins, he did have a certain appeal. "Very attractive," she said, mopping the damp folds in his neck with the sleeve of her jacket.

He responded by blowing a raspberry, his little pink tongue vibrating between his lips. A spray of spittle landed on her cheek.

Wiping her cheek with the back of her hand, she said, "Keep it up, pal, and I'm turning you in to the lost and found."

"He likes you," Lizzy said, with a slight smile. "Do you mind if I leave him with you for a minute?"

"You're not thinking of going back there, are you?"

"Of course not. I just need to use the bathroom."

"Can you wait until we get this rest of the stuff? I don't think we should separate."

Lizzy thrust a scrap of paper into Signy's hands. "Here's a list of what we need. I'll meet you at McDonald's in ten minutes." She clutched at her abdomen. "I'm sorry, I really need to go."

Signy watched Lizzy disappear through the narrow racks of brightly coloured baby clothes. "Alrighty then," she said to Justin, "looks like it's just you and me. How about we get you loaded up."

Scanning the list, Signy was relieved to find that she recognized almost everything on it. Still, it took almost ten minutes to gather all the items and another ten before she finally made it to the front of the checkout line.

Eyeing the colourful array of candy conveniently arranged at eye level, Justin popped his thumb out of his mouth and shrieked.

"Oh, no you don't," Signy said, plucking a packet of dental floss from the shelf and rattling it in his face. She willed the cashier to pick up the pace, but it still felt like hours before she finally collected her change, tucking her pink wallet back into her jacket pocket. Late for her rendezvous with Lizzy, she zoomed toward the McDonald's outlet.

Crossing under the golden arches, she scanned the small space but found no sign of Lizzy Stone. She stepped back into the Superstore and, standing on her toes, did a quick visual search. It was no use. Everyone looked the same. Woolen hats pulled low over ears, heavy boots dragging across mud-splattered floors, pasty faces starkly lit by the overhead fluorescents. Every person she saw looked old, tired, and ill. Not one of them looked like Lizzy Stone.

Trying to quell a sudden bad vibe in the pit of her stomach, Signy gnawed on her bottom lip. It had been almost twenty minutes since they'd separated. Lizzy had probably come to the restaurant and, not finding them, had gone back into the store to look for them. The best thing to do would be to wait right here for her to return.

Signy pushed Justin back into McDonald's and joined the line at the counter. A few minutes later, she bit into a Big Mac, the fat-laden calories helping to buoy her spirits. Stabbing a fry into a pool of blood red ketchup, she examined Justin propped in the high chair that she'd dragged over to the table. He was gumming an arrowroot cookie, smearing more of it onto his face and hair than he was keeping in his mouth.

Signy swallowed reflexively and glanced away. Why people were so desperate to embark on the whole parenting journey, she had no idea. She fully intended on putting off baby making until the last minute and maybe even beyond.

Not that she had any prospects in that direction. The vagaries of her life as a conductor on the Line had done nothing to improve her already impoverished social life. Sucking in a mouthful of extra-creamy chocolate shake, she thought about texting Ben and then remembered that her phone was in a million pieces out on the interstate. Great.

Signy checked her watch. It had been almost thirty minutes since Lizzy had claimed she needed to use the facilities. Where was she? Lizzy's terror had been palpable in the car and her reaction to the creepy religious freak over the top. Was she losing it? Signy felt her stomach churn, the fast-food lunch settling like a brick inside her stomach. She checked her watch again.

"Where's your mommy?" she asked Justin.

The baby responded by mashing a thick glob of wet cookie into his ear. Almost immediately, his eyes welled up and he started to cry.

"No, no, no," Signy pleaded, digging out the soggy paste with the tip of her finger and then wiping his face with a moist towelette.

"Can I help?" A white-haired woman sitting at the next table smiled at Signy.

Shaking her head, Signy hauled the baby out of the high chair.

"I remember those days," said the woman, watching Signy stuff Justin into his new, lightweight snowsuit. "It was a wonderful time, but also exhausting."

Captivated by the older woman's grandmotherly smile, Justin's cries hiccupped to a halt.

Signy glanced at her watch. Had Lizzy's trip to the bathroom been a ploy? Had she abandoned her son? Worse, had Dr. Stone somehow managed to track his wife to the Superstore? Signy felt adrenaline explode inside her chest. How was she going to explain to Grace that she'd lost their passenger?

Suddenly aware that the people in the restaurant had gone very quiet, Signy watched the elderly woman's sharp eyes flick toward her and then settle on Justin. A quick glance around the small space proved the old lady wasn't the only one who seemed to be taking an inordinate amount of interest in the baby.

A table of young mothers was whispering among themselves, doing little to disguise their interest. In a back corner, two male Superstore employees, clad in blue vests, were also watching them, the younger man speaking urgently into his cellphone.

Feeling increasingly anxious, Signy gathered up the scattered remains of her meal. As she hustled over to the garbage to dump the refuse, she glanced at a massive-screen TV mounted on the wall in the corner of the restaurant and tuned to the Fox News Channel. Despite the distracting multiple screens, Signy had no problem picking out exactly what had piqued the interest of her fellow diners.

A large picture of Lizzy Stone holding baby Justin, his distinctive pumpkin head a dead giveaway, dominated the main screen. Underneath, scrolling in a continuous feed, two dreadful words. AMBER ALERT.

"Oh, shit," Signy whispered, tossing the empty tray onto the dirty pile. As she hurried back to the table, almost everyone in the place turned toward the plate glass windows that looked out over the parking lot. Glancing over her shoulder, she felt her heart jump inside her chest.

A line of New York State Police cruisers had just careened into the parking lot, sirens blaring.

Chapter 26

The first thing the Tracker did upon deplaning was to make his way to a men's room, where he changed into a pair of jeans and a T-shirt, taking care to transfer his cellphone from his suit pocket into his jeans. After riding the shuttle out to the car rental area, he picked up a nondescript white sedan and within minutes was driving south on I-95, cruise control set at a moderate sixty miles per hour.

He hadn't been grandstanding when he'd told the repulsive little mayor that he already had everything he needed to find the hapless Mr. Screed. Frightened amateurs usually equate distance with safety, although nothing could be farther from the truth. A successful runner plans meticulously, erases every scrap of his former life, then chooses to hide in a place that no one, not even his own mother, would think of.

He'd once found a crooked Wall Street executive busting horses on a small ranch in Wyoming. He'd still be there too, if he'd been able to give up the day trading. Holding on to the past was the second biggest mistake a runner could make.

Donating to the Pomeranian Rescue Society, resuming a coin-collecting habit, ordering that Hollywood rag everyone knows you love to read, or feeding your TV addiction. It was all gold to a man like him. Might as well wave a white flag over your head.

A quick search of the Intelius database had uncovered everything he needed to know about the unfortunate Mr. Screed. Most people lived under the illusion that as long as they kept their firewalls up to date, changed their passwords every few weeks, and purchased the latest data encryption programs, they were safe from prying eyes. Wrong again.

For a small fee, anyone can access every detail about anyone else—age, address, credit record, criminal record. Hell, even shoe size, if that's what floats your boat. For those pertinent details that you expected big companies to keep private, a couple of quick calls usually do the trick.

He'd discovered that Screed had a lengthy criminal record, which meant Canada and Mexico were out of the question. Most likely, the man had fled to either Florida or California. Both states were about as far away as he could run, and both were warm, a considerable bonus in the winter months.

He considered Los Angeles first. It was a massive city. With luck, Screed might manage to disappear for a month or two. On the other hand, Florida was relatively nearby. For a man without two pennies to rub together, bus fare to California would be a stretch.

With Florida the more likely bet, he googled TV providers in South Florida and found that three companies provided cable service while only two offered satellite. Cable was cheaper, so he started there.

Using a throwaway phone, he dialled the first company on the list. A young female service rep answered the line. He'd have preferred a male—they were far easier to scam—but young women were manageable too, if you struck the right note. Middle-aged women were a no go; better to hang up and try your luck again.

The Tracker began his pitch to the young rep using an awkward, pimply voice. "Hey, uh, ya? My name is Lenny Screed. I signed up for cable a couple days ago and I think I gave you the wrong address. I was going to move into a place on South Avenue but changed my mind. Can I check if I gave you the South Avenue address or the new one?" The Tracker laughed nervously. "I'm moving in with my girlfriend. Getting the place ready. I'm a little nervous, I guess."

"Really? That's so sweet," said the young woman.

Bingo.

"Gee, thanks," said the Tracker. "She's a pretty great girl and I want to make everything perfect, know what I mean?"

"I'm sure she'll love the place."

"I sure hope so," said the Tracker, "and thanks for the moral support, I needed that." He laughed. "Oh, sorry, what was that address again?"

"We have you at 64785 North Federal Highway, unit seventeen."

"Told you I was nervous," said the Tracker, writing down the address on the hotel scratch pad, "I did give you the right one. Thanks so much."

"No problem. Is there anything else I can help you with today, Mr. Screed?"

As the Tracker took the exit for Atlantic Avenue, which would take him down into Delray Beach, home of 64785 North Federal Highway, he felt almost guilty. Sometimes it was just too easy.

Deep in the back of his mind, he felt the whisper of his uncle's warning voice, *Pride goeth before a fall, boy,* but he brushed the memory away. He didn't make mistakes. He might as well have a licence to print money. Grinning, he turned onto the North Federal Highway.

Lenny Screed didn't know it yet, but his life was about to take a nasty turn for the worse.

Grace glanced at the clock on the dashboard and touched the gas. She'd been on the road for almost an hour. Barrelling east on I-90, she'd stopped only once to purchase a couple of candy bars and a bag of chips. The long, straight interstate, bordered on both sides by endless forest, was mind-numbing, and the flat winter light reflecting off the snow added a squint-inducing glare to the low-hanging cloud cover.

She was starting to worry that she'd missed her turnoff when she spotted the exit to Manchester. She peeled off the highway, heading north on Highway 21. Less a highway than a sleepy two-lane country drive, the road wound through low hills covered with leafless hardwood trees and deep layers of snow shrouding the ground.

As the car nosed down into a pretty valley, a flash of light high on the eastern hill caught her eye, and the sight of a golden statue, soaring almost two storeys into the sky, startled her. Depicting a cloaked figure, holding a book in one hand, the other raised above his head, the statue looked religious.

She confirmed the notion a few seconds later when she read a huge sign welcoming visitors to Hill Cumorah, birthplace of the Mormon faith. Grace made a mental note to check out this place on the Net when she got home. Kim loved this historical stuff.

Kim. She stared straight ahead, unseeing, her hands and feet on automatic pilot. She pawed about on the passenger seat, searching for the bag of potato chips. Ripping the bag with her teeth, she shook a few chips into her mouth. Chewing without tasting, she wondered, for the umpteenth time, how her life had spiralled so far out of control.

She slowed the car as she approached the tiny village of Pultneyville on the shore of Lake Ontario. The bag of chips rattled in her hand as she read a sign announcing that this unassuming place was the terminus of the Underground Railroad. She shoved more chips into her mouth and chewed furiously in an attempt to still a niggling apprehension running down her spine. She had enough real things to worry about.

Turning north on the Seaway Trail running parallel to the lake, she passed a collection of whitewashed clapboard houses clustered like ducks along the water's edge. Scattered about, sturdy homes of hand-carved brick and leaded glass windows sat like blind sentries to the past.

As the town site disappeared in her rear-view mirror, the territory changed again. Great orchards of apple and pear trees dominated the landscape. Row upon row of carefully pruned apple trees, their tortured branches fixed to V-shaped supports, resembled nothing more than an endless Golgotha. Grace shuddered. She wished she were home, Chivas curled up beside her on the couch, Kim reading by the fire.

Before long, a growing wilderness usurped the ubiquitous orchards. Dense forests lined both sides of the road and the orienting sight of the great lake disappeared. She flashed by a well-marked road sign, then glanced at her notes. Her memory was correct.

Dr. Stone's estate was coming up fast.

Chapter 27

Hauling the baby out of the high chair, Signy hightailed it out of the restaurant, leaving the stroller along with all their purchases behind. With the cops about to stream in the front entrance, she had nowhere to go but back into the store.

Her exit almost went unnoticed, as almost everyone had turned to watch the ominous blue and gold tide of New York State police cruisers. It was the one pair of eyes not watching the action outside that worried Signy.

Standing near the entrance, the Bible freak with the pockmarked face had his opaque eyes glued on the tiny figure of Lizzy Stone.

"Thank God," Signy said, waving at her errant passenger.

"Where have you been?" Lizzy demanded. "I've looked everywhere."

"No time," Signy said, dragging the woman through an empty checkout aisle.

"What is it?" Lizzy cried, as she tried to keep pace with Signy's much longer stride.

"Amber Alert" was all Signy had to say and the colour drained from Lizzy's face as though all the blood in her body had suddenly evaporated. Signy thought for one dreadful moment that the girl might faint. "Keep moving," she hissed from the corner of her mouth.

"What about the car?" Lizzy cried.

"Too late," said Signy. "Cops are everywhere." The two women dodged left and right through a maze of tightly packed clothing racks. Taking refuge behind a bank of centrally located change rooms, Signy paused for a half second to get her bearings. "They'll have the side entrance covered soon," she said, indicating the auto repair area located on the east side of the building, "but we might be able to make it out through the loading docks."

Too tiny to see over a rack of bulky men's parkas, Lizzy stood on tiptoes.

"Right now we have a more immediate problem," said Signy, looking over her shoulder.

Striding up the aisle, not twenty feet behind them, the surprisingly agile religious nut had the two women firmly in his sights.

Grabbing two parkas from the rack, Signy pushed Lizzy forward.

The baby seemed to take great delight in their wild flight, letting loose with a steady stream of excited babbling as he bounced up and down on Lizzy's hip.

Clutching the jackets to her chest, Signy raced toward the hardware department located on the west side of the building. Emerging from the relative cover of the clothing racks, the trio hurried across an open space, then veered up a smaller aisle containing shelves laden with screwdrivers, hammers, power drills, and saws.

Glancing over her shoulder, she saw the skeletal man's bolo tie fly up and hit his cheek as he rounded the corner and entered their aisle. "This way," she whispered, dragging Lizzy around the corner and down another aisle that led toward the back of the building. She heard the intercom click on and was relieved when it turned out to be nothing more than a tinny announcement reminding shoppers that delicious Florida oranges were on sale in the produce department, only two dollars a bag.

Ahead, she saw two pimple-faced boys jousting with a pair of flimsy ski poles they'd snagged from a bin.

"Hey, you guys," she said, as the little trio scurried forward. "Can you help us? There's a weirdo following us. He keeps saying creepy things to her." Signy jerked her head at Lizzy.

Eyeing Lizzy and the baby, the skinnier boy uttered a quiet "Gross."

"Can you hold him up for a few seconds while we get out of here?" Signy asked.

The larger of the two puffed out his chest.

Signy graced him with a brilliant smile as she flashed by.

Rounding the final corner, she could hear a sharp exchange begin between the blank-eyed man and the two boys. Signy grinned. Her faith in the macho cockiness of the teenaged male was, once again, well placed.

Using clothing racks and display cases as cover, the two women weaved their way along the north wall until they came to a corridor marked Staff Only. Signy peered around the corner and, finding the hallway empty, stepped inside, followed closely by Lizzy and the baby.

Behind them, Signy heard an adolescent voice cry out in pain. "Dammit," she said, shoving the baby into Lizzy's arms. "Wait here."

"No," Lizzy said, clutching Signy's sleeve. "Don't go."

She shook off Lizzy's hand. "Don't move. I'll be right back."

She heard Lizzy whimper as she took off back toward where she'd stupidly asked her teenaged heroes to fight a grown-up battle. She felt sick, hoping that the skeletal stranger hadn't done any major damage.

She rounded a stack of fitness equipment just in time to see the bony man shove one of the youngsters backwards into a rack of snowsuits. For someone so frail-looking, the man was surprisingly strong, with the mindless power of a zealot.

On the floor, his arm cocked at an odd angle, the other boy cried out as he attempted to struggle to his feet. "Stay down," Signy said, stepping between the boys and the stranger.

The man turned his reptilian gaze on her.

Behind him, she could see tan Stetsons worn by the New York State Police bobbing through the aisles. The cops would be on them at any moment.

The stranger raised his face to the sky. "*Blessed be the Lord my rock, who trains my hands for war, and my fingers for battle.*"

Feeling the hair rise on the back of her neck, Signy cast her eyes about searching for anything she might use to disable him. She didn't have time for hand-to-hand combat and wasn't at all sure she would prevail in any case. Having just taken out the two boys, the man wasn't even breathing hard.

She was considering the idea of burying him under the useless rack of puffy snowsuits when, without a sound, the man leaped forward as though he had suddenly sprouted a set of leathery wings.

She turned and ran, pumping her legs, letting her big thigh muscles quickly put enough distance between her and her pursuer for her to enact a plan of sorts.

"*Resist the devil and he will flee from you*," shouted the man.

Signy paid no attention to his crazed ramblings, instead focusing on the stack of fitness equipment she'd noticed earlier, specifically, the pyramid of iron kettle balls. Round with a convenient handle, kettle balls were easier to swing and sling than traditional dumbbells, offering more bang for the buck, according to some fitness gurus.

Signy didn't care about any of that. She was interested in the slinging effect. Running past the display, she scooped up a two-pound ball, painted canary yellow. Slipping her fingers through the wide handle she pivoted on one foot, and then swinging her arm behind her, spun to face the man.

She could see his vacant eyes, his mouth twisting as he spewed his arcane invectives. She watched his bolo tie lash up and down as he swept toward her. Using the middle button of his starched white shirt as a target, she swung her arm out in a graceful arc, letting go of the kettle ball at the last instant.

She thought she tasted a hint of iron on her tongue as the yellow ball split the air, although the foul reek of the strange man's explosive exhalation was real enough as the heavy projectile hit him in the centre of his chest, the force of the blow dropping him to his knees.

Signy watched for the split second it took for the man to topple forward onto his face, completely winded. "Let he who is without sin, cast the first stone," she muttered, then turned and ran.

In seconds, she was back to the hallway where she'd left Lizzy and Justin, and was relieved to find the young woman rooted to the spot, still holding the two purloined parkas. "In here," Signy said, opening an unmarked door that proved to be the entrance to a utility closet.

Stepping inside, Signy pulled off her jacket, letting it drop on the floor, and then holding the baby while Lizzy did the same. The two women then donned the bulky parkas. Signy tucked the baby inside her jacket, a state of affairs he seemed to find comical. He chortled merrily and she could feel his chubby legs grip her waist.

Signy flipped up her hood and indicated that Lizzy do the same. As they exited the closet, Signy risked a quick glance back into the store. Her heart sank. The tan Stetsons she'd spied a few minutes ago had multiplied exponentially. All she could see now was a sea of cops, rolling right toward her.

Chapter 28

Grace slid the car to a halt and examined the imposing wrought iron gate. Situated between massive stone pillars and crowned with a neat row of sharpened metal spikes, the twelve-foot-high arch appeared designed to intimidate. It was certainly doing the trick. She felt a trickle of sweat run between her breasts. Inching the car forward, she rolled down the window and pressed the intercom button.

"May I help you?" A tinny voice streamed from a hidden speaker.

Grace leaned out the window. "It's Abigail Lieberman, from *Sift* magazine. I have an appointment with Dr. Stone?" She heard nothing but the slap of her windshield wipers and the wind whistling through the iron spikes. "Hello?" she repeated.

"Drive on up to the house."

As she wound her way along the rough driveway, her eyebrows

disappeared under the frizzy mop of her hair. She'd expected manicured lawns, ponds with footbridges, and discreet fountains. Instead, hemmed in on both sides by a natural barricade of tangled deciduous trees and scrubby brush, she was relieved when the car finally broke free of the dense woods.

Catching sight of the house, Grace felt her breath catch in her throat. Although the limestone construction was similar to that of Grand Central Station, the comparisons ended there. Maitland's house, with its wide chimneys and sloping copper roof, had a definite Tudor influence, while the floor-to-ceiling windows and swooping lines of the Stone home had a more organic feel. Grace thought it one of the most beautiful homes she had ever seen.

After tucking her phone into her coat pocket, she hurried up the front walkway. Before she was able to knock, the door swung open and Dr. Stone stood in the open space, his hand outstretched and a tentative smile on his face. "Ms. Lieberman? No problems finding the place?"

Grace found him handsome, almost to the point of prettiness. Thick dark hair sculpted into a fashionable peak, black eyebrows tweezed to form perfect arches framing startlingly blue eyes. A trendy five o'clock shadow. His slate grey suit was rumpled; the striped tie was loose at his throat.

Stone stood aside to allow Grace to enter.

Stepping inside, Grace stifled a gasp. If she'd thought the exterior was remarkable, the interior of the house was stunning. Strategically placed windows channeled sunlight throughout the open space, and a wide, sweeping staircase drew the eye up to a glowing cathedral ceiling. Tearing her eyes away from her surroundings, Grace said, "Thank you so much for making time to meet with me. You must be tired after your trip."

"My trip?" Stone repeated, shoving his hands into his pockets. He peered at Grace. "I take it you haven't heard?"

Grace took a step back. "Heard what?"

"My wife. She's disappeared with our son. The police have just issued an Amber Alert."

Grace felt sick, thinking of Signy. "My God, I didn't know. I'm so sorry. This must be a terrible time. Should we reschedule?"

Stone looked at her for several long moments and then shook his head. "I'd rather go ahead with the interview, if you don't mind. It wouldn't hurt for your Canadian readers to be on the lookout. She might have crossed the border."

"If you're sure you're up to it?" Grace, said, doubtfully.

Stone nodded. "I do better when I'm busy. May I take your coat?"

As Grace shrugged her parka into his waiting hands, she examined him more closely. He seemed much less imposing in person than in the austere photograph on his website. In person, his eyes were warm and open, and Grace felt her shoulders slide away from her ears.

Stepping over to the front closet, he slipped her coat onto a hanger.

"Your home is lovely," Grace murmured.

Stone followed her eyes. "It was a wreck when I bought it. It's taken years but I think I've managed to restore it to its previous glory."

"It was built in the organic style?"

"You know your architecture. A student of Frank Lloyd Wright built it in 1942. Unfortunately, after the original owner died intestate, it was abandoned and fell into disrepair."

"You've done a wonderful job on the restoration."

"That is kind of you to say, Ms. Lieberman," Stone said. He glanced at his watch.

"This is awful. Are you sure you don't want me to come back another time?" Grace said.

Stone wiped at his eyes. "No. Please. If there is even the slightest chance that Lizzy has run off to Canada, I'd like your audience to know as much as possible. Does that make sense?"

Grace could feel his desperation roll over her like waves from a toxic ocean. She had no doubt he was grieving, along with being terribly afraid. Tuning into the hairs on the back of her neck, she found them relaxed. "Absolutely," she said, "the more eyes the better."

Stone put his hands together in an attitude of prayer and bowed. Before leading her farther into the house, he turned and locked the front door, shooting home the deadbolt with a flick of his wrist.

Chapter 29

Stumbling into the truck receiving area, Signy pulled Lizzy to a stop in front of an employee notice board. Pretending to read the latest missive on workplace health and safety, Signy took the lay of the land.

Directly ahead, a burly employee dressed in a blue vest bustled about inside a standard, fifty-three-foot trailer backed into the loading dock, rolling cartons of Charmin toilet tissue down a conveyor belt. At the bottom, another man retrieved the merchandise, placing each carton on a large pallet truck. A scrawny kid, barely out of his teens, stood on a stool near the truck checking items off on a clipboard.

"What now?" Lizzy whispered.

"Keep your head down and follow me," Signy said. Zipping the parka up over the baby's head, she willed him to stay quiet as she marched straight toward the blue-collar conga line.

"Quit fuckin' around, men," the skinny kid yelled. "We don't have all day."

Sullen and bored, the two older men paid no attention to the kid or to Signy and Lizzy as they approached. Signy kept her head down, and they'd almost made it past when the kid called out in a high-pitched voice. "Hey, you two. We could use some help here."

Signy ignored the kid, keeping her pace steady.

"Hey, assholes. I'm talking to you."

Signy flipped him the bird, without turning around. She heard one of the worker drones snicker as the kid huffed and puffed from atop his little stool. Reaching the driver's access door, she shoved it open with a bang and then clattered down the iron stairway.

Pausing at the bottom of the stairs, she pulled Lizzy tight against the block wall. They looked at each other, their frozen breath rising above their heads like thunderclouds. "Wait here," Signy said.

Lizzy's eyes widened, but she stayed put as Signy stepped out onto the perimeter road.

Shoving her hands in her pocket, Signy scuffed her feet in the snow and looked around, just another a worker killing time. To her right, two trucks waiting to unload partially blocked the perimeter roadway, but to her left the road was open. The driveway disappeared around the side of the building, where, she presumed, it led out to the parking lot at the front of the store—and a heavy police presence.

A hundred yards in front of her, a snow-covered berm separated the back drive of the Superstore from the parking lot of a Sam's Club store. If they could make it across that berm, the Sam's Club lot was crammed with vehicles, ripe for the picking.

Glancing over her shoulder, Signy caught Lizzy's eye, then tilted her chin in the direction of the Sam's Club.

Lizzy nodded and stepped out into the roadway.

Inside her jacket, Signy felt the baby squirm. She pulled the zipper down just enough to allow his head to peek out the top, covering his downy pate with her hand as he craned his neck, his blue eyes fixed on the crystalline flakes of snow spiraling out of the oppressive sky.

"What now?" Lizzy asked.

"The cops will have found Walter and the two boys by now," Signy replied, setting off toward the Sam's Club parking lot. "We don't have much time." Arriving at the northwest end of the building, Signy halted, waving Lizzy to do the same.

The Sam's Club lot was less than fifty feet in front of them. Pressing herself against the wall, Signy peeked around the edge of the building, then immediately jumped back. The baby responded with a swift kick to her gut. She hissed through her teeth.

"What is it?" Lizzy asked.

"State cruiser, coming right at us." The two women turned and sprinted back toward the idling tractor trailers, slipping between the two big rigs just as the nose of the cruiser poked into view. Overhead, a roiling cloud of exhaust fumes billowed into the sky.

Checking their options in the other direction, Signy could see the busy four-lane road that separated the Superstore from the Salmon Run Mall. She cursed under her breath. Even if they managed to cross four lanes of traffic and the parking lot without being spotted, the mall would be crowded with people. With Amber Alerts delivered directly to smart phone subscribers, there would be eyes everywhere, all of them on the alert for Lizzy Stone and her baby.

She could hear the crunch of the cruiser's tires as it rolled toward the two idling trucks. She felt Lizzy turn to run.

"No," Signy whispered, placing a restraining arm on the girl, "we'd never make it."

"We can't stay here," Lizzy hissed. "We're sitting ducks."

Putting a finger to her lips, Signy took a calming breath. There had to be a way out. Beside them, running the length of the perimeter road, a concrete wall separated the Superstore property from a new subdivision. A viable escape route if she could solve the vexing problem of how to scale the smooth six-foot barrier.

Crouching down, Signy tried to spot the cruiser, disheartened to find that it had rolled to a stop inches from the truck behind which they were hiding. She waved at Lizzy to move back.

Flattening themselves beside the passenger side of the second truck, they inched backward until they were able to slip under the trailer. Hunkering down, they held their noses against the acrid stink of trapped exhaust fumes.

"Hey!" shouted the cop, "You there!"

Signy felt Lizzy grab her hand, and the two women stared at each other, eyes wide.

Justin kneed Signy in the solar plexus and let out a frustrated shriek.

"Hey, you," the cop shouted, punctuating his command by banging on the side of the truck.

Signy lurched backward, shoving Lizzy behind her. Her mind racing, she almost missed the six-foot-wide opening in the concrete wall right beside them.

"You there!"

Grabbing Lizzy by the arm, Signy burst out from under the

trailer, crossing the short distance between the truck and the concrete wall in just a couple of paces.

Boom. Boom. Boom. The cop smashed his fist on the side of the truck.

Crouched down in the bottom of the concrete stair well, Signy felt Lizzy make a sudden movement beside her. She looked over, hardly believing what she was seeing.

Lizzy Stone whipped a double-edged hunting knife from under her coat. Gripping it like an ice pick, she fixed her eyes on the spot where the cop would appear and prepared to strike.

Chapter 30

Grace closed her notebook. “I think that about wraps it up. I can't thank you enough for being so open during such a difficult time. It's not often that I get such a clear sense of someone on the first interview.”

“Not at all,” Stone said. “I only hope I didn't bore you.”

“I'm sure my readers will enjoy getting to know you not only as a scientist but also as a person. I certainly have.”

“I'm not usually so forthcoming about my personal life. It must be a testament to your skill as an interviewer, Ms. Lieberman.” Stone offered a wry smile. “I certainly have been a chatterbox.”

Grace leaned forward. “You know, I think the most exciting thing about your research is how widely applicable it seems to be. I'm not a war correspondent, I have little experience with catastrophic wounds, but I do have an aunt who lives with complicated diabetes. She wages a constant battle with sores on her legs and feet. Would your skin replacement help her?”

"You are very astute, Ms. Lieberman. A universally accepted skin graft will not only help burn and trauma victims but will also go a long way toward making life better for people with diabetes, skin cancer, and other infectious processes that destroy skin."

"Infections?" Grace interjected. "Like flesh-eating disease?"

"That is one example. Of course, necrotizing fasciitis is a rare disease but the damage can be horrific, although with the onset of superbugs like MRSA, I fear we will be seeing more and more patients in need of radical skin repair."

Shaking her head, Grace rose to her feet. "A frightening prospect. It seems your discovery comes not a moment too soon." She held out her hand. "It has been a pleasure, Dr. Stone."

Stone shook her hand. "The pleasure was all mine. It isn't often I am able to discuss my work with someone who understands the science so well. May I offer you something to eat or drink before you head out?"

"I really shouldn't take any more of your time," Grace replied.

"Please, I'd appreciate the company."

Grace checked her watch, using the minor distraction to come to a decision. He did seem to be a caring husband and father, but she'd met plenty of abusers who masked their hateful intent with a benevolent exterior. It wouldn't hurt to stick around for a few more minutes to make sure.

She smiled at Stone. "I'll need to make a quick call first. I have a colleague waiting for me."

Stone indicated a phone sitting on his desk. "Take your time. When you're done, please come through to the kitchen."

Walking toward the phone, Grace remarked on the array of electronic equipment purring on a set of glass shelving and was not surprised when he explained about the need for a sophisticated data backup system.

She waited until Stone had left her alone before picking up the phone and dialling Signy's burner phone. Almost immediately, she heard a mechanical voice telling her that the customer she was trying to reach was unavailable.

She glanced out the window. Snow was coming down hard. Perhaps the storm was wreaking havoc with the cell reception. Certainly, if the police had picked up Signy and Lizzy Stone, the grieving husband would have been informed.

Grace dialled Grand Central. When Henrietta picked up, she immediately asked if Signy had called in.

"She did," Henrietta replied, tersely.

"Was she okay?"

"She seemed fine."

"Have you heard about the Amber Alert?"

"We have, the news is all over the place."

"Good. I'm sure Signy must have, as well. Any updates from your end?"

There was a long pause before Henrietta answered, "We've had a bit of a glitch here but Maitland's on top of it."

"A glitch?" Grace asked.

"Nothing to worry about. I'm sorry, honey, but I really can't talk right now," Henrietta replied.

Grace bit her lip, knowing in the pit of her stomach that the debacle at the embassy was coming back to haunt her. "I understand. One last thing, though. If Signy does check in again, can you tell her that I don't know for sure at this point, but there is a good chance our new passenger's version of events may not be accurate."

"If I can. There's a possibility we'll be shutting down for a day or two."

"Damn. It's because of me, isn't it?"

"Don't be silly. Must go, honey. Talk soon." Henrietta hung up the phone.

A few minutes later, Grace made her way to the kitchen, a gleaming modern affair, decked out with all the latest appliances.

Standing behind a counter, Stone held up a bottle of red wine. "Do you mind? I can brew some tea if you'd prefer."

"Wine sounds just about right," Grace said, trying not to sound too eager as she shoved away any thoughts of what might be transpiring at Grand Central.

"Were you able to reach your friend?" Stone asked, as he attacked the seal with a metal corkscrew.

Nodding, Grace noticed that his hand was shaking. "Is everything okay?"

Stone shook his head. "I called the detective in charge of the case. He talked up a storm but he hasn't made any real progress." He opened the wine, found two large glasses, and filled them to the brim.

"Tell me about your son," Grace said, breaking the silence. "What's he like?"

"Justin?"

Grace nodded.

"Adorable," Stone said, with a crooked smile. "Curious, playful, smart, although I imagine all parents would say the same. He has a set of lungs on him, though. He suffered from colic for the first three months."

"I've heard that can be brutal. How did you cope?"

He handed Grace the brimming glass of wine.

Thanking him, she inhaled the complex yet delicate aroma.

"It's a 2010 Pinot Noir, from right here in New York."

She took a sip, allowing a delicious mix of strawberry, pine, and oak to melt on her tongue.

Stone poured a quarter of his own glass down his throat, "I'm sorry. I can't seem to stay focused. You were asking?"

"This is crazy. Is there someone I could call to come and be with you?"

"I keep picturing Justin having one of his crying jags and Lizzy losing her temper," he continued, as though she hadn't spoken.

"Losing her temper?"

"She's always been volatile. I'm sure she has some sort of problem, but I've never been able to convince her to see a professional." Stone rubbed his knuckles across the pristine counter top. "She's always felt things far more acutely than most people. She'll be giddy with joy over some little thing, and then burst into tears over a soppy commercial on TV. She's always been like that, up and down like a yo-yo. She can be prickly too. Say the wrong thing and the next thing you know she's accusing you of all kinds of nasty things. I've learned to live with it over the years, but when Justin came along, her behaviour got exponentially worse."

Looking into his sad eyes, Grace realized with some surprise that she believed him. She put her glass down.

"Never mind. I'm making myself crazy. The police will find her safe, and everything will be fine. Meanwhile, it really does help to have a little company. How about I take you on the fifty-cent tour?"

Feeling the Pinot Noir begin to warm her bones, Grace said, "Sure. Why not. If you don't mind. I'll take a few pictures. They'll help add a little colour to the article."

Stone offered her a pained smile. "You are a very kind woman, Ms. Lieberman."

"Please, call me Abby."

Taking her arm, he led her from the kitchen. As they passed through the door and into the hall, Grace watched him erase a small brown smudge from the floor with the tip of his shoe.

Chapter 31

"Hey you," the cop shouted, "this is your last chance. Come out of there, right now."

Eyes glittering, Lizzy Stone raised the knife.

Whipping out her hand, Signy clamped her fingers around the tiny woman's fragile wrist.

Rage flared in Lizzy's eyes, and she jerked away, struggling to maintain control of the weapon. For several long moments, the sharp blade slashed back and forth, just inches from the baby's head.

Signy was finally able to twist the smaller woman's thumb down until it touched the inner aspect of her forearm. The move had the desired effect. The knife slipped from Lizzy's numb fingers and into Signy's waiting hand.

Over the rumbling truck engines, Signy heard the cop slam his fist into the side of the truck.

Glaring at Lizzy, Signy dropped the knife into the snow, burying it with the tip of her boot. She risked a quick peek around the edge of the retaining wall. The cop was standing beside the leading truck, pounding on the driver's door.

"What did you do that for? Are you trying to get us killed?" Lizzy muttered, raising her fists.

Boom. Boom. Boom.

"If you don't shut up and do what I tell you, I'll turn you in myself," Signy warned.

They both flinched as they heard the truck door crack open with a squeal of rusting metal.

"*Che cazzo?*" shouted the driver, in a thick Italian accent.

"What the hell took you so long?"

"I was asleep in the back. What the hell you want?"

"Did you see a woman and a baby pass through here?"

"*Che diavolo sta succedendo?* A bambino in this dump?"

"That's not what I said. All I'm asking is whether you saw a woman and a baby come through here in the past five minutes," said the cop.

The trucker spat in disgust. "You wanna look? Come on up. I got nothin' to hide."

"Calm down. As I was saying—"

The trucker was only getting started, and while the cop endured the verbal onslaught in stoic silence, Signy pinned Lizzy's arm and shoved her forward. They raced up the concrete stairs before ducking along the flat path that led to the subdivision. They'd made it safely to the narrow space between two houses by the time they heard the irate truck driver sputter to a halt and slam his door shut.

"Look, I'm sorry," Lizzy said, "I didn't mean—"

"I told you to shut your mouth," said Signy, pulling her forward. As they ran, Signy unzipped her jacket, and the baby popped his head out like a joey kangaroo. His spirits had obviously improved. He was babbling a stream of experimental vowels and consonants.

She cupped the top of his head. He seemed warm enough even though her teeth had started to chatter. She wasn't sure if her shivering jaw was a result of the bitter cold, the icy snow flakes pelting her exposed skin, or the narrow escape they'd had from Lizzy Stone eviscerating a state trooper.

As they burst out from between the two houses, Signy's outlook improved slightly. A plumber's van stood idling in an unfinished driveway across the street. A few seconds later, having picked their way across the uneven construction site, Signy and Lizzy climbed into the truck and were rolling down the street, back out toward the road that ran between the Superstore and the Salmon Run Mall.

Providing Grace with much more than a fifty-cent tour, Solomon Stone was pleased to show off his home, from the extravagant living and dining rooms on the lower level, right through to the opulent bedrooms. Grace oohed and aahed, snapping pictures with the camera she'd brought. But coming upon a closed door festooned with gaily painted nursery rhyme characters, Stone paused, his face grey.

"What is it?" Grace asked.

Stone pushed open the nursery door and stepped inside.

"We don't have to—" Grace began.

Walking over to the white painted crib, Stone lifted a small brown teddy bear from a mountain of stuffed animals and hugged it to his chest. "Lizzy knows how much Justin loves this guy." He glanced at Grace. "Why didn't she take this with her?"

Seeing his stricken expression, Grace felt terrible for him. She wished she could tell him that Lizzy was safe, that his son was being well cared for. Instead, she croaked out a feeble assurance that she was sure everything would be fine.

He held the stuffed bear over his heart. "She was so young when I first met her. I was in my third year of residency. I had to pick up a family medicine rotation and decided to complete it in the community clinic." He looked up at Grace and smiled. "I've always had a penchant for excitement, and the free clinic was anything but boring."

"I know what you mean. Years ago I rode the homeless van in downtown Toronto." Grace shook her head. "It was wild."

Stone raised his glass in salute. "To a fellow adrenaline junkie."

Grace tipped her own glass, then motioned for him to continue.

"She was maybe sixteen when I first saw her. She presented at the clinic with a nasty laceration to her left arm. Classic defensive wound but she wasn't talking. My first impression was of a tough street kid, but she had a certain vulnerability as well. Her inherent intelligence screamed through the rough persona. She just didn't have the proper social tools, and it was obvious that if something didn't change soon, all that potential would be wasted." He looked at Grace and smiled ruefully. "Every once in a while one of them plucks at the heartstrings, you know what I mean?"

Grace nodded, an image of Signy flashing through her head.

"It took some effort but I managed to get her into a great program that was being offered for at-risk youth. The kids got a bed, three squares, and life-skills counselling. All they had to do was stay in school and put in some volunteer hours." He smiled. "Lizzy managed to complete the program and get her high school degree before the funding was pulled."

"You followed her progress?" Grace asked.

Stone tucked the teddy bear back among his stuffed friends. "You mean was I screwing her?"

Grace choked on a sip of wine.

"Of course I wasn't," he said, smoothing down his tie. "I got her into the program and that was the last I saw of her until she got in touch several years later. She'd taken a fashion course at college and was working at one of those big chain stores. American Apparel? Macy's? Something like that. She was hoping to become a buyer, take trips to Paris and Milan."

"You must have been very proud."

He looked away. "She was a very special young lady." Stone took one last look around the room, then flicked off the nursery light. "Shall we?" he said, leading Grace back toward the stairs. "That was part of the problem. She loved the bright lights and Rochester isn't exactly Manhattan."

"No," agreed Grace.

Stone shook his head. "I worked for Doctors without Borders for several years after I graduated. After that, I signed on to a practice in Seattle. It wasn't long after that Lizzy got in touch. She was twenty-one when she wrote and asked if she could thank me in person for helping her get into that program. I was happy to meet with her. I remembered her well. Wanted to see how she turned out." He smiled ruefully. "When she walked into the restaurant, I thought my heart might stop. She was so beautiful."

Grace smiled and followed Stone down the staircase.

"I was a goner," he said, running his hand along the banister. "Completely head over heels. I was more than willing to give her anything she wanted. For a while, that was enough. She liked Seattle. She knew a lot of people, had friends."

"So why the move to Rochester?" Grace asked.

"Purely selfish reasons, I'm afraid. I wanted my own practice. Seattle was swamped with plastic surgeons at the time, but Rochester was underserved, and it seemed like an ideal place to conduct my research." He guided her back to the kitchen. "I won't lie. The money is good. I've done well, although to be honest I would have been content to stay in the loft we owned downtown. Not Lizzy. If she was going to be trapped in a backwater like Rochester, she insisted on the big house on the lake, the sports car, the whole nine yards."

"Young people nowadays seem to have no concept of the value of a dollar." Grace ran a hand through her hair. "Listen to me, I sound like I'm a hundred years old."

They walked back into the kitchen. Grace stepped over to the floor-to-ceiling windows that looked out over the vast lake, but a wall of snow blurred the landscape, and all she could see was her own reflection.

Stone set their empty wineglasses in the sink.

"I'm not saying that I resented her," he said, "but when we moved east, things changed. She didn't need to work, of course, but I encouraged her. I thought that this much closer to New York she might find something exciting. It would certainly be a way to meet new people." He shook his head. "She did a little volunteering, but mostly she put all her energy into decorating the house."

"She has talent."

"It is lovely," he agreed. "But when the house was finished, she started shutting down, going into herself. After the baby was born, she came apart at the seams. I spoke to a psychiatrist friend of mine, and he believes it could be postpartum depression."

He stared out the window. "I should have seen it earlier. I should have been more proactive. I hired a nanny when I should have been finding a way to get her treated. Poor Katy." He darted a quick glance at Grace. "She's the nanny. I sent her home. She's beside herself." Stone shoved his hands into his pockets and bowed his head. "If anything happens to them, I'll never forgive myself."

Outside, the storm was raging, hard little flakes driving almost horizontally, snowdrifts accumulating against the side of the house. Grace thought it unlikely her flight to Toronto would take off in this weather even if she could make the drive back to Rochester. Did she really have to leave?

Lizzy Stone and her baby were safe with Signy. But Solomon was hurting. The poor man, through no fault of his own, had lost everyone he loved. She certainly knew how that felt. She made a snap decision. "When did you last eat?"

He sighed. "I don't remember."

"Food will help. Trust me."

"Are you sure? You don't need to get home?"

"No one there to miss me," she said, forcing a chuckle in order to take the sting out of the words.

"I see," he said, gently. "In that case I'd be more than happy to share a meal with you." He glanced out the window. "Good Lord. Much more of this and you'll be trapped here with me."

"I'm not worried," Grace said, surprised at her boldness. She wondered for a moment if the Pinot Noir was going to her head, then shrugged her concerns away. If there was one thing she had come to know over the course of the afternoon, it was that she had nothing to fear from Dr. Solomon Stone. She looked up into his kind eyes.

Nothing to fear at all.

Chapter 32

Signy drove east in silence. After stealing the plumber's van in the subdivision behind the Superstore, she'd simply driven back into the parking lot and pulled up beside her own car. The cops had been too busy searching inside the store to notice the little trio pile out of the van and into the rental.

She flicked her eyes at the rear-view mirror. Lizzy Stone sat quietly beside her sleeping son, gazing out the side window. Her annoying passenger had tried to open a conversation a couple of times, but Signy had shut her down. She didn't care what the girl was feeling; her stunt with the knife could have gotten them both killed.

She checked the gas tank. The gauge indicated that they were down below half full, and although she would have preferred to fill up, they were still within close proximity of Fort Drum, one of the largest military bases in the Northeast. The gas stations they'd passed were too exposed and far too crowded. She was hoping to find one off the beaten path as they got closer to Lake Placid.

Ten miles later, Signy could see a line of hills ahead, and the road began to wind through bleak stands of aspen, ash, and maple. Circles of wild turkeys congregated in the windswept fields like black-cloaked morticians. She shook off the resultant heebie-jeebies.

Before long, they began to climb the long ridge, and as they drove through the village of Black River, traffic slowed to a halt, allowing a yellow school bus to discharge its passengers by the side of the road. On her right, Signy saw a cemetery, each headstone covered in a mound of white snow and sporting a plastic replica of the Stars and Stripes. She waited impatiently for the school bus to get moving, her eyes darting left and right, watching for anyone who might be examining them too closely.

She glanced at the dashboard clock. Grace would have flown home by now. She wished she could give her a call to let her know about Lizzy Stone's odd behaviour. She shook her head. Grace had enough to deal with given the mayhem at Grand Central. No matter. They would be at the chalet soon. She could handle the girl until then.

After suffering through several more school bus drop-offs, Signy was relieved when the bus moved onto the shoulder, allowing the long line of traffic to move past. As they continued east amid a fairly steady stream of traffic, she noticed that the road flattened out again and thought it felt very much like driving in Ontario.

It wasn't until they'd passed through the village of Fargo that traffic finally began to die away. Up ahead, she spied a lonely, overgrown apple tree standing close to the road, its tenacious fruit gleaming yellow against the dark sky. A survivor, Signy thought, just like Lizzy Stone. She tried to push away her feelings of irritation with the girl.

Driving past the apple tree, she blinked with surprise. Half buried in snow, an assault rifle was fixed to a wooden table, its barrel pointed high into the sky. Signy followed the strange sight with her eyes, even craning her neck to look over her shoulder once the SUV had flashed past.

"Welcome to the boonies," Lizzy said quietly from the back seat.

"Did I really see that?" she asked, deciding she'd given the girl the silent treatment for long enough.

"Weird, huh? They probably think they're doing their part for home and country."

"They figure they're going to shoot down foreign fighter jets or something?"

"I doubt it." Lizzy shrugged. "I think they're more worried about Washington."

"Militiamen?" Signy asked, feeling a slight shudder run down her spine.

"I wouldn't be surprised. There are probably more of them out there than we imagine."

Signy returned her attention to the road. They'd crossed into the Adirondack Park a while back. With the exception of the occasional touristy spot, there was not much in the way of civilization. All alone with the crazies. Perfect, she thought, shaking her head.

The snow was coming down in earnest now, and Signy wondered if perhaps her earlier assessment that the storm would peter out over the Atlantic had been a bit premature. She saw a sign that said to tune to 107.2 for local weather updates but when she did so got nothing but static. She kept a tight grip on the wheel. The SUV was handling the conditions with ease, but other vehicles had not been so lucky. She'd already passed three cars that had slid into the ditch.

Cresting the top of a high hill, she saw a sign pointing to a scenic overlook. She imagined the view would be gorgeous if she could see anything through the driving snow.

"Listen," Lizzy said, "I really am sorry."

"That's why you disappeared in the store, right?"

"I didn't mean to take so long. It took ages for me to find someone to unlock the case where they keep their hunting knives."

"And you thought what? That you'd slit a cop's throat and we'd just walk out of there?"

"I know. It was stupid. Old habits kicked in, I guess."

Signy contemplated that loaded statement as the sweet odour of woodsmoke drifted into the car. She glanced in the mirror.

Lizzy was holding up two fingers in the universal peace sign.

"All right," Signy said, "truce. Just don't pull anything like that again, okay?"

Lizzy nodded. After a while, she asked, "How long now?"

"We're on the Olympic Scenic byway, which leads right into Lake Placid. I'd say about another hour and a half, max." A powerful gust of wind buffeted the side of the car, and Signy struggled for several hair-raising moments to bring the vehicle back under control.

"Wow," Lizzy said, leaning forward and gripping the back of the passenger seat. "It's not getting any better out there, is it?"

"Nope."

Lizzy peered out the window. "And the cops will figure we can't have gotten too far."

Signy nodded. "I wouldn't be surprised if they've brought in reinforcements. Not to mention that the sun's about to go down. It'll be pitch black in a few minutes."

"Oh, shit."

"Couldn't have said it better myself," Signy said, her knuckles white on the wheel.

Chapter 33

Number 64785 North Federal Highway proved to be another of the ubiquitous mobile home parks that dot the American landscape. A faded pink and white sign proclaimed Coral Gables as a family-friendly community offering short- and long-term rentals.

The Tracker turned in to the complex. The park consisted of forty to fifty identical mobile homes, situated on a grid of gravel drives. Each unit consisted of a single-wide trailer with attached carport, white siding, and a single window in front. Perched over each front window, a tan canvas awning. Postage-stamp front yards laid with sun-baked, broad-leafed grass added the only hint of colour.

In a central courtyard, desiccated palm leaves floated on the dark surface of an unmaintained swimming pool. Coarse brown coconuts littered the patchy turf of a desultory three-hole mini putt course.

Ignoring the Visitor Parking at Rear notification, he continued further into the compound, executing a series of left and right turns before finally sliding past unit 17. At first glance, there was no sign of life. The only vehicle in the driveway, a rusted child's tricycle toppled on its side.

He parked his car a couple of doors down, then donning a ball cap emblazoned with a TV Cable company logo, strode up the driveway to unit 17. He breathed in the sweet scent of hibiscus the neighbours had planted in abundance around their unit. The sun was warm on his bare arms and he could hear the piercing whistles of two cardinals duking it out in a palm tree. He felt his neck muscles relax. It was very good to be back in the South.

He saw blackout curtains drawn across the windows of unit 17, and the front door secured with two deadbolt locks. "Cable company," he called, rapping on the metal door. There was no sound from inside the trailer. The only thing he could hear was the insistent buzz of a cicada high in the palm branches.

Taking a step back, he surveyed the building. The freshly swept front stoop, the empty mailbox, and a small hibachi sitting on a metal stand brimming with white ash spoke to recent activity. Walking around to the back, he saw more evidence of habitation: bags of potting soil, a couple of shovels, a plastic wading pool, but no sign that the resident or residents were currently home.

Walking back to his car, he flipped open his computer and performed a quick Google search. He was looking for local gambling parlours where a man down on his luck might slip a few quarters into a machine. Lenny Screed had a fondness for the slots, and nothing could calm jangled nerves like a few pulls on the one-armed bandit.

Checking the results, he learned that although the state of Florida had passed legislation banning the playing of computer-type slot machines in adult amusement centers, nearly a thousand of the small arcades were still in operation. Worse, it seemed a good number of those were within driving distance of Delray Beach.

He pinched the bridge of his nose with his fingers. Might as well start with the closest location. Punching the address of Beachside Bingo and Arcade into his onboard GPS, he slipped the car into drive and headed toward downtown Delray.

The sun was low on the horizon by the time he'd checked out two arcades, an Internet café, and the back room of a smoky restaurant where five machines allowed patrons to try their luck while they ate. No sign of Mr. Screed. He decided to try one more place before taking another pass by unit 17.

The Tropicana Flea Market and Arcade was located in an old warehouse off Atlantic Avenue. The place was a dump, reeked of black mould, and judging by the greenish-black fungus that clung to the damp ceiling tiles, was probably toxic. *Stachybotrys chartarum* perhaps.

Holding his nose, he worked his way through dense aisles crammed with racks of five-dollar T-shirts, faux designer jewelry, and booths laden with sketchy-looking electronics.

Deftly sidestepping an aggressive vendor hawking *quality* Roll-ex watches, he located the shining bank of slot machines that lined the back wall of the market. He scanned the players. Five elderly women perched side by side on leather stools, chatting from the corner of their mouths as they tried their luck. Two younger men, one dressed in jeans with a set of headphones plugged into his ears, the other mumbling to himself and scratching at an open sore on his face.

Ducking behind a concrete support pole, the Tracker examined the final patron. A big man wearing a loud floral print shirt stretched tight over a serious beer gut, late forties give or take, with a scrap of salt and pepper hair twisted into a rat-tail at the back of his neck. Nasty sunburn across the back of his neck shouted snowbird.

Lenny Screed.

The Tracker slipped his hand into his pocket, fingering the garrotte he'd fashioned using a length of wire and two golf pencils.

"Hey, mister."

He felt a small hand tug on his sleeve. A boy, dressed in a pair of worn cotton shorts and nothing else, stared up at him with big brown eyes. He had his grubby hand out.

"You gimme some money, señor?"

"Get lost, kid." The Tracker tried to turn away, but the kid grabbed on tighter.

"Ah, come on, mister. I need to buy medicine for my sister."

"Jesus Christ," said the Tracker, wrenching his sleeve away from the kid's filthy fingers.

"*Mi madre está muerta*, you gringo prick."

The Tracker cuffed the side of the kid's head. Hard.

The kid took off, spewing a string of filthy Spanish invectives.

The Tracker watched until he was sure the kid had left the arcade. He turned back to the slot machines.

The man in the loud floral shirt was gone.

Chapter 34

Deep in the Adirondacks, the dark was absolute. Signy was almost grateful for the hypnotic reflection of driving snow off her headlights. At least it gave her something to look at.

"How much longer?"

She flicked her eyes at Lizzy. "At this rate, I'm guessing another hour or so." She tipped her head toward the sleeping baby beside Lizzy. "Do you think he'll make it?"

"As long as we keep moving. He loves the car."

Signy returned her eyes to the front. Up ahead, a faint glow appeared in the trees off to their right. As she got closer, she saw that it was another of the decrepit roadhouses that dotted this neck of the woods.

A hand-drawn sign stuck down by the road advertised the Patriot Club. It was a low building with a flat roof, constructed from roughly hewn log planks, sitting hard against the base of a rock cliff. A fluorescent sign advertising Miller beer swung precariously from a corner of the roof. There were at least ten vehicles parked diagonally across the front of the building.

"Looks like a hangout for the 'live free or die' crowd," Lizzy said.

Signy nodded, the memory of that creepy-looking assault rifle pointing into the sky sending a shiver down her back.

They drove in silence for another few minutes as Signy concentrated on the sliver of road she could see through the mesmerizing tunnel of driving snow. She kept her eyes pinned to the white line running down the middle of the highway, trying to keep the SUV from straying into the oncoming lane.

Lizzy leaned forward. "So, what happened back there?"

"What do you mean?"

"At the Superstore. How did you get rid of Walter?"

Signy shrugged. "It was nothing."

Lizzy stared out the window for several minutes, then said, "I'd like to do what you do someday."

"What? Be a conductor?" Signy kept her eyes glued to the white line.

"There are so many street kids out there, just ripe for the picking. Abusive parents, sexual predators, pimps—the list is endless." She paused. "Every once in a while, I'd just have to bring a kid home with me for some extra TLC."

"Really?" Signy couldn't keep a note of skepticism out of her voice. She believed in maintaining professional boundaries between workers and clients. Crossing lines could result in messy situations—for both parties.

"I know what you're thinking," Lizzy said, "but for some of

these kids there simply was no other option. Someone had to do something. Solomon understood. He would never admit it, but I know he enjoyed having the kids around."

I'll bet he did, Signy thought.

Lizzy leaned forward. "And for a couple of them, just having a safe place to regroup made all the difference."

Signy didn't know how to respond. Solomon Stone had hardly provided a safe place to Lizzy when she'd been a child. It was as though the adult Lizzy Stone had blinkers on her eyes.

"Oh no," Lizzy whispered.

Signy peered into the darkness. They had just crested a high hill, and down at the bottom, not two hundred feet away, a state police patrol car was parked sideways on the highway, blocking both lanes. Signy hit the brakes, her heart rate rising at the eerie sight of the red, white, and blue emergency lights reflecting off the falling snow.

"Roadblock." Lizzy's voice caught in her throat.

The SUV's headlights lit up the cruiser, and Signy could see a bulky figure standing near the front of the car, swinging a flashing light back and forth.

"Do you think they're looking for me?"

Signy inched the car down the slope. "I think we have to assume they are."

"Can't you turn around?"

She checked the rear-view mirror. There were no cars behind her, but there was no way she could make a sudden U-turn in the middle of a steep downhill slope without arousing suspicion. She tossed the parka she'd stolen from the Superstore into the back seat. "Tuck this around you and pretend to be asleep," she said.

"Grab that bag of clothes in the back. I think there's a pink sweater in there. Throw that over the baby. If they get close, maybe they'll think he's a girl."

Lizzy did as instructed.

Tucking her distinctive braid down the back of her sweater, Signy rolled slowly down the hill, squinting against the blinding emergency lights. "Hang on," she said. "Here we go."

In the back seat, Lizzy burrowed under the jacket.

Signy stopped the SUV about twenty feet in front of the cruiser, her headlights trained on the lone cop. Several inches of snow had built up on his heavy parka and a fur hat. At first glance, he looked like the abominable snowman. She peered closer. He had his gloved hands tucked under his armpits and he was stomping from foot to foot in the deep snow, trying to keep warm. Under his hat, she could see bright eyes and smooth cheeks. He wasn't more than a kid.

Hoping her headlights would blind him, she opened her door and stepped outside before he had a chance to come to her. "What's going on?" she called.

Her only answer was the howling of the wind.

Head down, the cop took a few steps forward.

Wrapping her arms around her body, Signy walked toward him, trying to ignore the frigid snow spilling inside the top of her boots. To the cop, she would appear to be a very cold, very young woman with short hair, her facial features obscured by the glare of the lights at her back. She covered her mouth and nose with her cupped hands as the cop approached. "Hi, there," she said.

"Bad accident up ahead," the cop said, drawing to a halt a few feet in front of her. "Road's closed."

Signy felt a second of relief until she remembered that, aware of the Amber Alert, he'd be on the lookout for two women and a baby. She tensed up again as she watched him give her a professional once-over.

"I'm trying to get to Plattsburgh," Signy said.

The cop shook his head. "You can't get through tonight. Snow's too heavy. You'll want to grab a motel for the night and start out again in the morning."

Signy stomped snow from her boot and nodded. "Okay," she said, "thanks." She was turning to go when she heard the distinctive wail of a baby coming from inside the car.

She watched the cop frown and then take a step forward.

"You travelling alone?" he asked.

Signy opened her mouth, hoping her brain could provide an explanation.

The cop raised his flashlight, playing the beam of light over the SUV.

He took a step forward just as a thumping hip-hop rhythm began inside the SUV. Ludacris singing something about hollow-point bullets. The cop stared at the vehicle.

A figure in the passenger seat was bouncing to the music like a demented puppet.

Signy glanced at the cop and rolled her eyes. "My brother," she said. "This is the last time I drive him to a hockey tournament, I swear to God."

Over the hill behind them, another car approached, lighting up the interior of the SUV.

The cop watched Lizzy pumping her shoulders up and down, one hand to the side of her head, as though she were holding headphones close to her ear. The music screamed louder.

"Sorry about that," Signy said, shaking her head. "What a jerk." She leaned around to watch the other car slow to a stop behind the SUV. "I'd better get out of the way. Stay warm." She started to walk back to the driver's door, taking care to step inside her own footprints. She was about to pull on the handle when the cop called out again.

Signy held her breath. She turned around, a polite smile plastered on her frozen cheeks.

"How are you for gas?"

Barely able to hear him over the ear-shattering music, she gave him a thumbs-up.

"Just checking," he called. "There's only one way out of the park, and no gas stations open for at least thirty miles. You'll be okay until then?"

"What's goin' on?" A middle-aged man wearing a fluorescent orange hunting jacket had exited his car and was walking up to join the little party.

Signy took the opportunity to jump back inside the SUV. As the hunter approached the cop, she put the SUV in gear and turned the vehicle around. They had crested the hill before Signy reached out and turned off the radio.

In the back seat, the baby wailed.

Lizzy leaned over the seat and popped a soother into his mouth.

"Close call," Signy said.

Lizzy held her hand out. "Look at me, I'm shaking. Did I do okay?"

"You did great."

"That was the only radio station I could find. I almost had a heart attack when it started playing that song."

"It was perfect. I told him you were my idiot kid brother." Signy laughed. "You can really bust a move, by the way."

Lizzy let out her breath in a long shudder.

"Anyway, the cop was right. We'll have to find someplace to stop for the night." She checked the gas gauge. "And we'll need to top up too."

"Did I hear him say no gas for thirty miles?"

Signy nodded, then shoved her hand into the pocket of the parka, fingers probing for the pink wallet.

"Do we have enough to get that far?" Lizzy asked.

Not finding her wallet in the first pocket, Signy jammed her hand into the other one. Her fingers met only a deep, empty space. She was casting about the floor when the realization hit her like a two-by-four to the side of the head. Her hands went slick on the wheel, the back end swung out, and before she knew it, the SUV was sliding sideways down the highway.

Lizzy rocked sideways as one of the back wheels slipped over the edge of the road and into the ditch.

Signy gunned the engine and, yanking on the wheel, steered the Tahoe toward the oncoming lane in a desperate attempt to free the back wheel from the suffocating grip of the snow-packed ditch. The SUV screamed along the edge of the road before the back wheel caught and the vehicle bumped up and out of the ditch. Heart pounding, Signy pulled to a halt.

Lizzy stared at her, wide-eyed.

"My wallet," Signy said, barely able to believe what she was about to say. "It was in the pocket of the coat I dropped in the Superstore."

"What?"

"Cash, credit cards, all gone. My ID too." Signy smacked a hand on the steering wheel. "By now they'll have discovered when and where Ms. Carole White rented this SUV. It probably has GPS tracking too. It's only a matter of time before they pinpoint our location."

Behind them, the baby spat out his soother and howled.

Chapter 35

"Dammit!" Signy shouted, pounding her fist against the steering wheel.

Pumping his legs inside his snowsuit, Justin Stone wailed at the top of his lungs, the ebb and flow of his furious shrieks adding a strident car-alarm quality to the fireworks.

"How could I have been so bloody stupid?"

Giving up her attempt to quiet the baby, Lizzy leaned over the seat and rummaged in her bag, producing the last bottle of formula. She gave it a vigorous shake, then popped the nipple into the baby's mouth. He immediately began to suck, fat tears rolling down his cheeks as he stared wide-eyed up at Lizzy.

"Stupid, stupid, stupid," Signy chanted, banging her head against the wheel with each syllable.

"Stop. It's not your fault." Lizzy said.

Signy ran her hand down her long braid and then nodded.

"How bad is it?" Lizzy asked, tipping the bottle up. Justin had drained almost half the formula.

"Pretty bad."

"I have about thirty bucks left in my wallet, if that helps," Lizzy said. "And I brought a few extra diapers in my bag."

"I can't believe I could be so stupid." Signy bit her lip.

"I've done worse. Believe me."

Parked on the edge of the road, hazard lights on, Signy watched the car that had come up behind them at the roadblock drive by. "All right," she said, sitting up straighter, "we have thirty bucks in cash, a couple bags full of women's clothing in the trunk, a few extra diapers, and zero food for the baby. Is that about right?"

Lizzy nodded.

"On the plus side, the cop at the roadblock didn't twig to the SUV."

"He probably couldn't see the plates."

"Either that or they haven't found my wallet yet. Which means we have time."

"Time for what?" Lizzy asked.

"First thing we have to do is get rid of the SUV."

Lizzy frowned. "Can't you just disable the GPS? Unplug it or something?"

Narrowing her eyes, Signy examined the dashboard. "The devices are built into the car. I wouldn't know where to look."

"Great," Lizzy said, shoving her hands into her armpits. "How are we supposed to find a new car? We're in the middle of nowhere."

"Not exactly," Signy said, putting on her turn signal, then crawling slowly back onto the highway. "Remember that roadhouse, awhile back? I'm sure someone there will be happy to lend us a car."

Lizzy stared at her. "You're just going to walk into the middle of a bunch of crazy militants and ask to borrow a car?"

Signy smiled tightly. "Not exactly."

Ten minutes later, Signy saw the eerie glow of the Miller beer sign just ahead. She touched the brakes but still almost slipped past the driveway to the Patriot Club. At the last second, she managed to swing the SUV into the lot, blasting through almost a foot of unplowed powder.

She was heartened to see a few more cars had joined the row of vehicles parked in front of the windowless building. Something must be going on inside that was important enough, or pleasurable enough, for the patriots to brave the wintry conditions. Probably a gun show.

Easing the SUV past the line of pickups and cars, she found what she was looking for snugged in between two pickup trucks. A vintage Chevy Malibu with a standard V-8 engine, it would be powerful enough to handle the snow, and seemed in relatively good condition.

She drove to the end of the parking lot and tucked the SUV into the last remaining spot. She put the car in park, then turned to Lizzy. "You can drive, right?"

Lizzy nodded.

"I need you to take the wheel," she said, as she pulled on her heavy parka.

Justin, having drained his last bottle of formula, was watching the two women with interest.

Lizzy didn't ask any questions.

Signy was starting to like Lizzy Stone. Her overreaction with the knife notwithstanding, she was a real asset. No shrinking violet, she kept her wits about her and didn't require endless explanations. She took in the implications of a situation quickly and did as instructed.

"You know how to hot wire a car?" Lizzy asked.

Signy pulled open her door. "I'm hoping it's like riding a bike." She climbed down into the deep snow and then stomped around to the back of the SUV. Opening the hatch, she rummaged about in the bag of clothes she'd purchased on her way to Rochester that morning and pulled out a wire hanger. "Once I get the car going," she said to Lizzy, who was watching her with interest, "follow me. We'll drive for a bit, then ditch the SUV."

"Okay," Lizzy said. "Good luck."

Signy shut the hatch, then pulled the hood of her parka tight around her face. She slogged back along the row of vehicles, keeping her eye on the entrance to the club building. Over the front door, made of the same wood as the log building, a single halogen bulb cast a sickly amber glow through the falling snow.

Sidling up alongside the Malibu, Signy felt a rush of warmth run down her spine when she saw the driver's door was unlocked. She hadn't been looking forward to having to jimmy the lock. After taking a minute to scrape the snow off the windows, she opened the door and slipped inside.

The interior of the car reeked of nicotine, although with the exception of an overflowing ashtray and a few candy wrappers, the rest of the car was relatively clean. She hoped that a neat car meant a conscientious owner, and that a conscientious owner equaled a full tank, but she'd just have to wait and find out.

She opened the glove compartment and swept her hand around inside. Not surprisingly, she failed to find a charged-up cellphone, a roll of twenty-dollar bills, or anything else she could use. She shut the glovebox with a snap, then examined the steering column.

Rubbing her hands together, she recalled the last time she'd boosted a car. She'd had a spare period at high school, and when she'd gone outside for a quick smoke, Zef had been waiting for her. She could still picture him leaning against the brick wall in his faded blue jeans, the black T-shirt showing off his muscular shoulders, and the light brown hair falling over his eyes.

He'd kissed her long and deep, right there in front of the smoker's corner crowd, and she remembered the thrill of feeling all eyes on her. She could almost imagine what they'd been thinking. Where did that freak Signy Shepherd find such a gorgeous guy, and what's he doing with *her*?

She hoped they imagined all sorts of romantic stories. What she would never tell them was that he was just another of the unfortunate kids that moved in and out of David and Sarah Shepherd's foster home on a regular basis.

Zef had arrived at the Shepherds' about six months earlier, and Signy had fallen in passionate, teenaged love with him from the minute she laid eyes on him. They'd hooked up soon after, and he'd taught her everything he knew, including how to hot-wire a car.

"Remove the access panel," she whispered to herself, running her hands under the steering column until she felt the concealed clips that held the panel in place. She slipped her fingers under the clips and the panel popped off into her hands.

She shot a quick glance at the entrance to the clubhouse. The front door remained closed. She reached up and flicked on the interior lights. She'd need to be able to see for the next part. Leaning down, she peered up under the steering column until she located a bundle of multicoloured wires. She pulled out the two red ones and, using her teeth, stripped a bit of the red plastic off the ends of each one, then twisted the two ends together.

She heard Zef's voice in her head as she peered back at the bundle of wires. *The ignition wire is usually brown. Take it out and touch it to the two red wires. Remember to rev the engine when you touch the wires together.* She found the brown wire and was about to touch it to the others when she heard voices. Male voices, at least two, coming right at her.

She clicked the overhead light off and, slipping the access panel back into place, sank down into the seat, pulling her jacket up over her face.

"I tell ya, brother, I'd kill the motherfucker."

"Ya, I know. But the little prick is Sharon's kid brother."

"Too fucking bad. Asshole disrespected you. He needs taking care of."

"Ya, fuck. I know."

"You don't want them miserable sons of bitches thinking you is pussy-whipped."

Signy held her breath. The two men had stopped right behind the Malibu. She could hear the scratch of a match as one of them lit a cigarette.

"I'll take care of it."

Signy felt a thump as one of the men leaned against the Malibu.

"Make it look like an accident. Fuck with his brakes or something. Asshole's always driving into the ditch. Sharon will never know the difference."

"Ya, maybe."

"I'm just sayin', brother. You let that piece of shit get away with that crap, and before long it's you what'll end up with a hole in your head."

"Jesus, would you look at the snow? I'm heading home."

"Just don't let any grass grow under your feet, brother."

"Ya. Fuck. Whatever."

Signy could smell cigarette smoke and hear the crunch of boots. One of the men was stomping back the way he'd come, the other was moving up between the pickup truck and the Malibu. Signy cursed under her breath.

Hearing the sound of a key slipping into a lock, she balled her fists.

But it was the door to the pickup truck that swung open, and she heard the man climb up behind the wheel. She stayed perfectly still. One glance out his window and she'd be hard to miss, lying sideways on the driver's seat, her hands gripping the access panel of the steering column.

She heard the roar of the engine as the man pumped the gas. A few seconds after that, the pickup rolled back out of the parking spot, its headlight slicing through the interior of the Malibu.

Signy waited until she heard the truck roar out onto the highway before she let the access panel slip down to the floor. Retrieving the brown wire, she touched it to the red, immediately getting the spark she was looking for. She revved the engine, thrilled to hear the big V-8 rumble to life. She was even more thrilled when she saw the gas gauge rise well past the halfway mark.

Flicking off the interior light, she backed the car out of the parking spot, the old boat plowing through the snow with ease.

She looked up into the SUV and saw Lizzy wave. She put the car in drive, then eased out of the lot and back onto the highway.

She drove slowly, the only light the occasional glare of an oncoming car and the steady beam of Lizzy's headlights in her rear-view mirror. She needed to find somewhere to ditch the SUV. Slowing to a crawl when she saw a brown sign indicating that a canoe access route was just ahead, she slid the Malibu onto the shoulder just before the entrance to the access road.

Lizzy stopped just behind her.

It took only a few minutes to transfer everything from the SUV over into the Malibu, including Justin, still snug in his car seat. Signy spent another few minutes wiping down every surface, including the exterior door handles.

While Lizzy pointed the Malibu headlights down the canoe access road, Signy revved the SUV engine and plowed along the road until she was no longer visible from the main road. Yanking on the wheel, she drove the rental off the road and into the deep snow.

Not sure whether she was wasting her time, she popped off the panel that covered the fuse box, and removed all the fuses, tossing them out into the snow. She knew there was another set of fuses under the hood, but she didn't have enough lighting to locate them. If there *was* a GPS tracking system, all she could do was hope that one of the fuses she'd tossed would do the trick. She used a sleeve to wipe down the fuse box panel, then hopped down out of the SUV and slogged back to the main road.

When she climbed back into the Malibu, Lizzy had shifted over to the passenger seat. Lizzy spent a couple of minutes blurting out how scared she'd been when the two men had approached the Malibu in the parking lot of the roadhouse.

"I thought about heading back to Priya's," Signy interrupted, "but the cops will be watching all the shelters. They'd nab you before you made it inside." The image of the little white card and its ten-digit phone number, tucked inside the cherrywood box at the bottom of her closet, flashed through her mind. She pushed it away.

"I was thinking the same thing, but I know where we can hide out for a bit," Lizzy said. "There's a place near Henderson Harbor, on the shore of Lake Ontario. Very secluded. The man who owns it is in the South of France for the winter. The only problem is we'll have to go back the way we came."

Signy put the car in gear. "It's not like we have much of a choice. We'll make a quick stop when we hit one of those small towns, see if we can't find ourselves a new licence plate."

As they drove in silence, Signy's thoughts kept drifting to the cherrywood box. She shook her head.

There had to be another way.

Chapter 36

Stone pushed his plate away and leaned back in his chair. "I think that might have been the best omelette I've ever eaten."

Grace smiled. His worries about the contents of his fridge had been unfounded, and it hadn't taken long to whip up a fluffy egg-white creation stuffed with an assortment of fresh veggies, a sprinkling of prosciutto ham, and some creamy goat cheese. She'd argued that healthy eating be damned, he needed comfort food, and had insisted on frying up diced potatoes and sweet onions in a large dollop of butter.

He checked his watch.

"Do you want to give the police another call?"

He shook his head. "It's only been a half-hour."

"I'm sure they'd understand."

"No," he said, getting to his feet, "it's better if I let them do their job. Meanwhile, I'll get these dishes done."

They stood at the sink together, Grace elbow-deep in soapy water, Stone wielding a tea towel. After a while, Grace said, "My brother had a mental illness."

Stone glanced at her, maintaining a mask of professional neutrality. "Really?"

"Schizophrenia," Grace said quietly.

"I'm sorry."

Grace shrugged. "Before he got ill? My God, he was something. Funny, brilliant, good-looking." She handed him a dripping pan.

"Older or younger?"

"Five years older. It was just the two of us. Our parents were gone a lot of the time, and he looked out for me." Grace smiled. "I adored him."

Stone wrapped the towel around the dripping plate and held it to his chest. "What happened?"

"He killed himself. Jumped off a bridge."

"Oh, Abby," Stone said, setting the plate down on the counter and turning to face her, "I'm so sorry."

She waved him away. "It was a long time ago. I just wanted you to know that I understand how devastated you must feel. It's terrible to feel so helpless."

Rocked by a gust of wind, the window over the sink rattled.

Grace jumped. "My goodness. It's getting crazy out there. I'd better be off."

"You're not seriously thinking of driving in this storm? I have plenty of room."

Grace looked at him doubtfully.

"Please," Stone said.

Grace glanced at the window. Snow had built up against the screen. Outside, the wind howled.

"That's settled then," he said, not waiting for an answer. "We'll have a fire. Keep the bad thoughts at bay."

"Are you sure? I don't mind driving."

"Perhaps a nip of cognac as well?"

Grace smiled. "I have to admit that sounds far preferable to ending up in a ditch somewhere."

A few minutes later, Grace followed Stone into his study. He was carrying a basket full of kindling along with a couple of large logs.

"There's a bottle of Courvoisier and some glasses on the bottom left." He nodded his head at a cherrywood cabinet.

Grace was opening the cabinet door when a phone rang.

They stared at each other for a second before Stone dropped the basket of wood onto the floor. "Excuse me," he said, running over to grab the phone from its stand.

Grace backed out of the room, knowing that Stone was likely receiving the bad news that Lizzy and Justin had disappeared without a trace. She wasn't sure she was up to acting surprised. In fact, with the amount of alcohol she had coursing through her system, she was afraid she might blurt out the truth.

Wobbling across the grand hall, she opened a door at random and discovered a well-appointed library. A series of cleverly disguised pot lights illuminated the mahogany bookshelves. Surrounded by six leather-bound chairs, a matching central table held a Tiffany reading lamp and a gold pen and pencil stand.

She stepped over to the closest shelf, expecting to find an overrepresentation of stuffy medical textbooks, but was impressed to find a breathtaking collection of American literary classics. Slipping out a copy of F. Scott Fitzgerald's *The Beautiful and the Damned*, she opened the front cover and was amazed to see that it was a first edition.

She cocked her head. She could hear Solomon talking on the phone. She hoped he wouldn't take the news too hard. He'd turned out to be such a kind man. She wished she could tell him that Lizzy and Justin were safe, that in all likelihood, he would have his son back very soon—but she couldn't. She would have to maintain the Abby Lieberman charade for a bit longer.

Tucking the Fitzgerald back into its spot, she meandered along the stacks, almost overwhelmed by the depth and breadth of the collection. She smiled when she came to not one but five copies of the entire Harry Potter series by J. K. Rowling. She plucked out a copy of the first book, *Harry Potter and the Sorcerer's Stone*, and opened the front cover, wondering if perhaps she had another first edition in her hot little hand.

Her attention was caught by a handwritten inscription on the inside cover. *To my dearest Janelle, No matter how difficult things might seem, never give up on your dreams.* It had been signed with what appeared to be a dramatic *S*.

Cracking open the next in the series, *Harry Potter and the Chamber of Secrets*, she was surprised to find the same inscription, written in the same hand and signed with the same wild flourish. Only the recipient's name was different. *To my dearest Amelia—No matter how difficult things might seem, never give up on your dreams. S*

Frowning, Grace examined several more of the Harry Potters and found that every one had been inscribed with the exact same phrase, and each signed with the dramatic, flowing *S*. The only difference, in each case, was the name of the recipient.

Janelle, Amelia, Muhubo, Kristen.

But it was what she read on the inside cover of *Harry Potter and the Order of the Phoenix* that caused the blood to drain from her face. *To my dearest Kit Kat, No matter how difficult things might seem, never give up on your dreams. S*

Kit Kat? A very unusual name, and one she'd seen very recently. Grace heard the door creak open behind her. She stuffed the book back into its spot. Affecting a cheerful smile, she turned to face Solomon.

He stood in the doorway, an odd expression on his face.

"Everything okay?" she asked, unable to trust her voice. Her knees wobbled, and she vowed never to touch booze again.

He walked over to where she was standing. He turned and ran his finger over the Harry Potter collections. "J. K. Rowling is a genius, don't you think?"

Grace cleared her throat. "Was that the police? Is there any news?"

"News?" he repeated, turning to face her. "Yes, as a matter of fact."

"Did they find them?" she said, taking a step back. She could feel the sharp spines of books pressing into her back.

He took a step into her personal space. "Not yet, but they came very close at a Superstore in Watertown. Apparently, Lizzy has an accomplice. A Ms. Carole White." He peered closely at her. "That name mean anything to you?"

Pressed back against the stack of books, and with nowhere to go, Grace stared into his eyes. "Never heard of her," she said evenly.

"Are you sure about that?"

Grace frowned. "Why on earth would I lie?"

"Why, indeed." Stone narrowed his eyes. "And yet it seems that Ms. White is a reporter for the same magazine you work for. An odd coincidence, don't you think? Two reporters from *Sift* magazine following the same story at the same time? Neither one knowing about the other?"

Grace shrugged. "I don't make those decisions. You'd have to speak with my editor, Rachel Carson. I can get you her number if you want."

Solomon studied her eyes. "Most people don't know this, but when a person lies, their pupils dilate. They can't help it. It's an autonomic response."

Grace reached behind her, her fingers scrabbling along the row of books, searching fruitlessly for anything she might use as a weapon.

"And yours, my dear Abby, are as big as saucers."

Before Grace had time to blink, Stone drove his fist into her face.

Grace saw a flash of white light, and then her world went dark.

Chapter

37

Signy and Lizzy drove back through Watertown, bypassing the more heavily travelled arterial routes through the centre of the city. At the last possible opportunity, they rejoined the stream of traffic crossing the bridge over Interstate 81. Continuing west on Highway 3 toward Lake Ontario, they passed by the Superstore. Signy was not surprised to see vehicles cramming the expansive parking lot, the police presence long gone.

They'd made good time considering the blizzard conditions, the heavy Malibu cutting through the fresh snow, if not like a knife through butter, then at least like a knife through butter frosting. They'd made only two stops, taking care both times not to cut the engine. Signy wasn't sure she'd be able to repeat her hot-wiring feat.

At the first stop, at a grocery store in the village of Black River, where they'd used Lizzy's remaining thirty dollars to stock up on baby food, candy bars, a ten-dollar prepaid phone card, and a slot-head screwdriver. In addition to their legitimate purchases, Signy had also pilfered a generic cellphone.

After leaving the store, they'd driven up and down a few side streets until Signy found what she was looking for, a minivan lodged in a snowdrift behind an elementary school. She'd used the screwdriver to remove the minivan's licence plate, then attached it to the Malibu. She waited until they had driven some distance away from the town before she slid down her window and whipped the Malibu's original plate out into the storm.

Leaving Watertown behind them, they drove west until they reached the edge of Lake Ontario. At the town of Sackets Harbor, Lizzy directed Signy to take the Seaway Trail. As they drove south along the edge of the lake, gale-force winds howling in off the water rocked the Malibu from side to side.

Signy appreciated that Lizzy had gone silent, allowing her to concentrate on her driving. Drifts were settling like sand dunes across the highway. She let out a breath she didn't know she'd been holding when Lizzy pointed out the road that led to the cottage. She slowed to a crawl, negotiating the turn inch by inch. On both sides of the unplowed back road, dense tangles of cedar brush served as a snow fence of sorts, and they were able to push forward. Still, the going was treacherous, and it took almost ten minutes to travel the final mile.

"There it is," said Lizzy, pointing out a small track almost completely hidden by a natural rock cairn on one side and overhanging cedars on the other.

Signy gunned the engine. She couldn't see anything, but Lizzy explained that they were travelling onto a narrow spit of land that jutted out into the lake. The Malibu roared, starting to feel the effects of the wintry punishment. Snow had caked up under the wheel wells, and she could feel the drag on the steering wheel.

Sweat was beading on her forehead by the time she caught sight of a huge grey mass directly ahead. She snugged her car as close as she could to the stone cottage. Turning off the engine, she thought she caught a whiff of burning rubber. She patted the wheel and sent a silent thank you to the god of internal combustion engines.

She picked up the screwdriver, then turned to Lizzy. "Stay here. It might take me a few minutes to get the door open."

"No need," Lizzy said. "I know where Bill hides the spare key."

"You're positive your husband doesn't know about this place?"

Lizzy shook her head. "Bill has a successful legal practice in Rochester. He does occasional pro bono work for the kids at the shelter. He lets us bring the kids out here for swim parties in the summer. I never mentioned anything about it to Solomon."

Signy nodded, then hauled on her parka and grabbed as much stuff as she could carry. The lashing wind tore at her face as she struggled through high drifts toward the front door. Behind her, Lizzy followed in her footprints, the baby clutched tightly to her chest.

The grey building was less a cottage and more a compact stone mansion. Constructed of hand-hewn grey stone blocks, it rose two storeys into the sky. A miniature glacier of snow shimmered on the sloped roof, and icicles hung like inverted daggers from the eaves. Signy stopped in front of a thick wooden door fitted with a very modern-looking deadbolt lock.

"Open the mailbox," Lizzy said, shouting to be heard over the roar of the waves. "You'll feel a little hole on the bottom near the corner. Stick your finger in there and pull it up."

Signy did as instructed and had no trouble locating the key. Within seconds she had the door open and they tumbled inside. Brushing her fingers along the wall, she found the switch and flicked it on. At least they had electricity.

Stomping snow from her boots, she looked around. The place was an airy showpiece. Open concept, with ten-foot ceilings and a huge picture window overlooking the front lawn, it sported French doors leading out to a wraparound cedar deck that jutted out over the lake. She thought the view must be spectacular in summer.

While Lizzy took the baby upstairs to get him changed, Signy conducted a quick reconnoiter. Inside a utility room located off the kitchen, she found a propane furnace running on low to keep the water pipes from bursting. She turned the furnace up and cranked the water temperature.

With the problem of heat and water taken care of, she turned to the next item on her list. Returning to the front hall, she keyed in the number on the prepaid phone card to the stolen phone and added the ten dollars' worth of chat time. She immediately punched in Grace's number.

She frowned when the call flipped over to voice mail. Flicking back the sleeve of her sweater, she checked the time on her watch. Almost eight o'clock. She pushed away the sickening thought that their performance at the embassy might have consigned Grace to a jail cell in Ottawa by now. She considered checking in with Grand Central but nixed that idea. With the lines at Grand Central tapped, whoever was watching would pinpoint her location in seconds if she didn't destroy the phone.

And getting rid of the phone was not an option. She thought

about Ben. She'd been deluded to think she could make their date tomorrow night. At the rate this case was going, she'd be lucky to be home before next week. She pictured him showing up at her house and finding it dark, heading over to Winston's, thinking that maybe she'd decided to meet him there. He'd grab a table and wait, probably send her a few puzzled text messages, and then give her a call. He'd get that automated voice telling him that the customer he was trying to reach was unavailable.

Would he be angry that she'd stood him up, or worried that she wasn't answering her phone? Ben was a cop. She had no idea how he'd react. The only thing she did know was that she couldn't afford to have him come looking for her. She started to tap out a quick text message, then realized that his number was on the phone she'd tossed under the wheels of an eighteen-wheeler earlier that day.

Barely resisting the urge to shriek with frustration, she glanced over at the meagre supplies they'd purchased at the grocery store. The baby needed proper food and a lot more diapers. They could use something more substantial to eat as well, but she'd found no food stores in the kitchen if you didn't count the salt and pepper shakers and a small tin of Fry's cocoa powder. They'd have to stick to candy bars for now.

She sat down, leaning her elbow on the kitchen table. She sensed that she was squeezing further and further between the proverbial rock and a hard place. As much as she was loath to admit it, she needed help. Preferably from someone with money who wasn't afraid to get his hands a little dirty.

She knew of only one person that fit that particular bill, and he was the last person on the planet she wanted to call. She spent another useless few minutes trying to formulate an alternative solution but came up empty. She stared at the phone for a few seconds, recalling the ten-digit number scrawled on the little white card in her cherrywood box.

Cursing under her breath, she dialed.

Chapter 38

Slumped behind the wheel in the visitors' parking area of the Coral Gables mobile home park, the Tracker had a clear view of unit 17. He'd been listening to a Spanish language radio station and had enjoyed a two-hour retrospective on twentieth-century classical Cuban guitar music. Unfortunately, the afternoon music shows had been replaced by evening talk radio. Only five minutes in, he was already sick of a rant on the evils of leftist politics.

With the exception of a few people arriving home from work, there had been little movement in the park. In unit 17, he could see a sliver of light where the curtains on the front window didn't quite meet, and the occasional shadow of someone walking back and forth inside.

He doubted it was Lenny Screed. As soon as he'd lost the fat man in the floral shirt, he'd raced back to Coral Gables. There was no way Screed could have made it back to the park ahead of him.

He figured good old gambling Lenny must have moved on to a luckier spot while he'd been distracted by that foul-mouthed urchin.

He almost missed a flicker of movement to his right. Turning his head, he caught sight of a bulky figure on a ten-speed bike, wheeling into the park. The Tracker flipped off the radio and rolled down his window. He could hear the hiss of tires on the gravel drive as the bike sped past.

The floral shirt was unmistakable, as was the grimy salt and pepper rat-tail plastered to the back of his sweaty neck. The Tracker watched Screed steer the bike to the front of unit 17, then heave one bulky leg over the seat and toss the bike on its side onto the front lawn. The big man leaned forward, hands on thighs, gasping for breath.

Slipping the garrotte from his pocket, the Tracker watched as the front door to unit 17 swung open and a rectangle of light illuminated the scrubby front lawn.

Frowning, he let the slim wire fall from his fingers. A petite bottle-blonde clad in a pair of short shorts and a tube top rushed down the stairs. Judging by the brief but intense confrontation that followed, the woman had been waiting for Screed. As soon as she showed signs of calming down, Screed drew her into his arms, tipped her face up toward his, and kissed her.

The Tracker shook his head. How could the man have drawn a woman into his shitstorm? Switching the overhead light to the off position, he retrieved the garrotte and clicked open the door. The selfish fool deserved what he got.

He was about to slide out of his vehicle when he saw the screen door crack open once again. His heart skipped a beat as he watched a curly-haired heartbreaker toddle out onto the front stoop.

"Son of a bitch," he muttered under his breath.

The toddler negotiated the wooden steps on her hands and knees. Safely on the ground, she hauled herself to her feet and wobbled toward Screed and the woman, her tiny toes digging into the dusty driveway, her arms akimbo as she struggled for balance.

The Tracker felt his throat tighten with anger. Why hadn't he known the runner had a kid? Not just some kid, but a little girl. "Son of a bitch!" he repeated, sinking lower in his seat when he realized that he had shouted aloud.

Feeling a rush of heat flare in his chest, he cranked the engine, then turned the air conditioner on high. He shoved his hand back into his pocket, winding the garrotte between his fingers.

After a moment, he relaxed his fists and sucked in a calming breath. He had a duty to carry through with this assignment. The resultant boost to his bank account would go a long way toward discovering the identity of the mysterious Dr. Jekyll and just how he was involved in the murder and disappearance of his mother and father. He owed it to himself. He owed it to Signy.

Signy.

He squeezed his eyes shut and almost immediately felt the dreaded misty red cloud descend. He was six years old again, slipping backward in a pool of scarlet, the stench of copper tearing at his nose and throat. Holding his mother's hand, her skin fiery against his, sweat beading like poison on her forehead, her blue eyes fading, even as she begged him to keep his sister safe.

The cellphone in his back pocket rang.

His eyes flew open, his heart thumping painfully inside his chest. He'd given the number to only one person, and after four months of waiting, he had begun to despair she would ever call.

The phone rang again, and then twice more before he finally managed to dig it out. "Hello?" he said, hearing nothing but the sound of breathing on the other end of the line. "Is that you?"

"Hello, Alex."

"Signy! I'm so glad you called," he said, his face cracking into a wide grin.

There was a long pause, and then, "This isn't a personal call."

"I see," he said, melting inside despite her chilly tone.

"It's just that I'm in a bit of trouble."

One corner of his mouth turned up. *Plus ça change, plus c'est la même chose.*

"Long story short, I have a woman and her child with me. I need to get them to California but I've lost my money and my ID."

"No problem. I'm coming."

"No," she said, "no way. I can handle this myself."

"I can fly out tonight. Where are you?"

"Look, Alex, you don't want to get involved. There's an Amber Alert out for the child."

He paused.

"If you can just send me some money, I'll take it from here."

"Please, let me do this for you." He held his breath.

"We're holed up in a cottage near Watertown, New York," she said, finally.

While she rattled off the directions to the place, he scribbled the particulars on the back cover of the vehicle manual he pulled from the glove compartment. "I'll fly out tonight. I should be there by noon at the latest." He waited in vain for a response and thought she'd hung up, when he finally heard her say, "See you tomorrow." Before he had a chance to say anything else, the line went dead.

It was a minute or two before he'd calmed down enough to remember the mayor and the moronic Lenny Screed. He glanced over at unit 17. The blackout curtains had been pulled tight in a vain effort to keep the boogeyman from the door.

Fingering the garrotte in his pocket, he stared at the dark front yard for several minutes before tearing a page from the vehicle manual. He scribbled a phone number in the margin, then exited the car. With his ball cap pulled low over his eyes, he marched up the walk and pounded on the door. He could hear a flurry of movement from inside and then nothing.

He knocked again. "Screed?" he called through the closed door. "I have a message from an old friend of yours. Open up."

After a moment, Lenny Screed poked his nose out. "Look, I don't have the damn video."

"I couldn't care less about your dirty little movie."

A wave of confusion passed across Screed's face. "Then why are you here? Is he finally going to fork over what he owes?" Screed smacked a fist into his open palm. "I knew he'd cave eventually."

"For God's sake," said the Tracker, "I don't have time for this."

"What?"

"You're a fool."

"What the—?"

"But that doesn't mean that little girl in there should be made to suffer."

"Girl? I never—"

"Shut up." Even as the words left his lips, the Tracker felt the stab of cold steel in his back. He froze.

"No, you shut up," a feminine voice instructed. "Len, open the door."

The Tracker heard the ominous scrape of metal as the woman cocked the gun.

Baring a row of yellowing teeth, Screed danced with rage as the woman prodded the Tracker inside the trailer. “Who’s the fool now, eh, fucker? Who’s the fool now?”

The Tracker winced. Even an idiot like Lenny Screed was bound to call one right every now and then.

Chapter 39

Grace could hear an intermittent squeaking, like rats shrieking underfoot. Her ears were ringing, and she felt stuffed up, as if she had the worst head cold of her life. There it was again. That damn squeal. She tried to turn toward the sound, but the only result was a shocking dart of pain across the bridge of her nose.

She let out a frightened yelp. "Where am I? What's going on?"

There was no response. The squeaking sound got louder. With a sense of growing dread, her brain finally made the connection. She was rolling down a hall on a gurney, which could only mean one thing. She was back in the hospital.

"No," she shrieked, "this is a mistake. I'm okay. I want to go home."

There was no answer. She tried to sit up and discovered to her horror that both her arms and legs were immobilized. The restraints were not painful, but they were effective. Overhead, she could see industrial fluorescent lights whiz by. The walls appeared to be made of cinder block. What kind of a hospital was this?

"Hey," she said, twisting violently. The movement caused a knifelike pain through her head. She groaned. The gurney slammed through a swinging door. She could see an IV line dangling above her head and realized that the ache she felt in the back of her hand must be the entry point of the IV needle.

She started to hyperventilate, her breaths coming in short, harsh gasps through her mouth.

The squeaking ceased. The gurney jolted as the brakes slammed into place. Her eyes rolled wildly in her head. The room was chilly, several degrees below her comfort zone, and there was a caustic bite of chemicals in the air.

Hands clad in thick white gloves came down from above her head and pulled up the green sheet a little tighter around her chin.

"Don't touch me," she gasped, spittle spraying from between her cracked lips. She could hear the hiss of oxygen and the clatter of metal tools. Her nose felt horribly stuffed and she was starting to swallow constantly against a metallic-tasting postnasal drip that trickled down the back of her throat. Blood? She struggled to remember the accident. It had been snowing. She could remember that. Perhaps she had slid off the road.

A blur of white swept past on her right. She cranked her eyes and saw a figure dressed in a full body suit, the kind used by forensic workers at a crime scene or scientists in a biocontainment laboratory.

The white figure turned toward her, and in the reflective surface of the visor sewn into the hood, she could see her own face peering back at her.

Panic clawed at her throat. Both her eyes were black, her upper lip looked split, and her nose was most definitely not where it had been this morning. She'd seen enough beating victims to know that her nose was broken, the upper half swollen and displaced.

Gloved hands reached out.

"Leave me alone," she cried, trying to wrench her head away but finding herself powerless against the tight restraints. She shrieked as the hands tented into a triangle pushed against the swollen tissue of her broken nose. She could taste bloody mucus pouring down the back of her throat as the cartilage cracked violently back into place. Tears poured from her eyes, and she felt suddenly nauseous. She fought the sensation. With no way to turn her head, throwing up could be deadly.

She swallowed convulsively as layers of gauze were applied none too gently across the bridge of her nose, followed by thick surgical tape. Air moved freely through her nostrils again, and she tried to slow her breathing. "I want to go home," she said, trying not to cry.

"Soon," said a voice from behind her head.

"Who are you? What happened? Where am I?" The words spilled from her lips in a desperate rush. She watched an ice pack settle across her eyes and was grateful for the momentary blindness. She didn't want to see what she was already beginning to suspect. She felt a coldness in her arm as something entered her bloodstream through the IV line. "What are you doing?" she asked. "What is that?"

She heard the sound of footsteps and the bang of the door, and then the orderly was gone. She was alone. Overwhelmed by a wave of sleepiness, she was unable to call out. Within seconds, she slipped into darkness again.

Chapter

40

The Tracker heard a soft click as the woman closed the door behind them. Cranking his eyes to the right, he could just make out the silhouette of the petite bottle-blonde. She had a short-barrel shotgun centered on his right kidney.

"Kill him, Darlene," Screed spat.

"Shut up, Len," said Darlene, prodding her prisoner forward.

The Tracker stumbled into the room.

"That's far enough. Keep your hands where I can see them."

Raising his hands over his head, the Tracker said, "Stay calm, please. I'm here to help you. You and your daughter."

"Debbie?" asked the woman, her growing alarm evident in her shrill tone.

"Come on, Darlene. Get rid of him."

The Tracker raised his hands high in the air and slowly turned to face the woman.

"Hold it right there, asshole," Screed said.

"Shut up, Len," Darlene repeated, tilting the barrel a fraction of an inch in his direction.

"What the fuck, Darl?" he said, after taking a step backward. "Whose side are you on?"

Ignoring the fat man, Darlene stared at the Tracker. "What do you want with my daughter?"

He shook his head. "The same thing as you. That she stays safe."

The Tracker watched a crease form between Darlene's blue eyes. He nodded his head toward Screed. "Your boyfriend here has got himself into some pretty bad trouble. Did he tell you about it?"

Darlene's eyes flicked toward Screed.

"He's lying, Darl. It's all bullshit."

"I didn't think so," said the Tracker. "You don't seem like the kind of person who would endanger her own child."

"Don't listen to that lying sack of shit. This is me talking." Screed held out his hands, palms up.

"Seems good old Len here took a video of a pretty powerful mayor getting it on with a couple of underage girls."

"Mayor?" Darlene's eyes narrowed. "You mean that sexcapades creep?"

The Tracker nodded. "And that creep didn't take kindly to his old buddy here trying to sell the video to the highest bidder."

"Len?" Darlene said, turning to glare at Screed, the gun following along with her.

Screed backed further away, upsetting an ashtray piled high with cigarette butts. The chemical odour of nicotine and ash permeated the cramped space.

"That's why I'm here," the Tracker said, his attention on Darlene.

Darlene swung the barrel of the gun back, levelling it at the Tracker's chest.

"I was hired to get rid of the problem." The Tracker glared at Screed. "Permanently."

"Are you fucking kidding me? That perverted son of a bitch wants to kill *me*?" Screed shouted.

"So it's true?" Darlene settled the weapon expertly against her shoulder.

The Tracker nodded. "Lenny here has been using you."

"No, Darl. That's not true. It's just that I didn't know where else to go." Screed bounced inside his shoes.

"Listen to me, Darlene. It took me less than a day to find you, and there are others out there who are even faster," he lied. "And you can be sure the mayor will send someone else if I don't get the job done. He won't stop until everyone associated with that video is in the ground. Your daughter included."

Tears sprang into Darlene's eyes.

"May I?" the Tracker asked, pointing at his pocket.

Darlene tipped her chin almost imperceptibly.

Sliding the garrotte from his pocket, he dangled it from his fingers, allowing her a good look before dropping it to the floor.

"Jesus," Screed said, staring at the sharp wire.

Reaching into his pocket a second time, the Tracker removed the torn page on which he'd written the phone number. He stepped slowly toward the woman and, easing the barrel of the shotgun away from his chest, pressed the shred of paper into her hand. "Call this number. Tell the man who answers that the Tracker sent you. He'll get you and your daughter relocated. You can even take him, if you are so inclined." He shot a contemptuous glance at Screed. "But whatever you choose, I suggest you do it immediately."

Darlene held the scrap of paper to her heart.

"Now, if you don't mind, I have a rather important meeting I must make." He took a tentative step toward the door, his eyes trained on the shotgun.

But Darlene had already shifted her attention to her lover, and from the looks of it, life was about get even more challenging for the hapless Lenny Screed.

Sidling past the furious woman, the Tracker exited the house, his mind already a million miles away by the time he started his car.

He had a plane to catch.

Anthony Lupo, known to his intimates as Tony the Wolf, held his son's hand tight inside his. Beside him, his wife, Angie, continued the verbal barrage she'd begun the minute they'd left for the airport. There was veal Parmesan in the fridge, potato salad in the crisper, and ziti done five different ways in the freezer. She didn't expect to come home to a dump, so he'd better remember to use the laundry hamper for once in his life.

"Daddy?"

Tony the Wolf smiled down at his son. Only four years old, and he'd already learned to ignore his shrew of a mother. Tony felt he might burst with pride.

"Does Nonna D. have TV at her house?"

"Don't worry about it. In Los Angeles, if you don't have at least three TVs in the house, the feds start bustin' heads."

Little Tony giggled.

"Anthony," Angie warned, "you're scaring the boy."

Tony the Wolf looked down at his son and rolled his eyes.

"Daddy,"—the boy was pointing at a magazine kiosk up ahead—"can I have some Hot Tamales?"

"No candy," barked his mother. "I want you to sleep on the plane."

Tony glanced at the candy counter, wondering how he might load the kid up without his wife finding out, when he caught sight of a blond man waiting in line to buy a pack of gum. He narrowed his eyes. He recognized a no-good rat when he saw one.

"Your mother's right," he said, dragging the kid past the kiosk, keeping his face turned away.

Angie looked at him in surprise.

Disengaging his hand from Little Tony's, he passed the boy over to his mother. "Take him," he said. "I'll be back in a few minutes." When she opened her mouth to protest, Tony shot her a fierce look from under his heavy black brows.

Angie nodded and then dragged the boy away, shushing his protests with a swift swat to his behind.

The one good thing about Angie, she knew not to interfere when he was working. He walked over to a line of plastic chairs and, grabbing a discarded *Miami Herald*, sat down and pretended to read.

When the guy walked right by him a couple of minutes later, Tony could hardly believe it. The asshole was whistling. One of those stupid nursery rhymes his mother used to sing. Something about Johnny coming home from the fair. The guy was oblivious. Nothing like his legendary reputation. Tony tossed the paper, then stood up and followed at a discreet distance. He needed to find out what the dumb prick was up to.

Ten minutes later, Tony the Wolf shoved a calling card into a pay phone and dialed a Miami number. When the line picked up, he said, "It's me. I'm at the Fort Lauderdale airport. Angie's takin' Little Tony to visit her mother."

He listened for a minute, then his shoulders slumped. "Ya, right, sorry, Boss. So anyways, you're never gonna believe this but the Tracker is here." He frowned, then said, "Ya, that Tracker. The pretty boy what got your brother popped." Tony the Wolf beamed. "*Grazie*, Boss. You gotta pen? Lemme give you the details."

Tony waited for a moment, then said, "Okay, so he's using the name Alex Hunter. He bought a ticket to Chicago. He lays over there for a few hours, then flies on to Rochester in the morning." He stopped talking, interrupted by the person on the other end of the line. "Ya, Rochester, New York, and no, I don't know why. Alls I'm saying is you might wanna have a guy waiting for him in Rochester." Tony listened for another few seconds, then nodded. "I hope you tear his nuts off. Vito was good people."

After hanging up the phone, Tony the Wolf pinched away a growing erection, then walked over to the kiosk to fill up on candy for his son.

Chapter 41

Signy stood at the window, looking out over the pristine snow that blanketed the front yard. She was relieved to see that the driveway appeared passable, the tangled cedar forest on either side providing a natural snow barrier. The old Malibu stood where she'd left it, although it now sported an eight-inch layer of fresh powder on its roof. The sky was gloomy, the feeble morning light fighting a losing battle against the thick cloud cover. At least the damned snow had stopped falling.

She stared down the drive, keeping her eye on the spot where it disappeared around a small bend. Her stomach flipped, and not because she'd only eaten a candy bar for breakfast. Justin Stone had wailed off and on all night. Signy had heard Lizzy fix a bottle, sing lullabies, and walk the floor for hours.

Not to mention the snowmobiles. She heard them racing through the fresh powder well into the night. She hoped Alex was bright-eyed and bushy-tailed because she wanted to get on the road as soon as possible, and she certainly didn't feel rested enough to take the first shift of driving.

Alex. Signy's stomach lurched again. He'd sounded happy to hear from her on the phone, but what did that really mean? As much as she didn't want to admit it—they shared genetics after all—the man was probably a psychopath. How could she trust anything he said or did? Still, her heart skipped a beat when she caught sight of a movement near the bend in the driveway, although it was only a jackrabbit hopping through the deep snow.

"Good morning."

Signy turned back into the room. Lizzy was coming down the stairs with baby Justin snugged onto her hip.

"Did you sleep at all?" Lizzy asked.

"A lot better than you, I expect," Signy said. "I have his breakfast all ready to go in the kitchen."

"Thanks," Lizzy said, coming over to stand by Signy at the window.

Signy glanced at the young woman. Her hair hung limp down her back, and there were dark circles under her eyes, otherwise, she seemed in good shape.

"When do you expect your friend?" Lizzy asked, looking out the window.

"Sooner rather than later, I hope. We can't stay here much longer. With all the snowmobiles and the ice fishermen we saw out on the harbor, it's only a matter of time before someone figures out we're here."

"Will he be coming all the way with us?"

"Alex?" Signy shook her head. "Only as far as Chicago. We'll move quicker on our own after that."

"You're lucky."

The baby buried his fist in Signy's braid and yanked.

"Ouch," Signy said, plucking Justin's hand out of her hair. "Lucky? How do you figure that?"

Lizzy shrugged. "Nice to have someone care about you, I guess."

Signy felt a fizzy sensation in her chest. "How about that breakfast?"

"Sure," Lizzy said.

Signy smiled, grateful that Lizzy wasn't going to push her on the subject. The woman seemed to have an intuitive sense of when to take a step back. "I warmed up some baby cereal for Justin," she said over her shoulder, "but I hope you can manage with another chocolate bar."

"A Kit Kat for breakfast?" Lizzy grinned. "Solomon would be demented."

"Mum . . . mum . . . mum . . . mum," Justin chortled.

"That's right," Lizzy said, tickling him under the chin. "Aren't you a clever little thing."

Threading his way through taxis and buses idling outside the arrivals entrance of the Rochester airport, the Tracker wrapped his wool scarf tighter around his neck and pulled his cap down low over his eyes. Dark clouds roiled in the charcoal sky but at least the snow had let up.

He was surprised at how rested he felt. The plane had only been half full and he'd been able to stretch out across a row of three seats. There had been a long layover in Chicago, but he'd managed to catch a few winks in the departure lounge and had slept again on the shorter hop to Rochester.

As he stepped through a set of sliding doors and into the parking facility, he inhaled a mix of gas fumes, rubber, and stale air. He found the noxious stew oddly comforting. Cars and trucks, concrete and steel. Solid, everyday things.

As he made his way diagonally through the rows of parked vehicles toward the rental section, he wondered how angry Signy still was, and whether that anger would cloud her judgment. If she wanted his help, she was going to have to trust him.

He grimaced underneath his wool scarf. He would have to make her understand that for him, his pursuit of Elena had been just another job. He wouldn't apologize for that; he couldn't. It was the life he'd been given, the life he'd been trained for.

He located the black GMC Yukon he'd rented, and pushed the button on the key fob, the click of the locking mechanism echoing in the deserted underground lot. He tossed his bag onto the passenger seat and climbed in.

He turned on the GPS, inputting the address Signy had given him. Looking over his shoulder, he backed the big truck out of the parking spot and eased down the aisle toward the exit. He swallowed back a frisson of anxiety.

Despite months of watching, he wondered how much he really knew about the real Signy Shepherd. She was skillful in many ways. She had an uncanny ability to think on her feet. She had a black belt and was a good driver under pressure, but outside of her work life, she was an enigma. He smiled. Perhaps they weren't so different after all.

In any event, he was glad they had a mutual goal upon which to focus their attentions. If she wanted the woman and her kid to disappear, then he would take care of that. Hell, if she wanted him to fly them to the moon, he'd find a way to make it happen. He'd be damned if he'd fail her again.

As he approached the exit, he felt an almost imperceptible hum vibrate in the space between his conscious and subconscious minds, but with his thoughts consumed by Signy Shepherd, he brushed aside the errant sensation with as much awareness as he would flick a mosquito off his skin.

He also failed to notice that when he'd climbed into the Yukon in the car rental area a few minutes before, there had been no rumble of motors, no footsteps in the distance. Yet now, as he bumped over the theft prevention device that separated the rental lot from the main parking garage, a white pickup truck appeared out of nowhere, slipping in tight behind him.

Oblivious, he pointed the car north toward Signy.

Chapter

42

Grace swirled back into consciousness. Feeling the bite of the restraints on her wrists and ankles, she remembered the silent orderly, and the gurney ride through the deserted hallways. She rolled her eyes, checking out her surroundings. With its array of medical equipment, the space looked like a hospital room, but she knew with sudden clarity it was anything but.

Adrenaline exploded inside her chest. She remembered everything. The pixie on the treadmill, the long journey up from Rochester, and the lonely drive to Dr. Stone's estate. The pleasant conversation during dinner and then the terrible discovery of the inscriptions inside the Harry Potter books. She'd recognized some of the distinctive names from the ongoing missing women reports that littered her office. Overcome by a wave of self-loathing, she banged her head against the gurney.

How had she been so stupid? She'd fallen for his bullshit—

hook, line, and sinker. Had she been so desperate for a little human compassion that she'd let down all her defences? The only thing she could be thankful for was that this monster's wife and child were safe at the chalet in Lake Placid.

Behind her head a machine beeped, stopped, and then beeped again. She was well acquainted with the warning tones of a heart monitor machine. She'd been hooked up to one for several days after she'd been shot. She could feel similar wires attached to her chest. It must have picked up her racing heartbeat and sounded the alarm. She tried to calm her breathing.

She wrenched her fists against the soft ties that held her arms firmly to the bed. She felt her heartbeat quicken again as she contemplated the dreadful possibilities that Stone had in mind for her.

Hearing the door screech open, she cranked her eyes to the left and saw the white-shrouded figure enter the room. "What the hell is going on?" she demanded, with far more bravado than she felt.

The figure loomed into view, and from under the white hood, she heard a cheery Dr. Stone call out, "What are you up to, Abby? Your pulse is far too high and your cardiac output is erratic."

"Why are doing this?"

With a gloved hand, he reached out and peeled back the sheet.

She realized to her horror that she was wearing nothing but a skimpy blue hospital gown.

He pulled off the white hood and stepped out of the protective suit. Underneath he was wearing a pair of soft brown corduroy slacks and a cream turtleneck sweater. He had a stethoscope around his neck.

"My editor will be wondering where I am. I wouldn't be surprised if the cops come looking for me anytime now," Grace said.

"I was hoping to start the harvesting procedure this morning." Stone glanced at the white suit he'd hung on a hook. "But with your heart rate all over the map this way, I'll need to conduct a physical exam first. It's essential that you are capable of withstanding the process." Bending down, he ripped open the top of her gown.

Watching his greedy eyes roam over her naked breasts, Grace whimpered.

Stone glanced up at the cardiac monitor, which had begun to beat wildly, then placed the two ends of the stethoscope in his ears. He warmed the round end against his palm, then brought it to her chest. He pressed it firmly between her breasts and listened.

"Get off me," cried Grace, struggling to move inside the restraints.

Ignoring her, Stone cupped her right breast in his hand and, moving it to one side, placed the stethoscope just under her armpit.

He removed the instrument, then jerking her face toward his, leaned down. "This will be much easier if you just relax."

Her momentary rage extinguished by debilitating fear, she hated the sound of her own voice as she pleaded with him. "No, don't. Please."

He palpated her breast, squeezing gently. "Don't worry. If you're in relatively good health, you'll easily survive the tissue harvest. Most subjects do. It's the next phase of the process that can be a bit tricky. We need you to be in tip-top shape for that."

Squeezing her eyes closed, Grace turned her head away. She didn't want to know anything more.

Stone continued his examination, moving the stethoscope all over both sides of her chest before placing it on the left side of her neck. She watched his face as he listened to the blood flow through her carotid artery. The sight of his moist tongue protruding between his lips made her want to vomit.

He replaced the stethoscope around his neck. Grace was about to let her breath out in a sigh of relief, when he peeled the sheet down further, revealing her stomach, pubis, and the tops of her thighs. She wrenched against the restraints.

Attempting to inspect her abdomen, he paused, obviously irritated as she flinched away from his probing hands. He slapped her face. Hard.

She went completely still, shocked at the sting of his hand on her cheek.

"This will go much more smoothly if you behave yourself."

"Go to hell," she said, and snapped her teeth at the fingers that had strayed too close to her face.

Whipping his hand out of the way just in time, he turned to the metal cabinet and opened a drawer. "If that's the way you want it, I'm happy to oblige. I really can't have you hurting yourself."

Recoiling as he turned back toward her, Grace stared in horror at the rubber ball and Velcro restraint he had clutched in his fist. She clamped her mouth shut.

Stone responded by jamming his fingers into the meaty muscles where her jawbone met her skull. The force was enough to wrench open her mouth.

Feeling the press of hard rubber against her tongue, Grace squeezed her eyes shut as he secured the strap across her forehead. Trying to breathe around the obstruction in her throat, she willed herself not to vomit.

He resumed his examination. Her legs were already wide open, the ankles tied to either corner of the bed, and he had easy access to her vagina. He started by inserting a finger inside her and pressing down on her lower abdomen.

"You have a small uterine fibroid. Nothing to worry about. To be expected in someone your age. But I think we should take a closer look, just in case." He removed a large metal speculum from a metal tray on top of the cabinet, holding it up so she could see it clearly.

Grace squeezed her eyes shut, hot tears pouring down her cheeks.

"Now then, Abby dear, just try to relax."

She winced when she felt his gloved fingers spread her open and the bite of the metal as it probed for the opening.

"Lift your hips, please."

She pushed her bottom into the bed.

"Lift your hips, Abby," he repeated, "or I will lift them for you."

Although every muscle in her body screamed in protest, she complied.

"That's a good girl," he said, spreading her open once again.

Lying perfectly still as he slid the speculum deep inside her, she flinched as he cranked open the mechanism. Stone slid a powerful light over and positioned it between her legs, taking an inordinately long time to examine the inside of her vagina. She heard the rip of paper and then a nasty pinch as he used a long wooden stick to scrape cells from her cervix.

"I might as well do this while I'm here," he said, giving the stick another vicious twist. "Regular Pap tests are a woman's primary defence against cervical cancer."

Grace groaned as she felt a stab deep inside her abdomen.

"I should bring you up to date," Stone said in a conversational tone. "The police were able to track down the SUV your colleague was driving. It was found abandoned just off a forest route in the Adirondacks Park."

The only bright spot in this nightmare, suddenly extinguished. Signy and Lizzy had not made it to safety at the chalet. Grace closed her eyes.

"The police are searching the area for them, but I don't think they'll find them. I think your Carole White is a most resourceful woman. I think as soon as she realized that the police had her identity, she ditched the SUV. Probably stole another car. Am I right, Abby?"

Grace exhaled as she felt the speculum slide free of her body.

Stone tossed the instrument into a metal sink along with the soiled latex gloves. He rolled the stool up toward Grace's head until he was looking down into her face. "Where has your friend taken my wife and son?"

Grace opened her eyes and stared up at him.

"You and Ms. White were working together. I'm guessing your role was to keep me occupied so as to give your accomplice a head start?" Stone shrugged. "Nonetheless, the jig is up, my dear, and it will go much easier on you if you just tell me what I want to know."

Grace made a choking noise behind the gag.

"Of course, silly me," Stone said, undoing the Velcro strap and removing the gag.

Grace gasped for air.

"They can't have gotten far," Stone said, leaning forward. "The Amber Alert, the snow. You must have had a place to stash them nearby if worse came to worst. So tell me, Abby. Where are you keeping my wife and son?"

"I'll tell you," Grace whispered. "Just don't hurt me anymore."

"That's a good girl."

Grace tried to speak, but her mouth was so dry she could hardly make a sound.

Stone walked over to the sink and filled a small cup with water. After releasing the Velcro restraint, he placed a hand behind her neck and lifted her head in a manner that seemed almost tender.

Sipping from the cup, Grace beckoned him closer.

Stone leaned forward until their lips were almost touching. "Where are they, Abby?"

"Go fuck yourself," she said, and then spat in his face.

Chapter 43

Standing on her toes, Signy peered through the small round window. It was freezing in the tiny attic room, and it smelled like mouse droppings, but it gave her a much clearer view of the long road that snaked back along the spit toward the mainland.

She'd left Lizzy and the baby downstairs. She could hear Justin babbling experimentally as Lizzy tidied up. In the distance, she caught a shimmer of white through the cedars. She blew on the window, clearing the frost. It was probably another of the ubiquitous white-tailed deer she'd seen desperately pawing under the snow, searching for something to eat.

She wiped her palms on her jeans. She had no idea what she was going to say to him. The last time she'd seen Alex, they hadn't left on the best of terms. She'd arrived home the night Grace had been shot, weary beyond belief, to find the man she'd known as Jay Hunter sitting at her dining room table.

She remembered her growing rage as she listened to him try to explain away why he'd led a Russian assassin right up to Grace Holder's door. His lame excuses had only fueled the fire. When he went on to tell her that she was the sister for whom he'd been searching for over twenty years, she had slapped him across the face. Hard.

Her own cheeks burned at the memory. There was no doubt that he was her brother; the proof was in the DNA results he'd sent to her. That didn't mean he was family. Quite the contrary. He was a stranger who had shown up in her life purely by accident. She owed him nothing, certainly not scintillating conversation.

She pressed her forehead to the cold glass and saw a puff of white rising above the cedars not far from the house. A vehicle was coming up the drive, and it was kicking up a whirlwind of snow. Showtime. She took a few calming breaths and then headed for the stairs.

By the time she reached the main floor, her confidence had deserted her. She peered through the front window, biting her lip.

The baby was playing on the floor with a red plastic teething ring.

"Is that him?" Lizzy asked.

Grabbing her parka, she pulled open the door. "I'll be right back."

The baby smacked the hard plastic into the bridge of his nose.

Ignoring the resulting hysteria, Signy stepped outside. Icy wind slashed her exposed cheeks, and she drew her hood tight around her face. With the solid door pressed against her back, she watched a black Yukon roll into view and make short work of the unplowed drive. The SUV pulled up directly in front of her. She peered up into the driver's seat.

Alex Nakai smiled down at her.

She found the smile disturbing, although she wasn't sure why. Indicating that he should stay where he was, she pushed her way through the drifting snow. She opened the passenger door and climbed inside. Leaving her hood up, she sat for a moment, blowing warm air onto her fingertips.

"Hi," he said.

"Hi. Sorry to drag you out in this storm."

"Signy Shepherd smack dab in the middle of chaos? How could I resist?"

She felt him grinning at her the way a stray dog does when it realizes there is a treat hidden in your pocket. That uniquely canine blend of frantic pleading and "Give me the damn bacon strip or I'll snap your fingers off." She'd learned to tread lightly around strange dogs and didn't feel inclined to act differently with this man.

He inhaled deeply and she could see his shoulders relax. He'd left the vehicle running, the heat on high. He was dressed in a pair of faded jeans and a navy blue hoodie emblazoned with the Arizona State University logo. He'd spent the entire night cooped up in an airplane, but his thick blond hair did not appear to have a single strand out of place. Another strike against him.

"Did you have a good flight?" she asked.

"Not bad, considering."

"I was worried the airport might have been closed."

"Got lucky, I guess. Florida was heaven compared to this."

"Florida?"

Without losing the freaky grin, he nodded.

"I thought you lived in New Mexico?"

"I was working."

"Oh," she said, wanting to shut down that line of conversation before it got started.

They sat in silence for almost a minute. Signy leaned over the heater, warming her hands, wracking her brains for something to say.

Alex broke the impasse. "I'm glad you called."

She felt a clutch in her throat. Something she couldn't identify. She stuffed it back down. "What the hell," she said, throwing off her hood. "Can I say something?"

"Sure."

"Is it just me, or does this feel really weird."

"Bound to be strange at first, but we can make it work, don't you think?"

She looked directly into his blue eyes for the first time. "Cards on the table? There's something I think you should know before we go any further."

His intense smile faded a few watts.

"I called you because I had nowhere else to turn." She cleared her throat. "I'm not interested in a family reunion, especially not with you."

His smile faded a little more.

"So, if that's what you think this is all about, well . . ." She let the sentence go unfinished.

"Oh," he said.

"I'm sorry if that sounds harsh, but I need you to know where I stand on all this. If you're looking for some kind of hearth, home, and apple pie scenario, you're barking up the wrong tree. That's just not me."

She watched him look away. When he turned back again, the

silly grin was gone, replaced by the more sober expression she remembered.

"I understand," he said, putting his hand over his heart. "I'm here to help, nothing more." He looked out the window toward the house. "Is the girl inside?"

Signy felt an equal measure of relief and sadness at his abrupt change of tone, but she answered quickly in the affirmative.

"Right," he said, pushing open his door. "Let's get this show on the road."

Climbing out of the SUV, Signy led the way up to the house.

Chapter 44

"All set?" asked Alex, placing his hands lightly on Lizzy's shoulders.

Seated on a solid oak kitchen chair, Lizzy said, "Don't I get to watch?" She tugged at the towel she'd wrapped around her neck to protect her shirt from the dripping wet brown hair hanging halfway down her back.

Alex shook his head. "I think this will go a lot more smoothly if you hold off on the screaming until we're done."

"That bad, huh?" asked Signy, who was watching from a comfy chair in the living room. She had the baby in her lap. He was sucking on her braid with evident pleasure.

Rummaging in the bag of beauty supplies he'd purchased on his way to the cottage, Alex withdrew a pair of barber's scissors, clicking them open and shut experimentally.

"Oh, God," Lizzy said, holding her hands over her eyes.

"Not to worry, madame," said Alex, in a faux French accent, "I spent a couple of months working as an apprentice at a well-known salon in Austin."

"Oh, come on. Is that true?" Signy asked.

"Would I lie?"

"Do you really want me to answer that?"

Alex cleared his throat. "Probably not."

Watching Alex butcher Lizzy's hair, Signy had to work hard not to show her dismay. Disappearing was hard enough, but losing her hair could be even more traumatic for a young woman.

"Don't look yet," Alex said. He set aside the scissors, then handed Lizzy the box of hair dye. "Go have a shower, then use this. I'll finish it up once you come down."

Lizzy gazed down at the mounds of hair at her feet, then brought a tentative hand to her head.

"Go," said Alex, tilting her chair forward, forcing her to stand up.

"I don't mean to be a pain, but we do want to get out of here as soon as possible," Signy added.

"I'm going," Lizzy said, dragging her feet as she climbed the stairs, the box of hair dye hanging loosely in her fingers.

Alex watched her go, then walked over to where Signy was sitting with the baby. He leaned over and let Justin pull on his finger. "Wow. The kid must take after his father."

Signy looked down into the baby's face. "If his dad is George Clooney."

Alex coughed into his fist.

"Stop it, he's adorable."

"Come on. He looks like a cross between a baby orangutan and Kim Jong Un."

Signy examined the wisps of gauzy hair protruding from Justin's pumpkin head and couldn't suppress a smile.

"Ow," cried Alex, extracting his finger from the baby's mouth. "No one said he had teeth."

Smiling sweetly, Signy shook the baby's tiny hand. "Good boy."

Alex sat down in the chair opposite Signy.

Turning away from his intense gaze, she pretended to play with the baby.

"This is nice," he said, finally.

Plucking at her sleeve, Signy maneuvered her lips into a polite smile.

They sat like that for several minutes, both of them feigning great interest in the antics of the baby. Finally, Alex said, "Something very odd happened to me yesterday, and it might involve you."

"Me?"

"You were too young to remember the day our mother was killed, but I've looked into it, off and on, over the years. Up until recently, I had nothing to go on, no leads to follow." He leaned forward. "When I found you, I thought I finally had somewhere solid to start."

He searched her face for several seconds, then continued, "I was finally able to determine the approximate date she was murdered, and judging by how long we were in that car, I have some idea as to where." He scrubbed the top of his head with his hand. "I searched police and newspaper records from that time period, all over the region, and found nothing. Nada. No body, no murder, no investigation. It was as though she never existed."

"How can that be?"

"I don't know," he said. "It was a bloodbath. Not something that would go unnoticed."

Signy looked at him. His eyes had taken on a faraway look. "Don't take this the wrong way, but is there any chance that you might be wrong about what happened?"

He shook his head. "If anything, I wish I could forget."

"I'm just saying, the laying down of memories can be a tricky thing during a traumatic event, especially for children."

"I know what I saw," he insisted.

"There can't have been that many women killed during that time period. Why couldn't you find her?"

"The only thing that makes sense is that a third party swooped in and cleaned up. Erased every last shred of evidence that she'd ever been there."

Signy frowned. "You know about Occam's razor?"

"Sure, with two competing solutions to a problem, the most obvious is probably correct. The idea seemed far-fetched to me too." Alex leaned forward. "Until yesterday."

"Yesterday?"

"Someone figured out that I'd been looking into her murder. Whoever it is has been dogging my online footsteps, watching what I do, where I go. For all I know, they've figured out where I live."

Upstairs, they heard a loud thunk as Lizzy turned off the water in the shower.

Signy stared at Alex. "But why?"

Alex bent over and picked up a set of plastic keys the baby had just dropped on the floor. He jingled them in front of Justin's face until the child reached out a pudgy hand, then he let the boy pluck them from his fingers. "Have you ever read the book *Dr. Jekyll and Mr. Hyde*?"

"*Dr. Jekyll*? Maybe in high school. Why?"

"I'm not sure." Alex shook his head. "Someone seems to be sending me a message."

Signy hugged the baby close to her chest, her thoughts whirling. Overhead, the floorboards creaked.

Alex's eyes flicked upward. "First things first, though. I did a background check on her before I caught my flight. It's amazing how often people hold back crucial information."

She narrowed her eyes. "Have you done one on me?"

"Never," he grinned, crossing his heart. "But I did find something very interesting about Mrs. Stone. It seems that before Lizzy hooked up with Solomon Stone, there was no record of her having existed at all."

Signy frowned.

"Hey, you guys look intense." Lizzy Stone stood on the stairs, a towel covering her hair. "Everything okay?"

Signy shifted the baby onto her knees. "Just getting caught up."

"Come on down," said Alex, in a hearty tone. "Let's see the damage."

Lizzy resumed her seat in the kitchen chair, and Alex proceeded to dye her brows to match her newly blond hair. When he was done, he handed Lizzy a bag of clothes. "I had to guess at your size, but I think these might fit."

Lizzy peeked inside the bag, and a wide grin split her face. "It's been a long time since I've worn anything like this."

Alex smiled. "Go ahead. Let's see what happens."

As soon as Lizzy shut the bathroom door, Alex turned and walked back over to Signy. Dropping to one knee beside her, he said, "From what I've been able to find, Lizzy Stone never existed before she married Solomon Stone."

"What about her maiden name?"

"I found the marriage certificate easily enough and got her maiden name from there. Elizabeth Smith."

"Smith?" she said, skeptically.

He nodded. "That's what I thought as well. There are thousands of Elizabeth Smiths in the USA. Luckily, only two of them shared the birthdate that was on the marriage certificate."

"So?"

"One died in a drowning accident as a child, and the other lives in a convent."

"I doubt this Lizzy has ever been a nun," Signy said.

"Not to mention that Elizabeth Smith, the nun, is almost six feet tall and has no body hair."

"No hair?"

"Alopecia. Chronic hair loss. She's had it since she was fifteen."

Signy stared at Alex. "How do you know all this?"

"My guess? Your Lizzy took the identity of the drowning victim."

Signy stared at the floor. "She said she was a street kid and that she left home at thirteen when her stepfather began sexually abusing her. Maybe she wanted to leave that part of her life behind forever."

Alex tipped his head sideways. "Could be."

They both turned at the sound of the bathroom door cracking open.

Signy turned to look, Alex's disturbing revelation momentarily forgotten. Lizzy was transformed: platinum blond hair standing up in stiff spikes, her huge brown eyes obscured by dark eye shadow, a silver nose ring clipped onto one nostril. She was wearing black leather pants tucked into a pair of heavy Doc Martens boots. A matching leather motorcycle jacket studded with chains completed the ensemble.

Alex walked over and turned up the collar of Lizzy's jacket, adding a further air of menace to her already dangerous look. Standing back, he surveyed his work. "You'll do," he said, finally.

"I like it," said Lizzy, running a finger across her lips.

Heaving the baby onto her hip, Signy walked over to where Lizzy was examining herself in the mirror over the hearth. "I doubt even your husband would recognize you."

Lizzy tilted her head. "It's amazing, isn't it?"

Signy glanced at Alex, who was sweeping up the mountain of hair with a broom he'd found in the kitchen. "Is there anything you can't do?" she asked.

Chuckling, he bent down to sweep the hair into a dustpan. "I guess you could say I'm a jack of all trades."

"And modest," said Signy.

"And hungry. I think we should eat something here before we go. The fewer stops we have to make on the road, the better. What about you, little man?" Alex picked up the baby. "Do you want to help your Uncle Alex make some lunch?"

"We only have a couple of candy bars left," Signy said.

Alex touched the side of his nose. "I think I can do better than that. You two stay out here."

Signy eyed him. "You're just full of surprises."

He hoisted the baby onto his hip and walked into the kitchen.

Chapter 45

Grace swam back into the light. Her mouth felt dry, her tongue sticking to the roof of her mouth. Her eyelids were sticky, and it took some effort to peel them open. Her head felt like a hundred-pound weight and she let it fall to one side. Her eyes slowly focused. She could see the IV tube still connected to her arm. She ran her tongue over her lips, feeling the dry, bumpy ridges.

"Welcome back."

Her eyes snapped toward the voice. Stone was once again suited up in the white infection-control suit.

"Sorry about the little nap, Abby, but you were being such a bad girl, and I needed you to stay quiet for a bit. I injected a fast-acting neuroleptic. The effects will wear off shortly."

"What?" Grace lifted her head. Her arms and legs were still pinned to the bed, but at least her head was free. She looked down at two large rectangles sketched on her thighs with black marker. "What is this?"

Stone ignored her. Using a pair of forceps, he dipped a large cotton pad into an iodine solution, then spread the liquid over the rectangular markings on her thighs, scrubbing the area thoroughly.

Grace's flesh shivered in response.

"It is unfortunate that you refuse to cooperate," Stone said. He moved over to the cabinet and selected a tray laden with large needles. Picking up one of the needles, the doctor held it to the light and depressed the plunger a fraction of an inch.

"Wait." Grace rolled her eyes. Just to her left, she could see a cabinet laden with sharp instruments, glassware, and needles, any of which would be adequate to disable the insane doctor. Unfortunately, with her hands secured to the stretcher, they were of no use whatsoever.

"You're too late."

Grace coughed. "No. Something feels wrong in my throat."

He eyed her cautiously. "No more spitting. I don't want to have to knock you out again."

Grace inhaled sharply. "I'm having trouble swallowing."

Stone frowned and then set the loaded needle back down on the tray. "You may be experiencing a reaction to the drug. Open up."

Coughing, Grace opened her mouth.

Stone bent down until his forehead was almost touching hers. Using a light, he looked into her open mouth. "I don't see any swelling—"

Grace jerked her head up, driving her forehead into the bridge of his nose.

Stone dropped to his knees.

Grace thrashed against the restraints, screaming with frustration when she couldn't make the straps give even a tiny amount. She recoiled in horror as Stone hauled himself back to his feet. His nose dripped blood, and she could feel the warm splatters on her cheek.

Grabbing a bandage off the tray, he held it to his nose. He looked down at her, a pained expression on his face. "That was a very silly thing to do."

"Go to hell."

Stone pulled the bandage from his nose and looked at it. "No permanent damage."

Grace watched with disgust as he twisted a bit of tissue into a ball and stuffed it up his nostril.

"I was going to give you some pain medication. I'm not a monster, but you've really begun to irritate me, Abby. I think a little reality check is in line." Tossing the needle aside, he picked up a much larger bore needle.

Grace recoiled.

"I'm loading this with a simple saline solution." He filled the huge needle with clear liquid, then scraped the sharp needle along one of the black lines on Grace's thigh. "I'll inject this under your skin, to make it easier to harvest the necessary samples."

"No, please."

Stone probed the balled-up tissue in his nostril. "Think of it this way: at least your paltry little life will have meant something in the end." He bent over and shoved the tip of the needle inside the rectangle just under the surface of Grace's thigh, slowly depressing the plunger until he had injected the entire contents of the needle.

Grace bit down on her bottom lip until it bled.

Stone filled the needle again. "On the other hand, we could stop this right now. All you have to do is tell me where Lizzy has taken my son."

"I told you. I don't know where they are," Grace said, banishing any thoughts of Signy from her mind.

Stone sighed. "As you wish."

The jab and stick process continued until the flesh on her thighs was puffy with liquid. Tears ran down her cheeks, soaking the bed sheet underneath her head.

Through it all, Grace never uttered a sound.

Chapter 46

Leaving Alex to putter about in the kitchen, Signy and Lizzy went upstairs to tidy up. Signy did not want to leave any traces of their presence in the cottage. While Lizzy cleaned the bathroom, Signy used a roll of paper towels and some cleaning fluid to wipe down all the surfaces they might have touched in the bedrooms.

As Signy cleaned the master bedroom, she thought about what Alex had discovered. Lizzy had assumed the identity of a dead girl before marrying Solomon Stone. Had she been that desperate to escape the trauma of her childhood and life on the street? Remembering the flash of rage in Lizzy's eyes during those tense few seconds as they'd struggled for the knife, and the criss-cross of self-inflicted wounds on the inside of her arms, Signy frowned. Like freshwater icebergs bobbing out on the lake, there appeared to be much more to Lizzy Stone than she allowed the world to see.

As she wiped down the windowsill, Signy looked out over the

front yard, squinting against the glare of the flat white light. Her eyes burned, three nights of poor sleep catching up with her.

She was about to turn back into the room when she thought she saw a flurry of snow rising into the sky about halfway down the peninsula. She opened her eyes wide. Hidden by a dense thicket of cedar forest on three sides and the wide expanse of the lake on the other, the goings-on in the cottage should have been invisible to prying eyes. There should not be a vehicle heading this way.

She peeked out the window again. The double tracks left by Alex's SUV were visible in the new snow. She supposed it was possible that someone had taken note of the fresh tracks and sounded the alarm. She watched wide-eyed for several more minutes, but there was no further sign of movement. Maybe it had been just another snowmobiler out for a joyride.

Turning away from the window, she caught the scent of something delicious wafting up the stairs. She felt her mouth water. Leaving the bedroom, she decided not to mention anything to Alex and Lizzy. There was no use putting them on the alert for what was probably no more than a figment of her overwrought imagination.

She popped her head into the bathroom on her way out. "Smell that? Don't tell him I said this, but it looks like Alex can do anything. Ready for something to eat?"

Lizzy smiled. "He really is amazing."

"Soon as we're done, we'll get going," Signy said, as they headed back downstairs. "I don't want to push our luck by staying here any longer than we have to."

The air in the kitchen was redolent with the scent of sautéed onions and garlic. Alex stood at the stove, stirring a pot full of bubbling tomato sauce. On the back burner, pasta boiled in a deep pot of water. At his feet, Justin sat propped against a cupboard door, gumming a potholder.

"You win," Signy said, "Where did you find all this?"

Alex tossed a handful of dried herbs into the pot. "On my way in, I noticed corn stalks sticking up out of the snow out front. I figured they must have a garden in the summer. Where there are fresh veggies, there is often a cold cellar. Especially in a place this size."

"You even set the table," Signy said, noticing the red and white checked tablecloth.

"No wine, I'm afraid. I figured with the long drive ahead, we better stick to water." He reached into the fridge and produced a bottle of chilled San Pellegrino. "At least I found a bottle of the good stuff."

"Feels like a party," Lizzy said. "What are we celebrating?"

Alex twisted the cap from the bottle of sparkling water. "Oh, I don't know," he said, filling each glass in turn. "New beginnings, I guess." He shot a glance at Signy from the corner of his eye.

"I'll drink to that," Lizzy said.

"I'm just glad to be eating some real food," Signy said, as she rummaged through the cupboards. Finding a colander, she joined Alex at the counter.

Lizzy retrieved Justin from the floor and sat him on her lap. Before long they each had a plate of steaming spaghetti and marinara sauce in front of them. Lizzy and Signy tucked into their food with gusto, while Alex proceeded at a more sedate pace.

Signy offered the baby a strand of spaghetti and watched with amusement as he tried to make sense of the sticky noodle. She laughed when, having lost track of his prize, he pursed his tiny lips. Peeling the strand from where he'd plastered it to the top of his head, Lizzy handed it back. His eyes crossed as he examined his new toy.

Avoiding the topic of Lizzy's identity, Signy discussed their plans for the next couple of days. They would dump the Malibu in the woods, where, with luck, it would remain hidden until spring. Then they'd take the Yukon to Chicago, where with even more luck, they'd hook up with the Midwest conductor. If not, Signy would proceed with Lizzy on her own.

Alex had suggested that it would make more sense for them to travel as a group all the way to California, as the authorities were looking for two women and a baby, not two women, a baby, and a man. They'd gone back and forth on the subject, Signy arguing that she'd have to check with Maitland when she could, but they hadn't reached a resolution by the time their plates were clean.

"We should get moving," Signy said, checking her watch.

"How about you and I do up these dishes, while Lizzy gets the baby changed and ready to go," Alex said.

Lizzy tucked a finger down the back of the baby's diaper and sniffed. "Good call."

After Lizzy left the room, Alex used a napkin to gently lift Lizzy's water glass from the table.

Signy shot him a puzzled glance.

"I don't like loose ends." He carried the glass over to his computer.

As she filled the sink, Signy watched him examine the glass.

"It's not necessary to have a high-tech crime lab in order to retrieve fingerprints," Alex said. He held up the small tin of Fry's cocoa powder.

She watched with fascination as Alex dusted Lizzy's water glass with a fine film of the dark cocoa powder. When he was done, he held the glass up and she could easily see the perfect outline of Lizzy's unique thumbprint. He took a picture of the print with his cellphone and then sent the image to his computer.

"Amazing," Signy said, unable to hide her admiration. "Now what?"

Alex winked and tapped in a few commands on the computer keyboard.

Signy looked over his shoulder as she dried the last of the pots.

"Now we wait to see if there's a match with IAFIS," he said. "Shouldn't take long." He walked over to the dish strainer and grabbed a handful of cutlery.

"IAFIS?"

"The FBI fingerprint database. We'll be able to compare Lizzy's prints to over seventy million records."

Signy twisted a tea towel in her hands. "You're hacking into an FBI database?"

"*Hacking* is a dated term. What happens is—"

She held up the towel. "It's probably better if you don't tell me, don't you think?"

Alex smiled. "Probably."

Shaking her head, she walked back over to the strainer, and started in on the last glass.

Alex tucked the two pots inside one another and shoved them back into a drawer under the oven.

"Tell me about the Painted Desert," she said.

He glanced at her, a quizzical expression on his face.

"You told me that was where you grew up."

He nodded.

"Sounds exotic. How did you end up so far away?"

He shrugged. "That, I'm afraid, is the sixty-four-thousand-dollar question."

Signy flicked her eyes to the ceiling. "Right, sorry."

"Anyway, I loved it. Nobody around for miles in any direction. Just my mother and I, all alone in our hogan. It was a good childhood. What about you? Were you happy?"

"Your mother?" Signy asked.

"My adoptive mother, I guess you'd say, although I doubt there was anything formal put down on paper. She didn't work that way."

"She's gone now?"

"Almost ten years ago."

"I'm sorry."

"And you?"

"Foster parents. David and Sarah Shepherd. Both gone. Cancer."

"Rough. You miss them?"

"Sometimes, but when you're only one child among so many others, you don't establish the same tight bond. You were lucky."

"I'm not sure *lucky* is exactly the right word." Alex shrugged.

"Maybe not. But given what we both went through, life could have turned out a lot worse." Signy wiped off the counter with the dishtowel, then hung it neatly on the rack where she'd found it. "You do seem to be fairly accomplished."

"True," he said, grinning at her.

She rolled her eyes. "Seriously, though, it would be cool if you'd teach me some of that computer stuff."

A pinging alarm coming from the computer caught Alex's attention. "I'd be happy to, but only if you teach me some of those crazy winter-driving skills of yours. That was some display you put on at the embassy."

"The embassy?" Signy's smile died.

Standing in front of the computer, Alex froze.

"What are you talking about?" she said.

"What? Nothing."

"How do you know about the embassy?"

"How about you forget I said anything?"

"Hold on. You were there?" Signy felt her voice rise a full octave.

"Can we talk about it later?" Alex said, his eyes fixed on the screen.

"Oh my God. Are you kidding me?"

"We really have to talk about this another time," Alex said, a note of urgency in his voice. "We got a hit on Lizzy's prints. Look at this." He pointed at the screen.

Cheeks flaming, Signy reluctantly moved closer in order to look over his shoulder. The first thing she saw was a picture of a woman with red hair and blue eyes. The chin was different, and the face was rounder, but there was no doubt it was Lizzy.

"Read that," he said, pointing at the screen.

Signy scanned the text below the picture of a young Lizzy Stone. "That can't be right."

"IAFIS doesn't lie. Looks like your passenger has some explaining to do," he said.

Upstairs, they heard Justin Stone scream.

Chapter 47

Signy stared at Alex. "Justin Stone isn't Lizzy's baby."

"He can't be," Alex agreed.

"Then who the hell is he?" Signy bit her bottom lip. "And where is his mother?"

"An interesting question."

"I'm going to go talk to her. You stay here."

"Is that wise?"

Signy pursed her lips. "I can take care of myself."

Alex sighed. "I never said you couldn't."

"Whatever," Signy said, stomping away from him.

"Signy, wait."

"Oh ya," she said, over her shoulder. "When this is over, you can explain why you've been stalking me."

"I haven't been—"

Signy pushed through the kitchen door and into the living room, cutting off his lame reply. Lizzy was coming down the stairs, bag in hand. Tucked into his car seat, the baby waited by the front door.

"Where's Alex?" Lizzy said, looking over Signy's shoulder.

Signy glanced toward the kitchen door. "He's just finishing up, but hey, can we talk for a minute?"

Lizzy reached into the closet and grabbed her parka. "Sure," she said, turning back to Signy, "what's up?"

Signy took a seat on the couch and patted the spot beside her.

Lizzy picked up the car seat and walked over. "Sounds serious," she said, as she set the baby down at her feet.

Signy looked down at the baby, then back up at Lizzy. "There's no easy way to say this."

Lizzy frowned. "What is it? What's wrong?"

Signy leaned down and gripped the baby's tiny fingers inside her own. "Justin isn't your baby, is he?"

Lizzy backed away.

Signy watched her closely. "It's true. Justin isn't your baby. He can't be."

"You don't know what you're talking about," Lizzy cried, shaking her head.

Please come and sit down. I just want to talk to you."

"No. To hell with you. I'm out of here." Lizzy turned to flee, grabbing her coat off a hook by the front door.

"When you were thirteen," Signy said, quietly, "you were repeatedly raped by your stepfather. You were injured so badly that the doctor had to remove your uterus in order to save your life."

Her eyes bright with tears, Lizzy let the coat slip from her hands.

"He was sentenced to ten years, and your mother went away for six months for failing to provide the necessities of life."

"No, please—" Lizzy held up her hands.

"You ended up in the foster system, but you ran away, didn't you? That part of your story was true."

Signy watched Lizzy open her mouth to speak, but no words came out.

"As was the fact that you were a survivor. You did what you had to in order to stay alive. I get that."

"That foster home, the father—" Lizzy whispered.

Signy's mouth twisted downward. "I can guess."

"I couldn't let them take me back."

"I know," Signy said. "I would have done exactly the same thing if I'd been in your shoes."

Tears spilled down Lizzy's cheeks, and she took a step forward.

"But, then the police found you in a motel room with a john. You'd been badly beaten."

"Son-of-a-bitch tried to kill me," Lizzy said, her voice ragged.

Signy walked over and picked up Lizzy's hands in hers. "So you stabbed him."

Lizzy's chin fell onto her chest.

"You killed him before he could hurt you anymore?"

Lizzy nodded.

"Then you disappeared before the investigation was complete."

"I had to." Lizzy hung her head. "I couldn't go to jail."

Signy drew Lizzy into a hug.

The two women stood that way for some time, Signy murmuring gentle words, Lizzy as rigid as a block of wood inside her arms.

Finally, Signy took a step back and looked into Lizzy's swollen eyes. "Who is he?" she asked, glancing at the baby.

Lizzy collapsed onto the couch as though all the air had gone out of her.

Justin babbled at her. "Mum . . . mum . . . mum . . . mum . . ."

Lizzy sniffed. "After the attack, I had to go to the free clinic for weekly follow-ups. Bandage changes, antibiotics, that sort of thing. That's where I met Solomon." Lizzy glanced up. "Everything I told you about him was true. He was the first man I'd ever met who loved me for me. He was sweet, kind, and gentle. He felt so terrible about everything that had happened to me, and he couldn't do enough to make me feel better. He knew how terrified I was of prison, so he told me that if I wanted, he could change my appearance and we could run away together."

"He must have seemed like a knight in shining armour."

"Not just seemed," Lizzy said, "he was. He rescued me from hell on earth."

"And the baby?" Signy asked, glancing at Justin, who was pumping his legs and writhing inside the car seat.

Lizzy sat up straighter. "We moved to Seattle. He changed my appearance, and I became Lizzy Smith. When I was old enough, we got married. Solomon never stopped being a compassionate advocate for street kids. I loved that about him. As I said, we've often had kids come to stay in our home for a few days, sometimes even longer. And Solomon never stopped giving a few free hours a week to the local clinic, no matter where we lived."

Justin clawed at his restraints, squawking in irritation.

"He did that in Rochester too?" Signy asked, poking the baby in the belly in an attempt to distract him.

"That's where he found Katy." Lizzy drew in a ragged breath. "Justin's biological mother."

The two women turned as Alex slipped into the living room from the kitchen.

Lizzy stared at Signy.

"It's okay. He knows."

Alex smiled at Lizzy. "How about I bounce him around for a bit? Get him good and tired for the car?" He bent down and unhooked Justin from the car seat, then flipped him up and into the air. Justin squealed with delight.

Lizzy squeezed out a grateful smile.

"Katy?" Signy prompted.

"She came to stay with us about a year ago. She was a sixteen-year-old runaway. Her parents were from Russia. They'd come into the country illegally. Katy had no passport, had never been enrolled in school, and she was four months pregnant. Solomon asked if he could bring her home, and of course I said yes." Lizzy sighed. "Solomon had always wanted us to have children, but we couldn't go the normal adoption route."

"Because of the outstanding murder investigation?" Signy asked.

Lizzy nodded. "I'd never pass the rigorous background checks. With enough digging, Solomon believed, they'd eventually discover my real identity."

"He was right," Alex said.

"So we made a deal with Katy. We'd let her stay with us through her pregnancy. Solomon would give her all the medical care she needed and would deliver the baby. In return, she'd let us raise her child as our own without having to go through any formal adoption process."

"Sounds reasonable, I guess," Signy said.

"It was, until Solomon discovered something special about Justin," Lizzy said, wringing her hands inside her lap. "Have you heard what he found?"

Signy nodded. "He's discovered a technique that will revolutionize burn repair. Some kind of biological tissue replacement."

"Not just that," Lizzy said. "The stem cells he used to develop the tissue replacement are rare. Almost unheard of, as a matter of fact."

Alex tilted his head. "Meaning?"

"Most cells have a set lifespan, especially in the lab. It's hard to keep a cell line going for more than a few months. But not this one. As long as he keeps it in the right conditions, it will go on forever."

"Hold it," Alex interjected. "I read something like that a couple years ago. A woman with cancer, wasn't it?"

Lizzy nodded. "Henrietta Lacks. She was dying of cervical cancer, and when they took a specimen to study, they discovered that her cells just kept on going."

"Right, I remember now." Alex nodded. "HeLa cells. They still use them for cancer research don't they?"

"Not only cancer. HeLa line became *the* human cell line for all sorts of scientific inquiry. Aging, vaccine development, understanding viruses, in-vitro fertilization, you name it."

"So, let me get this right," Signy said. "You're saying that your husband discovered another immortal cell line? Different from these HeLa cells?"

Lizzy nodded. "Only this new line originated in the foreskin of a baby."

Signy stared at Lizzy and then glanced over at the baby, tucked safely inside Alex's arms.

Lizzy nodded. "As soon as Solomon discovered what he had with this baby, everything changed. He couldn't let Katy go, for one thing."

"Of course not. She was the baby's mother," Alex said. "She might also have the mutation that caused the immortal cell line."

"Exactly," Lizzy confirmed. "He started running tests on her, taking skin biopsies, that kind of thing."

"Why didn't she just take the baby and run?" Signy asked.

"Solomon threatened her. Said if she tried anything like that, he'd kill Justin." Lizzy shook her head. "But not before he harvested every last strip of skin from his body."

"Where is she now?" Alex asked.

Lizzy paused for several seconds, looking down at her hands. Finally, she raised her head and looked straight at Signy. "The day that Solomon left for the conference, Katy disappeared. She just left the baby and ran. I knew that Solomon would blame me. Katy and I never really got along. I wasn't lying when I told you earlier that Solomon prefers younger girls."

"But you haven't been exactly truthful either," Alex said.

"I have. I am. I've told you everything."

"Not quite."

"Alex?" Signy asked, frowning at him.

Keeping one eye on Lizzy, he turned to look at Signy. "I checked further into Lizzy's juvenile record while you two were talking. Before she ever met Solomon Stone, Lizzy had quite the history."

"No. That's not true," Lizzy said.

"Court records don't lie, I'm afraid."

"What are you talking about, Alex?" Signy asked.

"Before she was fourteen, Lizzy was convicted in juvenile court of aggravated assault."

"You don't understand," Lizzy said.

"Not once, but three times," Alex continued. "In one case, the young lady that Lizzy attacked suffered permanent brain damage."

Signy's heart sank as she remembered the flash of rage in Lizzy's eyes when they had struggled for the knife outside the Superstore. "Lizzy? Is this true?"

Lizzy wiped her mouth with the back of her hand. "What do you want me to say? You have no idea what it's like to have enough money in your pocket to buy some food, only to have someone come along and steal it from you. Or to put your trust in someone, only to find out that her plan all along has been to sell you to her pimp."

"Two of the girls were much younger that you," Alex said quietly.

Lizzy glared at Alex. "You think I'm lying, don't you? About my husband, Katy, the baby? Everything?"

"Honestly?" Alex said. "I don't know what to believe."

Lizzy jumped to her feet. "I can prove it. After Katy disappeared, I went to Solomon's lab to see if she was down there. She sometimes helped him with his work. She wasn't, so I logged into his computer to see if I could find some sort of clue as to where she might have gone."

"And?"

Shaking her head, she fished in her pocket and pulled out a USB key.

"What is it?" Alex asked.

Lizzy turned to Signy, tears spilling from her eyes. "Those kids we took into our home? Those kids that trusted him with everything? He used them like lab animals." Her hand was trembling as she held up the USB key. "I copied this from his computer before I left." She threw the key at Alex.

Alex caught it in one hand.

Lizzy glared at Signy, a miserable expression on her face.

Retrieving his Mac Pro from the kitchen, Alex slipped the key into a port, then tapped in a couple of quick commands.

When the screen flickered to life, Signy barely had time to pull a chair under her before her legs collapsed.

Chapter 48

Dr. Stone set aside the tray of empty needles. "That wasn't so bad, was it?" He probed the swollen tissue in her thighs.

Grace moaned.

"Oh, by the way. In all the excitement, I forgot to mention that the police called. Apparently, your colleague Carole White is proving elusive. Either she's using a fake identity or she's some sort of ghost." Stone bent over the tray of instruments on the cabinet and selected what appeared to be some type of medical-grade cheese slicer.

Grace squeezed her eyes shut.

"I'm a man of science, of course. I don't believe in spirits. I don't think you do either, Abby, if that really is your name." He held up the instrument. "Are we ready?"

"No," Grace said, "don't."

Stone touched the blade of the cheese slicer to Grace's swollen thigh. "It's up to you."

Grace shook her head. "I don't know. I don't."

"Let's see if we can't change your mind." Stone flipped down the visor of his decontamination suit, then drove the slicer into Grace's flesh.

A flare of pain flashed up Grace's spinal column and she felt the tendons in her neck stretch to popping.

Stone bent to his work, inching the slicer up with one hand, using the pen mark as a guide. With the other hand, he caught the inch-wide strip of flesh he'd trimmed from Grace's thigh.

A deep moan escaped her lips.

"Good," Stone hummed. "Very nice." He laid a six-inch strip of Grace's flesh onto a tray lined with damp gauze. Using forceps, he wrapped the gauze gently around the excised skin, then placed the little package inside what looked like a steel pot.

Grace could not believe the agony. Even on her worst day after the shooting, the pain had been nothing compared to this. She could hear screaming in the distance and wanted to tell whoever was carrying on so to shut the hell up.

"Who is Carole White?" Stone placed the slicer on Grace's skin, parallel to the first cut.

Grace wrenched her neck until she thought her spine would crack. The screaming in the distance got closer. She clamped her jaws shut.

Stone slid the slicer deep into Grace's flesh.

Grace felt a warm heat suffuse her body. She smiled and opened her eyes.

"Crazy, isn't it?"

She turned toward the familiar voice. "Ethan?"

"Hi, Gracie."

Grace stared at her brother. They were standing on the Bloor Street Viaduct, high over the Don Valley Parkway in Toronto. Far below, cars whizzed by. "Is it really you?"

"In the flesh," he said, with a chuckle. He flicked his fingers, stirring a fine white mist that seemed to blur the outline of his body. "Sort of."

"But, you're—?"

Her brother smiled and looked over the railing. "Long way down, isn't it?"

She peered over the edge. Far below, she could see gorgeous fall colours lighting up the ravine on either side of the highway. Grace felt a burning pain in her legs. She winced.

He placed an arm on her shoulders and drew her close.

She snuggled against his thin chest, noting with amusement that he was wearing his Question Authority T-shirt. She ran a finger over the words embossed on the soft cotton fabric.

"What are you up to, little sister?"

"I'm tired." Grace did feel tired. More exhausted than she had ever felt in her life. It was as though a great weight had been fixed to each of her limbs, and the cars whizzing past so far below made her feel dizzy.

"You've been keeping secrets again, haven't you, Gracie?"

"No," she said, sticking out her bottom lip.

Ethan punched her playfully on the arm. "Liar, liar, pants on fire."

Grace giggled and shoved him away. "You're not the boss of me."

Laughing, he climbed up onto the railing.

"Ethan, stop it. That's not funny." Grace stomped her feet.

He grinned down at her and lifted his knee until he was balancing on only one foot. White mist swirled like smoke around his head. "No more secrets, Gracie." He danced on the railing, his arms flailing.

"Stop that," Grace cried. "I can't."

He jumped back down and swept her into his arms. "You're not me, Gracie. You can do anything you want."

"I'm too tired," she said.

He looked over his shoulder and then touched each of her eyelids with the tip of his thumb. "We have time. Why don't you rest for a bit? You'll feel better when you wake up."

He sat down on a bench and pulled her down beside him. Putting his arm around her, he laid her head down on his lap. The last thing she felt was his gentle touch on her hair.

Solomon Stone pointed the flashlight into his patient's eye and saw her pupils fixed and dilated. "Damn," he whispered. He pulled a stethoscope off the cabinet and checked her heart and lungs and found everything normal, but when he tried to move her fingers, he found them rigid. He pinched a bit of skin on her breast and twisted, but she gave no reaction to the stimuli. Neither did she react when he poked a needle into the soles of her feet.

Stone stood back from the stretcher and ripped off his gloves. He looked down at the naked woman, the open wound on her thigh pulpy and oozing fluid. "I don't have time to play hide-and-seek, Abby," Stone said with disgust. "Come out, come out, wherever you are."

Grace didn't answer.

Chapter 49

Sitting side by side on the couch, Signy and Alex watched the video Lizzy had taken from Solomon Stone's computer. What appeared at first to be a perfectly ordinary hospital room swam into focus, a Stryker bed, its white plastic sides fully raised, a green oxygen tank standing alongside. Blood pressure and cardiac monitors, IV hooks and a tangled array of wires and tubes dangled from steel poles at the head of the bed.

The picture was shaky, but it soon became clear that this was no typical hospital room. Underneath the array of equipment, a young girl writhed amid twisted sheets, her wrists fixed by thick leather straps to the sides of the bed, her ankles similarly immobilized.

"Subject 27" scrolled across the top of the screen in white lettering. "I picked this one at random," Lizzy said. "There were many more just like it."

"Christ," Alex muttered.

Long, dark hair tangled around the young victim's face. Mid to late teens, more or less. Her head thrashed back and forth, her mouth opening and closing with what appeared to be panicked screams.

Signy was grateful that there was no sound on the video. "Hold on a sec," she said. Leaning forward, she pressed the pause button. "I've seen this girl before."

Lizzy glanced at Signy. "I don't know how you could have. Her name is Sandra. I remember her from a couple of years ago. Solomon brought her home for a few days. She was kind of quiet, but nice."

"Sandra," Signy repeated, staring off into space. "Yes, I saw her picture on a missing persons poster in Priya Subramanian's office." She glanced at Lizzy. "Surely you must have seen it?"

Lizzy shook her head. "Even if I had, I would have assumed that Sandra had simply fallen back into her old ways."

Signy nodded, then leaned forward and restarted the video. A figure clad in a white biological protection suit strode into the picture, back to the camera. The girl's lips moved frantically, but the shrouded figure answered her pleas by shoving a black ball about the size of a large plum into her mouth.

Over the next few minutes, Signy watched a nightmare unfold. The figure in white used long-bladed scissors to cut off the girl's clothing. She wore a navy sweater over a long-sleeved pink shirt and a pair of worn jeans. Her feet were bare. Signy felt tears prick behind her eyes when the figure snipped off the girl's underwear, a pair of white, low-rise briefs printed with tiny pink hearts.

She was mildly obese, the weight of her heavy breasts dragging them down to either side of her chest, the loose flesh of her abdomen and upper thighs criss-crossed with silvery stretch marks. Both knees appeared badly scraped and her feet were black with grime. Her painted toenails were chipped.

Alex stopped the video. "Had she recently given birth?"

"Solomon helped. Once she was back on her feet, he told me he'd taken them both to a young mothers' centre."

"Another baby?" Alex glanced at Lizzy. "More stem cells? How many pregnant women did he have out there?"

"Some." Lizzy glanced at him. "But I didn't know what was going on, I swear." She twisted round to look at Signy. "You have to believe me. If I'd known . . . I mean, my God."

Biting hard on her lip, Signy restarted the video.

Removing a felt-tipped marker from his pocket, the figure flipped off the cap, then bent down and drew the tip across the girl's left thigh, outlining a large rectangular shape. The girl bucked, causing the marker to slip and an errant line to criss-cross the neat rectangle. A latex-covered hand whipped out and twisted her breast viciously. When the pen outlined a similar rectangle across her second thigh, the girl remained perfectly still.

The shot faded to black.

Lizzy Stone reached out and paused the video. "It gets a lot worse from here. Are you sure you want to keep going?"

"Play it," Alex said.

Lizzy looked at Signy.

Signy nodded.

Lizzy pushed the start button. "You can tell from the time signature that several hours have passed since the last segment."

"Oh my God," Signy said, as she realized that she was looking at the same young woman, nude and tied down to the bed. Only now, all the skin flayed from her thighs, her flesh was a pulpy, bloody mass, oozing with clear bodily fluids. The doctor pried open an eyelid.

"Why is he doing this?" Signy whispered.

"You'll see," Lizzy said.

Immobilized on a gurney, the girl was wheeled down a dark hallway. There was still no audio, but Signy could almost imagine the screech of the wheels against the concrete floor echoing in the narrow space.

The girl was naked from the waist up, her lower half clothed in heavy white pants, her feet encased in boots made of the same material. Signy looked closer, then felt the hair on the back of her neck rise. She was sure she'd seen protective clothing like this before.

The girl bucked against the four-point restraints as the gurney came to an abrupt halt.

A figure, clad head to toe in the same white material, moved into the shot and unbuckled her arms and legs. When she flew from the bed and tried to rush past the ghostly figure, a gloved hand lashed out and caught her a glancing blow on the chin. She dropped to the floor.

Bending over, the figure hauled the girl to her feet and dragged her over to the wall. Embedded in the cinder block at shoulder height were two metal shackles. The figure clamped the girl into the restraints, her face to the wall, her naked back exposed, and then placed a helmet on her head, using thick black electrical tape to secure it around her neck.

What happened in the next few seconds was more horrific than Signy could have ever imagined.

The figure shuffled into a corner, lifted what appeared to be a propane tank, and slung the attached harness over his shoulder. Reaching back, the figure unclipped a metal nozzle from the tank and aimed it at the girl's naked back.

A white-hot flame shot out, hitting the girl squarely on her back. The figure played the flame back and forth over her back and arms until the flesh turned red, bubbled up, and finally cooked into a black crispy layer. The charred flesh peeled away, hanging in sheets from her back and arms. Melted fat ran down her back.

The girl had slumped in the restraints. On both sides of her upper back, the white tips of her scapulae were showing through red layers of exposed muscle tissue. The hanging skin covered the seat of her white pants like a black sweater tied around her waist.

The figure halted the flame and shrugged off the tank. Placing it on the ground, he moved forward and inspected the damage. Satisfied, he unhooked the unconscious girl from the manacles and laid her face down on the gurney.

The figure undid the zipper, then stepped out of the protective suit. As he turned toward the camera, Signy could see Dr. Solomon Stone, licking his lips.

Scrambling to her feet, Signy fled into the bathroom.

Alex lunged for the stop button.

Alex and Lizzy stared at each other, listening to Signy heave up her lunch. Signy reappeared a few minutes later, wiping her mouth on a tissue.

"Do you believe me now? If you watched a bit further, you'd see him use the skin that he harvested from her thighs to try and repair the burns on her back."

Signy waved a hand. "I can't."

"That's why Katy took off. That's why I had to take Justin and run."

Signy nodded, dumbly.

"Before I left, I trashed his lab. I dumped every single container of his precious cells down the drain. It was all I could do to try and stop him."

Signy looked at Alex. "Any more questions?"

Alex stared at the blank screen. The heinous content notwithstanding, something else about the video was bothering him. Try as he might, he couldn't put his finger on what it was. He shook his head.

"Okay," Signy said, "let's get the hell out of here."

"Thank God," Lizzy whispered. She reached for the USB key, but Alex had already slipped it into his pocket.

Chapter 50

Listening to the police detective explain at length why they still had no idea where Lizzy and Justin might be, Stone thought he might smash the phone onto the concrete floor. You couldn't find your dick if you were holding it in your hand, he felt like shouting to the thick-headed fool. Instead, he played the role of grieving husband and father, agreeing to stay close to home in case Lizzy decided to come back on her own. It took every ounce of self-control he possessed to thank the cop for his hard work and gently hang up the phone.

Stone glared down at his unconscious patient. He was sure that Abby Lieberman knew where the elusive Carole White had taken his wife and son, but the damned woman had outwitted him by taking a voluntary trip to never-never land, and nothing he did was able to rouse her.

He'd need to take another tack. If Muhammad couldn't go to

the mountain, then he'd make the mountain come to Muhammad. Perhaps if Ms. White learned that Abby was his unwilling guest, she might be willing to make a trade. He needed to make contact with Carole White. How?

He started with the land line. Abby had used his phone to place a call earlier. She'd told him she needed to let a colleague know that she was going to be late. Carole White perhaps? Checking the call history on the phone display, he found that she had in fact made two calls.

He dialled the first number but was frustrated when the only response was an automatic voice telling him the customer was unavailable. A call to the second number yielded the same result.

Stabbing the off button, he went looking for Abby's cellphone. He made a circuit of the house, checking in all the rooms she'd visited, pausing in the library to replace the Harry Potter volumes. He shook his head. He knew she'd read the inscriptions. Too bad he'd been unable to tell her how badly she'd misinterpreted what she'd read. She might have helped him had she known.

It was a moot point. Hindsight was 20/20, and if he wanted to salvage the situation, he needed to find her damn phone. Exiting the library, he remembered hanging her coat in the front hall closet. A few seconds later, he found what he was looking for inside her coat pocket.

After powering up the device, he looked at the screen and almost screamed with frustration. The bitch had password-protected the damn thing. Overwhelmed by a growing desperation, Stone tore down the stairs, racing through the maze until he reached the treatment room.

Striding over to the patient, he performed a rough exam, checking for signs that she might have regained consciousness. Still out. Taking a deep breath, he resisted the urge to bash her head in. He needed that password.

He glanced around the room. The usual treatments hadn't worked. He'd have to find something a little more productive. His gaze fell on the portable defibrillator he kept handy for those odd occasions when patients tried to check out early. He selected his subjects with care, ensuring that they were as young and healthy as possible. Much older, and they might not survive the devastating injuries. Still, every once in a while, a weak heart would give out.

He turned on the machine and removed the paddles. He watched the gauge, waiting until the electrical current had built to its maximum voltage. Squirting gel onto each paddle, he held them over her ample breasts. "Wakey, wakey, sleepyhead," he shouted, and then slammed the paddles down onto her chest.

"Breakfast is ready, *pollito*."

"Stop calling me that," Grace said.

The older woman screwed her face into a mock scowl.

"I'm turning fifteen, you know," Grace said, eyeing with cautious respect the tea towel the woman was snapping against the side of her leg.

Bushy dark eyebrows disappeared under a helmet of coarse, salt and pepper hair. "*Dios mío!* I hadn't heard."

Grace rolled her eyes, then turned back to the screen. Hearing the squeak of Eugenia's crepe soles draw closer, she turtled her head down between her shoulders, steeling herself against the business end of the twisted cloth. Instead she felt only the rumble of suppressed laughter against the back of her neck.

"What are you studying?"

"Deductive reasoning."

"Logic? You?"

Grace narrowed her eyes. "I'll have you know I'm top of my class."

"Uh-huh."

"Doubting Thomas," said Grace. "You asked for it." She poked an index finger into the air and assumed a professorial tone. "I think we can both agree that all *pollitos* are baby chickens."

"*Sí*," said Eugenia, with a wide grin.

"And I believe we can take it as a given that *I* am neither a chicken nor an infant."

Eugenia nodded her head, solemnly.

"Ipso facto," Grace said, "you should stop calling me your *pollito*."

"Ipso facto," Eugenia repeated, rolling the unfamiliar words around her tongue.

"It means—"

"I know what it means," said Eugenia, grabbing Grace's cheeks between her meaty hands and giving her a face a tender squeeze. "It means that someone is feeling a little fowl this morning."

The giggle forming in Grace's throat died. "What's that?" she asked, jerking her head toward the sound of screaming coming from downstairs.

Eugenia brought a hand to her throat. "*Qué es eso*?" She rushed from the room.

Grace stood motionless, hands over her ears.

"Gracie? Can you hear me?"

Seeing her brother standing in her doorway, she rushed across the room and into his arms. "Ethan? What's happening? Why are you home from university?"

He squeezed her tight. "Mummy's had some bad news."

"News?" Grace pushed him away and covered her eyes with her hands. "What day is it?"

"Wednesday."

"Wednesday's child is full of woe," Grace whispered.

"Gracie, I'm so sorry."

Grace looked at her hands. "These can't be mine. Look at the skin. It's all spotty."

He grabbed one of her hands and placed it over his heart. "Your skin looks beautiful. You're beautiful. I'm so proud of you."

Grace glared at him. "You left without saying goodbye."

"I couldn't help it. I would have stayed if I could."

Grace felt her spine stiffen. "That was the last time Eugenia called me her little *pollito*." In the distance, she heard the screaming again. It didn't sound like anything she'd ever heard before. She turned toward the sound.

"Don't," said her brother, drawing her back into his arms. "Don't look."

"Is someone in trouble? Is it Mummy?"

"Mummy is fine. She's here with me." He patted her head. "Go back to sleep. I'll be here when you wake up."

"Do you promise?" She looked up at him and felt like her neck might snap.

He pressed her cheek to his chest, and she relaxed, the terrible cries fading into the misty darkness.

Stone almost danced with rage. He'd shocked the fat bitch three times, and she still wouldn't wake up. Three times was all he could do. Any more and he'd risk killing her. As much as he wanted her gone, he couldn't take that chance. He needed to get inside her phone.

He'd have to find something else. He stalked over to the chemical closet where he kept a delightful assortment of particularly nasty acid solutions. If she needed additional incentive, he could provide that. In the end, his new strategy proved unnecessary.

Over on the metal table, Abby Lieberman's phone rang.

Chapter 51

After taking a few minutes to recover from the horror they'd just witnessed, Alex, Signy, and Lizzy exploded into action. Alex packed up his gear while Lizzy got the baby refastened into his car seat. Signy ran around the house doing a last sweep to make sure they had left nothing behind and wiping off any last surface they might have touched.

Standing at the master bedroom window, she peered outside. She could see the Malibu and Alex's Yukon, parked side by side in front of the cottage. With the exception of the single set of ruts left by the Yukon, and a few rabbit tracks, the snow was unbroken. She turned to head downstairs but found Alex blocking her way.

"What is it?" she asked, her eyes darting out into the hall.

He stepped into the bedroom and closed the door. "Listen, I'm all for getting that poor girl the hell out of here, but I have to ask, shouldn't someone call the cops?"

"I've thought about that," Signy said. "As soon as we have Lizzy relocated, I'll send the video to the state police. Tell them the whole story."

"Won't they want to interview Lizzy?"

"I don't know about you, but I think she's had enough trauma to last several lifetimes. Have you seen her arms?"

"The scars?" The Tracker nodded. "I'd say she used to cut herself."

Signy nodded. "You and I might have had an unlucky break when we were kids, but nothing like what she's had to face. Do you really want to subject her to any more?"

He shook his head.

"Then let's go."

She hustled back down the stairs, Alex trailing behind.

"Everything okay?" Lizzy asked, her eyes darting between Alex and Signy.

"We're getting you the hell out of here," Signy said, firmly.

"You believe me," Lizzy said, her knees wobbling. "Thank you, thank you."

"Alex? If you can get the SUV loaded, I have to make a quick call. I need to let my boss know what's happening. I'll toss the phone after I make the call." Ever since viewing the horrific video, Signy had had an overwhelming urge to make sure Grace was okay.

"Can't you do that later?" Lizzy asked, pulling on Signy's sleeve.

"Come on," Alex said to Lizzy, "you can help me load the car."

Signy shot him a grateful look, then turned her back and punched in Grace's number. Her heart leaped in her chest when she heard the line pick up. "Grace, it's me." She heard nothing but breathing on the other end of the line. "Grace? Are you there?"

"Good morning. Is this Carole White?"

Dumbfounded, Signy couldn't utter a sound.

"Hello, Ms. White."

"I'm sorry, I must have the wrong number," Signy stammered, her finger poised over the off button.

"Don't hang up, Ms. White. My name is Solomon Stone. I think you'll be interested to hear what I have to say."

Signy waved frantically at Alex.

"What?" he mouthed, dropping his bag.

"I'm listening," she said, into the phone. She crooked her finger at Alex.

"It's simple, really. You have my wife and son. I want them back."

"I don't know what you're talking about."

Lizzy Stone stared at her from across the room.

Alex moved up beside Signy and she held the phone up between them so they could both hear Stone's words.

"Let's not waste time, Ms. White. You have something I need, and I have something you want."

"You have nothing I could possibly want, you sadistic bastard."

"I see you've bought into my wife's lies."

"I saw the video. I know what you've been doing."

There was silence on the other end of the line, and then Stone said, "Lizzy is resourceful, I'll give her that."

"You are one sick fuck."

"Actually, it's a good thing she showed you my experimental work," he said, "because now you understand what will happen to your friend if you don't return my wife and son to me immediately."

"My friend?" Signy whispered, feeling raw panic slash at her throat.

"She told me her name is Abigail Lieberman, but I'm guessing you call her Grace. Either way, she's proving to be an excellent donor." He chuckled. "Plenty of surface area on those thunder thighs."

Signy uttered a strangled cry.

"Here's the deal and I'll say this only once. You bring back my wife and son by tonight or I will burn your lovely Grace alive."

"Tonight?" Signy dug her fingers into Alex's forearm, her mind racing. "Don't hurt her. Please. I'll bring them. I promise. But I need more time."

"Stop wasting *my* time. The whole world is looking for you. I'd be surprised if you're more than a few miles away. Oh, and Ms. White? No cops, or I'll break her bones before I put the torch to her."

"Wait," Signy said, but Dr. Stone had already hung up.

Chapter

52

Signy fell backwards into the living room, collapsing in a heap on the couch. She put a hand to her throat, unable to catch her breath.

Alex rushed to her side. "We'll get her back. We'll get her."

"Get who?" Lizzy cried. "That was him, wasn't it? It was Solomon."

"My God," Signy said, "that psycho bastard has Grace."

Forgotten inside his car seat, baby Justin wailed.

"We'll get her," Alex said, "I promise."

Signy looked into his eyes. "He called her a donor. What do you think that means?"

"I don't know," he lied.

"He's going to hurt her like he hurt that poor girl," Signy said.

"Get who back?" Lizzy said. "Tell me what's going on."

Kicking his legs out in front of him until they were as rigid as iron pipes, the baby screamed.

Pointing a finger at the baby, Alex glared at Lizzy. "Pick him up, for God's sake."

"Oh, Grace," Signy whispered.

"Tell me right now," Lizzy said. "Is he out there? Is he coming?"

Alex rounded on Lizzy. "If you don't shut that kid up in the next few seconds, I'll throw you both in the car and dump you at the police station myself."

Lizzy held his eyes for a few moments and then looked away. She removed the baby from the car seat and, holding him to her chest, walked him around the room.

Alex returned his attention to Signy.

"I called Grand Central yesterday afternoon. She was there." Signy stared down at her hands, remembering that Henrietta had never actually answered her query as to whether Grace was present for the embassy investigation.

Behind them, Lizzy had succeeded in getting the baby calmed down.

"I'm okay," Signy said, finally. She stood up and turned to Lizzy. "Your husband is holding another conductor hostage. Alex and I are going to go and get her out."

"What?" Lizzy shouted, setting off a new round of caterwauling from the baby. "Are you out of your minds?"

"No choice," Alex said, as he opened up his bag.

"What about me?" she said. "You just can't leave me here."

Alex pulled a prepaid credit card out of his wallet and handed it to Lizzy. "If we're not back in a few hours, take the Malibu and go."

"There's no key," Signy said.

Lizzy glanced at Signy. "You're not the only one who knows how to hot-wire a car."

"When you get to Chicago," Alex interjected, "find a used car lot. Dump the Malibu and buy something else." He glanced at the prepaid card. "That is exactly the same as cash. Use it. Keep driving. When you get to LA, find a cheap apartment and pay cash. Pay cash for everything. Don't use the phone, Internet—nothing."

"You have the new ID I gave you," Signy added. "If you need help in the future, get in touch with me using that name. I'll come." She scribbled a number on a piece of scrap paper she had in her pocket and shoved it into Lizzy's bag.

"You won't be back," Lizzy said, burying her cheek in the baby's soft neck. He clawed at her face, his eyes swollen from crying.

Alex smiled. "We will."

"Ready?" Signy said. She had her hand on the door.

"Wait," Lizzy said, hustling over to Signy. "Do you have any more paper?"

Signy fished another folded scrap from her pocket.

Lizzy grabbed the paper. Shoving aside a glass vase full of colourful beach sand, Lizzy set the paper down on the hall table and sketched a quick drawing. When she was done, she handed it back to Signy. "It's a map of the basement."

"What's this?" Signy asked, pointing to a large open room at the north end of the basement.

"Crematorium," Lizzy said. "It's where he burns the medical waste. Oh, and by the way," she continued, ignoring Signy's appalled expression, "he has security cameras everywhere. There's no point giving you the code to the front gate, he'll know you're there. Besides, he changes it every day. You'll just have to drive up and wait."

"Thanks," Signy said. She stuffed the map in her pocket, then tipped a few handfuls of the beach sand into her pocket.

"What's that for?" Alex asked.

"An old trick."

"New to me."

Grabbing hold of the doorknob, Signy turned to Alex. "Listen, I just want to say—"

"No need."

"No, seriously. I'm glad you're coming with me."

He smiled. "Do you really think I'd let you go alone?"

"Let me?" She arched a brow.

"Poor choice of words?" he said, a smile playing around the corner of his mouth.

She narrowed her eyes, then turned and pulled open the door. She stopped dead.

"Are we going or what?" asked Alex.

"Ah, man. Could this day get any worse?" she said.

"What is it? What's wrong?"

"We have company."

Glancing over her shoulder, Alex frowned. A white pickup truck was roaring up the driveway, heading right for them.

Chapter 53

The white truck pulled to a stop not ten feet from where Signy and Alex stood side by side at the front door.

"Who is it?" Lizzy asked. She was standing just behind the pair, the baby bouncing on her hip.

"Take Justin and go into the kitchen," Alex said, his eyes trained on the newcomer.

"Oh God. Is it him?"

"Go."

They heard Lizzy's footsteps as she retreated to the kitchen.

The icy wind biting at her exposed skin, Signy pulled up her hood. "What do you think?" she asked.

"I don't know. Could be the caretaker, I guess."

"The owner's name is Bill. I don't know his last name."

They watched the driver's door creak open and a large man

wearing a light-grey parka exit the vehicle. Pulling his hood over his head, he tramped his way through the dense drifts.

"Cop?" Signy said, quietly.

Alex shook his head. "I don't think so."

"Howdy, folks." The man stood in front of them, his face shielded by a thick layer of fur ringing the hood on his parka, his hands shoved deep inside his pockets.

"Good afternoon," Alex said. "Can I help you?"

"Didn't expect to see people out here." The man took another step closer.

"We're friends of Bill's," Alex said.

"Seems a little late in the year to be hanging out at the cottage."

Alex shrugged. "We like the snow."

The man shuffled forward another step. "My name is Gerry Hanniwell. Bill hired me to keep an eye on the place. He didn't say anything about having visitors."

"It was a last-minute thing," Signy said.

"You don't say." The man turned his head toward Signy. Through the furry tunnel of his hood, she could see a pair of flat dark eyes.

Alex pushed Signy behind him.

A gust of wind tore through the small group, rocking them sideways.

The man smiled. "Cold as a witch's tit out here." He shuddered theatrically and took another step closer. "Mind if we step inside?"

"I do," Alex said.

Whipping his hand out of his pocket, the man pointed a large handgun at Alex. "Keep your hands where I can see them and move back into the house. Both of you."

Signy felt Alex's hand on her arm, pushing her back into the house. She could smell the crisp newness of his jacket as he crowded into her, and heard the crunch of his boots on the crusty snow. She stepped back inside the house, her view of the gunman obscured by Alex's body.

"What's this about?" Alex asked, watching the gunman use his free hand to shut the door.

The gunman shrugged. "How many people in the house?"

"Just the two of us," Alex said.

Signy stepped out from behind Alex, ignoring the exasperated look he directed at her. She unzipped her coat and tossed it on the floor. "Did Stone send you?"

"Signy," Alex warned.

The gunman stared at Alex. "I have no idea who Stone is, but it wouldn't surprise me if this asshole has more than a few enemies."

"This is about him?" Signy said, her voice rising. Turning her back to the gunman, she winked at Alex.

One corner of his mouth twitched upward. "Shut yer mouth, ya crazy broad," he said, with more gusto than necessary.

Whirling on the gunman, she jammed her fists into her hips. "What's he done now?"

He flicked his eyes at her. "Your boyfriend here messed with the DeMeo family."

"This is about Sal?" Alex said.

"This dumb-ass is not my boyfriend," she said. Pushing forward until she was standing between the gunman and Alex, Signy poked a finger into Alex's chest. "You son of a bitch. You promised me you weren't doing that shit anymore."

"Ah, come on, doll. Whose side are you on, anyway?" Alex said, channelling Lenny Screed.

"At least the skank knows a fuck-up when she sees one."

"Hey! Who you callin' a skank?"

"Move," said the gunman, jabbing Signy in the ribs with the barrel of the gun.

"Whatever. I don't give a shit what you do with him; just leave me out of it." She waved her hands wildly in the air as she spoke, pleased to see the gunman's eyes following her gestures.

Unfortunately, he kept the gun pointed squarely at her chest.

"The feds turned Vito DeMeo, you moron," Alex said. "Sal needed his brother gone before he did any more damage."

"Bullshit," said the gunman, his eyes darting between Signy and Alex.

"DeMeo?" Signy said, in an incredulous tone. "You fucked with the DeMeo family?"

Ignoring Signy, Alex said, "It's true. The only reason he sent you to kill me was so nobody would find out that he had his own brother popped."

Signy saw a cloud of confusion pass across the gunman's eyes, and she whirled toward Alex. "You bastard!" she shrieked, stiff-arming Alex until he stumbled backwards.

"Sal DeMeo murdered his own brother!" Alex shouted, pretending to lose his balance. He fell to his hands and knees.

"Enough!" roared the gunman. "Get outta the way, bitch."

She whirled back to face the gunman. "You wanna take him out? Be my guest." She took a step to her left, her eyes fixed on his. She saw him shift his weight onto his left foot.

"Go ahead," she said, "Kill him."

"I'm getting real tired of people pointing guns at me," Alex said, skittering backward on the floor. "Can't we have a conversation like civilized people?"

"Come on. Do it," Signy said, clutching at the gunman's sleeve.

"Get off me."

She yanked harder, and taking advantage of the downward momentum, chopped her other arm down onto his wrist, forcing the gun down.

The assassin pulled the trigger.

The concussive force of the blast almost knocked Signy off her feet. Ears ringing, she wheeled around, scanning her brother for any signs of injury. She exhaled with a whoosh when she saw that the bullet had torn a harmless chunk out of the floor.

"Signy!" Alex shouted.

She remembered the gunman a fraction of a second too late.

He'd regained his balance and, not bothering with any fancy moves, slammed his body into hers, sending her flying halfway across the foyer. She fell onto her butt. Eyes wide, she watched the gun swing back around toward Alex. "Look out!" she shouted.

Her warning was moot. Alex had bounced to his feet and was flying through the air. Before the gunman was able to pull the trigger again, Alex was on him.

Signy watched, unable to breathe, as the two men struggled. She'd lost sight of the gun but knew it had to be somewhere between the two writhing bodies.

Grunting with effort, Alex twisted to one side in an effort to unbalance his opponent, but he might have been trying to dislodge a cement wall. The assassin responded with a well-placed blow, smashing Alex's body against the wall. The two men glared at each other for what seemed like an eternity.

The gun boomed again.

Signy sucked in a breath with a loud whoop.

Alex stared ahead, eyes wide.

She scrambled to her feet and rushed across the small space. "Alex?" she called.

His eyes rolled back in his head, and he slid down the wall, the gunman following him all the way to the floor.

Chapter 54

"Alex?" Signy shouted.

The two men lay motionless, tangled in a heap on the foyer floor.

Lizzy peered through the kitchen door. "What's happening?"

"Stay there," Signy said, taking a cautious step forward. An alarming amount of blood was pooling beneath the two crumpled bodies, but she thought she caught sight of a hint of movement amid the tangle of arms and legs.

One of the men groaned.

Signy fell to her knees. The gunman was lying on top. Grabbing the hood of his parka, she heaved, the inert body resisting at first, then suddenly shifting toward her. Vivid scarlet stained his parka. Confused, it took her a second before she saw the knife protruding from the right side of his chest. She touched a finger to his carotid artery. Nothing.

She turned her attention to Alex, placing her ear to his mouth, reassured by the sound of steady breathing. His pulse was strong and steady, although his eyes remained closed.

"Lizzy?" she called, over her shoulder.

Lizzy banged through the kitchen door. She set the baby down, then stared at the lifeless body of the gunman. "My God, is he dead?"

"Never mind that. Alex is out, and I don't know why. We need to get his coat off."

Tearing her eyes away from the dead man, Lizzy hustled over. Together the two women tugged Alex's arms out of his parka. Signy examined his head, front and back. He had a nasty lump on the back of his head where the gunman had slammed him into the wall, but a quick probe with her fingers did not reveal any lacerations or fractures. She moved on to his neck, chest, and abdomen. Finding nothing, she said, "Let's roll him over." With Lizzy supporting his back, Signy pulled on Alex's shoulder, rolling him onto his side.

"Anything?" she asked Lizzy, who had a clear view of Alex's back.

Lizzy shook her head. "Clean."

As they lowered him gently onto his back, Alex groaned.

"Alex?" Signy said. "Are you okay?"

His eyes fluttered open, and he looked up at her.

Lizzy rolled up Alex's pant leg, revealing a gaping wound in his calf.

Signy felt her stomach heave. She could see shredded red muscle fibres and bits of white bone where the bullet had torn across his tibia.

"Ow," Alex said, in a relatively clear voice.

"Hey," said Signy, looking into his eyes. "How are you feeling?"

"Like I got hit by a Mac truck. What happened?"

"You took a blow to the head. You were unconscious for a few seconds. But it looks like your leg took the worst of it."

Alex struggled up onto his elbows, wincing as he caught a glimpse of his wounded leg.

"You'll need surgery," Lizzy said, "but I can wrap it up for now, hopefully prevent any infection."

Signy glanced at Lizzy. "You sound like you have some nurse training."

Lizzy shook her head. "Advantages of being a doctor's wife. I'll run upstairs and see what kind of supplies Bill keeps in the medicine chest." She got to her feet and raced up the stairs.

Alex rolled his head toward the gunman. "Is he—?"

Signy nodded.

"God, that hurts." He clutched at his leg, then grinned up at her. "Dumb-ass?"

"Crazy broad?" she countered.

Alex croaked out a chuckle. "You were great, by the way. I almost bought your little act, myself."

"I thought if I could distract him long enough for you to reach that knife you keep strapped to your leg, you might stand a fighting chance."

"You remembered," he said, flicking his eyes toward the eight-inch Italian stiletto. "Still, that was a crazy risk you took."

Signy shrugged. "What choice did I have?"

Alex nodded. "He'd have killed you as soon as I was down."

Lizzy tripped down the stairs carrying a bundle of bandages and other assorted medical supplies.

"Listen," Signy said. "I have to go."

He frowned.

"I'll call an ambulance," Signy added.

"No, you can't," Lizzy said. "They'll see me."

"Look at him," Signy said. "He needs a doctor."

Alex clutched at Signy's hand. "Don't go."

"Listen to him," Lizzy said. "Your friend is dead by now. Help me get him in the car, and we can get out of here before we all end up the same way."

Signy pulled on her coat. "I have to try."

"She's right, Signy. The man's a psychopath. I can't let you go there alone."

She narrowed her eyes and glared at him. "Let's get one thing straight. You don't *let* me do anything. I decide what I do or don't do." She glanced at his leg. "It's not like you're in any position to help. I guess tracking people down was bound to catch up with you sooner or later." She watched his already pale face lose even more colour.

"Give it a rest, would you? I didn't mean to imply you weren't capable. It's just that I have people I can call. Backup."

"Seriously?" She eyed him. "You have people?"

He checked his watch. "They're based in Washington. They could meet you at Stone's place in less than three hours, if we're lucky."

She shook her head. "Too long."

"Signy, please. Don't do this. It's a mistake."

"Duly noted," she said, zipping up her coat.

"If I'd known having a sister would be such a pain in my ass . . ." Alex muttered under his breath. He leaned forward and unbuckled a leather sheath he had strapped to his uninjured calf and handed it to Signy. "Take this." He glanced at the dead man. "And his gun, too."

She accepted the contraption and, after a brief examination of how it worked, managed to fix it to her left calf. She turned and began to pull the knife out of the gunman's chest. It took a surprising amount of force to loosen the blade, and by the time it slid free, she was sweating. Wiping the blade on the gunman's parka, she slipped the blade into the sheath.

Signy looked at both of them. "I'll be back. I promise."

"I wish you wouldn't go," Lizzy said miserably.

The baby looked at Signy and laughed.

She leaned over his car seat. "You really are a smart little guy, aren't you," she said, tapping him on the nose.

"Signy?" Alex said.

She raised a brow.

"Be careful, okay?"

"Don't worry," she said with a tight grin. "You and I have unfinished business."

Nodding, he wheezed as he let out a croupy laugh.

As she opened the door, she heard him whisper a few words in a strange language. *Ayóó ánóshí, Shideeszhi*, she repeated to herself, trying to commit the strange syllables to memory.

If she got out of this alive, she wanted to ask him what the words meant.

Chapter

55

Swearing under her breath, Signy focused on the road ahead. What she could see of it, anyway. It had been easier than she'd expected to manoeuvre Alex's SUV down the track leading from the cottage and out onto the main road. She had followed the fresh tracks created by the white pickup, but out here on the main road, the going was tough.

The wind whipped in off the lake, the snow drifting horizontally across the road. Great white dunes had accumulated wherever there was an open stretch of road, and although the plows had been through at least once, the drifts were filling in as quickly as the plows tore them down. Whenever she caught sight of a mountain of snow, she'd slam her foot on the gas and barrel straight on through, sending an explosion of white powder out behind the SUV.

In an effort to keep her thoughts from straying into dark territory, she deliberately turned her mind away from Grace, thinking instead about the gunman. She'd never heard of the DeMeo family, although she had a good idea what they might be. Certainly, if one of their lieutenants was found dead in his truck at the bottom of Lake Ontario, the cops would jump to the obvious conclusion—just another gang hit. There would be nothing to point to her, or to Alex Nakai.

A sudden vision of Grace hanging from a hook on the wall slammed into her brain. The car rocked from side to side, as she struggled with the wheel. Gritting her teeth, she tried to limit her attention to the road in front of her.

Sweating by the time she arrived at the Stone estate, she slid to a halt in front of the wrought iron gate and rolled down the window, oblivious to the icy sleet that pelted her cheeks.

"Carole White?" She barely heard the tinny voice over the howling wind.

Signy flipped off her hood and stared into the lens of the security camera.

"Where are they?" the voice asked.

"Close by," she called out. "Lizzy demanded a neutral location to make the exchange."

"No. I want them here."

Signy shrugged. "Your wife is a stubborn woman. This was the best I could do, and if I don't see Grace alive and well in the next ten minutes, the deal is off."

A long pause and then the intercom clicked off. A moment later, the gate began to swing open.

Taking a deep breath, Signy steered the SUV up the long drive. A plow had been through not too long before and the driving was easier between the dense trees than it had been out on the road.

Still, there were at least two or three deep drifts she had to blast through, and she struggled to maintain her grip on the wheel.

It took almost five minutes to traverse the mile-long drive, and when the big house finally loomed into view, sweat was flowing freely down her back. Reflexively, she touched the gun inside her jacket pocket.

Pulling to a stop in front of the imposing entrance, she turned off the car and looked around, trying to memorize the lay of the land in case she needed to beat a hasty retreat. Taking a deep breath, she yanked open the door and stepped outside.

A treacherous sheet of ice lay beneath the snow, and she almost went down a couple of times before finally making her way up the stairs to the front door. She was about to knock when the door swung open and she was looking into the handsome face of Dr. Solomon Stone. He had a gun pointed at her chest.

Keeping her eyes trained on the weapon, Signy raised her hands.

He stood to one side and gestured for her to move inside.

As soon as she had passed the threshold, Stone slammed the door.

"Nothing happens until I see Grace," she said, acutely aware of the cold steel weighing down her right coat pocket.

"You're in no position to give orders here," Stone said. He waved the gun in her face.

"Where is she?" Signy asked.

"You don't get it, do you? As far as the police are concerned, you aided and abetted child abduction. One phone call from me and you're finished."

Signy dropped her hands. "If I don't see Grace in the next

few seconds, you can kiss your miraculous skin donor goodbye." Keeping her eyes focused on Stone, she slipped her hand into her pocket, her index finger probing for the safety switch on the gun. She winced when she saw his eyes catch sight of the tiny movement.

"What have you got there?" he said, moving forward and jamming his weapon into the side of her neck.

She slowly drew the gun out of her pocket.

"Put it on the floor and slide it over here."

Every muscle screaming in protest, Signy complied.

Without dropping his eyes from hers, Stone stopped the gun with the side of his shoe and then kicked it into the far corner of the foyer. "Stupid move."

"Look," she said, "you give me Grace and I'll tell you where Lizzy is. Otherwise, you might as well just shoot me now."

"Enough." He aimed the barrel of the gun directly at her heart, then gestured for her to move.

As they walked together down a long hallway, Signy kept her eyes on the man. He had a serpentine feel about him. She could see his muscles bunch and contract under his expensive suit. She had no doubt that when he struck, it would be lightning quick.

"She's down there," he said, coming to a stop in front of a stairway leading down to the basement. He waved Signy ahead.

She took the steps slowly, trying to scope out the lay of the land at the bottom. If she remembered correctly from Lizzy's rough map, Stone's lab was located near the south side of the building, while the crematorium was situated on the north wall. In between, a maze of hallways and smaller rooms. She wondered which way he would lead her.

Stone turned right, toward the crematorium.

Overwhelmed by the nightmarish vision of Grace chained to a wall, Signy bit back a wave of nausea. The sight of fluorescent biohazard warnings didn't help, nor did the sickly sweet odour of cooked meat.

Stone came to a halt at an open door.

"In here," he said.

Keeping one eye on him, she peeked inside the room. Grace was lying in a hospital bed, a white sheet tucked up under her chin and an IV tube running down into one arm. She appeared to be asleep. Glancing at Stone, Signy took a cautious step inside the room.

Grace's face was white, dark circles like black bruises under both eyes, a yellow crust building up on her lashes. She had a bloodstained gauze bandage plastered across her nose, and her lips were dry and cracked. "What have you done to her?"

"Nothing a little heat therapy won't fix," Stone said.

He'd sidled up close behind her, and she could feel his breath like fire on the back of her neck. "You sick son of a bitch," she whispered.

Stone responded by shoving her farther into the room. "Time to join your fat friend in hell, Ms. White. I hope you like barbecue."

Chapter 56

Alex lay on the couch, his leg propped on a blanket Lizzy had found in a box by the fireplace. He was rereading Lizzy Stone's troubling history when he heard her coming back down the stairs. He shut the computer off and pretended to sleep.

"You awake?"

He allowed his eyes to flutter open.

"What should we do about this mess?" she asked, draping a coat over the dead gunman.

He cocked a brow.

She shrugged. "Just being realistic."

"There's a team on the way. It'll be a few hours, but they can deal with the body when they get here. And if Signy isn't back by then, they'll go get her."

Lizzy shook her head. "I should be gone by then."

"What have you got there?"

"I wanted to find some rubbing alcohol before I got started on your leg. How are you feeling?"

Allowing himself to tune in to the pain in his leg, he realized it was getting worse. "I've been better."

Sitting in his car seat on the floor beside Alex, the baby fussed.

Lizzy handed the baby the set of plastic keys, then kneeling in front of Alex, opened the first-aid kit.

He saw with some dismay the rolls of white gauze and gleaming sharp scissors.

She sliced open his pant leg, exposing the wound.

Watching her eyes, he said, "Bad?"

"Let's just say this is going to hurt."

Propping himself on his elbows, Alex got his first real glimpse of the injury. He felt his stomach lurch.

"Could have been worse, actually," she said. "It looks like bullet only grazed the bone." She looked up at him. "Ready?"

Alex nodded, then hissed through his teeth as she sloshed rubbing alcohol into the gaping hole. Jerking his head to one side, he came eye to eye with Justin, who was watching the proceedings with great interest.

Lizzy jabbed at the wound with a clump of bandage, cleaning away any remaining debris.

"Jesus," Alex said, "do you have to be so rough?"

Ignoring him, Lizzy crammed cotton balls soaked in alcohol into the wound.

Trying not to scream, Alex let out a high-pitched hoot of agony.

Justin responded to Alex's screwed-up face with a round of hysterical laughter.

"Here comes the hard part," Lizzy said, calmly.

"The hard part?" Squeezing his eyes shut, he gritted his teeth when she jerked his leg up in order to wind layers of white gauze around his calf. He fought to stay conscious, the searing pain like nothing he'd experienced before.

"Men are such babies when it comes to a little discomfort," Lizzy muttered.

Discomfort? As soon as he got back on his feet, he'd like to find out how much torture this crazy woman could tolerate. Alex's agony-induced thoughts were interrupted by a loud ripping sound. Cracking open one eye, he saw that she had a roll of grey duct tape in her hands.

She tore another long piece off with her teeth.

"What's that for?" he managed to grunt.

"The duct tape seals the wound. Keeps it anaerobic. No oxygen equals no bacteria."

He tried to breathe as she wound the sections of duct tape round and round. His leg felt like it was on fire. Finally, she was done. He collapsed back on the cushions.

"This should keep you until you can see a proper doctor."

He looked down at the neat wrapping of duct tape. "Where did you learn to do field dressings?"

She handed him four white pills. "Tylenol with codeine. I found them in the medicine cabinet."

He popped all four into his mouth and swallowed them dry.

Gathering scraps of bandages into her lap, she asked, "I want to be gone by the time your reinforcements get here."

"I understand," he said. "You still have the cash card?"

She nodded.

Alex tilted his head at the corpse. "You could take his truck. It'll be safer than the Malibu."

Rising to her feet, she said, "By the way, can I have my USB key back?"

Glancing up at her, he saw her hands were shaking—and just like that, all the pieces fell into place. "Christ," he muttered, staring up at her.

"Something wrong?"

"What? Oh. Nothing." He patted his jeans. "It's just that I could have sworn I put the key in my pocket."

She frowned.

Pretending to glance around the room, Alex slid his hand down his leg, reaching for his stiletto, and then remembered he had given it to Signy.

He turned back to her, and they locked eyes.

"You know. Don't you," she said.

He nodded.

"How?"

He glanced down at her hands.

Following his gaze, she slipped her shaking hands into the pockets of her new jacket.

"It was obvious if I'd been thinking clearly."

"It's not what you think."

"From the quality of the picture, it's easy to see that the video was shot using a hand-held camera."

She swallowed reflexively.

"I assumed from the beginning that Stone filmed himself using a camera on a tripod. But he couldn't have done it that way. The picture was too shaky." He held her eyes. "Someone else was in the room."

"You don't understand. He made me do it," she said, tears pooling in her eyes.

"Maybe. Maybe not." He peered closely at her. "You're either another victim of that sick bastard or a walking nightmare. I just don't know."

She watched him for several seconds. "So what now? You call the police?"

Alex struggled to a sitting position. "That's up to you."

"Why? What do you have in mind?"

"A trade."

Narrowing her eyes, she leaned forward. "I'm all ears."

Chapter

57

Stone pointed the gun at Signy's head. "So, what's it going to be, Ms. White? Are you going to tell me where to find my wife and son, or do we have to do things the hard way?"

Signy squinted at the gun. It was a small nine-millimetre but it felt like she was staring down the barrel of an elephant gun. "The hard way, I'm afraid."

He sighed. "I see you've bought into my dear Lizzy's tale of woe. About how the evil doctor is out to have her declared insane?"

Signy's lips twisted in disgust.

Stone frowned. "You've got it all wrong."

Grace moaned. Her eyelids fluttered open, but it was clear there was nobody home.

"What have you done to her?"

"A small procedure. Nothing really."

"Then why isn't she awake?"

"That's a bit of a puzzle, actually. She's seems to have voluntarily checked out."

Signy bit her lip, remembering Grace's strange behaviour at the embassy. If she was going to make a move against Stone, she needed Grace alert and mobile.

"My methods may be unorthodox." He shrugged. "Nevertheless, I share Aristotle's philosophy that the needs of the individual must sometimes be sacrificed for the higher good."

"You call staking a woman to a wall and burning the flesh from her body the higher good?"

Stone's eyelid twitched.

"Lizzy copied videos before she left—lots of them. If anything happens to me or Grace, Lizzy will give them to the cops."

"Oh, I don't think so, Ms. Shepherd. That wouldn't suit my dear Lizzy. That wouldn't suit her at all."

"That's not what she says," Signy said, with a bravado she didn't feel.

"I can see you're confused," Stone said. "Why don't I show you exactly what my dear Lizzy has been up to? Perhaps then you'll understand how important it is to get my son away from her before she does him irreparable harm." He pointed the gun at Grace. "You push your fat friend there. We'll take a walk down to the animal holding pens."

Stepping over to the gurney, Signy peered into her mentor's blank eyes. There was no response.

Behind her, she heard the door squeak open and Stone call out for her to move. Standing behind the gurney, she pushed and pulled until she angled the rolling bed feet-first toward where Stone was standing in the open door.

"Shall we?" he said, beckoning her forward.

As Stone retreated into the hallway to allow the gurney to pass through the door, Signy leaned down and whispered into Grace's ear. "Knife—strapped to my left calf." There was no reaction, not even the twitch of an eyelid. Signy felt a deep despair grow inside her chest.

Jabbing the barrel of the gun into her back, Stone directed Signy through a maze of corridors. He said little, opening his mouth only to bark directions. Eventually they arrived at what appeared to be an underground animal stable.

"I get no pleasure out of my human trials, believe me," he said. "I mourn each and every one of the young people that have given their lives for my research. But in this case, Ms. White, the end truly does justify the means."

"You can tell yourself whatever you want, but the fact remains you're nothing but a pedophile that gets off on torturing children." The wheels of the gurney squeaked hollowly inside the narrow hallway. Up ahead, Signy could see a dark splotch marring the concrete floor. The smell of singed meat was getting stronger, and she tried without success to ignore it. She tasted vomit in the back of her throat.

"It is very easy to be high and mighty," Stone said, "but if you'd seen the horrific damage that man wreaks upon his fellow human beings, you'd appreciate why I had to expedite my research."

Signy shook her head.

"I tried working with pigs. They are a decent stand-in for humans—

their skin is quite similar as a matter of fact—but nothing compares to the real thing when one is trying to refine a new technique."

Signy ran the gurney over the long, dark streak that she recognized as dried blood. She felt her knees wobble.

"Does she seem like a good mother to you?"

"If you're implying that Lizzy is not Justin's biological mother, I know all about it."

"Do you? Lizzy never fails to surprise me." Stone shook his head. "Ever since I first laid eyes on her, she's been a bit of a wild card. That's what I loved about her. You never knew what she'd try next. Her sexual appetites were prodigious." He stared off into space. "She was off the charts in terms of deviant creativity. The things she could do with that tiny body." Stone hummed.

Signy faked a bored shrug.

Stone chuckled without humour. "You're right. Perhaps those are tales for another time. The best thing about my darling Lizzy was that she was willing to do whatever it took to help me in my work. And if that involved procuring human subjects, then she was happy to comply."

"I don't believe that."

He smiled. "Who has better access to society's most vulnerable than a shelter worker? It was easy for her to befriend young girls and bring them to me." He shrugged. "Those poor girls were doomed from the day they were born. At least this way, their lives had a purpose. Lizzy understood that."

"I'll tell you what I understand. You're an evil bastard. If you think I'm telling you how to get your filthy hands on either Lizzy or Justin, you're even more out of your mind than I thought."

"Unfortunately, all good things must come to an end," Stone

said, as though he hadn't heard her. "For Lizzy, her obsessive jealousy proved to be her undoing. Despite all the love I've shown her over the years, despite everything I've done for her."

"You mean the way you carved her body up until she looks like a Barbie doll?"

"Oh, dear. Have we been bitten by the green-eyed monster?" Stone shoved Signy roughly forward.

She stumbled against the gurney. Grace's inert body rocked slightly, but she might as well have been a lifeless puppet for all the awareness she was exhibiting. Signy felt a terrible cramp grip her lower abdomen as she began to realize that there might be no way out of this hellhole.

Stone sighed. "The last subject that Lizzy brought home was a real beauty. It wasn't until I completed her physical exam that I determined she was pregnant."

"With Justin?" Signy said, without thinking.

"Exactly." Stone beamed. "Pretty little Kit Kat. After I found out about the baby, I couldn't go ahead with the procedure. Lizzy and I both agreed. We would wait it out. Fetal tissue stem cells can be a treasure trove. No need to let them go to waste."

Signy grimaced, remembering the distinctive name from the newspaper article on Maitland's iPad, as well as the missing persons poster on Priya Subramanian's wall.

"A child would add legitimacy to our situation in any case."

"Kit Kat?" Signy said.

"I called her Katy, of course. Kit Kat is a ridiculous name."

Signy squeezed her eyes shut.

"But wait. If Lizzy told you about Justin, I assume she mentioned the lovely Katy?"

"She told me Katy ran away," Signy said.

Stone threw back his head and laughed. "Is that so? I'm going to take you to meet Katy. Perhaps then you'll be more inclined to tell me exactly where I can find my son. Hopefully, for your sake, and the sake of your fat friend here, he'll be safe and unharmed."

Signy thought she heard Grace say something. Hope flared in her chest, and she leaned forward. The wheels of the gurney shrieked on the concrete floor. "Grace?" Signy whispered.

"Ethan?" Grace muttered, her eyelids fluttering open and closed.

Signy felt a surge of hope rise in her chest. "Please wake up."

Grace's eyes rolled back in her head, and she said nothing more.

Chapter 58

Grace dangled her legs over the edge of the railway overpass. She heard a whisper, like a mosquito in her ear. She waved it away. Far down below she could see the cars going by on Mount Pleasant Road. She was wearing a tank top and a pair of cut-offs. Her thighs felt hot.

"You're going to get burned," her brother said. He was sitting beside her, the skin on his thin legs tanned a healthy nut brown.

She punched him playfully on the arm. "You're as bad as Kim. Worry, worry, worry."

"I wish I could have met her."

Grace glanced over at him. "You'd have liked her. She's a pain in my ass, just like you."

"Feel that?" he said, putting a hand on the rail.

Grace nodded. She'd been aware of the rumbling for a while now.

"Train coming," he said.

Grace shrugged and tilted her head up. The sun warmed her face as she watched a hawk drawing lazy circles in the bright blue sky.

Sighing, Ethan leaned forward to watch the cars zip past.

"Grace?" Grace heard a female voice call her name. Frowning, she glanced at her brother.

Overhead, the hawk shrieked.

She leaned back and peered up the tracks. She thought she saw the brilliant light of the engine, playing through the trees on the other side of the bridge.

"Not long now," Ethan said.

"I don't care."

He rolled his eyes. "Remember the day Eugenia caught us up here?"

Grace chuckled. "We almost didn't make it that time. Poor Eugenia thought she was going to see both of us splattered all over the tracks."

"You were fearless."

"Hardly. I don't think I've ever run so fast in my life."

"You sure about that?"

Grace frowned. "What are you doing here, anyway?"

He picked up her hand and placed it on the rail.

She could feel the deep rattling through her entire body.

"Some things you can't outrun," he said, "no matter how hard you try."

Grace snatched her hand away. "You should know," she said.

"The damned illness took me away, Gracie. There's nothing anyone could have done."

The warning shriek of the whistle broke through her lethargy. The train was on the bridge now, its vivid headlamp burning her eyes.

"You're different than me, baby sister. You have a choice."

She scrambled to her feet, pulling her brother along with her. "We have to go."

"Go?" Ethan placed his hands on her shoulders and turned her around until her back was to the oncoming locomotive.

Grace gasped. Ahead, the tracks disappeared into a dense fog bank. All she could see was her own silhouette staring back at her.

"Grace Holder, you have always been far more than a shadow on the wall," Ethan said.

The train whistle screamed.

"You are fearless."

"Ethan?"

"Yes?"

"Will you stay with me?"

"Always," he said.

"Grace!" Over the roar of the throbbing engine, Grace heard Signy call to her. "Please wake up."

"All right," Grace said.

Ethan grabbed her hand, and they turned to face the train together.

Chapter 59

"Here's the deal," Alex said, his eyes fixed on Lizzy's. "If you want to disappear without a trace, you're going to need to travel fast and light."

She nodded.

"The cash card I gave you is preloaded with thirty thousand dollars, untraceable."

"That much?" She arched one brow.

He nodded. "That should get you where you want to go, with enough wiggle room to get set up."

"So what's the trade?"

He tilted his head toward the baby. "Him."

She took a step back. "No way, he's—"

"Your bargaining chip, I get that."

"I was going to say my responsibility."

"Right," he said, peering at her from under half-closed lids.

"I can't leave him."

"You can't afford not to. Look at you. New hair, new clothes. You have a good chance on your own. If you take the baby, they'll pick you up in a New York second."

Squatting down on her haunches, she peered at Justin, a speculative expression on her face.

"I understand what you're going through," he said.

"You don't know anything about me."

"I know this much. You want your husband to suffer."

She shook her head. "Like I told Signy, he was going to kill me."

"How do you know that?"

"Katy told me. The night before he was due to come home. She laughed when she told me that he was going to make it look like a suicide." Lizzy wiped her nose. "She always hated me."

Alex peered at her. "She hated you because you were the one that lured her out there in the first place, isn't that right?"

"What? No." Lizzy glared at him. "She hated me because I had what she wanted. Solomon."

"What happened after she told you what your husband was planning?"

Lizzy's eyes held his. "I went up to my room, packed a bag, and left."

"And yet you said earlier that Katy ran off alone, leaving the baby with you."

"That's right," Lizzy said, clasping her hands together to stop them from shaking.

"It doesn't add up, Lizzy. If what you say were true, why would she give up her chance to become the next Mrs. Solomon Stone? And why leave her child behind?"

Lizzy flew to her feet. "How am I supposed to know what that bitch was thinking?"

"I think you took the baby because after you trashed his work, Justin was the only thing that would allow Stone to start over. That's what this is all about, isn't it? Revenge?"

"No."

"And you copied the video for added leverage."

"You're making me out to be some kind of monster." Lizzy paced back and forth. "If you're right, if I am some kind of terrible person, why wouldn't I just kill Justin?"

"Why indeed?" Alex stared at her. "I think you kept the baby with you because you are basically a decent person who got caught up with the wrong man. You were only a girl when he got his hooks into you. He took an unformed child and made her over into his version of the perfect woman. Like some sort of perverted Pygmalion, he changed you surgically, taught you how to walk, talk, and dress, how to be everything he wanted."

Lizzy glared at Alex.

"I think the real you is holed up inside and waiting to come out."

"You don't know anything."

Alex stared at her. "What if I could guarantee that Stone never gets his hands on the kid? That would solve all your problems, wouldn't it? Solomon would be ruined, and you would be free to start over."

"You can't promise that." She got to her feet. "Look at you. You're a wreck." She strolled across the room until she was standing in front of the fireplace. She picked up an iron poker from the stand.

Alex reached down and placed a hand on the car seat. The baby, thankfully, was nodding off, the little keys limp in his hands.

"The fact is," Lizzy continued, "Signy will be dead soon, but not before he's forced her to give up our location." She checked her watch. "I expect Solomon will be breaking down the door long before your reinforcements arrive." She dragged the pointed end of the poker through the ashy remains of an old fire.

Alex watched her with the same intensity that he afforded the rattler that lived under the front steps of his trailer.

"Not only is the baby the only source of the immortal skin cells, he's also the only thing standing between me and a very painful death." She shook her head. "He's coming with me."

Hauling himself into a sitting position, Alex smacked the wound on his leg with an open palm. "It's an interesting thing, really. Pain is really is no more than a series of electrical impulses flashing along nerve tissue, nature's way of letting the brain in on the big secret that a part of the body has experienced an injury and needs tending."

"So?"

He rose up, standing solidly on both feet. Towering over her, he said, "When you know what it is, pain is easy to ignore."

She narrowed her eyes.

"If you go now, you'll have a decent head start. You can start over, Lizzy. Have a better future." He hoped she couldn't see the sweat popping out like pearls on his forehead.

She let her eyes slide down to his injured leg.

"You've proved you are an intelligent woman, Lizzy. You won this battle. Why risk losing the war?"

She stared at him for several seconds before finally dropping her eyes. "Just make sure he finds a good home, okay?"

"Count on it."

She tossed the poker back into the stand. "I'll just go grab my stuff."

After watching her climb the stairs, he glanced at the front door, where her packed bag sat on top of the baby's gear.

"I don't know about you," he said, looking down at the sleeping baby, "but I don't want to be around when Eliza Doolittle comes back. God knows what she's planning next." Slipping the USB key from his pocket, he tossed it onto the coffee table where Lizzy would be unable to miss it.

Overhead, he heard Lizzy's Doc Martens thudding across the floor like distant cannon fire. Telling himself that he wouldn't be taken down by a few annoying electrical impulses, he bent over and picked up the car seat. He clamped his jaw tight and limped across the room, the pain from his cracked tibia almost too much to bear.

Chapter 60

"Last stop," Stone said, pointing the gun at a heavy steel door.

Signy allowed the gurney carrying Grace's inert body to roll to a halt.

Stone swiped his access card, and the door whooshed open.

As Signy pushed the gurney through the doors, her heart sank: she recognized the green concrete walls from the video and saw the gas canister sitting on the concrete floor. She felt her knees almost buckle when she caught sight of the iron manacles embedded in the wall. The smell of cooked flesh was stronger than ever.

"That's far enough," Stone said, swiping his access card again. The big door swung shut.

"Now would be a good time, Grace," Signy said, loudly.

"I wouldn't look to your fat friend for help, Ms. White. She's down for the count."

Stone sidled up behind Signy, and she could feel his breath on her neck. "Are you two lovers?"

Signy felt her hands ball into fists.

"I only ask because if you play for the girls' team, you would have loved to have seen Lizzy at her best. The way she used her body with another woman? My God. It was perfection."

Signy thought she saw Grace wiggle her toes.

"Lizzy had a flair for sexual creativity that went beyond the pale, and if at first the young ladies weren't willing to throw themselves into it, they eventually fell into line. God," he said, "they were beautiful to watch."

"You're a sick fuck."

"Please, Ms. White, there's no need for crudity," he said. Stone poked the gun into her spine, and Signy stumbled forward, moving alongside the gurney until she was parallel with Grace's midsection. "I only tell you this because I want you to understand that I loved them all, especially Katy. That was something Lizzy couldn't tolerate. As the baby grew inside Katy, Lizzy's rage deepened. The only way I could keep her under control was to promise to get rid of Katy once the baby was born."

Closing her ears to Stone's mad ramblings, Signy concentrated on Grace, certain she saw a hint of movement in her fingers.

"Of course, once I discovered the immortal skin cells in Katy's baby, I couldn't do it. What was it about her that had given rise to such an extraordinary child? I had to know more."

"And the fact that she was still almost a child herself was just an added bonus, right?" she said, knowing she was baiting him but unable to help herself.

Stone slammed a fist into the small of Signy's back.

As she toppled forward onto the gurney, Signy managed to snag the end of the Velcro restraint holding Grace's right hand. She gave a cry of pain in order to mask the ripping sound.

Yanking her up by her long blond braid, Stone twisted her toward an unopened door. "Before you say another word, take a look at what that crazy bitch did to my beautiful Katy." He pulled open the door.

Signy screamed as a badly charred body cascaded out of the closet, bone by bone. The torso and lower limbs were black, the arms contracted up into the classic pugilistic pose often observed in death by fire. The smell was overpowering. Besides the charred odour of seared pork, there was an acrid reek of smoked liver and the coppery smell of boiled blood.

But it was the girl's face that almost brought Signy to her knees. Untouched by fire, Katy's lips were drawn back in a rictus of agony, while her colourless eyes stared into space from beneath singed lashes and brows. Signy stared at the death mask, knowing that she'd seen that face before. Kit Kat. The young girl in the missing persons poster.

"And you think I'm the monster," Stone said, shoving Signy's face closer to the horrific sight.

Signy groaned aloud as she recalled the number of faces that lined Priya's wall, all of them young, all of them pretty. Just like the burned corpse at her feet.

"Do you see what she did? Do you want to be responsible for Justin's death? Because if I don't find him soon, I have no doubt she'll do exactly the same thing to him."

She had a sudden image of Alex, hobbled by the bullet in his leg, alone with Lizzy Stone in the deserted cottage. She pushed it away. "Bullshit, why would I believe you? I saw what you did to the girl on the video, and by now, I'm guessing, so have the police."

Stone narrowed his eyes.

"That's right," Signy said, quickly, "she's been talking up a storm. She said she'd rather die in prison than down here in this hellhole. I wouldn't be surprised if the cops come crashing through your door any second."

She watched a worried expression cross his face, and then his eyes cleared. "Nice try," he said, then used the gun to prod her back into the room.

To her dismay, Grace was lying motionless on the gurney, her blank eyes staring at the ceiling. Worse, her restraints appeared to be firmly in place. "Oh, Grace," she said.

"It's a shame about that," he said, tilting his head toward the unconscious woman on the gurney. "I'm sure I'd be able to persuade her to cooperate if she'd only wake up." Stone pursed his lips. "You see your friend found some J. K. Rowling books up in the library. Lizzy used them as part of her grooming regimen. What kid can resist Harry Potter? Unfortunately, Grace read the inscriptions and assumed, wrongly, that I wrote them. An honest mistake on her part. Lizzy's signature *L* looks a lot like an *S*."

Signy's eyes flicked to the nine-millimetre dangling loosely in Stone's right hand.

As though he'd read her mind, he jerked the gun up until it was once again leveled directly at her heart. "There's no reasoning with either of you, is there? Over there," he said, gesturing at a steel door on the opposite wall. "Open it."

Signy walked over to the door and pulled it open. Inside, she found an empty space about eight feet by four feet. She glanced up, her heart sinking at the sight of coiled metal piping. On the floor, identical patterns of coils underneath an iron grate.

Stone flicked a switch on the wall beside her.

Signy reared backwards as a series of white-hot flames jetted from the pipes on the floor and ceiling.

"I'm done wasting time," he said. "Either you tell me where I can find my son, or you wheel your comatose friend here into the fire." He flicked his eyes at Grace, and his mouth dropped open.

Grace was upright, all five feet, eleven inches of her, quivering with rage. Before his mind could make sense of what he was seeing, she hammered his face with her fist.

Stone reeled backwards.

Grace pressed her advantage, grabbing Stone's gun hand in both of hers, then using her broad shoulder to crush him into the wall.

Blood poured from Stone's nose, but he did not go down. He and Grace wrestled for control of the gun.

Signy stood unmoving, unable to believe what she was witnessing. It took too many seconds before she bent down, pulled up her pant leg, and reached for Alex's knife. The case was empty. Cursing, she shot back up.

Fatigued from the drugs that had not yet had time to clear her system, Grace was quickly losing ground in her struggle with Stone. She maintained her grip on the nine-millimetre, but Signy could see that Stone was slowly twisting the barrel back toward her mentor.

Reaching her hand into the pocket of her jacket, Signy pulled out a fistful of the beach sand she'd tipped into it back at the cottage. She rushed forward and, screaming with all the fury of a wild banshee, flung the gritty particles into Stone's eyes.

He cried out, temporarily blinded.

The brief distraction was enough for Grace to regain control of the gun, but as she spun away from Stone, she lost her footing and the weapon popped out of her hands.

Signy watched helplessly as the gun skittered under a metal shelving unit. She turned back just in time to see Stone charge forward, knocking Grace off her feet and flinging her into the air.

Grace fell against the gurney, sending it crashing perilously close to the open door of the fiery crematorium. Her feet tangled in the wheels and she went down hard onto her hands and knees. With a cry of rage, Stone rushed toward the fallen woman.

Signy reacted. Intercepting Stone, she slammed the heel of her hand up toward the bridge of his nose, hoping to drive the tender cartilage directly into his brain. She missed, the blow passing harmlessly along the side of his jaw. Off balance, she toppled forward, right into Stone's waiting arms.

Digging his fingers into Signy's throat, Stone cut off her air and blood supply. He bared his teeth, his eyes wild. "Burn in hell, you meddlesome bitch."

Fireworks exploded behind her eyes, but she managed to plunge her hand once again into the pocket of her coat. Bringing the fistful of sand up, she ground the sharp granules directly into his face, but her strength was deserting her along with her breath. The irritant had no effect.

Stone pushed forward, forcing her body closer and closer to the fiery conflagration. Her fists punched ineffectually at his well-muscled torso. Her mouth was wide open, her tongue protruding as she searched for air. As the light began to fade, she almost didn't see Alex's Italian stiletto streak through the air.

Stone's body jerked as Grace plunged the knife into his back, and although Signy could see a hint of confusion cross his eyes, he did not let up the pressure at her throat. She could feel the brutal heat of the crematorium licking at her back.

The knife flashed again, and Signy felt a sickening thud zing through the end of Stone's fingertips as Grace buried the knife up to the hilt in his back. She heard Grace howl in triumph.

Glassy-eyed, Stone loosened his grip on Signy's neck.

She slipped free.

Again, the knife slashed down. Stone reached out behind him, probing with his hand at the small of his back.

Gasping for air, Signy watched with sick pleasure as Grace grabbed Stone by his arm and, using his own momentum, spun him across the room. He toppled onto the gurney, and she was on him again. Slashing down with the knife, slicing into his chest and neck, until great clots of dark blood poured from his mouth.

"Grace!" Signy cried.

Grace was beyond hearing. Her eyes glittering in the reflected glow of the raging fire, she charged forward, driving the gurney into the flames.

Chapter 61

Signy turned away as a sea of flames engulfed the corpse of Solomon Stone. She couldn't bear to watch as wave after wave of searing fire reduced his clothes to cinders, roasting the flesh off his bones.

Signy heard Grace's ragged voice. "Time to go."

Haggard and dressed only in a blue hospital gown, Grace stood tall. Staring at the inferno, the gas canister cradled in her arms, she glanced at Signy. "Are you okay?"

Signy brought a hand to her swollen throat and took a few experimental breaths. "I'm fine."

Grace nodded. She raised the canister over her head, her wild hair shivering.

Signy stared in amazement as Grace cast the propane into the inferno.

The metal cylinder rolled into the flames, coming to rest directly under the body of Solomon Stone.

Screaming the word "Run!" Grace ran toward the door.

Signy followed, and then realizing that Stone's access card was still around his neck, the women wasted a nightmarish minute trying to figure out how to override the locked exit. Over the roar of the flames, they heard his bones snapping like firewood as they tried and failed to force the door.

While Signy continued to fling her body against solid metal, Grace stood back and examined the problem. Placing a hand on Signy's shoulder, she pointed to a sensor on the ceiling.

"What?" Signy asked.

Grace's only answer was to run back into the room, where she fumbled about in Stone's medical cabinet before finding a roll of cotton bandages. Picking up the roll with a long clamp, Grace soaked the roll in alcohol, then lit it with a butane lighter. The roll burst into flames.

Signy watched with growing comprehension as Grace held the flaming ball up to the sensor. Within seconds, an alarm began to sound, and the doors unlocked with a metallic click. The two women ran for their lives through the maze of corridors, Signy hoping that her recollection of Lizzy's crude directions was accurate.

It felt like forever but was probably no more than thirty seconds before they found the door leading upstairs. While Grace grabbed her jacket and boots, Signy shouted, "How much time do we have until it blows?"

"I'm not waiting to find out," Grace replied.

Signy placed a restraining arm on Grace. "Stone took videos of everything. Lizzy trashed his computer, but surely he must have made backups?"

Looking up at the ceiling, Grace plunged her fingers into her hair. "His office," she shouted. She flew across the grand hall and into Stone's office, finding what she was looking for amid the array of computer equipment still humming on the glass shelves. "Backup hard drive," she muttered, ripping the black box from the shelf.

A deep rumbling sounded below their feet.

"Go," Signy shouted, and the two women raced out of the house, just as the acrid odour of smoke and cooking flesh wound its way up the stairs from the basement.

Signy led the way back to the cottage, Alex's powerful SUV plowing through the drifts that had spread like fingers across the long driveway leading out to the main road. She checked her rear-view mirror repeatedly, and every time Grace was still there, following close behind, her eyes firmly on the road, her car steady on the icy surface.

They were almost at the road when they saw the flash and heard the first explosion. A few seconds later came a series of even more powerful eruptions as the big exterior propane tanks erupted. A black mushroom cloud billowed high above the trees.

Spinning the SUV onto the main road, Signy tried to think. Stone claimed that he'd used Lizzy to lure young women to the estate, that it was Lizzy who had brutally murdered young Katy. As much as she didn't want to believe him, his words had had a ring of truth. She pressed down on the gas pedal, terrified of what she might find at the cottage.

In her rear-view mirror, she watched the Stone estate burn, the flames lighting up the western sky.

The darkness was absolute by the time Signy turned down the small road that traversed the length of the peninsula. A light snow was falling, but the wind had finally died. She picked her way carefully along the snow-packed road, the tracks that she'd followed on her way out having drifted over.

The headlights in the rear-view mirror were blinding as Grace dogged her steps down the narrow track, and she tipped the mirror down. Through the trees, she could see a dim light shining in the front window of the cottage, and she allowed it to guide her around the final bend in the road.

As her headlights swept the area in front of the cottage, her heart sank. The stolen Malibu was where she had left it, but the dead assassin's truck was gone. After parking the SUV, she grabbed her parka and joined Grace inside her vehicle.

"Where are we?" Grace asked. "What is this place?"

Catching sight of a pink-stained bandage wrapped around Grace's left thigh, Signy said "My God. Are you all right? Did he—"

"I'll live," Grace replied. "It stings like a bitch, but it's superficial as far as I can tell."

Signy nodded. "Okay, look. I have to tell you something. When we couldn't make it to your chalet, Lizzy brought us here. It belongs to a friend of hers. It's safe enough for now."

"Good." Grace reached for the door handle.

"Hold on. I don't know how to say this except straight out. There are two men inside. One is dead, and the other has been shot in the leg."

"What?" Grace's eyebrows disappeared up under her frizzy mop of hair.

"The guy with the leg wound is a friend of mine." She glanced over her shoulder at where the white pickup had been. "There's a vehicle missing. What if what Stone said about Lizzy was true? What if she—"

"There's only one way to find out," Grace said, zipping up her jacket.

The two women climbed out of the car. Wearing nothing but a hospital gown under her jacket, Grace was shuddering with cold by the time Signy pushed the front door slowly open.

Signy peered inside. The main floor was a maze of incomprehensible shadows. Other than the dim glow cast by the stove light in the kitchen, there was no other illumination. "Alex?" she called. There was no response.

Signy flipped on the light switch, and she and Grace stepped inside together.

Leaving Grace to make a cursory examination of the body by the door, Signy rushed over to the couch where she had left her brother. The only thing she found was a blood-soaked rag and a half-empty bottle of medicinal alcohol. The baby's car seat was also missing.

"Lizzy?" Signy yelled, tilting her head as she waited for a response. Nothing.

Letting the blanket fall back over the dead man's face, Grace rose back to her feet. "Maybe they're upstairs?"

Signy nodded. The two women climbed the stairs with Signy leading the way to the room that Lizzy and the baby had shared. Bursting inside, she switched on the light. The room was clean. There was no sign of Justin. Her shoulders slumped.

"How badly was your friend hurt?" Grace asked.

"Bad. I can't imagine how he could walk on his own."

"Maybe she called an ambulance?"

Signy thought about that for a moment, then shook her head. "She wouldn't risk it." They stared at each other for a long minute. Through the double-paned window, they could hear the roar of the storm-swept waves crashing into the shore. The despair Signy was beginning to feel crept into her voice. "Dammit."

"Don't panic," Grace said. "Maybe they called someone else."

A spark of hope flared inside her chest but faded when she checked her watch. "He did say he had people he could call, but there hasn't been enough time." She bit her lip. "Besides, if they had been evacuated, don't you think he would have left a note?"

It was Grace who had the courage to ask the obvious question. "Do you think Lizzy did something to them?"

Signy stared into space for several seconds and then shook her head. "No. I can't believe it. There has to be another explanation. You check the rest of the rooms up here, I'll try downstairs." She hustled away, pausing when she reached the door. "There's a bag of women's clothes down in the front foyer. There should be something in there for you to wear." Signy turned and raced back down the hallway.

A few minutes later, they met up in the living room. With a shaking of heads, both announced that their respective searches had turned up empty. Alex and Justin were gone.

Signy sat heavily on the couch and dropped her head into her hands.

Chapter 62

Wincing, Grace lowered herself onto the couch beside Signy.

"You okay?" Signy asked.

"These pants are too tight. They're pulling on the bandage." She was wearing a black sweatsuit she'd found in the bag of clothes Signy had purchased. "At least I'm warm."

"God, I'm an idiot. He didn't trust Lizzy from the get-go. I should have listened to him."

"Listened to who? Who is this friend of yours?"

Signy peered up at Grace. "Do you remember the name Jay Hunter?"

"Hunter? You mean Volkov's thug?"

Signy cleared her throat. "That's the one."

"What about him?" Grace said, sharply.

"Okay. You're not going to believe this, but it turns out that he's my brother."

Grace jerked in her seat. "Come on. Jay Hunter?"

"I'm serious."

"*The* Jay Hunter?"

"If you mean the one that Leonid Volkov hired to track down Elena? The Jay Hunter who almost got you killed? Yes, that's the one."

"I don't understand." Grace narrowed her eyes. "What the hell are you saying?"

Signy scrubbed at her forehead with the palm of her hand. "His real name is Alex Nakai. Turns out he's been searching for me for years. It was sheer coincidence we met during Elena's case."

"But how could you have a brother? They found you all alone in that Dumpster." Grace's voice had risen a full octave.

"It was Alex who put me in there."

Grace's mouth dropped open. "What?"

"He was six and I was about two when our mother was murdered and we were abducted. When the killer stopped for a red light, Alex opened the door, grabbed me, and ran. He managed to hide me in the Dumpster before the kidnapper found him."

"My God, why didn't you tell me?"

Signy glanced up at Grace. "I guess we've both been keeping secrets."

Grace plucked at the tight fabric rubbing against her injured leg. "Post–traumatic stress disorder. That's what the shrinks call it. If I'd said something sooner, maybe none of this would have happened. I'm so sorry."

They sat quietly for a couple of minutes, both of them lost in their own dark thoughts.

"Leaving aside the whole sibling thing for a minute," Grace said finally, "how did he end up here with you?"

"When the Amber Alert was called, we had to make a quick getaway. I lost all my ID and money. I called Grand Central but things were going crazy over there."

Grace sucked in a breath. "Christ. I forgot about that. It's about the embassy, isn't it?"

Signy nodded. "We tried to make it to Lake Placid, but the road was closed because of the storm. With the Amber Alert out for the baby, I didn't know who else to call."

Grace pointed her chin at the shrouded body. "What about him?"

Signy shrugged. "Apparently, when you're in Alex's line of work, the customer complaint process can get nasty."

"Jesus Christ," Grace muttered.

"Grace?"

Cocking her head, Grace held up a hand. "Did you hear that?"

"What?"

Grace sat quite still for several seconds and then shook her head. "Never mind. My imagination seems to be working overtime lately. What were you going to say?"

"Do you think he's dead?"

Grace sat up straighter. "Let's look at this rationally. You said that this so-called brother of yours didn't trust Lizzy?"

"Not totally, no. He did a background check on her and found some troubling things in her history."

"If he believed that she was dangerous, why not just let her go? Especially if he was injured. Why wouldn't he just let her walk away?"

"The baby," Signy said.

Understanding flooded Grace's face. "The baby belongs to that poor woman in the crematorium."

"Kit Kat."

"And you think Lizzy was using the baby to . . . what? Punish her husband?"

"Justin is the source of the immortal skin cells. She knew how desperate Stone was to get the baby back. She must have been terrified when I went to the estate, knowing Stone would likely torture me until I gave her up. She thought that it was only a matter of time before he stormed the cottage."

"And after she was gone, he'd get to live happily ever after with Justin," Grace added.

"And win the Nobel Prize."

Grace peered at Signy. "How far do you think she'd go to keep the baby away from Stone?"

Signy gnawed on her bottom lip. "God. I don't know. She seemed like a good mother. She was fine with Justin, but she did tell me that I had no idea how easy it was to cross over to the dark side." Signy held Grace's eyes. "As for Alex, I can't believe he would let her hurt the baby."

"You said he was shot. Even if your faith is well placed, and frankly, I'm not convinced that it is, how much could he do?"

"That's what I'm afraid of," Signy said, twisting her hands together in her lap. "He sacrificed himself for me once, and I think he might have done it again."

Grace's eye darted over to the bloodstained couch. "Right. We need to call the police," she said, getting to her feet. "Assuming Justin and . . . that man aren't already at the bottom of the lake, the cops need to know the whole story if they're to have any hope finding the baby alive."

Signy's shoulders slumped.

"Is that working?" Grace asked, pointing at a land-line phone sitting on a table near the front door.

"I think so. Unless Lizzy cut the line."

Grace walked over to the phone and picked up the receiver. She was just about to dial 911 when a high-pitched whine twisted thinly through the house. Pressing the receiver to her chest, she stared at Signy. "Surely you hear that?"

"Listen." Signy cocked her head. The sound came again, louder this time, and more insistent.

The two women exploded into action.

"It's coming from over there," Grace cried, pointing toward the door that led to the kitchen.

They banged through the kitchen door together and skittered to a halt. There was no sign of either Alex or the baby. Signy hauled open the side door, but other than a blast of frigid air, she could see nothing. The thin wail came again and both Signy's and Grace's eyes snapped to the floor. "I didn't find any sign of a basement when I searched this floor," Grace said.

Signy spun around in confusion. The baby cried again, louder now. It was definitely coming from under the floor. She spied the walk-in closet where she'd found the washing-up stuff earlier. Striding over, she pulled open the door and stepped inside. Every inch of wall space appeared crammed with shelves of cleaning and paper products. There was no door.

She gritted her teeth in frustration as she heard the baby shriek just below her feet. Beside her, Grace fell to her knees.

"Here," said Grace, using her finger to trace the outline of a small panel embedded into the wooden floor. She flipped up the panel, revealing a brass ring.

Signy bent down and together they lifted the door. It opened with a loud creak, releasing a puff of air that smelled of sweet onions and squash, crisp apples and damp. Before Grace managed to secure the door, Signy was already dashing down the short flight of steps that led into the darkness. “Alex?” she cried.

There was no answer.

She waved her hands in front of her face, moving in the direction of the baby’s cries. She felt something cold brush against her palm and, recognizing it as a hanging light switch, yanked down hard. A bank of fluorescent lights flickered to life. She turned toward the sound of the baby crying and spotted Justin and Alex.

Alex sat propped against the back wall, surrounded by boxes stuffed with preserved fruits and vegetables. Cradled in his arms, the baby squirmed furiously.

Signy walked in a crouch beneath the low ceiling until she reached the pair. Falling to her knees, she plucked the crying baby from Alex’s icy hands. Justin’s skin was chilly, but he appeared unharmed. Signy handed him over to Grace, who had followed her down into the cold room.

While Grace raced the baby back into the relative warmth of the kitchen, Signy turned and examined Alex. His face was a frightening shade of white, and despite the almost freezing temperature, his blond hair was plastered to his head. His injured leg, wrapped in grey duct tape, sat propped out in front of him.

With trembling fingers, she touched an index finger to the side of his neck. She almost gasped when she felt how cold his skin was. Overhead she could hear the baby screaming. Unable to find a pulse, she stabbed her finger up under his jaw.

He moaned.

"Alex?" she said, relieved when she saw him crack open one eye.

"Huh?"

"The baby's fine. You're going to be all right."

"Signy?"

"Yes, it's me," she said, raising her voice so that he could hear her over the baby's furious cries.

He clutched at her hand. "Tell me."

"What?" She leaned in closer.

"Tell me," he repeated, smacking his lips together as he tried to get them to follow his commands. "Tell me, Signy. Does that kid never shut up?"

She reeled back on her haunches.

He was grinning up at her, blue eyes sparkling with laughter.

Chapter 63

While Grace tended to the baby, Signy dragged Alex out of the cold cellar. Her muscles were screaming by the time she had him propped on the couch and covered in blankets she'd torn off the beds upstairs. His teeth were chattering, and she hoped that his uncontrollable shivering was not a sign of impending shock.

She was rubbing his hands, trying to get some warmth back into his extremities, when Grace limped out of the kitchen carrying a mug of steaming hot tea for Alex and a warm bottle for the baby. She handed the mug to Signy, then took a seat opposite the couch. She settled the baby carefully onto her lap, taking care to avoid her ravaged thigh, then plugged the bottle into his mouth.

Signy handed Alex the warm tea.

As he drained the mug, his muscles relaxed, and colour began to flood back into his cheeks. He hauled himself up on his elbows. "Thanks for this," he said, holding up his mug and nodding at Grace.

"Don't thank me," she said, her tone flat.

"Grace," Signy said.

Grace shot Alex a furious look. "Where's the girl?"

"Long gone," he said. "I gave her the cash card and the USB key and suggested she take off."

"Why the cold cellar?" Grace asked.

Alex eyed the fireplace poker. "I had a bad feeling."

Signy leaned forward. "Did she try something?"

He shook his head. "After I got Justin down the steps and closed the trap door, she stomped around for a good five minutes. She was obviously trying to find him. She was angry. I heard her curse a few times, but other than that, she didn't say a word. I heard the front door bang, but I couldn't take the chance she was lying in wait, so we stayed down there." He shuddered.

Signy tucked the blanket in around his feet, ignoring a sniff of distaste from Grace. "Do you think she meant to hurt the baby?"

Alex shrugged. "Do you remember the way the video picture shook?"

Signy nodded.

"It took me a while, but I realized that for the picture to shake that way, someone had to be holding the camera. Lizzy admitted that it was her."

Grace shot Signy a doleful glance. "So, Lizzy Stone was involved in the torture of those girls?"

"She claimed that Stone forced her to do it, that she was as much a victim as the rest of the women," Alex said. "But the way she dressed my leg? That took hands-on medical experience."

"You think she did more than just hold the camera?" Signy asked.

He shook his head. "I don't know. I couldn't read her. So I decided it would be prudent to err on the side of caution."

"So that's it? She just walks away?" Grace said, outrage creeping into her voice.

"Leave her to me," Alex said, cryptically. He turned to Signy. "What about Stone? How did you get out of there?"

Signy filled him in on the events at the Stone estate.

When she was done, Alex looked at Grace. "You are a remarkable woman."

Pursing her lips, Grace rose slowly to her feet, the baby clutched to her chest. She limped about the room, patting Justin's back.

"I can do that for you if you like," Signy said.

Glancing over her shoulder, Grace shook her head. "No, thanks. I can manage on my own."

Signy was wracking her brain for something to say, when she heard the growl of a vehicle pulling up to the front of the cottage.

"That would be the cavalry," Alex said. When Grace turned toward the window to look, Alex smiled at Signy and flicked imaginary sweat off his brow.

Signy opened the door. A wiry woman, with a frizz of salt and pepper hair cropped close to her skull, entered first, followed by two bulked-up men, wearing black paramilitary clothing.

Introducing herself as Kathy Barrow, the doctor moved toward Alex, but he waved her away, insisting she check out Grace and the baby first. Dr. Barrow smiled at Grace. "Who said chivalry was dead?"

"Is that what you call it?" Grace said, under her breath, before taking a seat on a chair.

After giving Grace a couple of tablets for the pain, the doctor removed the gauze bandages that Stone had wrapped around her thigh.

Signy's stomach flipped at the sight of the angry red welt.

"Looks good," said Dr. Barrow, smiling up at Grace. "This new dressing will help control the pain and will aid in the regrowth." She ripped open a foil packet labelled Scarlet Red.

Grace sucked in her breath while the doctor applied the dressing.

"You will notice some significant oozing over the next few weeks. That's normal. Have the dressing changed regularly, and you'll be fine."

Dr. Barrow checked out the baby next and pronounced him healthy, then turned to Alex.

Having had her fill of gore for one day, Signy walked back out to the front foyer. She watched the two men drag the now-fragrant body of the assassin out to the Malibu, where they stuffed it inside the trunk.

"What do you think they'll do with him?" Grace asked, joining her.

"They didn't say, although I imagine the local police won't be terribly shocked to find a guy like that at the bottom of the lake."

"Or buried in a landfill," Grace added.

They stood in silence as the two men hooked up the Malibu to the back of their oversized van.

Triggered by the sight of the old Malibu, Signy retrieved her burner phone and punched in the number for the New York State Crime Stoppers. She left an anonymous tip, reporting that she'd overheard two men planning a murder. She gave the general location of the Patriot Club and went on to say that one of the conspirators had a wife named Sharon and that it was Sharon's younger brother who was the intended victim. She hung up the phone, feeling alternately silly and hopeful that she'd prevented further bloodshed.

By the time she walked back downstairs, the two men were standing by in the foyer with a stretcher, and Dr. Barrow was packing up her gear.

"How is he?" Signy asked.

The doctor smiled. "A little loopy right now, but he'll live."

Alex rubbed his eyes. "Good old Helen always comes through in a pinch."

Good old Helen? Signy knelt down beside him, wondering just how many *people* he had at his beck and call. "You'll be right as rain in a few weeks."

"I'm pretty awesome right now," he said.

At least that's what she thought he said. His lips were rubbery, his words slurred. Smiling, she narrowed her eyes. "That's a good thing, because we still have a lot to talk about."

He tried to push himself up straight but didn't have the strength. He leaned forward instead, his eyes serious. "You must suffer me to go my own dark way."

"What?"

"My own dark way, that's what he said. Dr. Jekyll. I don't care. He can't make me stop looking."

She flicked her eyes to the doctor.

The older woman shrugged.

Signy returned her attention to Alex. "You need to get some rest."

"Yes, Helen," he said, and then his chin fell forward onto his chest.

Taking that as their cue, the two men pushed the stretcher into the living room.

After he was strapped in, Signy took his hand.

He cracked open one blue eye.

"Will I see you again?" she asked.

He grinned.

She squeezed his fingers, taking care not to dislodge the IV port. "Thanks for being there when I needed you." She paused and looked into his eyes. "Every time."

He made a raspberry noise with his lips, and then he was on the move. He was almost out the front door when Signy shouted for them to wait up.

"Hey," she said, trotting up alongside the gurney. "This morning you said something to me in Navajo. At least I think it was Navajo." She looked into his blue eyes. "*Ayoo*? *Anoshi*? Something like that?"

He grinned up at her. "*Ayóó ánóshí, Shideeszhi.*"

"What does it mean?"

He squeezed her hand. "*Ayóó ánóshí, Shideeszhi*. I love you, little sister."

Then her hand slipped from his, and he was gone.

Chapter 64

After dropping Justin Stone with Priya Subramanian with the instructions that authorities be informed that the baby had been abandoned at the shelter by person or persons unknown, Grace and Signy settled into adjoining rooms in a hotel out by the Rochester airport. Over a late night dinner of pepperoni pizza and diet Coke eaten on Grace's bed, Signy finally mustered the courage to ask the question that had been plaguing her.

"Who's Ethan?"

Wiping tomato sauce from her mouth with a napkin, Grace said quietly, "My big brother." She glanced at Signy. "He helps me out now and then."

"I didn't know you had a brother."

"His name was Ethan."

Noticing Grace's use of the past tense, Signy remained quiet.

"He died. Suicide, actually."

"I'm sorry," Signy murmured, unable to think of anything else to say.

"Don't be," Grace replied. "No matter what meds the psychiatrists tried, they were never able to get his hallucinations under control. For Ethan, every day was an agony of nasty voices and frightening visions."

Signy winced.

"He's happier now." Grace glanced at Signy. "Don't worry. I may have PTSD but I'm not crazy."

"I didn't think you were."

"I did." Grace smiled. "For years, I've confused my symptoms with those of schizophrenia. I was terrified. I thought I was going to go the same way as Ethan."

"It didn't start with Volkov?"

"Sooner than that. Probably since the day Ethan died. But the symptoms really ramped up when I was stabbed in the arm by the husband of one of our clients."

"Stabbed," Signy said, shaking her head. "I knew something had happened, but I didn't know the details."

"He opened up my brachial artery. If it hadn't been for Kim, I'd have bled out in seconds. I managed to keep my symptoms a secret from almost everyone." Grace shrugged. "Kim knew, of course, and when the thing with Volkov happened, well, she just couldn't take it anymore."

"That's why she acted so strangely when I went to see her," Signy said, and then realizing what she had revealed, bit her bottom lip.

"It's okay," Grace said, patting Signy's hand. "You were only trying to help. I should have listened."

Signy felt her shoulders relax. "So the fugue state at the embassy was something to do with your PTSD?"

"Blackouts are part of it, yes." She stared off into space for a moment. "So is the rage. When my brain gets overloaded, I need a calming presence to help me through."

"Ethan?"

"God, I looked up to him," Grace said. "Before he got sick, we used to do everything together. It was the two of us against the world. When he died, I couldn't deal with the reality that he was gone, so I decided to keep him around to act as the sane little voice that helped keep me stable." She tossed her napkin into the garbage can. "Water under the bridge. Right now we have other things to discuss."

Signy nodded. "The fire at the estate was huge. It will have destroyed any trace of the victims."

"But thanks to you, we have the backup hard drive."

"Do we take it to the police?"

Grace peered at the ceiling. "At this point," she said, finally, "there's nothing to tie either of us to Lizzy or Justin, or to Stone's demise. I'd rather keep it that way."

"The world has to know," Signy protested. "At least the families of all those poor girls. They deserve to know what happened."

"Of course," Grace replied. "We'll send the hard drive to the *New York Times* in the morning."

As for Lizzy, that outcome remained murky. Grace leaned toward Lizzy's being the monster that Stone had portrayed, while Signy couldn't shake the feeling that she was as much a victim as the other young women, caught up in the web of a very powerful spider. In the end, they came to no conclusion. Unless she resurfaced someday, Lizzy Stone would remain what she had always been, an enigma.

The conversation about Justin Stone fell even further into dark territory. The baby's cells were unique. In the hands of ethical scientists, the possibilities were endless, Grace argued. Equally passionate, Signy decried the idea of handing the poor child over for doctors to experiment on, as if he were some kind of lab rat. The debate raged until both were too exhausted to continue. They agreed to present the dilemma to Maitland and let her make the final decision.

Signy stumbled into her room but kept the adjoining door open. As she climbed under the covers, she heard Grace talking on the phone at length with Maitland McGuinness. Signy tried not to listen, but she did hear Grace say that they would be home the following day to help in the ongoing investigation of events at the Ottawa embassy. She was pleasantly surprised as well to hear Grace freely admit to Maitland about her ongoing struggle with post–traumatic stress disorder: her behaviour had interfered with the embassy mission, she was solely to blame, and she would answer to any consequences.

Signy yawned, tension building in her shoulders. She couldn't settle. The pizza was sitting heavy in her stomach. The room was too hot, the air dry. Down the hall, someone was filling ice buckets from the machine every five minutes. When she tried to close her eyes, she was rocked by the image of Solomon Stone's body being consumed by flames.

When she heard Grace pick up the phone and make another call, she pulled a foam pillow over her head. She finally fell asleep listening to the indistinct drone of Grace's calm voice talking well into the wee hours of the morning.

Chapter

65

The next morning dawned cold and clear. Signy squinted against the bright sunlight pouring in through the hotel window. Outside, the snow was white and crisp. Picking up the copy of the *Democrat and Chronicle* outside her door, she read the headline announcing the happy news that Justin Stone had been safely located. The story went on to say that the police were still searching for Lizzy Stone, worried for her welfare, especially after the tragic fire that had taken the life of her husband, the esteemed Dr. Solomon Stone.

After a quick shower, she went downstairs and joined Grace for breakfast in the lobby of the hotel.

"Maitland's springing for us to fly home," Grace announced.

"That's good news. I'm not sure I feel up to the drive. It's been a brutal few days."

Biting into a stale croissant, Grace nodded her agreement. "And she had even more good news to share. Binah Jakende is safe out west somewhere and the embassy has given up the pursuit. As soon as the ambassador was presented with hard evidence as to the proclivities of his press secretary, he had no choice but to send the bastard home."

"Will Binah be able to return?"

"Would you? Given the choice?"

Signy shook her head. "It's so unfair. Sometimes life really blows."

Grace raised her coffee cup in an ironic salute.

Later, after dropping Grace's rental car at the airport, the two women caught a flight to Toronto. Stretched out in her first-class seat, Signy stared out the window and thought about Alex. By the time the plane landed at Pearson International Airport, Signy had come up with all sorts of ways she might engineer a trip down to New Mexico. Grabbing her bag from the overhead compartment, she wondered if she would ever make it happen.

As they made their way through customs, both of them looked like they'd gone three rounds with Mike Tyson. Not that the other passengers looked much better. Airport lighting was much like a Superstore's, Signy decided; everyone looked as though they'd just stepped off the zombie express.

Signy was relieved she'd had the foresight to bring her real passport inside the false bottom of her backpack. Even with her face plastered all over upstate New York, she had slipped through Canadian customs without incident.

The two women stepped through the sliding doors that led out into the arrivals lounge.

Signy heard Grace gasp. Not ten feet away, Kim Blackwater was waiting with a huge grin on her face.

Grace flew into her lover's arms.

Their reunion was sweet to watch, or would have been if Signy hadn't been feeling so disheartened—and lonely.

Eventually, Kim and Grace walked back over to where Signy sat, slumped in an uncomfortable plastic chair. Kim was the first to speak. "Hi," she said.

Signy offered a weak smile.

"I heard you had a long couple of days."

Signy shrugged.

"I just wanted to say. You know. The other day? At the hospital?"

Signy's throat suddenly felt very dry.

Taking a deep breath, Kim continued, "I just wanted to say I appreciated the heads-up."

Signy turned to Grace. "Listen, I didn't mean—"

"Don't worry," Grace said, holding up a hand, "I applaud your courage. Listen, there's something I need to tell you."

"Don't tell me, there's another red file?" Signy asked in mock horror.

Grace chuckled. "Good Lord, I hope not. Quite the opposite, as a matter of fact. I'm retiring from fieldwork for a while."

"For a while?" Kim frowned.

"It will mean more responsibility for you," Grace added. "Are you okay with that?"

Signy didn't know whether to laugh or cry, so she just sat there clutching her hands together in her lap, nodding like a fool.

"Great," said Grace, fishing the keys to her Prius out of her pocket. "Could I ask you one more huge favour? Would you mind driving my car home?"

Signy jumped to her feet.

Grace drew her into a deep hug.

"Can I say something stupid?" Signy whispered.

"Of course."

"Maybe Ethan really did come back to help you. Brothers can be a pain that way."

Grace squeezed her tighter. "Thanks, honey. Oh, and feel free to kick my butt anytime you think I need it. You'll always be my dear friend, no matter what."

Signy felt tears spring to her eyes, but before she had a chance to embarrass herself, Grace and Kim had turned away. She watched them walk arm in arm toward the exit, their heads touching.

The sun was low on the horizon by the time she pulled Grace's Prius into her driveway. After parking around back, she shrugged into her parka and pulled open the door. Frigid air seared the delicate tissues inside her nostrils.

God, she hated winter. Holding the sides of her hood together, she trudged up the alleyway between the houses and around to the front. With the blustery wind whistling in her ears, she almost didn't hear the deep voice call her name.

Startled, she flipped off her hood and looked up. Her eyes popped open.

Ben Tran was standing on her veranda holding a takeout bag in one hand, a broad grin on his face.

"Ben?" Her foot slipped on a patch of black ice, and she windmilled her arms.

Dropping the bag, Ben jumped nimbly down the stairs and caught her.

"What are you doing here?" she asked, once she'd regained her balance.

"When you didn't show on Saturday, I figured you were on the job."

"Really? I thought you might think I'd stood you up."

"Why would I think that?" He peered at her quizzically.

Signy felt a sparkling sensation as though a match had flared to life inside her chest.

"Anyway, I left a message with Grace asking her to let me know when you'd be back. I hope you don't mind that I came over?" He glanced up at a takeout bag he'd dropped on the wooden porch. "It's not quite Winston's, but I figured it would do for now. Do you like Chinese?"

She smiled up at him. "That sounds perfect."

Tucking her arm inside his, she led him inside. As they climbed the stairs together, Signy felt warm inside for the first time in years.

Acknowledgments

Disappearing without a trace is a herculean task in this age of surveillance, although not impossible. I am grateful to the following experts for their illuminating books: *How to Disappear: Erase Your Digital Footprint, Leave False Trails, and Vanish Without a Trace* by Frank M. Ahearn with Eileen C. Horan; *"Soldier of Fortune" Guide to How to Disappear and Never be Found* by Barry Davies, BEM; and *The Art of Deception: Controlling the Human Element of Security* by Kevin D. Mitnick and William L. Simon.

A sincere thank-you to the passionate and informative volunteers who operate the North Star Underground Railroad Museum, located in the Town of Chesterfield Heritage Center, NY. A heart-breaking array of poignant exhibits tell the stories of fugitives from slavery who passed through northeastern New York and the Champlain Valley on their way to Québec and Ontario, Canada. My visit gave me a glimpse into the incredible courage and strength exhibited by the fugitives, and by the men and women who helped them along the way.

Many thanks to my writing buddies, Phyllis Diller Stewart and Tanja Hillis-Ormiston, who provided thoughtful feedback and joyful cheerleading throughout the process. You guys are the best. Deep thanks, as well, to Becky Toyne and Alison Clarke. Your insightful suggestions and thoughtful editing are evident throughout these pages. I continue to be amazed by the hard work and dedication of the entire Simon & Schuster Canada team, especially Rita Silva, Brendan May, Loretta Eldridge, Nita Pronovost, and my ever-patient copyeditor, Peg Haller. A special thank-you to Anne McDermid, agent extraordinaire.

To my children, Andrew, Sarah, and Abby; and my son-in-law, Kurt, I am especially grateful. Watching you spread your wings has been a privilege. I am thrilled that each of you has had the courage and passion to follow your dreams. LYLY

Finally, eternal love and gratitude to my husband, Steve, who cheerfully reads every word I write, and never fails to hit the nail on the head. Your kindness, creativity, and wisdom continue to make me a better writer and a better person. You truly are a man among men.